THEORETICALLY STRAIGHT

AMY BAILEY
ALEXANDER C. EBERHART

THEORETICALLY STRAIGHT

Copyright © 2023 Amy Bailey & Alexander C. Eberhart

All rights reserved. No part of this publication may be reproduced, stored in a retrieval system, or transmitted, in any form or by any means (electronic, mechanical, photocopying, recording, or otherwise), without the prior written permission of the publisher.

This book is a work of fiction and does not represent any individual living or dead. Names, characters, places, and incidents either are products of the author's imagination or are used fictitiously.

FOR THE QUEER KIDS LIKE US
WHO QUESTIONED THEMSELVES UNDER A STEEPLE

ONE
THEO

Sunday, September 3

"For the last time, Dad, I'm not going! End of discussion!"

"That is most certainly *not* the end of this discussion, young lady!"

"Well, it most certainly is for me!"

"Don't take that tone with me, Sarah Grace!"

The rising volume of my father's voice makes me flinch on my sister's behalf. It must be bad if Dad is dropping her full name in an argument.

I hear the unmistakable sound of stomping coming from the living room and try to relax. At least the war is raging in another room, allowing me to continue my quiet breakfast in the kitchen. I scoop up another spoonful of cereal with one hand and scroll mindlessly on my phone with the other—all part of my peaceful Sunday morning routine.

"You know, I honestly don't even have to come home at all!" Grace shouts, suddenly storming into the kitchen. Strands of her multi-colored curls hang messily in her hazel eyes as she yanks open a cabinet for a coffee mug.

I tense as Dad enters the kitchen soon after, frustration painted across his fairer features. He runs a hand through his short, graying blonde hair and sighs as he watches Grace pour her coffee.

Well, so much for my peaceful Sunday breakfast.

Dad takes a calming breath. "Look, Grace, there's just no need to—"

"Actually, you know what?" Grace interrupts, spinning around to face him again. "Maybe I should just commute to work from campus on the weekends from now on if this is what I have to look forward to every Sunday!"

"We're not saying that, Grace," my mother pleads as she joins us in the kitchen. Her big brown eyes brim with empathy, brows furrowed with worry as she approaches Grace and tentatively reaches for Grace's hand. "Of course we want you here!"

"Then stop pressuring me to go to church with you!" Grace demands, recoiling away from Mom's touch. "I told you I hate it there!"

Fortunately, no one seems to notice that I'm even in the room, sitting perfectly still at the table with my half-finished breakfast. As long as I don't make any noise or sudden movements, I can only pray that this shouting match will blow over soon, or at least maybe migrate into another room so that I can escape back upstairs.

"We're just worried about you, honey," Mom begs again. That's Mom—always trying to be the peacemaker in these situations, desperate to ease the tension and calm everyone back down.

"We want what's best for you," Dad adds sternly. He is the far less accommodating parent, unwilling to back down when he believes he's right.

Grace rolls her eyes. She definitely gets her stubbornness honestly. "I'm an *adult*, you don't get to—"

"You may be an adult," Dad cuts her off, unrelenting. "But when you're living under our roof, you respect our rules. You know that."

"So, is that a rule now? That if I'm here, I have to attend church every Sunday?"

Dad hesitates, but only briefly. "Maybe it should be."

Mom places a hand on Dad's forearm. "Michael—"

"Oh, well, that settles it," Grace barks out with a laugh, clapping her hands together. "I'll just commute to work from campus and not bother visiting anymore. Problem solved!"

My eyebrows shoot up. I have to admit it's kind of impressive how far Grace is willing to push my parents when they get into fights like this. I can't even imagine pulling that kind of stunt with them. Not in a million years.

"Oh, come on, don't be dramatic—" Dad says, exasperated.

"Wait, sweetheart, hang on—" Mom pleads again, her grip on Dad's arm tightening. "I'm sure we can work out a compromise, don't you—"

"Absolutely not," Dad counters, shaking his head. "Grace, you're being ridiculous. I mean, really—" he glances around the room, and his eyes suddenly land on me. "Theo and Nathaniel don't have a problem with going to church every week."

I freeze—a spoonful of cereal in mid-air, my mouth hanging open and my eyes wide. Oh crap.

"Isn't that right, son?"

All eyes in the room are suddenly on me. I blink. "Um. What—what was the question?" I stutter.

"Don't drag him into this, Dad!" Grace snaps. "That's completely unfair. He's not an adult yet, so he doesn't get to choose, but I do!" Her glare softens as her eyes meet mine.

"She's right, Michael," Mom says gently to Dad, then offers me a sympathetic smile. "Go on upstairs and finish getting ready for the day, sweetie."

I briefly glance at Dad—an unspoken attempt to make sure I'm safe to leave—and he pinches the bridge of his nose. "Go ahead," he sighs with a single nod.

I don't need to be told twice. I swiftly dump my dishes in the sink and make my way upstairs to continue my Sunday morning routine. I can still hear the argument droning on until I hop in the shower, turning on some music to drown it all out.

As soon as I'm out of the shower, I retrieve my phone and scroll through my notifications, checking the socials to see if I missed anything. My group chats are quiet, Twitter is dead, and I only have a few dozen new likes on the TikTok I posted yesterday. The only thing new is a text message from the only person my age who still sends SMS messages.

SIENNA: Good morning Theodore!! Happy Sunday! Can't wait to see you this morning and tell you all about the trip!! <3<3

I roll my eyes and ditch my phone once again to continue getting ready for the day. After a heavy application of deodorant, I toss on some clothes—dark cropped blue jeans and a gray short-sleeve button-down shirt—and my trusty high-top gray Converse. It's going to be insanely hot because it's freaking September in Georgia, but I imagine my parents might object if I dared to wear shorts to church. I briefly check my reflection in my bedroom mirror one last time. Geez, I need a haircut—my black curls are dangling just above my eyebrows. I reach for the small tub of whatever hair product Grace insisted that I start using, rub it into my hands, and spread it through my hair. At least the curls are less frizzy, more defined, and not falling into my eyes. Good enough.

By this point, the chaos downstairs has ended, so I assume Grace has locked herself in her bedroom, and my parents have probably already left for church or are just about to.

I don't think I've thanked You enough that I have my own car, by the way, I pray silently. *So... Thanks again for that.*

As I make my way down the stairs as quietly as possible, I hear my parents speaking in hushed tones in their bedroom. I grab a caffeinated soda from the fridge and clear my throat. "I'm heading to church. See y'all there."

"We love you, Theo!" Mom replies. "Drive safe!"

"Love you, too," I call back and head out the back door, already scrolling through my Spotify playlists in search of the perfect vibe for my fifteen-minute drive.

"Can I ride to church with you?"

My younger brother's voice from behind me startles me, and I jump. "Holy sh—" I snap my mouth shut before I finish the expletive, recovering quickly. "Crap, dude, you scared me."

Nathaniel is staring intently at his Nintendo Switch and can't be bothered to acknowledge anything I have to say other than an answer to his request. I roll my eyes. "Sure, come on."

Sundays are my least favorite day of the week, and I feel extremely guilty about it.

It's not that I don't love my church. Church is a lot like extended family members—I've known them my whole life, and I'm supposed to love them, so I do. They might not always be the most interesting and exciting people to be around, but they're your family. It would be wrong not to love them, right?

And it's not that I don't *like* going to worship God and learning more about the Bible every single week. Of course I like it—it's all I've ever known. Sure, the lessons get a bit repetitive and boring sometimes, but doesn't everything? I mean, it's truly the least I can do to thank God for literally sending His son to die for my sins. I really have no reason to complain at all.

Plus, it's easy. It's routine. Going to church isn't always fun or enjoyable, but it's definitely not the worst way to spend my Sunday mornings. Most importantly, my presence at church means the world to my parents. Thanks to Grace, I have witnessed firsthand what it would be like if I decided to stop going to church. And quite frankly, I would prefer to skip that drama entirely if I can.

But sometimes—if I'm really honest with myself—I wish I could skip church like Grace, too. It would be nice to essentially have two full days between each week of school instead of just one. An extra day to sleep in? Or to hang out with my friends? That would be amazing.

But really, I shouldn't even be considering the idea of skipping church. Just the thought of it causes that old familiar twist of guilt to curl in my stomach as I drive.

I'm beginning to wonder if becoming an adult—particularly a Christian adult—will primarily consist of feeling guilty all the time. Because, as a recent seventeen-year-old, that's been a surprisingly big chunk of it so far. I guess I'll have to see.

"I guess Grace isn't coming to church anymore."

Nathaniel's gruff voice startles me again. He's so freaking quiet lately, which is still a weird adjustment from his prepubescent personality. Only a few months ago, Nathaniel was a wildly energetic and hyperactive kid who was constantly chattering and making fart noises every chance he got. Now he's suddenly reserved, calm, and generally apathetic. It's creepy like someone body-snatched the real Nathaniel and replaced him with this freakishly tall boy with acne and social anxiety.

"Yeah, I guess not," I finally reply.

"Is it because she's going to college now?"

I briefly glance at Nathaniel's face. He's still deeply engrossed in his Minecraft game with no discernable expression apart from his new blasé exterior. "Maybe. I don't know, Grace never really fit in at church anyway, you know?"

"Hmm," is the only response I get, and the remainder of the drive is only soundtracked by Djo and Dayglow.

I find a parking spot as close to the exit as possible so that Nathaniel and I can make a quick getaway once church is out, and we start making our way to the Foundation—yes, the very trendy, cool name of our youth center. My phone buzzes in my pocket.

HARRISON: You at church yet?

THEO: just got here, I'll be down in a sec

Nathaniel and I meander to the entrance of the very intentionally industrial-looking building separated from the main sanctuary. Every few years or so, they try to make the structure look "cooler" or "trendier," but it never quite makes it. A few months ago, they covered the front entrance with wood paneling and put the logo in all lowercase letters, but now it just looks like a corporate office that's trying too hard to be hip. It's more than a little funny if I'm being completely honest, but I would never say anything aloud about it. Except maybe to Harrison.

It takes a few extra seconds for my eyes to adjust to the relative darkness of the main room compared to the blinding September morning sun, but I'm immediately scanning the room for Harrison.

"Theo, my man!"

I'm greeted with a clap on my shoulder by Chase, the spiky-haired youth pastor. I put on a friendly smile that I can only hope is convincing. "Hey, Chase."

"How is it going, brother? How goes the TikTok account?"

I try not to visibly cringe. "It's fine. Same old, same old."

"Nothing viral yet, huh?"

I spot Harrison standing alone across the room, and as our eyes meet, he looks like he's stifling a laugh. I quickly look back to Chase. "Nope, not yet."

"Well, let me know if you want me to start promoting you on my account! And don't forget, I'm still looking for someone to run the Foundation's TikTok account. Are you sure you're not interested?"

"Thanks, but I've got a lot going on right now, and I don't want to overcommit." It's my practiced excuse to get out of most things, and it works like a charm on adults.

"Understood. Well, good luck! I'll catch you later!"

I offer another smile and slide past him to get to Harrison—finally.

"How's Chase?" he asks as his eyes look past me to Chase with a smirk. "Still asking about managing the Foundation's TikTok account?"

I roll my eyes now that Chase has moved on to the next student on his greet list. "He means well, but geez."

We both find our usual spot towards the back of the room and slide down the wall to sit on the cold concrete floor. "How's yesterday's video doing?" Harrison asks quietly as he pulls out his phone again.

I shrug and do the same. "Not great, but I'm not sure what I expected."

"Yesterday, you were convinced this was the one," Harrison argues, frowning over at me.

"Nah, I think the one we make this Saturday will be the one. We just have to get the timing right. TikTok isn't the best platform for editing."

"Bro! I've been saying that for weeks!" Harrison scoffs, pushing his glasses up on his nose. "YouTube is superior in literally every way, and I have way more editing software for real videos. TikTok is shit, and you know it."

My eyes widen, and I shoot him a stern look.

He rolls his own eyes in response. "*Crap.* TikTok is *crap,* and you know it."

"I know, but even you have to admit it's more fun than YouTube. Only old people and little kids are on YouTube. We need to be on GhostTok."

"Yeah, yeah, yeah," Harrison mumbles and turns his attention back to his phone. "Whatever, I'll still bring my Sony a6000 on Saturday so that we might actually capture something."

For the first time all day, I feel a jolt of excitement. Just the possibility that we might catch something, *anything*, on video that even remotely resembles the paranormal is exhilarating in a way that only my close friends really get. I lean my head back against the wall and smile at the thought.

"Hey, you know Sienna's back today, right?" Harrison practically whispers, raising one of his eyebrows.

In an instant, the excited feeling of anticipation is gone, and the twist of something else in my stomach is back. "Yeah, I know."

"She's going to have that post-mission trip high," Harrison adds quietly, turning his gaze back to his phone. "I've been trying to mentally prepare myself all morning."

I sigh and scroll aimlessly on my phone. "I think she's still upset that I didn't go."

"To South Africa? Seriously? She knows those trips cost money, right? Like, a *crap* ton of money? And not everyone has rich parents and rich family friends that can just—"

"Yeah, yeah, I know," I interrupt. "But apparently, there were some fundraising things I could have done, you know, like the yard sales and car washes and stuff. I don't know. God would have provided the funds if I had just had a little faith, right?"

Harrison scoffs. "Yeah, sure," he replies, sarcasm dripping from his tone.

I shrug again. "I don't know, maybe she's right. Maybe I should have gone. I've been needing some…" I trail off, trying to find the words. "Spiritual recharging? I don't know. I didn't even try."

Should I have tried? I pray silently. *Did You really want me to go?*

Unsurprisingly, I don't get a discernible answer.

"I don't think your parents would have gone for it," Harrison adds. "Mine wouldn't have."

"I don't know. With the right convincing, they would have, right? I mean, if God called me to go on a mission trip, I'm pretty sure my parents would drop everything to make it happen."

Harrison chuckles dryly. "Mine wouldn't."

I consider this for a moment. The guilt—*conviction*, I should say—makes my stomach tighten. Did God try to call me to South Africa? Would I have even realized it? *You would have made it obvious, right, God?*

"Theodore!"

I recognize the sing-song voice immediately, and my heart lurches in my chest—ugh, I really wish it would stop doing that. I pocket my phone and awkwardly scramble to my feet. Sienna is skipping over to me with a big toothy smile, her rich copper hair bouncing with every step. "Ahh, I missed you so much!" She practically tackles me in a hug, almost knocking me back down.

"Sienna! I missed you, too!" I wrap my arms around her and give her a light squeeze. She reeks of vanilla and sugar—so sweet it's almost sickening. "How was the trip? Was the flight okay?"

Sienna pulls herself out of the hug and beams at me, her blue eyes sparkling. "Oh, Theo, everything was amazing. God is doing so much in that little village, and I'm just so, so blessed that I was given the opportunity to witness it!" She pokes me solidly in the chest. "We need to have coffee one night this week to talk about how the Spirit is moving and what He's laid on my heart about what we can do right here in Specter!"

I nod eagerly, wearing the most genuine expression I can muster. "Oh yeah, definitely! I just need to check my work schedule. I'll text you!"

She arches an eyebrow. "You better, mister!" Her eyes finally release their hold on me, and her gaze turns to Harrison. "Aww, Harry! Good to see you too!" She wraps her arms around Harrison with a little less enthusiasm than she had with me.

"Hey, Sienna," Harrison says, his eyes meeting mine as they embrace. He gives me a sympathetic expression, and I immediately look away. I know what he's getting at, and I refuse to acknowledge it. Nope. Not today.

"Well, I've got to go get ready for worship, but save me a seat for the lesson, okay?" Sienna flashes me another perfect smile, and I nod in response. With that, Sienna takes off towards the front of the room where the band is setting up.

"You good?" Harrison asks.

"Yes, dude, I'm fine," I grumble. "It's been like two months at this point. You're the only one that ever brings this up, and quite frankly, that makes it weirder than it already is."

"Okay, okay," Harrison raises his arms defensively. "My bad. I'm just trying to look out for you, man."

I can feel my jaw clench, and the twist of guilt in my stomach is acting up again. The temptation to drive home or escape to Starbucks for a while is strong, but I shake it off. I choose to change the subject instead. "Is Elise coming today?"

Harrison slides back down to sit on the floor again. "Nah, she's with her dad this weekend."

Ah, the woes of being a child of divorce. That, and Elise doesn't have her own car yet. Harrison and I are the only ones in our friend group who were fortunate enough to gain our freedom right away. Harrison's car—a fifteen-year-old white Toyota Corolla—was a hand-me-down from his older brother. Mine was a product of good old-fashioned hard work, surprisingly legal teenage labor, and a small loan from my dad. The deal was that as long as I started working part-time at fifteen and was responsible enough to keep that job for a year while also maintaining decent grades, my dad would help me put a down payment on a car of my choice (within reason). It's the American way, after all. Who needs a childhood when you can have a car? And to his credit, my dad kept his word. I applied at a local restaurant as a busboy a week after my fifteenth birthday and worked a couple of nights a week and almost every Saturday for over a year, saving almost every penny I earned. Then, about a month after my sixteenth birthday, I finally found an affordable but sleek used red Honda Fit. It was love at first sight. I named her Eileen after my favorite song from the 80s. My mother was not pleased, but I thought it was perfectly appropriate.

Not long after Harrison and I resettle on the floor, Chase is at the microphone on the stage up front. "Good morning, Foundation family! Let's gather around for worship!"

Worship is honestly what makes going to church worth the effort. Worship is where it all feels more real, more tangible. The music starts playing, and it feels as though the presence of God is no longer a question. He's just...*here* with me. He's here with everyone, and sometimes, it even makes everything else fade away. All the stress about school, about work, about my future, about social media, about my love life—or enormous lack thereof—everything all takes a backseat to simply being present in the moment with God. And it makes it all worth it.

So, as the music plays, I lose myself in the best way. I close my eyes, sway to it, even occasionally feel my hands lift into the air. Sometimes, I'm a little self-conscious about how the music affects me, worried others might think I'm putting on a show for attention, but I'm honestly not. In fact, attention is the last thing that I want. Music just *moves* me. It always has. For some reason, God chose not to give me any musical talent, so unfortunately, I can't really sing or play any instruments, but man, does music still move me. It's the best part—maybe even the only good part—about church, and I never want to miss it.

Today, however…

"We are so blessed this morning to have Miss Sienna Watts back from South Africa! How cool is that?" Chase says excitedly into the microphone and the youth group cheers. Harrison and I are lingering towards the back, but even from back here, I can feel the radiance oozing off of Sienna, her post-mission trip glow outshining the bright spotlights overhead. "She and the team just flew in on Friday, so she really is a trooper for even being here today, let alone leading us in worship!"

I focus my gaze on a point on the wall behind Sienna and begin tuning out altogether. Sienna's singing voice—albeit angelic and beautiful and freaking perfect as always—tends to pull me out of the pleasant trance that worship usually provides.

After a few minutes, I feel Harrison looking at me again. Sure enough, when I glance at him, he's got that Concerned Best Friend expression. Damn it. I'm overwhelmed with the urge to escape to the bathroom, but that will only make Harrison more worried. I check my watch. 10:12 AM. Less than an hour to go. It's fine.

When worship is finished, we all grab seats to listen to the Sunday School lesson provided by an overly caffeinated Chase. As promised, I save a seat beside me for Sienna, who slides in politely with her gigantic purse that looks more like a book bag. Inside, she has a massive Bible, full of different colored highlighted verses and handwritten annotations in the ledgers, as well as an ornate journal that has seen better days. She eagerly pulls both out, somehow balancing both on her skinny thighs, and then she pulls out a small pouch full of pens, pencils, and highlighters.

Two months ago, I found all these little quirks about Sienna charming, endearing, adorable even. Today, however…not so much.

I try to focus on the lesson. I really do. My proximity to Sienna makes my skin itch, and that familiar guilt twists in my gut again. The worst part is that Chase's lesson is one of those very fundamental Bible stories that I've heard at least a thousand times before, so my mind wanders easily. Surely, there's something new I can glean from this old story, right? Sienna must think so based on how furiously she's taking notes and marking the verses in her Bible.

The rest of church is a blur of uneventful, mundane routine. We gather for more worship in the sanctuary with the adults. I spot my parents a few rows over from where I sit with my peers. The sermon is more or less the same as it always is, and I only almost nod off once this time.

Harrison sticks by my side, and eventually, so does Nathaniel, although I barely notice his silent arrival between services. I avoid Sienna, which is actually easier than I expected, but given that she's just returned from a mission trip, many people want to talk to her.

Thanks for keeping her busy, by the way, I pray. *You know better than anyone how weird this whole thing has been. Also, sorry for saying "damn it" in my head earlier. And also sorry for being bored during Sunday school. And the sermon. And for the less-than-pure thoughts about the college girls at the end of the row. Anyway, thanks again for Harrison and Eileen. And Nathaniel is pretty cool, I guess, for a little brother.*

Before the closing song is over, Harrison, Nathaniel, and I slip out the back door and head for our cars, escaping to freedom.

TWO
CALEB

Thursday, September 7

"What makes you think he likes you?"

Freddy stares back at me from across the lunch table, his phone in one hand and the grossest sandwich I've ever seen in the other. The thing is practically dripping with pickles.

I give a shrug, using my fork to shuffle around the pile of tater tots on my tray. "It's just a feeling. I don't know how to explain it. He handed me a basketball in P.E. yesterday, and it was this slow, deliberate thing. Full eye contact the whole time. Like he wanted me to know he knew what I knew that he knew."

Freddy blinks back at me, the cogs under his dark curls whirring hard enough I think there's smoke coming out of his ears.

"Did you have something on your face?" Wren asks, sliding in beside Freddy with their lunch bag and tossing blue-black bangs out of their eyes. "Because if this was yesterday, that zit on your forehead looked like it was ready to go Chernobyl. He may have been worried about being in the fallout zone."

Freddy groans, dropping his sandwich on the table. "Really, Wren? I've asked you a hundred times not to mention nuclear disaster while I'm eating. I don't want to think about people's skin sloughing off."

Wren pulls a slice of translucent deli meat from their sandwich, holding it out. "Too real?"

Freddy slides his lunch across the table. "Yeah, I'm done."

I drum my knuckle against the table. "Focus, people. This is serious business. I need your help in trying to solve the age-old question of 'Is that cute boy into me, or am I just desperate?'"

Freddy rolls his eyes, dragging the pickle-infested sandwich back to his side of the table. "You're not desperate, Caleb. But jeez, why don't you crush on someone easy for a change? There are, like, seven guys in our grade that are out and available. Which I'm pretty sure is a record for our sleepy little Specter."

"Yeah, and they've all dated you at some point. I'm not interested in your sloppy seconds, Freddy."

"Sharing exes is just part of the gay experience," Freddy continues. "Especially when the pickings are slim. Didn't they go over that in your introductory email?"

I roll my eyes. "I must have skimmed that section."

Wren snorts a laugh. "Okay, enough snarky banter. We get it. You're both very witty. Now, fill me in. Who are we talking about?"

"Logan McCreadie," I remind them, immediately jumping on the defensive. "And before you say anything, yes, I know he's not officially out or anything, and yes, I know he was dating Sarah Schultz over the summer, but they're definitely not together anymore, and he's been throwing these vibes at me all week."

Wren doesn't look convinced. Which, to be honest, may just be their face. They kind of have a permanent scowl. "Explain these supposed vibes."

"Well, the first time I noticed it was in Geometry when he looked over at me and did this thing with his foot under the desk."

Freddy and Wren exchange a confused look.

"He did a thing with his foot?" Freddy repeats.

I prop a sneaker up on the bench beside me, trying to replicate the seductive foot motion. It doesn't really do the original justice, but I think it's passable.

Freddy raises a thick eyebrow. "So, he was stretching his Achilles' tendon? He was probably sore from the drills we've been running at soccer practice. Coach Reedy is trying to kill us this season."

My foot hits the floor with a *thud*. "Oh. Well, that's fine. Then what about Tuesday when he was waiting by my locker after third period, and told me that he liked the *Hudson's Haunted Habitats* pin on my backpack?"

Wren jumps in on this one. "Isn't Sarah's locker, like, three down from yours? Do you think he may have been waiting to talk to her?"

Shit. That's right. Oh my god, have I dreamt up this whole thing?

"Yeah, I guess that does make more sense," I admit. "He was still there when I headed to Biology. Well, heck. Here I go again, making something out of nothing…."

Wren reaches across the table to offer me their ring-studded hand. "Don't beat yourself up. I was convinced that Abby Sears was into me last year when she kept winking at me during English Lit. Turns out she just has Tourette's, and apparently, her ticks went wild while we read Emily Bronte. I mean, *Wuthering Heights* also makes me twitch, but that's for completely different reasons."

"Why is my brain like this?" I ask, taking Wren's hand and slumping down onto the table. "Why can't I just like a boy who can, theoretically, like me back?"

"Tatt's vat I'm sayin'," Freddy agrees through a mouthful of sandwich.

"This will be the year," Wren says, backing up their pep talk with a pitying hand pat. "You'll find your perfect, moody boyfriend and drag him into our friend group like a demon dragging an innocent soul through the gates of hell."

I crack a smile, the embarrassed heat in my cheeks cooling. "Not how I would have phrased it, but I claim it all the same."

Leave it to Wren to compare high school romance to eternal suffering. I'm sure most people would have to agree.

Freddy grabs his phone as it lights up, tapping out a message. "And if the stars align, and we turn out to be wrong about Logan wanting to hop on it, then I'll be the first to admit it. Also, I'll be the first person in line to date him after the tragic but unavoidable breakup—ow! That was my kicking foot, Wren!"

"And if you want to keep kicking, you'll grow a heart. Can't you see our little Caleb is in emotional turmoil?" Wren looks at me and nods their head with wide eyes like they're asking me to play along.

I clutch my chest. "What will become of me? I shall be single for the rest of my days…."

Freddy polishes off the last of his sandwich, wadding up the plastic bag and tossing it into his faded Pokémon lunch box. "Maybe you should just lower your standards. It certainly has served me well."

Maybe he's right. Freddy is far more experienced than I am when it comes to dating and… *other things*. Hell, I haven't even kissed another guy, let alone had a hookup. It's not that I'm afraid of sex or anything like that. It's more like the opportunity hasn't presented itself.

Or at least, that's what I keep telling myself. I'm afraid the truth may be far sadder.

"And where do you think he should lower these so-called standards to? The basement alongside yours?" Wren gives me a wink before looking back at Freddy. "Not everyone is equipped for the fast and loose lifestyle of Freddy Desoto."

Freddy snickers at that. "Fast and loose? Sounds like last Saturday night."

"Oh please," Wren says through a laugh. "We all know where you were Saturday night."

"Stuck on the couch between us," I chime in, "watching that cheesy horror movie from Wren's mom's collection."

Freddy shudders, his constant smile inverting to a grimace. "Don't remind me. I'm still trying to get the blood stains out of my brain. Why do you two always make me watch those movies? You know how I get."

"In my defense," I say, holding both hands out in a gesture of goodwill. "I didn't know it would be a horror movie when I agreed to watch."

Wren crosses their arms. "What exactly were you thinking a movie called *Slumber Party Massacre 4* would be about?"

"I must have tuned out the massacre part," I admit. "I expected a little more gossip and a little less gore. Also, I wasn't prepared for so many topless scenes. What was with people in the nineties? It seems like there were just tiddies everywhere."

"Not that we think women shouldn't be able to show off their bodies," Freddy adds quickly. "We're not those kinds of gays who think the female body is gross. Right, Caleb?"

"Right, all I'm saying is that I don't want to see tiddies for the sake of tiddies. Give me tiddies with backstory. Tiddies with heart. Fully-developed-as-characters tiddies. I think I just really enjoy saying the word 'tiddies.'"

Wren rolls their eyes. "You two are ridiculous, and I would force you to watch the first three *Slumber Party Massacre* movies if I wasn't positive someone destroyed all copies for the sake of humanity. So there go my plans for the weekend."

"Funny you should mention that," I say, reaching for my phone. "I actually wanted to see if y'all were interested in a little field trip on Saturday. I was watching the preview for the latest episode of Triple H last night, and Hudson is going to talk about the old Catholic Church over off of Holly Street. Apparently, it sparked so much interest in the place that they've started up ghost tours after dark. Doesn't that sound awesome?"

Freddy's face blanches, but Wren's toothy grin is a good sign.

"I'm totally down," they say, checking their phone. "And I'm free."

"I have a game that day," Freddy says, his gaze falling down to his hands on the edge of the table.

"Yeah, at like two o'clock," I remind him. "And it's a home game. Come on, Freddy. We'll come to cheer you on, and then we can go get pizza after the game before we get scared out of our minds at an old catholic church. How does that sound?"

Freddy lets out a sigh. "Sounds like I'm running low on excuses."

"At least there won't be any pointless tiddies," Wren offers, giggling at the word.

Freddy slides to the opposite end of the bench. "Okay, that does it. The next person who says tiddies buys the pizza on Saturday."

Wren gives me a sly look, then turns back to Freddy. "Well, don't get your tiddies in a twist."

Freddy pushes back from the table, fighting a smile. "Oh my god, I'm so done with you both. And Wren, I'm ordering an extra-large just for that little spectacle."

Wren shrugs, still giggling to themself. "Worth it."

The bus runs late, so it's almost five by the time I get home. Usually, I hitch a ride with Wren—I'm not exactly what you'd call a "good" driver, so I still don't have my license—but they had a therapy session after school. Mom's at the kitchen table with Lola when I walk in, the two looking up at me from what I can only assume is a serious case-related conversation.

Lola's my sister, three years my senior, and is a sophomore at Georgia State University getting her pre-law undergrad. She's been living at home, but you wouldn't know it with the amount of time that she spends between school and her internship at Mom's office. Her bedroom is practically a ghost town these days.

"Hey, Cal." Lola waves from the table, her curly hair tied back off her face. Mom always said the two of us could be twins, but I honestly don't see that much of a similarity between us. Sure, we've got the same coppery hair color, and our noses both have a slight upward slant. And yes, we both burn like unattended bacon in direct sunlight, but that's Mom, through and through. Dad somehow managed to contribute a zero-sum to our complexions and jokes to this day that he was just an innocent bystander to Mom's pregnancies.

Mom looks up from the stack of paperwork on the table and then checks her watch. "Was the bus late again? I'm sorry, honey. You could have called!"

"It's fine," I say, grabbing a pitcher of tea from the fridge and pouring myself a glass. "It's just karma for my piss-poor driving record. Plus, I got to catch up on my geometry homework."

"That's my boy." Mom nods, her attention falling back to the workload. "Lola, I've got to run back to the office for a bit. Can you go over the Henderson file and let me know just how many times Mrs. Henderson called the cops over the last year? That should be a good starting point."

"You got it," Lola replies, grabbing a thick manilla folder from the stack on the table before Mom starts shoveling the rest of them into her bag.

"Your dad's on set late tonight, so you guys just call me if you need anything. Oh, and put in our normal order at Egg Rollz when you get hungry, okay? I should hopefully get back before my food congeals."

"Got it," I agree, sliding onto the bench across from Lola.

Mom kisses the top of my head and then heads out the door to the garage. Lola sighs, slumping down in her seat and shoving the folder away.

"This internship has convinced me to never get married. Like, ever."

"That bad, huh?"

"Worse than you can imagine. Straight people are vicious, my dude. I can't spill too many details, obviously, but let's just say if I had to choose between mediating divorce proceedings and shoving a nest of angry hornets up my ass, it would be the latter."

"Then why are you working with Mom? She literally only works divorce cases."

Lola folds her arms on the table, resting her chin on top. "It's just a foot-in-the-door situation. I'll pay my dues, get my credits, get my dream job working for the EPA, and never touch another divorce case as long as I live."

I reach across the table to pat her arm. "Think of all the trees you'll save.

You'll be one of the reasons we'll still have oxygen in a hundred years."

"Yeah, or at least I'll get to stick it to an oil baron. God, it'll be so satisfying." She leans back in her seat, cracking her knuckles. "But I've still got a billion credit hours to go, so I should probably keep focused on the here and now. What's going on with you, little bro? You seem down-in-the-dumps."

Here I was, thinking I was doing a passable job at hiding my teen angst. Should have known Lola would be able to see through me. She's got older-sibling x-ray vision.

"I realized that a boy I thought was flirting with me at school was really just existing near me while not actively trying to assault me. A common mistake."

Lola snorts a laugh. "Yeah, I'm sure it happens all the time. I always think people are flirting with me when they don't immediately punch me in the face."

With a sigh, I deflate down to a puddle on the table, folding my arms under my head. "It's not fair. Why am I only interested in the boys who can never like me back? It's like a curse. I'm forever doomed to unrequited crushes."

Lola shakes her head, sending her curls bouncing. "You're sixteen, dude. I think it's a little early to be talking about 'forever.'"

"You know what I mean. You had a boyfriend at fifteen. Freddy has had too many boyfriends for me to count at this point. Even Wren had a summer romance with that girl after they both painted each other's faces to look like swamp creatures and did that photo shoot crawling out of the mud. I mean, where's my swamp creature? I want it so bad that it hurts sometimes. I just feel unwanted."

Lola's expression softens. "I'll always want you around, Caleb. I know it's not the same, but it's true. Even if you're terminally alone for the rest of your life, and you end up one of those creepy old men that sit at the Waffle House reading their newspaper for hours every morning while slurping watered-down coffee and making passes at the servers."

I grimace. "You really know how to paint a picture, don't you? Do me a favor and put me out of my misery before I start sexually harassing people who are just trying to serve waffles to the masses."

"I'll keep that in mind. In the meantime, is there really no one at school that you'd think is a dateable option? I've always thought you and Freddy would make a cute couple."

I cringe, leaning back into my seat. "Gross. He's the annoying brother I never wanted, and I don't see that changing, like, ever."

"Okay, so not him. But for real, there's no one else?"

"No one that's shown an interest. I mean, there are a few guys that are out. Most of them are seniors, though, and that's super intimidating. Plus, Freddy's already gotten to most of them, so it might make it weird between us. Despite his blasé attitude, I think he cares about some of them more than he lets on. I don't want a boyfriend at the price of losing my best friend."

Lola nods along, her honey-brown eyes squinting. "Sounds rough, little bro. All I can say is if you really want it, you have to put yourself out there. Take a chance or two, and maybe you'll get lucky. But be smart, please. Don't go up to some homophobic asshole and get your teeth knocked in. Mom and Dad paid too much money to get them straightened out."

She's probably right. I can't expect a boyfriend to fall into my lap, although it would be so much easier. I've watched too many rom-coms.

Real life isn't like that.

"I guess I can try. Who knows, maybe my future boyfriend is out there now, feeling the same way I do."

Lola makes a gross cooing noise. "Aw. That's kind of beautiful, Caleb. Now, if you'll excuse me, I have to go thumb through police reports from a lady calling the cops about her husband fucking an inflatable goat on the front lawn. Isn't love a magical thing?"

"That old-man-reading-the-paper fantasy is suddenly starting to look better."

She laughs, grabbing the file. "Would you mind calling dinner in?"

"I'm on it. May the Beef and Broccoli give you the strength to get through… all that."

THREE
THEO

"I can't believe you're being such a freaking idiot about this!"

"*Me?* I'm the one being an idiot? Elise, do you have any idea how impossible you are sometimes!?"

Harrison and Elise are already bickering rather loudly as I'm approaching our lunch table. Their weird version of flirting would be endearing if it wasn't a daily occurrence.

As soon as Oliver sees me, he groans loudly. "*Daaaad,* make them stop arguing. It's giving me a migraine!"

As usual, Harrison and Elise are sitting side by side on one side of the table, with Oliver directly across from Elise, so I take my seat beside Oliver and drop my tray of food on the table. "Now, Elise, why aren't we using our inside voice?" I ask sternly, feigning a frustrated fatherly expression.

Elise glares at me intensely, her mouth gaping. "Are you freaking *serious*, Theo? You *always* take his side! You don't even know what insane bullshit he just said, and yet you're already telling *me* to lower *my* voice!?"

"I mean, you are being significantly louder than—"

"*Theo!!*"

Harrison is rolling his eyes dramatically. "He doesn't even need to hear my case because I know he'll agree with me anyway."

Elise looks like she's about to combust, so I reach out and take both her hands in mine in an attempt to ground her to reality. "You're right, Elise, I'm sorry. I'll hear your side first. What does Harrison have an insane bullcrap take on?"

"This absolute *moron* has the audacity to still believe that subs are better than dubs. *Still!* In the year of our Lord 2023!"

"I don't see why the year matters," Harrison cuts in. "Subtitles are timeless. American dubs are notoriously bad, and Japanese voice actors are just superior. I like to experience the anime the way it was intended to sound, and I don't think any American voice actors can pull it off better than the original."

Elise inhales sharply. "You see what I mean, Theo? He's being an idiot! First of all, subtitles just get in the way and are distracting. I can't read everything on the screen and see each character's micro-expression at the same time!"

"Says the girl who hates subtitles on everything," Harrison mutters.

"Second, this isn't the freakin' twentieth century anymore!" Elise exclaims, her volume increasing again. "Dubs aren't an afterthought like they used to be! American voice actors are incredible! You can't sit here and tell me that Matt Mercer isn't a fantastically talented voice actor."

Harrison's face twists in confusion. "I would never say that. What does he have to do with—"

"Dude, come on," I interrupt. "Even I know that he's Jotaro in *JoJo's Bizarre Adventure*."

"See!?" Elise shouts. "Thank you, Theo! Finally, someone is making sense at this stupid table."

Harrison leans back, slightly defeated. "Okay, yeah, I forgot about that. But just because one voice actor on one show—"

"He's not the only one! Do you want me to pull up IMDB right now and drag you across this disgusting lunchroom floor? Dubs are just as good, if not better than subs nowadays, and if you're not willing to join us in this century and give them another try, it's your stupid loss."

Harrison turns to me in frustration, but I simply shrug. "Sorry, dude, I'm with Elise on this one."

"Ha! In your face, Harry!" Elise says excitedly, giving Harrison a flirty shove as she cackles at him. Before long, there's a big goofy grin plastered on Harrison's face, and even if no one else can tell he's blushing, I sure can. I smile at the two of them. Their flirting is cringe at best and grating at worst, but all things considered, I know that Harrison is loving every second of it. He deserves this. He deserves to be happy. To be in love.

And as if on cue, my phone buzzes against my thigh in my pocket. I frown in confusion—all the friends who I regularly text are sitting here at this table with me. Well, except for one "friend" who, of course, attends a private Christian school a few towns over.

Sure enough, the message is from Sienna.

SIENNA: Hey Theodore! Sorry I missed you after church last night! What's your work schedule like for the rest of this week? I'd love to get coffee and catch up! <3<3 Are you free tonight or Friday night?

I try not to roll my eyes as I type out a quick reply.

THEO: hey Sienna... darn, I'm actually working tonight and already have plans w/ family on Friday night... :(

There's an instant sense of relief that our schedules don't align, but it's immediately followed by a twist of guilt for that relief. Damn it. I swiftly type out another response.

THEO: what about next Monday?

Please, God, let her be busy Monday, please let her be busy Monday. Also, sorry for saying "damn it" again.

Why do I do this to myself?

My phone buzzes again, and I brace myself.

SIENNA: Darn it, I'm leading a Bible study on Monday night :'(What other nights are you free?? I miss you!

The same emotional whiplash occurs yet again—relief that promptly morphs into shame. I check my work calendar, and sure enough, I'm off Tuesday, too. Great.

THEO: I'm also off Tues, does that work?

SIENNA: Yay! Yes, next Tuesday is perfect! <3 It's a date then! ;)

A wave of anger washes over me with that last text. It most certainly is *not* a date. I close the messaging app without replying and shove my phone back into my pocket.

"Uh oh," Oliver says, gently bumping his shoulder into mine. "What was that about?"

I shake my head. "Nothing important. What did I miss?"

"*Blehhh*, just those two being disgusting," Oliver groans, gesturing towards Harrison and Elise, who fortunately are not paying any attention to either of us. "But hey, before we forget, we need to discuss Saturday."

"Umm, don't we *all* need to discuss Saturday?" Elise butts in. "Last I checked, we're all going to Saint Catherine's."

Oliver waves dismissively. "Yeah, but you two are just going to find a dark little closet and make out the whole time. Meanwhile, Theo and I have more important business to discuss."

Elise makes a loud sound of indignant protest, her cheeks flushed, but

Harrison just grins.

"So, what's the plan?" Oliver asks, his attention uncharacteristically focused on me.

"Okay, so obviously, we've all seen the Triple H preview of tomorrow's episode about Saint Catherine's and the whole haunted girls' school in the basement thing. The tour guide isn't going to take us there, so we're going to have to find a way to separate from the group."

"They're gonna kick us out," Oliver grumbles.

"Unless only one of us wanders away?" I say, raising my eyebrows. "Maybe just the one who has a decent following on TikTok?"

Oliver rolls his eyes. "Theo, two thousand followers is not a decent following on TikTok."

"Uhh, I beg to differ! How many do you have?"

"That's beside the point—"

"Nah, man, Theo's right," Harrison interjects, his mouth full of Doritos. "None of us have even close to that many. However," his eyes are on me again. "I think you need to use my camera if you want to capture anything good."

It's my turn to roll my eyes. "Dude, the tour guide is absolutely going to notice if the guy that has the fancy camera wanders off all of a sudden."

"Theo's right again," Elise chimes in. "Plus, it's freakin' TikTok. It's more believable if the quality is shit. That's how these people are."

While I hate to admit it, Elise is spot-on. TikTok viewers don't care if the quality is garbage. They just want to see a tiny ten-second clip of something incredible. That's what I need to get my account noticed. That's what I need to get a real following.

"Okay, then it's settled. I'll sneak off with my phone and try to capture what I can. You guys should still keep your eyes open for anything weird, though. You never know."

"Is Sienna coming?" Elise asks.

Harrison elbows Elise, who yelps loudly.

"No way," I answer casually. "Y'all know she's not into ghost stuff."

"Not unless it's the Holy Ghost," Oliver murmurs, smirking in my direction.

I laugh. "Exactly. She'd be the worst. I would never invite her to anything like this." I can feel Harrison is still eyeing me warily, so I continue. "Besides, we're all already on her prayer list—the last thing we need is her worrying that a demon followed us home or something."

Oliver snorts loudly and playfully punches my shoulder. "Dude, she totally would, no question. I still can't believe you two were a thing for so long."

"Come on, man," Harrison says sharply, shooting Oliver an intimidating glare.

"Harry, it's *fine*," I insist. "We broke up months ago. I swear I'm over it. Geez." I grin at Oliver. "I honestly can't believe it either sometimes."

"I mean, I get that you're both Jesus people, but she's like, *waaaaay* too into Jesus. You at least still have a personality, you know?" Oliver wraps an arm around my shoulder and gives me a shake. "And that's why we love keeping you around!"

I snicker and shove him off playfully, trying not to think too hard about what he means by that. "Oh right, that's the only reason, huh?"

"So, what do you guys think about getting pizza before the ghost tour?" Harrison asks suddenly. Classic Harrison. "Maybe Pizza Palooza?"

"That sounds amazing," Oliver replies. "We can't experience the paranormal without filling up on greasy pizza first."

"I couldn't agree more," I say right before shoving my peanut butter sandwich in my mouth.

"Sounds like a plan," Harrison says with a clap. "Just the four of us. Theo, can you pick us all up so we can carpool? Save on gas?"

I nod eagerly as I finish my bite of sandwich and swallow. "Of course! It'll be a tight squeeze, but Eileen is more than capable of handling our load."

"Theo!" Elise kicks my leg under the table.

Oliver spits out his drink onto the table, cracking into laughter.

Harrison snorts and shakes his head, grinning at me.

I can't stop smiling. God, I love my friends.

Bussing tables at Cathy's after school isn't my favorite way to spend a Thursday night, but it's not the worst, either. I'd much rather work a weeknight than a weekend, and fortunately for me, the managers at Cathy's are more than happy to give those weeknight hours to high schoolers. Weeknights also tend to be pretty slow, so only one person bussing tables is more than enough. While I typically prefer Cathy's to be at least a little busy because it makes the shift feel shorter, sometimes it's nice to be paid to stand around doing nothing for a few hours. It gives me time to think, text my friends, or even write or sketch a little bit to pass the time.

But for some reason tonight, I can't stop thinking about stupid Sienna and her stupid "it's a date!" text from earlier. I keep opening the message again and again, wondering if I should reply. Should I set the record straight and say something about it? Would saying anything do any good? Does Sienna think there's a chance we'll ever get back together? And if she does, am I going to stand up for myself and turn her down? What if Sienna didn't actually mean anything by it at all? Am I looking too far into things?

With a frustrated sigh, I close the text without saying anything and shove it back into my apron pocket.

"Uh oh," says a familiar feminine voice from behind me, startling me slightly more than it probably should have. "What was that about?"

Grace is way too perceptive. Annoyingly so. It's weird working this job with my sister, but at the same time, it's kind of nice. It's the only time we ever talk now that she's at school most of the time.

I turn around to face her and decide to act dumb anyway. "What was what about?"

She raises a darkened eyebrow. "You looked at your phone and very obviously saw something that made you mad." She stares at me with her thickly lined hazel eyes, then smirks. "Theo, I'm your big sister. I see everything."

I sigh and roll my eyes. "Fine, it was just Sienna being Sienna."

Grace's eyes widen, and she leans in. "Ahh. You guys broke up over the summer, though, right? You're not—"

"Yes, we broke up. No, I'm not still into her. She still wants to be friends, though, and it's…it's not really something I want. That's all."

Grace purses her lips and raises her eyebrows, looking impressed. "Okay, wow. Yeah, I believe you. Good for you, Theo."

I eye her suspiciously, but she returns to wrapping silverware. She's being sincere—she actually believes me, and it feels like she's going to drop it.

"So," I start as I move beside her to assist her with her side work. "I heard you and Dad arguing again. Earlier."

Grace snorts, avoiding eye contact. "Yeah, well. At least it wasn't as bad as Sunday's fight. I wouldn't be surprised if the whole subdivision heard that one."

I glance at her again before continuing. "Are you okay?"

She still doesn't look up from the utensils. "I'm fine. It is what it is. I might have to stay with Chloe on the weekends instead or something. I can't keep doing this every weekend, but I can't just quit. I need the money."

I silently remind myself to tread lightly. "What if you just…went to church?"

Grace bristles beside me.

"Now, hear me out," I add quickly, raising my hands up defensively. "I know you don't want to, and it sucks, and it's stupid. I swear I'm not trying to convince you to go for your soul or anything. I'm just saying—it would make everything easier, right? Just suck it up and waste a few hours of your Sunday to keep the peace? I mean, that's what I would do if I was in your shoes."

Grace finally looks up from rolling silverware and stares at me with so much intensity that it makes me squirm. After several agonizing seconds of silence, she finally opens her mouth to speak. "You may be too young now, but at some point, you're going to face a moment where you have to choose to fight for what matters to you. You won't want to 'suck it up'. You won't want to compromise. You won't care about keeping the peace. If you believe in something enough, it won't even be a question in your mind: you'll fight for it."

It's my turn to stare at her, but instead of intense introspection or whatever cryptic crap she has going on, I am completely confused. "So…what does that mean you're fighting for? The right to *not* go to church?"

"More or less," she replies thoughtfully, her attention turned back to the side work again. "You'll understand once you start going to college, I think. As long as you don't go to a Christian college or anything." She twists her face in disgust as she says the words "Christian college," and I'm honestly a little surprised. I knew she had grown to dislike church, but I didn't realize it had escalated again.

I give her a nervous smile. "Nah, Christian college is way too expensive. Plus, I'm not Christian-y enough for all of that. Just ask Sienna."

I don't mean for that last bit to slip out, but it does anyway. Shit.

Crap. Sorry, God.

Grace's eyes are on me again, but they've softened. "Good. Also, for the record, I never cared for Sienna, let alone her shitty opinions of your religiosity, so she can kindly fuck right off."

I can't stop the nervous, explosive laugh that bursts out of me. I immediately cover my mouth as customers and other staff members alike turn their heads toward me, which causes my face to burn and Grace to start giggling uncontrollably. From around the corner, one of the shift managers gives us a stern glare, and I silently mouth "sorry" and shuffle away to the kitchen to hide and regain my composure.

FOUR
CALEB

Saturday, September 9

"Maybe this pizza will fill the void in my soul."

Freddy holds up his slice of pepperoni, watching the grease drip from the end before shoving it in his mouth. Pizza Palooza is packed, as it always is on the weekend. We've managed to cram ourselves into a booth meant for two, but that means there's been a lot of elbows in uncomfortable places. Freddy has been pouting since he climbed into the back of Wren's Honda after the game. Apparently, it didn't go well. I guess I should have been able to tell that from the scoreboard, but honestly, who can read those things?

"It wasn't that bad of a loss," Wren says, picking a stray olive off of their slice. "It was close for the first two quarters."

"I cheered like you were winning the whole time," I add, knocking my shoulder into his.

Freddy snorts a laugh as he chews, swallowing before he says, "Yeah, I was wondering who kept screaming when the other team scored."

"I've said it before, and I'll say it again, they really need to label those goals. How am I supposed to keep up with who's on what side?"

"You could just remember the color of the team's jerseys. The goalkeeper stands in the goal box the whole game—"

Wren leans forward, their hand outstretched to cut Freddy off. "Remember, you're speaking to sports-challenged plebs here. We know as much about soccer as you know about Stephen King."

Freddy furrows his brow. "I'm not dumb. I know he made that old movie with the wrinkly alien."

"That's Steven Speilberg," I correct him. "Think scary."

"Oh, right. I meant the guy that wrote the musical about people getting made into pies."

Wren lets out a sigh. "Stephen Sondheim. You're getting even colder."

"Okay, okay, I get it. I don't know the difference between Stephens. In my defense, soccer isn't that complicated." Freddy folds his pizza in half, shoving the rest of the slice into his mouth.

"Sure," I concede, shrugging. "And we shouldn't tease you so soon after the smackdown you guys suffered. So, let me change the subject. Y'all were one hundred percent right about Logan. I spotted him down by—what did you call it? The hole box?"

"So close," Freddy says with a sigh. "Goal. G-O-A-L."

"Right, the goal hole," I say, giving him a playful wink just to let him know I'm in on the joke. Wren coughs into their soda, pinching their nose to keep it from spewing out. "Anyway, after the game, while you were changing, I saw him and Sarah tasting tonsils, so I guess that solves the mystery of 'does that cute boy like me?' Much like the last dozen times, the answer is a big fat 'no.'"

Wren wipes their nose with a napkin. "That sucks, dude."

Even Freddy gives me a pitying frown, for once not taking a weird delight in my melancholy. That sounds bad—I don't mean he's sadistic or anything. We just find the misery of others to be funny sometimes. Don't all sixteen-year-olds?

He reaches over to wrap his arm around my shoulder and pulls me into his side. "I'm sorry, Caleb. Are you okay?"

I stare at him, more than a little thrown off by the sudden tenderness. This is not normal Freddy behavior. "Uh, yeah. I'm fine. It's not like I was in love with him or anything. I'll just add him to my list of boys I thought were into me."

He nods, patting my shoulder. "I know it still stings, though. Hey, we'd totally understand if you wanted to spend tonight recovering emotionally. Maybe we could just go hang at Wren's and watch a movie or something?"

There it is. I knew something was up.

"Nice try," I say, giving him another gentle shove. "You're not getting out of the ghost tour that easy."

Freddy's feigned demeanor evaporates as he scrunches his nose. "Shit. I was so close."

"Yeah, for a second, I thought you cared about me."

"I *do* care about you, asshole," Freddy argues, punctuating his sentence with an elbow to my ribs.

Wren grabs another slice of their pizza, inspecting it. "Come on, Freddy. It's a tour of a cool old church. What's the worst thing that could happen? You get a splinter on an old pew?"

Freddy points a finger at them. "First of all, splinters are the leading cause of finger amputations, and secondly, it's a *church*. What if I get possessed by the vengeful spirit of a preacher who squeezes all the gay out of me, then tries to make me convert people? I mean, can you imagine me waking up one day and being like, 'I must make the gays repent.'"

Wren and I snicker at Freddy's preacher imitation. Honestly, it sounds just like the crazy pastors that show up on my TikTok from time to time. Their videos are usually stitched with creators tearing down their flawed ideology, but not always. Sometimes, it's just the hate coming right at you through the screen, and it's enough to make you want to throw up.

My family isn't involved with the church in any capacity, so I don't really understand where all the vitriol comes from. Mom grew up going to a huge Baptist church a town over, but once she moved away for college, she hasn't set foot in a church since. She doesn't really talk about it, but when the topic arises, she's quick to steer the conversation in another direction.

Wren's elbows rest on the edge of the table as she leans forward. "Okay, I'm actually with Freddy on this one, Caleb. That sounds like an absolute nightmare. What are the odds of one of us getting hijacked by brother Billy, the queer-bashing, Lord-loving, crucifix-carrying bible thumper who just wants to 'save' us heathen children?"

"But think about the positives!" I exclaim, drawing the attention of the table next to us. "We'd be able to get on triple H, no problem! Hell, we could make our own channel, something like 'Our Friend, the Ghost Bigot.' So, let's make a pact right here and now. If any of us get possessed by an evangelical ghost, the other two have permission to take full monetary advantage of them." I hold out both pinky fingers to them.

Wren and Freddy lock their fingers with mine.

"Agreed."

"One hundred percent."

The three of us laugh through the absurdity, returning our pizza and sodas and falling into the comfortable rhythm of our trio.

"Theo! Over here!"

A girl with dark, wavy hair pops up over the back of Wren's side of the booth, her furrowed brow and sneering frown rather intimidating. She looks familiar—which isn't saying much. Specter High is the only public high school in town, so I'm sure I've seen her around.

My eyes follow her gaze to the opposite side of the restaurant and the boy in the black band t-shirt and jeans. He gives the girl a slight wave, then shuffles awkwardly through the busy dining room. For some reason, I keep watching him as he squeezes between the tight tables, apologizing under his breath as he brushes against the patrons. There's something… cute about the way he moves like he's tiptoeing through the world, every movement measured. Deliberate. He reaches the booth with the girl and slides in, disappearing from my sight.

"Who are you looking at?" Wren asks, piling napkins on their tray till they've got a little pizza-stained mountain.

"Nobody," I say, shaking my head. "I just thought I recognized someone."

"Already moving on from the Logan heartbreak?" Freddy inquires, leaning into my shoulder again to try and get a glimpse.

I push him back into place. "No, I think it's just a guy from English Lit class."

"A cute guy from your English Lit class?"

"You really are like a dog with a bone, aren't you?"

Freddy shrugs. "Can't turn it off."

"I think his name is Theo," I say, careful to lower my voice since he's only one booth over. Then again, I don't think they're going to hear us over the noise of the dining room. The rest of Specter High's soccer team has shown up at this point, and they're not as demure as Freddy about their loss as they shout and launch packs of red pepper flakes at each other across the restaurant.

Boys can be so exhausting sometimes.

Wren leans forward, lowering their voice as well, so it feels like we're having this secret conversation. "Is it Theo Briggs? I had a Biology lab with him last year. He was my partner for all the dissections. He's nice. A little quiet, but there's not much to say when you're hacking up soggy animal carcasses in the name of science."

"Yuck," I say, pushing my last slice of pizza away. "Don't remind me. The smell of formaldehyde will haunt me for the rest of my life. If I didn't have Freddy as my partner, I wouldn't have made it through."

Freddy grabs the rejected pizza from my plate, unbothered. "Happy to help. So, do you think this guy is a viable option for our boy, Wren?"

Wren hesitates, biting their bottom lip.

"You don't have to answer that," I say, still worried Theo or his friends will hear us. "It's not like I'm actually interested. Besides, I'm thinking I should take Freddy's advice and only pursue guys I know one hundred percent are into other guys."

"Shee?" Freddy mumbles through a mouthful of cheese and pepperoni, "I'm herry vise."

Wren shakes their head. "You just agreed with Freddy. These are dark times, Caleb. Dark times indeed."

"What choice do I have? It's either this or accept the fact I'll be single forever."

"Forever is a bit much," Wren argues, echoing Lola's sentiment as they swipe a dark bang from their face. "But I get it. I have to ask, though, is being in a relationship really so important you'd consider jumping head-first into one you know isn't going to work?"

They have a point.

But ever since Freddy got his first boyfriend back at the start of tenth grade, I can't help but long for the same happiness (albeit short-lived) that he had. And with each new boyfriend of his, the jealousy has only gotten worse. Does it make me a shitty friend that his happiness makes me miserable? Maybe. But I can't talk about it.

Sometimes you just have to suck up the shitty feelings so you don't hurt the people you care about.

"I don't know," I admit, as one of the soccer boys bellows at the table beside us, raising his fists in the air in celebration. I raise my voice and add, "I just want to feel that spark, you know? I've never experienced it before, and at this point, I'm starting to wonder if I ever will."

"You're starting to sound like my mom when she's swiping on her dating app of the week," Freddy chimes in. "Give yourself a break, Cal. It's not like you're an old spinster."

"I know, you're right. *Jeez*, I will never get used to saying that to you."

Freddy sticks his tongue out at me, and Wren laughs. "I think what we're trying to say here is just relax, Caleb. The right guy will come along soon, and you'll forget all about how sucky it feels right now."

"What they said," Freddy adds. "And if you end up some old, unwanted, gay recluse, you can always come and stay with me and my fabulously wealthy husband. We'll prepare the guest house for you. You can be our pool boy."

Wren and I share a look across the table.

Oh, great. Another plan for my loveless future. I deflate with a sigh.

"It's the thought that counts, I guess."

FIVE
THEO

Saturday has finally arrived, and as planned, Eileen and I make the rounds to pick up my friends. Harrison is already at Elise's house, so I only have to make two stops. Predictably, Harrison and Elise cram in the backseat, holding hands and giggling to themselves occasionally, while Oliver, with his freakishly long legs, takes the passenger seat up front. Once again, it's a tight squeeze, but it's more than manageable.

When we arrive at Pizza Palooza, it's wildly busy. We have to split up right away so that Harrison and Elise can find a table while Oliver and I wait in line to order.

"God, they're sickening sometimes," Oliver grumbles to me as he watches Harrison and Elise flirting at the booth.

I elbow him. "Nah, you're just jealous. Once you find someone, you'll be just as gross."

"Yeah, yeah," Oliver says dismissively, then turns back to me with a grin. "Man, look at the two of us. The oldest of our friends and yet the lonesome bachelors." He smirks at me. "I mean, I know why *I'm* still single."

I raise an eyebrow at him. "Oh yeah? Why's that?"

"I'm too unapproachable," Oliver says while dramatically motioning a hair flip, even though all his sandy blonde hair is pulled back into a bun. "People are intimidated by my wit and charm. They always assume I'm far too hot and desirable to be single. I don't blame them. I'd be intimidated by me, too."

I roll my eyes. "Ah, yes, of course, that's the reason."

"But *you*? Why are you still single? You've been single for what, a month or two?"

"Yep."

"So, who's next? What's the deal?" For a moment, his expression softens, and there's a sliver of uncharacteristic seriousness. "Are you still actually, like, *into* Sienna? I know Harrison thinks you—"

I am already shaking my head vigorously as I interrupt him. "Not even in the slightest, dude. Harry's just being Harry. I'm one *thousand* percent over her. In fact, I'm not even sure I want to be friends with her anymore."

"Damn, that bad, huh?" Oliver whistles. "Then why haven't you been talking to any other girls?"

I shrug. "I don't know, man. There's not really anyone I really…*connect* with, you know? Like, I'm sure there are some hot girls in Specter, but none of them seem interested in the same stuff as me, or—I don't know. It doesn't seem worth the drama right now."

"So, what I'm hearing is that you're literally single for lack of trying," Oliver says with a grin.

"I guess?"

"Sounds like you might end up being our weird single friend after college who just lives alone in a studio apartment with like twelve cats or something."

"Twelve cats? That's how you see my future?"

"Exactly. Theo, the crazy old cat lady. But hey, if you want, we can make a pact or something. If we're both still single by thirty, I'll settle down and marry you myself." He grins as he wraps an arm around my shoulder and gives me a shake.

I laugh at an awkwardly loud volume. Shi—*crap*, that was too loud. Now it's weird. Now he's going to think I'm uncomfortable. Why would I be uncomfortable? Because I'm secretly gay or something? Obviously, I'm not, but even if I was, Oliver wouldn't care if I was gay—none of my friends would. Well, except maybe Sienna, but yikes, that's a whole separate can of worms that I don't want to touch right now.

Ugh, I've got to get it together. It's a joke. It's Oliver. Why am I making this weird?

"No homo, of course," Oliver adds with a chuckle, seemingly unaware of my inner panic.

"No homo," I repeat, trying to think of something funny to say, but suddenly I'm flustered about being flustered. Shit. Crap.

"Next!" the cashier calls out, her eyes meeting mine. I quickly but casually slide out of Oliver's grasp and escape to the counter to order my pizza.

Once we've regrouped at our table and are happily stuffing our faces, the weird feeling in my gut about Oliver's joke has passed, and all that remains is the insatiable hunger for greasy pizza and the anticipation for the evening's activities.

"Ugh, why are there only soccer people here?" Elise asks as she glances around the restaurant.

All our mouths are full of pizza, but Oliver answers anyway. "Nah, I saw Wren earlier. They were sitting with one of the soccer players and some red-headed kid."

"Who's Wren?" Harrison asks.

"They're the non-binary kid me and Theo had Biology lab with last year," Elise responds after a sip of her soda. "But yeah, they hang out with Freddy from the soccer team, so that's why they're here. But who's the other guy?"

I shrug. I'm not good at paying attention to anyone that's outside of our friend group. What's the point? It's not like anyone ever notices me.

Oliver shrugs. "I don't know. His hair's more like Sienna's color."

Elise's eyes light up. "Oh yeah! I think I know who you're talking about.

He's the cute curly-haired boy I had a crush on in ninth grade before I found out he was gay."

Harrison clears his throat aggressively and almost goes into a coughing fit. Elise smiles mischievously at me without looking at Harrison. The power this girl holds over Harrison is unmatched and, quite frankly, frightening.

"Do you think they're going to Saint Catherine's too?" Oliver asks. "I mean, I know there are more Triple H fans out there. I can go ask them. Maybe we can hang out with them."

"No way," I answer sternly. "We need to stay focused. We're here on a mission, after all."

"Shit, my bad, you're right," Oliver concedes. "Stick to the plan. The plan is still letting you wander off to the basement alone, right?"

I nod. "Just me. I won't be gone too long, and I may get caught and kicked out, but if I can capture something on camera, it'll be more than worth it."

"We all need to be super chill for this to work," Harrison chimes in with a very serious tone, mainly looking at Oliver. "We can't bring any kind of attention to ourselves, good or bad. As long as we blend in with the crowd, no one will even notice when Theo disappears."

"Agreed," Oliver says, his eyes and smile growing wider. "Holy shit, I'm so excited about this, guys! We might actually see some scary shit tonight! Can you imagine? Like a real ghost or demon or something!"

"I highly doubt it," Elise says, scrunching her nose in disgust. "I'm more worried that it's going to be super lame and educational. Like they're actually going to try to teach us the history of the church or something."

"Gross," I mutter.

"Hey, that could still be interesting," Harrison offers. "I'm sure there's a lot of history to unpack at a place like that, you know?"

Elise and I just roll our eyes, but Oliver tosses a packet of red pepper flakes at Harrison's face in response, and the table erupts into laughter.

SIX
CALEB

"This way for the tour! We'll be scanning your tickets at the door!"

The cracked and splintered parking lot outside the abandoned church is almost full. As we climb out into the sticky, warm air, a buzz of excitement hovers over the group of tour patrons across the lot. They form a rough line at the entrance to the sloped-roof chapel. I'll bet they're all Triple H fans, like us.

Beams of orange late-day sun streak across the dirty stained-glass windows of the church. Parts of the walls are actively crumbling from the years of neglect, but the waivers on their website stated protective measures are in place to keep people from being hurt during the tour.

I don't recall seeing anything about them covering possessions, though. Guess we'll have to cross that bridge if we come to it.

"This place is a shit hole," Wren says, pulling out their phone to snap a picture of the crooked steeple. "Good thing I've had my tetanus shot."

Freddy paces back and forth along the trunk of Wren's car, chewing on his thumbnail. "Why are we doing this again?"

"Because it's fun," I remind him. "Come on, aren't you at least a little curious about this place? It's been here forever."

"Curious?" Freddy shakes his head. "Not in the slightest. Weirded out?

Absolutely. My *bisabuela* used to talk about this place when we'd visit her in hospice. She went to school here when she was little. They ran a girls' school out of the basement back then. Of course, that was, like, in the fifties, so who knows what kind of crazy shit actually went on. She was eight when that fire broke out, and it destroyed all the classrooms. She told us it was because this place was, like, a gate to hell, and the devil himself was trying to crawl through."

Wren gives me a puzzled look. "Oh really? Because what I heard is that one of the nuns kept smoking behind the schoolhouse and flicked a cigarette into the bushes. But your story about a hell gate is much more entertaining."

"Either way," I say, stepping between Wren and Freddy and linking arms with them. "It's an interesting story. Now come on, we need to get in line before our time slot starts."

Freddy whines as we move towards the crowd of people lining the sidewalk leading to the stone steps of the church entrance. A faded wooden sign hangs crooked from a post, the faded letters spelling out "Saint Catherine of Bologna Catholic Church." Now, I'm not exactly an expert when it comes to saints, but it wouldn't surprise me if she were the saint of deli meats.

"Okay, so there was the fire in nineteen-fifty-two," Wren says, pulling out their phone. "Then there was that dead body they found shoved into the confessional in seventy-four. Then, in the eighties, a kid went missing from mass one Sunday, and they still have no idea what happened to him. Was that everything?"

"You forgot the priest that hung himself in sixty-two," I remind them.

"Ah, yes. We wouldn't want to forget them, would we?" Freddy groans, shaking his head. "I'm starting to think *Bisabuela* was onto something here. This place is a nightmare."

"Relax," I try to comfort him as we join the line. "Harry went through the whole list on his video, and most of the stuff has been hella exaggerated."

"Do you think he'll end up doing an overnight stay here?" Wren asks.

"Who knows? I'm sure he's got a lot more interesting places to visit than

Specter, Georgia."

The idea of Hudson coming here is honestly laughable. Let's face it, there's nothing particularly special about our town. Sure, it's close enough to Atlanta to attract suburban families, but it's also far enough away that there's plenty of backward thinking leftover from the generations before us. In other words—Specter is a little behind the times.

"Group thirteen, please gather in front of the stairs!" A short woman calls from the doors of the chapel. "Your tour will be starting in about five minutes!"

"That's us," I say, dragging the others along with me as we pull away from the rest of the crowd. "Lucky number thirteen."

Freddy rolls his eyes. "God, this is starting to sound like one of the terrible movies you make us watch, Wren. What's next, one of the groups goes off on their own and ends up unlocking the door to hell? Then we've got demons running around everywhere, and if they ruin my date with Andrew tomorrow, I'm going to be really pissed."

"Andrew who?" I ask, raising an eyebrow. Freddy hasn't mentioned an "Andrew" before.

"Rhiner," Freddy answers. "He asked me to go to the movies with him tomorrow after he gets out of church. I didn't want to bring it up before, what with your fragile emotional state and all, but now you've dragged me to this terrible place, and I'm not so much worried about your feelings at the moment."

I hold back a laugh. A date with Andrew Rhiner is not exactly something I would be jealous of, even in my current mood. The boy has the personality of a background character on *Friends*.

"I didn't know Andrew was a Jesus Freak," Wren says, looking up from their phone. "And he's okay with the whole liking another boy thing?"

Freddy makes a face, going on the defensive. "He goes to one of those affirming churches. I don't remember the specific denomination. They all run together after a while. But they have all the rainbow flags out front and go out of their way to show they're not assholes."

Wren nods, going back to their phone. "Good for him. If only they were all that cool."

"It still feels kind of weird, though," Freddy continues, turning his attention toward me as Wren is off in their own world. "I've never dated someone who's into the whole 'God' thing. Do you think he's going to be weird if I want to have sex?"

"On your first date? Yeah, I think that may freak him out."

Freddy gives me a gentle shove. "Not on the first date, Cal. I'm not an animal. I'm talking eventually. If we last that long."

"How the heck should I know? You're talking to the world's only gay virgin over here." I hold up my hand before Freddy can interrupt, "I'm kidding. But it does feel like that sometimes."

"You're no help," he says, crossing his arms.

I roll my eyes. "Look, just talk to each other about boundaries up front, then you'll be fine. If sex is that important to you, be sure to bring it up before you catch feelings, or else you'll just end up hurting each other."

"Wow," Wren chimes in, stowing their phone into their back pocket. "Listen to this guy. Have you been listening to that relationship podcast again?"

"*Why Won't You Date Me?* is not a relationship podcast," I defend myself. "Well, actually, I guess it technically is, but really, I just like listening to Nicole Byer talk."

"Group thirteen!"

The small crowd around us begins to move, gathering at the base of the stone steps and forming a single-file line up the stairs leading to the large wooden doors.

"Isn't that Theo again?" Freddy whispers to me, gesturing in front of us with a nod of his head. I stand on my tiptoes to try and get a better look, but a stranger steps in front of me and blocks my view.

"I can't see him," I say, stepping back. "But I highly doubt it. Why would he be here?"

"Why am I here?" Freddy poses. "Maybe he got kidnapped too?"

"We did not kidnap you."

"Yeah," Wren agrees. "If we did, I would have shoved a sock in your mouth."

"On second thought, maybe it's not too late?" I grin at Wren, and Freddy retreats a few steps away from us.

"You two have fun. I'll just go wait in the car."

"Come on, Freddy." Wren walks over to retrieve him, pushing him back into our spot in line. "I'll protect you from the demons."

"My hero," he replies, draping himself against Wren as he presses the back of his hand to his forehead.

It's our turn to go up the stairs, so I do my best to wrangle my friends. We let Freddy go first so he can't escape when we're not looking. Once our tickets are scanned, we follow the group into the entryway, the stone walls rising high above our heads.

"Welcome, everyone!" the short woman says, gathering us all into a clump. "The Specter Historical Society would like to thank you all for joining us on the tour of historic Saint Catherine church. Now, before we get started, I do want to remind you that pictures are allowed, but please do stay with the group as there are very clear indicators—"

"That's totally Theo," Freddy whispers, pointing to the dark-haired boy on the other side of the group. "He's cuter than I remember him being."

I crane my neck to get a better look. He's with the same girl from the pizza place—probably his girlfriend—and two other guys I recognize from school. One tall and lanky with his hair pulled up into a bun, and the other stocky with glasses and a friendly smile. I can't remember their names, though.

"They must be Triple H fans," I say, keeping my voice low.

"Do you want me to talk to him for you?" Freddy asks.

"What? No. Why would I want you to do that?"

"Because you'll never do it for yourself, and then we'll be right back to where we started with the whole Logan situation."

Heat builds in my cheeks. "That was different. Logan at least knew who I was. Theo hasn't given me the slightest indication he knows I exist. Plus, he's with someone already. So, no. Please don't talk to him."

"Mmm…" Freddy taps a finger against his chin. "Okay, fine. But if I accidentally bump into him at some point and the topic of you just happens to come up in conversation, you can't blame me."

"Alright, now everyone knows the rules. We're ready to begin our tour!"

Oh shit, was I supposed to be listening to that? I'm sure it'll be fine.

The guide leads the group into the main cathedral first, allowing us to fill a few rows of wooden benches as they tell us the story of Saint Catherine of Bologna. I spend most of the time scrolling on my phone and taking pictures of the cobweb-covered lamps that hang from the ceiling. Most of the windows have been boarded up, but a few of the stained-glass ones are still intact, and our guide explains how they were made in Italy and brought over during the church's construction in 1922.

"Are you going to talk about the hanging priest?" someone asks during a lull in the guide's story.

The short woman lets out a sigh before answering, "This is a historical tour of a landmark, sir. We will be sharing only the proven historical events that took place here."

"Are you saying he didn't hang himself?" someone else asks.

"That totally happened! My grandpa said he was the one that found him!"

"That's fake news!"

"What about the fire? Was the nun disgruntled?"

Quickly, the crowd turns on the guide, the arguing intensifying to the point where the guide has to shout.

"We will continue the tour through the parish! Please follow me and hold all questions till the end of the tour!"

Wren, Freddy, and I rejoin the group at the tail end.

"This is kind of lame," Wren mutters, pulling out their phone again.

"I thought at least we'd get some gory details. I was hoping to get some inspiration for a new look. All I've got so far is the overwhelming urge to fix our guide's insane eyeshadow."

"She does look wild," Freddy agrees. "Do you think she knows the eighties are over?"

"Sorry, guys," I say, a bit embarrassed as this whole thing was my idea. "I thought it was going to be way more entertaining."

"At least there haven't been any demon sightings," Freddy says, elbowing me in the ribs.

The group bottlenecks at the exit of the cathedral, leaving us to wait as everyone funnels through the narrow door to the stairwell that leads up to the parish on the second floor. Once inside, we wait patiently for the line to traverse the stairs. Across from us, another set of stairs descends, but a section of dusty velvet rope blocks the path, a sign taped to the rope reading, "Basement closed to the public."

"I wish we could go down there," I whisper, standing on my toes to get a better look at what lies at the bottom of the stairs. But it's too dark. There's a flicker of movement in the shadows, and my heart nearly jumps out of my chest. It's quiet all of a sudden.

"Did you see that?" I turn to ask Wren, but they've already disappeared up the stairs with the rest of the group. I look back down into the shadowy stairwell, giving myself a chance to come to my senses. A shuffling noise comes from below.

Am I really about to do this?

I duck under the rope and head down into the darkness.

SEVEN
THEO

It turns out that, unfortunately, Elise's cynical prediction about the tour being lame and educational isn't far from reality. The tour is extremely boring. While the Triple H episode has clearly brought quite a lot of attention to the historical site, it seems apparent that not all the attention has been positive or productive in the eyes of whoever owns the property.

Oh well. They're not going to stop me from exploring that basement.

There's eventually a perfect moment of chaos where the tour guide is just distracted enough by frustrated guests that I decide it's time to make my move. I exchange glances with Oliver, and he gives me a knowing nod. Harrison and Elise are once again too wrapped up in their own romantic pining to even notice, but that's okay because the fewer people notice my getaway, the better.

Thankfully, Oliver and I did our research ahead of time, so I feel prepared for this. We watched and rewatched the Triple H episode at least a dozen times last night and this morning, analyzing each and every scene to try to visualize the layout of the church before going in. We inspected dozens of other images and blueprints that we were able to dig up through hours of Google searches, so I'm pretty confident I know exactly where I need to go. I'm well aware that sketching out and attempting to memorize a floorplan of a century-old church building isn't quite the same as actually exploring it in the dark by myself while also trying not to get caught, but hey, it's definitely better than going in completely blind.

Slipping away from the crowd is surprisingly easy, but I still move quickly, my heart racing. There are two nearby entrances to the basement: one up ahead at the entrance to the parish and one that we've already passed at the entrance to the cathedral. As the tour guide begins guiding the group out through the parish up ahead, I sneak back to the entrance of the cathedral, duck under the velvet rope (complete with a sign that says, "Basement closed to public," no less), and head down the stairs.

Despite everything, I feel a surreal sense of calm about the whole thing as I carefully creep down each ominous step. It's kind of strange if I stop to think about it. When it comes to following the rules, this is my only exception. I am uncharacteristically determined to do whatever it takes to get some paranormal footage tonight, even if it means risking getting into legitimate trouble. Even so, what's the worst that could happen?

The basement is absolutely as creepy as the Triple H episode made it out to be, and possibly even more. Of course, there's no fancy camera work or professional lighting at all, so the actual darkness is far more foreboding. The distinct smell of mildew and dust lingers in the air, heavy and strong. Fortunately, there aren't as many cobwebs as I was expecting, so I continue as quickly and as quietly as I can.

For the most part, I use my phone's flashlight to guide my way, but up ahead, I spot where there's some light pouring in from the other entrance to the basement. I listen carefully for where the crowd is moving upstairs before crossing the opening, hoping all the party members have already passed. I pause for a moment, silently listening to see if anyone followed me, then keep moving forward.

I recognize a familiar length of scorched wall from my research, and I go ahead and pull out my phone, double-checking that it's set to vibrate.

Opening TikTok as quietly as possible (media volume down, media volume down!), I adjust the appropriate settings and prepare to record.

Suddenly, I hear something behind me. Movement. Footsteps?

Holy shit, is this it!?

Trying not to panic, I grip my phone tightly, press record, and whip myself around to face the source of the noise.

I almost drop my phone as my outstretched recording arm rams into a solid, living person. Something akin to a yelp escapes my mouth before I can stop it, and the other person gasps at the impact.

"Sorry," the stranger whispers. "I didn't mean to scare you."

I stare up at the person—a tall, lanky teenager with curly hair—and sigh with relief that it wasn't a corpse or a demon (or worse, a staff member). "It's okay," I whisper back, lowering my arm so I can stop the recording on my phone.

"What are you doing down here?"

I'm still trying to catch my breath as my brain finally registers that I vaguely recognize this guy from school. He's one of the ones Elise saw at the pizza place. *"He's the cute curly-haired boy I had a crush on in ninth grade before I found out he was gay."* Crap, what is his name?

"I could ask you the same thing. Did you follow me?"

"I saw some movement, and I, I thought it might be… something else."

"Something else?" I repeat, raising an eyebrow as I study him for a moment. "What, like a ghost or something?"

He shrugs. "Maybe."

Then it hits me. "Are you a Triple H fan?"

"Yeah, actually. It's the only reason we came in the first place." Even in the darkness, I can see his face light up with an enthusiastic smile, which instantly makes me grin back at him. The pale backlight from my phone screen casts shadows across his features as he leans closer, and something about his smile excites me.

"Cool, me too! So, you can probably guess what I'm doing," I raise my phone to show him the camera is still open, ready to record.

"You're trying to record a ghost? On your phone?"

I nod eagerly. "Or a demon, or just… Anything weird, you know? Can you imagine the views?"

"On what? TikTok?"

Uh oh. I know what's coming. The mocking, the condescending "TikTok is trash" comments, the disdain that people have when I express that I care about something as trivial as TikTok. I nod a little less eagerly this time, bracing myself.

"That's a great idea! With the right shot, you'll totally go viral!"

Oh. That's…different.

"Do you have anything so far?"

I blink a few times, trying to recover. "Oh, uhh—yeah, nothing yet. I just got here, but I think we need to head that way, right?" I gesture towards the main hallway. "That's where the fire started."

Curly-haired boy looks at me incredulously, his eyes glimmering in the phone light. "How do you know your way around this place?"

I glance down at my phone, suddenly feeling nervous again. "My friends and I did our research ahead of time. We knew the tour guide wasn't going to let us down here."

"Nice, that's smart," he says softly, still sounding impressed. "You really planned this whole thing out, didn't you?"

Once again, I just nod. Something about him makes me more nervous than usual. Maybe it's because he's a stranger, and even though he's being extremely nice and maybe even supportive, I have no way of really knowing his intentions.

Or, more likely, it's probably because I'm in the restricted basement of an extremely creepy and possibly haunted old church, literally hunting for ghosts. It's a mystery.

"Oh, I'm Caleb, by the way. You're Theo, right?"

I look back up at him in surprise. He knows my name? Should I have known his? *Crap.* "Yeah, I'm Theo."

"Cool, let's go catch ourselves a ghost!"

EIGHT
CALEB

Stumbling around in the dark basement of a haunted church with a cute boy is not how I saw my Saturday panning out, but hey, I'm not complaining. Even if the boy is impossibly straight.

"The fire started near here," Theo says, pointing down a narrow corridor that branches off the main hall. He holds his phone up higher so the light shines farther. "The blueprints we found said these were the classrooms."

"You looked up blueprints?" I ask, mimicking him and raising my phone over my head to illuminate the dusty space. "You aren't messing around, are you?"

Theo shakes his head. "Nope. I want this more than anything. I mean, come on, man. How dope would it be if we capture something? If we get enough views, Hudson may even ask us to be on the show."

"That would be insane. He's literally my favorite. I've been watching him since middle school when he was just making videos about urban legends. If I got to meet him, or hell, get the chance to talk to him, I'd probably pass out. Not to mention he's, like, so hot—" I catch myself, biting down on my lip. "Sorry, you probably don't want to hear about that."

Theo moves down the corridor, and I can't help but feel like he's running away. But he eventually shrugs and says, "It's fine." But there's a tightness in his voice that wasn't there a minute ago.

I follow him into the hall, thinking quickly to change the subject. "So, what got you into Triple H? Have you always been into paranormal stuff?"

Theo peeks his light into one of the doorways. "Nah, it's been pretty recent. One of his videos popped up on my For You page a few months back, and I got hooked. It was the one from that place in Baltimore, and he had those creepy voices on the recording."

I hang back, keeping my distance as he leans into the room, scanning from one side to the other. He reaches up to brush a lock of dark hair from his eyes.

Stop staring, Caleb. Keep talking.

"Oh yeah, the Smythe House. That place was wild."

"What's really wild were the views. He had, like, ten million views on his YouTube already, and double that on the TikTok clip."

He seems a bit obsessed with the numbers game. Is that all he's doing this for?

"I was sort of surprised to see you here, honestly," I say, wanting to suss out his intentions. "I didn't know if all this paranormal stuff conflicts with your religion or whatever."

Theo looks back at me, his brow furrowed. "Why would that matter?"

My cheeks burn as I look down at my feet like a scolded child. "Sorry if that sounded rude. I didn't mean it—I guess I'm just curious. My family isn't religious, so it's kind of foreign to me."

Theo nods, the harsh angles of his face relaxing. "Oh. Yeah, of course we believe in demons and stuff. I mean, I've never seen one, but they talk about them at church. The Bible asks us to believe a whole heap of stuff we can't prove, so why not believe in spirits, you know?"

"Sure," I reply, not really sure what else to say.

"Do you hear that?"

I freeze, holding my breath. The basement is quiet, with only the distant sound of footsteps coming from the tour group and groaning floorboards above us. I open my mouth to ask what he meant, but then I hear it.

I instinctively take a step closer to him. "What is it?"

"It sounded like a voice," Theo whispers, raising his phone to eye level, and opening the camera once again.

We stand still, and a few seconds pass before the noise happens again, shooting chills up and down my spine.

"It's definitely coming from in there," Theo says, pointing to the last classroom at the end of the hall.

Neither of us moves from the doorway. With our lights shining on the door frame, I can see the charred and blackened edges of the wood as well as the darkened marks on the wall above—no doubt from the fire.

"You can go first," I say, stepping to the side. "You know, to make sure you've got a clear shot of the room."

Theo doesn't seem thrilled, but after a deep exhale, he moves slowly into the room, his phone primed and ready to capture whatever is hiding.

I'm holding my breath, I realize, clinging to the tension in my gut as if I expect something to lunge out and snatch him. But he just does a three-sixty, pausing at the corners of the room, and just as he's about to turn back to me, he stops.

"Hey, come look at this."

The chills have morphed into straight-up heebie-jeebies at this point, but I enter the room as well, hurrying quickly over to Theo and shining my light in the same direction as his. There's a chalkboard on the scorched wall, with smears of faded chalk around the edges. In the center, a cluster of strange markings and symbols fills the board, making the shape of a five-pointed star.

"Whoa," I breathe, moving closer to the board. "What is all this?"

Theo moves beside me, shifting the direction of the light from his phone down to the floor. "Probably just kids, look there."

A fresh box of chalk sits on the ground, the top ripped open. Two energy drink cans lay on their sides beside the box, and a small pile of cigarette butts.

"Guess we're not the only ones that had the idea to come down here," I say, checking the time on my phone. I've been gone from the group for about fifteen minutes. How much longer till they come looking for me?

Theo lets out another sigh. "Lame. For a second there, I thought we'd found something—"

"This way!"

A voice echoes above our heads, reverberating through the empty space. I yelp, my foot catching on the uneven ground, and my hand grasps Theo's before I can even think about it. He tenses at my touch, and I pull away from him as soon as I'm steady again, muttering a quick, "Sorry."

What the hell are you thinking, Caleb? That's a good way to get punched in the face.

Theo shines his light up at the ceiling above us. An uncovered vent filled with cobwebs recesses into the ceiling. The voice echoes again, fainter this time, and I realize I recognize it.

"It's the tour guide," I say as the footsteps over our heads get louder. "They must be coming back downstairs from the parish."

"Damn." Theo pauses, making a sour face like the word tastes bad. "You're right. That must be what we heard earlier. Is it weird I was actually hoping for a demon?"

"Probably, but I won't hold it against you."

He lets out this weird, choked laugh and then falls quiet. I'm about to ask him if he's okay when my phone buzzes in my hand.

"Hey, Freddy," I answer.

"Where the hell did you go? I swear if you tell me you got dragged to Hell and you didn't even have the decency to tell us, I'm going to be very upset."

"I'm down in the basement," I explain, turning away from Theo. "And not to burst your bubble, but there's no portal to Hell. Sorry."

"Well, good. We'll just have to get in the old-fashioned way. Listen, the tour is about to end. Do we need to come rescue you or something?"

"No, I'll be up in a minute. Meet you outside the cathedral."

"Okay, sounds good. And I swear to god, if this is some demon pretending to be Caleb, I will annoy you so badly, you'll rue the day you ever crawled out of your sulfur pit, you hear me?"

"Loud and clear, Freddy. Loud and clear."

"Okay, byeee."

The call disconnects, and I turn back to Theo, who's looking around the room again.

"The tour is wrapping up, so I've got to head back upstairs. You may want to do the same."

He nods, lowering his phone. "Yeah, Harrison and Elise probably haven't even noticed I'm gone, but Oliver will be looking for me."

I'm starting to feel creeped out by the idea of walking through the basement alone, so I ask, "Did you want to come with me? I figure if we are caught, at least one of us can run away while the other distracts them."

Theo hesitates, his dark eyes wide. "Uh, sure. I'm just gonna take a quick video in here, and I'll be out. Maybe people will find the chalkboard interesting, at least."

"Sure, I'll be in the hallway."

I leave the classroom, stepping into the corridor. Out here, alone with my thoughts, I can't stop from circling back to me grabbing Theo's hand. I'm such an idiot. It's not like I did it on purpose or anything, but that isn't an excuse. I should be more careful. Even if he's not one of the loud, antagonistic religious types, it doesn't mean he won't react badly if he thinks I'm trying to come onto him.

But no matter how much I try to shove it out of my head, I can't stop thinking about how it felt to hold his hand, even if only for a split second.

Ugh. Annoying.

"You cool?"

Theo looks at me from across the hall, his light pointed down at our feet.

"Y-Yeah, sorry. Spaced out for a second."

"Come on, I think I can hear the next tour group. We can sneak out while they're in the cathedral."

I nod, following his lead as he heads towards the end of the hall and the stairs. Light pours down the dusty steps as we make our way to the main floor, Theo checking to see if the coast is clear before we duck under the rope and sneak into the cathedral. Sure enough, another tour group sits in the pews, a mixture of bored and frustrated expressions on their faces as they all realize that it won't be the ghost tour they expected.

The scariest part of the tour? It's too late for a refund.

Theo and I make our way back towards the entrance and slip through a side door into the muggy night air. The sun has long set at this point, and tall light posts hooked up to generators illuminate the parking lot. I spot Freddy and Wren waiting by the car.

"Sorry we didn't catch anything," I say, cautious of the distance between me and Theo. "I was getting really excited to meet Hudson."

Theo shrugs, stashing his phone in his pocket. "It is what it is. I'll just have to try something else, I guess. Maybe Hudson will come here himself, and then we can ambush him. How cool would that be?"

"Insane," I say with a laugh. "Hey, if you ever want to join us, Wren and I make it a thing to watch the new Triple H video every Friday after school at their place."

What are you doing, Caleb? That's probably the *last* thing he wants to do.

"Never mind," I say before he can respond. "Forget I mentioned it. I'll— uh—I'll see you at school." Turning my back on him, I haul ass over to the car.

"Hallelujah! He's alive!" Freddy yells at me from across the parking lot.

"Was that Theo?" Wren asks as I get closer, peering over my shoulder.

"Yeah, I don't really want to talk about it," I say, opening the door and climbing into the backseat.

Freddy and Wren share a look, then shrug and get in too.

This was nothing, Caleb. Just a run-in with a straight boy who definitely isn't interested.

I stare down at my palm as Wren cranks the engine.

This was nothing.

But if that's true…why can I still feel Theo's touch?

NINE
THEO

After Caleb runs after his friends—like, literally *runs* away quickly as if to get away from me as soon as possible—I try to shake off the weird warm haziness that I feel before regrouping with Harrison, Elise, and Oliver. It doesn't take long to find them casually chatting by Eileen in the parking lot. I did get a couple of texts from Harrison and Oliver while I was in the basement, but the overall vibe is still very relaxed as they wait for me. This was all part of the plan, right?

"Did you get anything?" Oliver asks eagerly as he spots me approaching.

"What was it like down there?" asks Harrison.

"Did anyone see you?" asks Elise.

I still feel like I'm in a daze. "Umm, so I don't think I got much of anything. No ghosts, just some creepy crap on a chalkboard, but surely that was probably the work of some dumb kids. Uhhh…yes, someone saw me but—"

It was that guy from school we saw at dinner tonight, I almost say. *Turns out he's pretty cool, and he's also into Triple H. He stayed down there with me, and we explored the basement together and talked, and then he accidentally held my hand for like two seconds, and it felt like my hand was being gently electrocuted, but it was fine because he said "sorry" when he let go, so it didn't mean anything.*

"—it was just Caleb. From school."

"Oh no," Elise says warily. "That's the curly-headed guy from earlier, right? Did he rat you out?"

"No."

All three sets of eyes are watching me, waiting for me to continue. Their confusion is understandable because my mouth is hanging open as I had planned on resuming my story, but my brain feels like it's on a slow internet connection, not quite buffered enough to continue.

"Theo?"

Time to shake it off. Time to act cool or I'll never get home. "Sorry, I'm a little spaced out. It was kind of intense there for a bit. I'll explain in the car, but yeah, let's head out."

As promised, I do try to explain what happened in the basement while we drive, ultimately deciding to leave out the one minor detail about Caleb touching me because it's unimportant, right? It's irrelevant—just a weird little thing that happened and nothing worthy of mentioning. When our eyes meet in the rearview mirror, though, I can tell that Harrison knows something is off. Fortunately for me, his car is at Elise's house, so I drop them off together before he can interrogate me further.

I catch another lucky break with Oliver because he is either completely oblivious to my weirdness or he has chosen to ignore it. Either way, I'm grateful as we talk about the eccentric tour guide, the ominous drawings on the chalkboard, and possible plans on how we can maybe revisit the church basement to try again in a week or so. Oliver gives me a fist bump as he hops out of my car, and I'm finally free.

For the first time since I've had a driver's license, I drive home alone in silence.

As soon as I get home, I head straight to my bedroom and review the footage I was able to capture one last time. After a few minor tweaks, adding some catchy captions and hashtags, I post it to TikTok. I barely pay attention to the video itself before posting it—because why bother if I was there—but I'm still hoping that at least it'll get me more followers.

Once it's out there, I change into some gym shorts and lay in bed, but I don't go to sleep. I'm not remotely tired. Instead, I stare at the ceiling and replay the events of the night in my mind over and over again.

He didn't mean to hold my hand.

It was a reflex. Caleb was just startled. Heck, I might have done the same thing.

So why can't I stop thinking about it? Why does my hand still feel like it's tingling when I remember it, even now, hours later? Why did it feel like that when we touched? What does it mean?

What the hell is happening?

Sorry, God, I know. But seriously, what is this?

I reach for my phone and pull up the first video that I took in the basement, the one I started recording the moment I heard footsteps and ended as soon as it was clear it wasn't a paranormal entity. It was just Caleb. I play it again and pause it just as Caleb enters the frame. Surprisingly, my phone does a decent job capturing Caleb's frightened brown eyes and his soft features. The low light just barely catches the reddish-copper tint of his curly hair.

Something happens in my chest as I watch the video—a slight burning sensation just behind my sternum that travels up and down my spine—and my heart skips a few beats before I forcefully stop the video. I close the app completely, lock my phone, and lay it on my chest, closing my eyes and taking a deep breath.

Crap, why am I acting like this? Maybe I just haven't made a new friend in a while. Surely that's it. I've been friends with Sienna and Harrison since elementary school and Oliver and Elise since middle school. I haven't made a new friend in at least five years. I have social anxiety. Making new friends is hard. That's all.

Also, now that I'm thinking about it, emotions were high in that place tonight. It was inherently scary, and what we were doing was risky. Even if there weren't any ghosts or demons, we definitely could have gotten into trouble with the staff. The stakes were high. Maybe Caleb and I are trauma-bonded now. Or something—I'll have to Google it.

That must be it. If we had met under any other circumstance, I'd feel super normal about Caleb and only kind of want to see him again like I would any other friend. We just had some stuff in common—the foundation of every budding friendship—and then we shared an intense emotional experience.

Hmm, I need to test this theory. Caleb and I need to hang out again without the threat of danger hanging over our heads. That's it. Just a normal, casual hang-out.

Okay. I just need to hang out with Caleb again. For science.

Sunday, September 10

The next morning, I am dragged out of sleep by the insistent buzzing of my phone over and over again. It's not my alarm, but just a constant, grating stream of buzzing. I groan as I groggily reach for my phone from my nightstand to stop the annoying sound—ugh, it's only 7:38 AM, it's too early—but then I'm jolted awake as I notice multiple frantic messages in my group chat with Harrison, Oliver and Elise (cleverly nicknamed "Oliver & Company").

> **OLIVER:** holy shit guys, theo's video is blowing up!! [attaches link and/or screenshot]
>
> **HARRISON:** *eyes emoji*
>
> **OLIVER:** theo, are you seeing this?

ELISE: AHHH Theo this might be the one!!
I'M SO EXCITED

OLIVER: yo is theo still asleep

HARRISON: Y'all know Theo doesn't wake up until like an hour before church starts, he's absolutely still asleep.

OLIVER: how could he sleep at a time like this
I mean it's not like Viral™ or anything but like
definitely his biggest so far

HARRISON: Yeah, no he's definitely still going to lose his shit over it.

OLIVER: ughhhhhhhh somebody wake him up

ELISE: Harry you should call him!! He's going to be so happy! <3

OLIVER: theeeeeeeeeeooooooooooo wake uuuuuuuuuup
theeeeeeeeeeeeeeeeeeoooooooooooooooooooooooo

I finally blink the sleep out of my eyes and type out a response because I know that Oliver will continue to spam the chat until I do.

THEO: okay okay I'm awake, I'm checking

My heart is already starting to race as I pull up the TikTok app. Sure enough, last night's video has already gotten more than eight thousand views and just under one thousand likes. Seventy-eight comments.

Huh? It doesn't make any sense. It's just a creepy chalkboard in a dark basement. What am I missing?

I scan through the comment section in hopes that something might clue me into what's going on, and the pieces finally start coming together:

"oooo spooky orb alert"

"YO WHAT IS THAT HOLY SHIT *scared emoji* "

"Fake orbs, lame"

"Did you see the orbs irl or did they only appear in the camera?"

"lmao you're gonna get haunted, rip"

"2spooky5me"

My eyes skim the rest, confusion overwhelming me. *Orbs?* What are they talking about? There weren't any—

I watch the video again, straining my eyes—and I freeze.

There, about sixteen seconds into the twenty-seven-second video, just beyond the chalkboard, are two strangely positioned orbs of light. One is floating to the left of the chalkboard, near the corner of the classroom, and the other lingers in the doorframe where Caleb is standing just a few feet out of frame. I watch it again and again, struggling to believe my own eyes, but every time, the orbs are there for a few seconds, and then they're gone. But they were definitely *there*.

My mind is racing. How had I missed that!? I know I didn't see anything with my own eyes while Caleb and I were down there. I don't even remember seeing them when I reviewed the clip before uploading it to TikTok!

How did this happen? What the hell is going on?

I jump back into the group chat.

THEO: did you guys watch the video?

OLIVER: yeah dude why didn't you tell us you got orbs???

HARRISON: You posted it after I was asleep so I didn't see it until this morning, but umm... What the fuck, Theo?

ELISE: ORBS?? WAIT

THEO: guys, there weren't orbs last night

OLIVER: what the hell man

THEO: I know that sounds crazy

ELISE: HOLY SHIT ASDKGKFHL

OLIVER: what do you mean there weren't orbs last night

THEO: I mean that there weren't orbs
    like I didn't see any orbs in the basement at all

HARRISON: Okay, we need to meet up after church today, you have some explaining to do.

OLIVER: what the fuuuuuuck, Theo got haunted!!

THEO: I just told you! I didn't see them! I would have told you if I did!

ELISE: THEO'S HAUNTED

HARRISON: Yeah but still you were weird last night, we need to get to the bottom of this.

OLIVER: ooooOOOOOooooOOOOO

THEO: Harry why wouldn't I have mentioned that I saw something ghostly? that's kind of my whole thing??

OLIVER: spoooooooooooky

ELISE: Oliver read the room, ffs

HARRISON: I'm coming over after church.

OLIVER: ooooooo theo's in trouble
can I come too actually I don't wanna be bored at home all day

Ugh, I don't feel like arguing with Harrison about this. During the entire conversation, I keep getting notification after notification from TikTok. More shares, more comments, more likes. This is crazy! Hell, Hudson might even see the TikTok if it gets enough engagement.

Caleb is going to lose his mind!

I'm taken aback as the thought crosses my mind. It's the first time I've thought about Caleb since last night, and there's a strange fluttering in my stomach at the thought of Caleb's brown eyes lighting up at the news that we might actually have something to show Hudson someday.

Wait... *Caleb might have seen something!* I need to talk to him. I need to show him the video and ask him what he saw. He wasn't in the room with me when I was filming, but maybe he saw something in the hallway or even the one lingering in the doorway. Maybe that's why he ran away so fast after we came outside—maybe he was freaked out! Maybe he was hesitant to tell me, given the conversation we had about religion, too. *Of course!*

My mind races as the reality sets in. If there was a ghostly presence that only my phone camera was able to pick up, that might explain why I felt so weird last night—why I still feel weird even now. An overwhelming sense of relief starts to wash over me. Maybe I'm not going crazy after all. Maybe I can make a friend like a normal person after all—this whole crisis has simply been a result of a paranormal experience.

Even so, I still think it might be a good idea to test my theory about it and plan a time to hang out with Caleb. You know, just in case. I need to make sure that I'm capable of making a friend in a normal capacity and that I'm not completely insane.

But how do I get in touch with him? I didn't get his number. I don't even know his last name or what grade he's in.

It's fine, I'll see him on Monday. We go to the same school—we might even share a class. How hard would it be to just find him in the hallways? Maybe at lunch?

Whatever, that's a problem for tomorrow. Right now, it's time to get up and start the day. Sunday. Maybe it won't be such a bad day after all.

As I make my way downstairs for breakfast, I can already hear rustling and movement in the kitchen, but quickly notice the distinct lack of yelling. This could mean one of two things: either the fight has already happened and Grace has locked herself in her room, or Grace has decided not to venture downstairs until after my parents have already left for church.

There's only one way to find out. I take a deep breath and enter the kitchen.

My mom is humming softly to herself by the kitchen sink, slicing what appear to be strawberries. She's still wearing her housecoat over her pajamas, so she must have only just woken up. My dad is seated at the head of the kitchen table with a hardcover book lying open beside his plate of scrambled eggs, reading glasses sitting low on his nose. He's in a white t-shirt and shorts, indicating that he, too, only just woke up. I warily take a few steps forward, clearing my throat to make my presence known.

"Well, look who it is!" Mom says cheerfully as she turns to me. "Good morning, *aroha*."

I smile at her. "Morning, Mom." She's clearly in a good mood if she's calling me *aroha*. It's the Māori word for "love" or "darling". Sometimes it makes me sad that Mom doesn't even act Māori most of the time. When her parents immigrated to the States before she was even born, they were determined to integrate into American society and raise their kids to be American first, Māori second. She doesn't talk about it much, but every now and then, little words and phrases leak through, and I think it's really cool.

"Morning, Theo," Dad mumbles, glancing up from his book with a polite nod. "Did we wake you up?"

I shake my head, opening the fridge for the milk. "Nah, my friends did."

Dad's head tilts forward so he can peer at me over his glasses with a furrowed brow. "Really? Why?"

I wince at my own slip-up. I hadn't intended to mention the video. Should I tell them about it? I mean, I might as well. They don't need to know how the video was made or that I had to break a couple of rules to make it. "Well, it looks like one of my TikToks blew up last night, and they were excited about it."

"Oh, Theo, that's wonderful!" Mom says excitedly.

Dad offers me an impressed grin. "Nice job, kiddo."

"Which video was it?" Mom asks.

"It was one I made last night at the Saint Catherine's Tour," I say, treading carefully as I make my bowl of cereal. "Just some spooky stuff that I saw. It was a cool place, so…" I trail off. Suddenly, I don't know what else to say. Am I lying? I'm omitting important details, sure, but…does this count as lying? The old familiar guilt twists in my gut again, but I try my best to ignore it.

"Nothing we should be concerned about, right?" Dad asks in a tone that could probably be interpreted as joking, but I can hear the suspicion in his voice. "You didn't get into any trouble, did you?"

"No, nothing like that," I answer honestly. "Just spooky old church vibes. TikTok loves spooky stuff."

"That's exciting! You'll have to show it to me later," Mom says, turning her attention back to her strawberries. The idea of my mom watching it worries me a little, but I'm pretty confident she's going to forget about it in a few hours, so I try to relax.

I sit down with my cereal at the table, catty-cornered with Dad, and begin eating. He hasn't stopped looking at me, and anxiety gnaws at my insides. Maybe he's just excited for me, that's all.

"So, how many views does it have?" Dad asks after a moment, shutting his book and sliding it away.

I swallow. "As of right now, about eight thousand."

My dad's eyes widen. "Eight *thousand*? Just overnight?"

I nod, unable to stop myself from grinning. "Yeah, isn't that cool?"

"Can I see it?"

I nearly drop my spoon as the blood drains from my face. How could I be so stupid not to know this was coming? Why did I bring this up at all? He's going to figure out that I was trespassing. He's going to see the pentagram and the creepy stuff on the chalkboard and think I drew those. He's going to think I was doing something demonic or evil or something. What if he sees the orbs? Will he think I'm possessed? *Am* I possessed? *Crap, crap, crap—*

"Unless there's something you don't want me to see," Dad presses again, eyeing me with clear suspicion now.

It's too late to back out now. I clear my throat again. "Oh, no, it's not—I mean, yeah, you can see it. Um, here, let me just—" I stammer, sliding my phone out of my pocket and reluctantly opening TikTok. Dad leans a little closer to me as I pull up the video, and I desperately try to will my fingers to stop trembling as I press play.

This is it. I'm going to be the one yelled at this morning. I'm going to get grounded. Dad's going to take my phone away and never let me make another TikTok again. He's going to take the keys to Eileen away. He and Mom are going to drag me to our pastor and have him exorcize the demons out of me. Maybe he should. Maybe I deserve it. I'm the one who broke the rules. I'm the one that messed with forces I didn't understand. I'm the one—

A second before the chalkboard is going to show up in the video, my dad's phone abruptly rings loudly on the table, and I nearly jump out of my skin. Dad snickers but turns away from my screen to glance at his phone with a frown. "Uh oh," he mutters.

"What? Who is it?" Mom asks worriedly.

"It's Pastor Mark," Dad answers with an expression of equal concern. He stands to his feet. "Sorry, kiddo, I need to take this."

I can hardly hide my relief. "Sure, Dad, of course," I say as I close TikTok and put my phone away completely.

Dad offers me an apologetic smile, then quickly heads out of the room, answering the phone with a "Morning, Mark. Everything alright?" before his voice fades away.

Whew. That was way too close.

The kitchen goes quiet for several moments, and I spend that time finishing my breakfast as quickly as possible so that I can get out of here before Dad returns.

"I hope everything's okay," Mom says quietly. I assume this is mostly to herself, but she turns around to glance at me before continuing. "Don't tell your father I told you, but I think Mark's calling about his daughter Ruthie."

"Hm," I offer as a reply, not sure why she's telling me this or why it's a secret. "What's wrong with Ruthie?"

"She's starting to have panic attacks," Mom practically whispers. "She's about the same age as you were when you started having your first ones, too, but Mark and Sarah aren't sure what's causing them."

I squirm in my chair. This morning just keeps getting weirder by the minute. "That sucks," I mutter.

"It does," Mom agrees. "Your panic attacks were very specifically linked to large crowds and overstimulation, so it was easy for us to resolve. Apparently, the Sheppards are having a hard time pinning down Ruthie's triggers."

I nod, shuddering slightly at the memory of the last panic attack I had about six months ago. It was a Phantogram concert—I should have known better, but it was a relatively small venue, so I had been confident that I would be fine. I was very wrong. I don't remember much of that night—just fragmented flashes of Harrison tossing me over his shoulder and carrying me out of the crowd like I weighed nothing at all, Elise cradling my head on her lap while dabbing my face with wet paper towels, and Oliver yelling at any poor soul who came within twenty feet of me.

It was awful, but my closest friends were there for me when I needed them most. Lessons were learned, too. I haven't been permitted to go to a concert or any place with a large crowd ever since. And while I'll always feel a little sad missing concerts, I'm perfectly okay with avoiding anything like that happening again.

"Her doctor wants to put her on medication, but she's so young," Mom continues. "So, for now, they're praying for a better solution."

I frown. "Isn't she like…twelve?"

Mom narrows her eyes at me. "Yes, but that's still way too young to be on anxiety medication. She's just a little girl."

I open my mouth to object, then think better of it. What Ruthie's parents do for her anxiety is none of my business and definitely not worth arguing with my mom about on a Sunday morning. Besides, I'm not even on anxiety medication myself, so what do I know?

"But Mark and Sarah remember when you were having panic attacks, so they've been coming to your father and me for advice. I just wish there was more we could do to help them. I remember how terrifying it was to…" she trails off, gazing at me sadly. "To watch your child experience such immense fear and have no way to protect them from it. It's just…awful."

I chew on my bottom lip, not sure what to say. "Yeah. I—I'm sorry I put you through that."

Mom shakes her head urgently. "Oh, my darling, don't *ever* apologize for that. None of that was your fault. It wasn't anyone's fault. And besides, we worked through it as a family and made it through the other side, right? Those panic attacks are ancient history."

"Yeah," I say softly. "Ancient history."

She's quiet again for a few moments, her eyes still studying me, and I almost think she's going to start crying until she inhales sharply and shakes her head. "Anyway, I don't want to hold you up by getting too emotional." She waves her hands, feigning dismissiveness. "You go on and get ready for church, okay?"

"Okay," I say, making my way to the sink, where I load my bowl and spoon into the dishwasher.

Before I can turn towards the stairs, my mom places a hand on my shoulder and pulls me in for a hug. "Just a real quick one, I promise. I love you, Theodore."

I return the embrace, rolling my eyes while she can't see me. "Love you, too, Mom."

"I'm proud of you, you know that?"

"I know."

She releases her grip on me and smiles warmly as she pulls away. "Good. Now, be free, *taku tama*."

I return her smile before swiftly bounding upstairs.

Man. Sundays are so weird.

TEN
CALEB

Monday, September 11

The cafeteria is especially loud today. Or maybe it's that I'm not quite reacclimated to the noise levels after my Sunday of laying around my room reading boys' love manga and listening to lo-fi.

"Freddy, for the last time, I'm not possessed." Wren sets their tray down across from me, followed quickly by Freddy beside them.

"You say that, but how can we trust you? You sneezed like, eight times during the tour. And as we all know, sneezing is the sound people make when they're trying to expel a demon from their body. That's why everyone is supposed to say, 'bless you.'"

Wren unscrews the top of their water bottle before brandishing it toward Freddy in a threatening maneuver. "That place was so dusty, half of the freaking tour group was sniffling and sneezing. I'm surprised they didn't try and sell us antihistamines out back."

"There was that guy selling t-shirts out of the back of his car. They looked pretty cool, right, Caleb?"

"Huh?"

I look up from my untouched lunch. Wren raises an eyebrow at me while Freddy is full-on staring me down. "What is up with you today?" he asks, unzipping his lunch bag. "You've hardly said a word, even when Ms. Gerty fell out of her chair in the middle of World History. I fired off that great quip about her not wanting to be upstaged by the fall of Rome, and you just sat there."

"I'm fine," I say, trying to shake whatever weirdness is weighing down my thoughts. It's like I've been in a fog ever since I left the tour on Saturday. I blame it on the numerous toxic chemicals I was undoubtedly exposed to in that basement. Who knows what all I inhaled down there?

"She fell again?" Wren asks, shaking their head. "At this point, you'd think the principal would cover that poor woman in bubble wrap."

The conversation continues outside of my focus, my thoughts drifting off again to the shadowy hallways under the Saint Catherine church. I haven't been able to get my mind off the weird symbol we found on the chalkboard, or the rush of terror that ran through me when we were in that classroom and the silence was broken by that voice. And the worst part, if I'm being one hundred percent honest, is I can't get Theo out of my head.

Which makes things very difficult when I notice he's walking straight towards me from across the cafeteria.

Oh, shit.

"Hey man," he says, hovering at the end of the table, his hands buried in his pockets. Standing in the pool of warm golden light filtering in from the skylight above, the ends of his curls are highlighted in tints of honey. "Not sure if you've seen, but the TikTok I posted went kind of crazy."

It takes me a second to catch up to what he's saying. "The basement video? Wait, did you actually catch something?"

"Kind of." Theo's gaze shifts to Wren and Freddy, who have paused their discussion of accident-prone teachers and are watching the two of us with a mixture of confusion and intrigue. He leans closer, lowering his voice. "Um, I wanted to talk to you about what went down, but I don't want to take up your lunch. Could we maybe meet up at Spookies after school?"

My brain short circuits, and I have to remember how to form words. "Y-Yeah, totally. We can do that."

Theo nods, his lips tilting into a half smile. Then he turns and walks back to the other side of the cafeteria, leaving me to face two very nosy friends.

Freddy practically teleports into the seat next to me, grabbing my hand and pulling it into his lap. "Here I was thinking that the recap of my date with Andrew would be the only thing we'd have to talk about. What exactly went on in that basement, Cal?"

"He said he didn't want to talk about it then," Wren reminds Freddy. "And I doubt that's changed. So, leave the boy alone."

"I'm sure it's just something about the video he recorded," I say, pulling my hand from Freddy's grasp. "We saw some creepy stuff down there, but it wasn't anything major."

Except, maybe it was. I need to find his TikTok account so I can see for myself. I pull out my phone and tap open the app, but then I get distracted by my own feed, and before I know it, the lunch bell is ringing, and I've not touched my food.

"I'll fill y'all in later," I tell Freddy and Wren. Grabbing my backpack, I dump my tray into a nearby trashcan and head for English Lit.

Relax, Caleb. Don't read into it. I'm sure he just wants to talk about the chalkboard or maybe ask if I saw anything before I bumped into him. Or maybe he wants to berate me for grabbing his hand in the dark.

Ugh.

I'm so wrapped up in my thoughts that it hardly even registers that Theo is sitting two rows away when I sink into my seat. Ms. Hyung moves down the rows of desks, handing out quizzes, so there's no time for me to notice how he chews on the end of his pencil between questions or how his leg bounces under the desk, alternating left, then right, then left again. And there's definitely zero time for me to watch as he flips the page of his quiz over and licks his lips before starting on the other side.

And shit, I've got seven minutes left for this stupid quiz.

I make a blinder for myself by cupping my hand around the side of my head.

Focus, Caleb. There will be plenty of time for staring at Theo later.

Spookies is only a couple of streets down from the school, so I decide to walk instead of asking Wren for a ride. Although, I wouldn't put it past Freddy to grab a table across the cafe to be the front-row audience for whatever Theo and I are doing.

The coffee shop in town is not actually named Spookies, but it's been affectionately nick-named that by the local kids since the time my mom went to high school here. Its real name is Java Beans or something lame like that, but they got the moniker Spookies after they decided to go all out decorating for Halloween one year and then got too lazy to take all the decor down. Since then, they've only added to the theming, hence the name. Now you can spot the inflatable ghost on top of the building from down the street.

The parking lot is already full as I walk up. I hope Theo can find a spot. The exterior windows are covered in faux cobwebs, and the bushes along the sidewalk are overgrown with Jack O'Lanterns and skulls sticking out at random intervals. Stepping inside, I'm greeted with the familiar smell of coffee and Spookies' famous pumpkin spice cake, which is on full display at the counter under a glass cloche. I do a quick scan of the cafe before getting in line to order, and I must miss him at first, but on my second pass, I spot Theo at a table in the corner, looking down at his phone. It doesn't seem like he's noticed me yet, so I give him a wave when he looks up, and he grins and waves back, which makes my stomach do this weird flipping thing.

Jeez, Caleb. You need to calm that down or this really will become Logan 2.0.

Once I've got my bloody lemonade—because I don't want to dump espresso on top of the anxiety that's already building in my stomach—I head over to the table in the corner and take a seat across from Theo.

"Hey."

He looks up from his phone, annoyance twisting his features as he swipes away something on the screen. "Hey, thanks for meeting me."

"No worries," I say, looking down at my sweating plastic cup. A line of red food coloring sticks to the side, looking almost like a wound. "Congrats on the video. I'm guessing that's what you wanted to talk about?"

"Thanks," Theo replies, any lingering irritation evaporating from his face. "It's crazy. I didn't think we'd even caught anything interesting in the basement, but I woke up yesterday to, like, hundreds of likes and people asking about what we saw."

"Can you show me? I tried to find it earlier, but I didn't have your handle."

"Oh, yeah. Duh. My bad. Here." He hands me over his phone, the tips of his fingers brushing against mine as he does.

I tap the screen to start the video. It's the classroom, of course, with the weird chalkboard and the singed walls. Then, about halfway through, a thrill shoots through me as I spot the first orb by the chalkboard, then the other just before the video ends on the other side of the doorway from where I was standing. It floats towards the camera and then vanishes as the video starts over.

"Dude, I was, like, right there!" I say, quickly realizing I'm being too loud and reeling it back in. I hand him back his phone, but not before making a mental note of his handle so I can find his page later.

"Right? That's why I wanted to talk about it with you. To see if you remember anything out of the norm while you were in the hallway?"

Out of the norm? I mean, not for a creepy, abandoned church basement. To be honest, I was too flustered by the fact that I just tried to hold a straight boy's hand, so I wasn't exactly present in the moment.

"Not that I can remember," I say with a shrug. "I was still coming down from the scare with the vent. Sorry."

"Damn," Theo mutters, then his eyes get wide, and he looks up. "Sorry, I mean darn."

I laugh, shaking my head. "It's fine. You should hear some of the colorful language that gets tossed around at our lunch table. These ears have heard far, far worse."

Theo smiles again, and I can't tell if he's just doing it to be polite or if he's actually enjoying himself. Why can't I be better at reading people?

"This is a great find," I add, steering the conversation back to the video. "I mean, I don't think they've had a lot of orb sightings at the location. It could be big news!"

Theo leans forward in his seat. "Right? I keep thinking about Hudson seeing it and coming down for a whole investigation. It would be so lit."

"Do you think he'd bring along Samantha and the entire crew, or would he do, like, a solo mission like he did at Alcatraz?"

Theo lets out an animated grunt. "Dude, the Alcatraz video messed me up for days. I still get chills just thinking about it."

"Me too! Can you imagine being locked up by yourself? But also, it was very educational. Like how I had no idea that Alcatraz means 'pelican.'"

"It's my number one fun fact," Theo says before sipping from his cup.

I do the same with mine, letting a silence bloom between us.

Did he only want to talk about the video? Maybe I should excuse myself now before things get awkward. I can go ahead and text Lola to come and pick me up. I mean, other than Triple H, what else could we possibly have in common?

"Hey, how did you do on Hyung's quiz today?"

I blink, confused by the fact Theo's still talking to me. "Oh, um… Okay, I guess? I kinda ran out of time, so I didn't answer the last three questions, but I got an eight-three. Thankfully, it was mostly review from last week's homework. What about you?"

"I did okay. I kept getting distracted by all the buzzing in my pocket. I had to sneak it out and silence my app notifications so I could finish."

Huh, so it seems like I wasn't the only one with a focusing problem today.

Theo leans back in his seat, his posture relaxed.

He doesn't really seem to be in a hurry to end the conversation, so I ask, "Why didn't your friends want to go down in the basement with you? Y'all went as a group, right? You could have had the whole gang down there like that old cartoon, snooping for clues. Although, you'd need a dog. A dog would totally have completed the experience."

Theo laughs, crossing his arms over his chest. "We were trying not to draw too much attention to ourselves, so I went down on my own. Then again, I must have been doing a bad job of sneaking because you found me no problem. Harrison would have totally come with me, but he was too busy flirting it up with Elise."

"Oh, wait, so Elise isn't your girlfriend?"

Theo scrunches his nose. "Elise? No way. I mean, she's great, don't get me wrong. But she's uh… a bit too loud for me. Just not my vibe, you know?" I do not know. I have no idea what his vibe is at the moment, which is exactly why I'm asking these questions. But I nod along like I understand.

"Yeah, so me and Harrison have been trying to figure out a way to blow up for the last couple of months, and I'm super into paranormal stuff, so it just seemed like a good plan. He keeps telling me we should make longer-form stuff for YouTube, but TikTok is where it's at right now. I mean, YouTube is nothing but reaction videos and old people trying to be relevant five years too late. Other than Triple H, of course. And that's what I keep—oh, sorry, man." He stops, scratching the back of his head as he looks down at the table. "I get really passionate about this kind of stuff. I didn't mean to rant at you."

"You're fine," I say with a laugh. "Everyone has their thing, you know? Like, my friend Wren and I love old horror movies, and they're super talented with special effects make-up, so they'll go on forever about the difference between practical effects versus computer-generated ones. Then Freddy will start talking about soccer, and he'll lose us both."

"Ugh, same. I will never understand people's fascination with sports. There are so many other things to do with your time that don't involve running balls back and forth."

"Literally, anything else is better. We went to Freddy's game on Saturday before the tour, and I'd be lying if I said I wasn't slowly dying in the stands. If I ever end up having to do community service, I feel like those two hours should count towards time served."

Theo laughs again, the edges of his eyes crinkling, which only adds to the swarm of buzzing nerves in my stomach.

"So, since we've established sports are a hard no, what do you like to do? You know, when you're not trespassing in old churches."

"The usual things," he replies, his posture suddenly going rigid again. "Hang out with the crew. Listen to music. Chill. Um, I go to church over at SCC. That takes up a lot of my spare time."

There it is. We've hit the inevitable wall of the conversation. Where can we go from here? Will he try to talk to me about my soul? Will he tell me I'm living in sin because I happen to crush on other boys? Will he offer to pray for me?

Honestly, all those options sound terrible. The anxious feeling in my stomach morphs into nausea as I hold my breath and wait for the onslaught to begin.

But Theo just sits there at the other end of the table, one hand clenched into a fist on the edge as he stares down at his knuckles.

"Cool," I say eventually, and it's like an exhale. Maybe I've been worried over nothing? Or maybe it's like Freddy said, and more churches are accepting of the whole queer thing?

Theo blinks, then shakes his head, some of the tension melting from his shoulders. "What about you?"

"Nothing special," I admit. "Hang with Wren and Freddy, mostly. I love old movies, so we'll usually raid Wren's Mom's VHS collection on the weekends for something terrible. And on rare occasions, I get to visit a set with my dad and see how they shoot stuff. I haven't been able to go in a while, though. He's a director of photography, so his schedule is kind of hectic."

"Whoa, seriously? Like, you've been on movie sets?"

I nod, swirling the ice around in my cup. "A few. He mostly directs with streaming shows nowadays, but it's all the same. The show he's working on now is filming just outside of Specter for a couple of weeks, so I'm hoping I'll be able to visit him sometime soon."

"That's so cool!" Theo grins again, leaning forward on his elbows. "God, I wish my dad did something even remotely interesting. Even his title, 'Project Manager,' sounds like a snoozefest."

"It definitely has its pros and cons," I admit. "Sometimes he's halfway across the world for weeks at a time. Between him being on set and Mom keeping late office hours, it stays pretty quiet around my house most days."

"I'd love a little peace and quiet sometime. Wait, that sounds bad. My parents aren't like crazy or anything. They just like to start sh—*crap* with my sister sometimes." He stops, then shakes his head. "Sorry, I don't know why I'm saying all this to you."

I shrug. "It's okay. I don't mind."

"You're really easy to talk to for some reason," he continues. "I usually only bring this stuff up with Harrison."

"Sometimes it's easier to tell things to a stranger."

"But you're not a stranger. At least, you don't feel like one." He makes a face. "Never mind, I'm not making any sense."

"I think I get it, don't worry. But if I'm not a stranger anymore, then what am I to you?"

Something flashes behind his dark brown eyes, but it vanishes just as quickly.

"A friend. If that's okay with you, I mean."

I swallow back the squeal that bubbles up in my throat.

"Sure. Friends it is."

ELEVEN
THEO

Friends. I try not to visibly sigh with relief at Caleb's confirmation. We're friends.

That should quell the storm within my stomach, knowing that this is the normal way to make friends and I'm doing just fine, but it doesn't. I still feel strange, like there's something more going on here. I shouldn't ask about the orbs again, but…if he's experiencing this, too, maybe I should.

No, I don't want to scare him off right away. I have to pace myself.

"Cool," I say with a smile, desperately trying to sound cool and casual about it, but words are tumbling out of my mouth before I can stop them. "So, do you want to hang out again sometime? Maybe this weekend we could watch a scary movie or something? We have a pretty dope theater room at my house with a nice sound system and smart lights and crap, and it's pretty cool, especially for scary movies. And we technically have seating for eight, so you could invite your friends too if you want since you said Wren likes scary movies too, right?"

Shit, why can't I stop rambling at him?

There's a flash of something in Caleb's expression—annoyance? No, maybe surprise? Dammit, why am I like this—but the corner of his lip twitches up into a half-smile. "Yeah? Sure, that could be fun."

I feel a grin take over my face. "Nice, okay! I mean, I'll have to check with my parents first. We all kind of use the theater room for our things, but it's usually just me and my friends now, but at one point before Grace went off to college, we had to establish a theater schedule because we all—" I stop myself, shaking my head. "Unimportant. Sorry. I'll just text you."

Caleb is fidgeting with his almost empty cup, a small smile still on his face. "You'll probably need my number for that."

"Huh?"

"You said you'll text me, but do you have my number? That might be helpful."

I rub my hand down my face, more heat rising in my cheeks. Is it possible to die from embarrassment? "Wow. Yeah, probably. Here," I open my messaging app and hand Caleb my phone.

I watch his fingers type in his number—his fingernails are…sparkling? Glitter nail polish? — and he sends himself a text from my phone before he hands it back. During the exchange, our fingers brush against each other for barely half a second, but the touch feels electric again. Just like it did at the church.

"Thanks," I mutter. Our eyes meet for a few seconds, but I look back down at my phone. There are a couple of seconds of silence, and I wonder if I'm boring him—or worse, annoying him. I'm not ready for this to end yet, so I scramble for something to talk about. A memory flashes through my mind about something Elise had said the other night that I hadn't really wanted to dwell on before, but maybe now was the time. "So, uhh…is Freddy your boyfriend?"

As soon as the words leave my lips, I regret them immediately. Caleb's eyes widen, and his mouth drops open, but before I can panic, he erupts in laughter. It's a contagious laughter that takes over his entire face, and I smile nervously, not sure if I should laugh with him, but man, do I want to. "Oh my God, that's hilarious," Caleb finally says, wiping a tear that's formed in his eye. "Absolutely not. We're just friends. I should probably tell you off for assuming the two gay kids are dating, but then again, I did the same with you and Elise, so turnabout's fair play."

I don't try to hide my relief this time. "Oh, okay. God. I'm so sorry, that was really shi—*stupid*—of me to assume you were—I mean, obviously just because two gay guys are friends doesn't automatically make them boyfriends." I can feel myself blushing with embarrassment again but it's so much worse this time, so I just keep talking and I can't stop. "I promise I'm not—I mean, like, I know Christians get a bad rap for being—I swear I don't care that you're gay, you know? Like, that's your business, not mine, and I think it's really—" I stammer—why can't I stop talking? "Well, quite frankly, I think it's shitty when Christians are homophobic. There. I—I'm going to shut up now."

Caleb stares at me, his face still a little flushed from his laughing fit from earlier, but whatever expression he has now, I can't decipher it, so I look back down at my phone.

Great. This is why I only have four friends. I should've quit while I was ahead.

"Dude, it's fine," Caleb says, still smiling, but his cheeks are definitely pinker than before. "I know you're not a bible-thumper or one of those nutjobs standing on the road with a bullhorn. I never got that impression from you at all. Trust me, I wouldn't be here now if I had."

I swallow, trying to release the tension in my shoulders. "Yeah. I—I know some people who can be weird about it and I just—I just don't want you to think I'm going to be weird about it." I meet his eyes again. "Except for now, of course, but hopefully I'm getting it all out of my system."

Caleb chuckles softly. "Yeah, but if this is as weird as it gets with you, I'm okay with that."

My head feels like it's buzzing, and my chest suddenly feels warm. Oh shit, it's happening again. I watch Caleb carefully to see if he's having the same reaction, but…he seems fine? Normal?

Should I ask him if he's felt strange since our encounter in the basement? Is he also experiencing light-headedness when he's around me? Has he felt the crackling energy when we touch? Does his body temperature rise when he thinks of me? I mean, how do I even ask about it without him thinking I'm insane? What if I'm alone in this? What if I am just crazy?

Honestly, he probably already thinks I'm crazy. I really don't want to make it worse, especially not this quickly.

I need to do more research on my own before pulling him into this. Yeah, that's what I need to do.

"You okay?"

Caleb's hesitant voice pulls me out of my thoughts. "Hm?"

He's studying me, one eyebrow raised. "You're…kind of staring at me."

"God, I'm so sorry. I—" I scramble for an excuse, anything. "I just remembered something that I have to do tonight. I guess I must have spaced out." I reach for my coffee and finish it off, turning my attention to anything, anyone but Caleb. I'm going to scare him off before I can get to the bottom of this. I just know it.

"Okay," Caleb replies casually. He's so cool and casual about everything, seeming so much more confident in himself than I am. Maybe that comes with being out at a public school in the suburbs of Georgia. I can't even begin to imagine the kind of courage that takes. I may not understand it, but I kind of admire him for it. "So, yeah, I guess you can text me about Saturday. I'll see if Wren and Freddy are free. Will your friends be there?"

"Oh, umm… Maybe. I'll have to ask them. But I'm cool if it's just us and your friends."

Caleb shrugs. "Either way is fine. Want me to bring anything?"

I shake my head. "Nah, you don't have to. My parents are used to hosting, so our fridge is stocked with drinks and the pantry is loaded with snacks. Unless there's something specific you want to bring."

Caleb smiles. "Cool."

"Well, I better head home," I hear myself saying awkwardly as I stand up from my seat. "Homework and all that."

"Yeah, me too," he replies, following my lead and standing to his feet as well. I think he's the same height as Harrison. Slightly taller than Sienna.

Taller than me, of course, because most people are taller than me, but at least he doesn't tower over me like a lot of guys do.

"Thanks for meeting me, though. I'll see you tomorrow?"

Caleb smiles again. "See you tomorrow."

CALEB: it's Caleb, here's my number :)

THEO: thanks man :)

Tuesday, September 12

Two afternoons in a row at Spookies isn't too out of the norm for anyone living in Specter, but it certainly is for me. I try not to go out too often or spend money haphazardly—a habit my dad strongly ingrained in me—and Spookies is only a treat for special occasions.

My trip yesterday was a special occasion, but this next one is not.

I arrive exactly on time despite knowing for a fact that Sienna will be at least five minutes late. My anxiety doesn't allow for tardiness, but Sienna is just one of those people who is perpetually running late no matter how hard she tries. I don't resent her for it or anything—it doesn't bother me to wait.

Besides, there are plenty of other things about Sienna to be bothered by.

Sorry, God—she's a perfectly lovely person, and I know You both are close.

After I order my usual—a syrupy, sugary iced monstrosity called The Witches' Brew because it's Halloween year-round at this coffee shop, and I need all the sweetness I can get—I notice that the same table where Caleb and I sat yesterday is available, so I grab it and wait. I check my phone, seeing that even though another day has passed, I'm still getting thousands of new likes on that Saint Catherine's video. I wonder for half a second if I should bring up the video to Sienna but immediately dismiss it. Sienna never understood my obsession with Triple H or with becoming TikTok famous. Only a handful of people do, and now Caleb has been added to that shortlist.

The thought of Caleb brings a tiny smile to my face, and I open my messaging app to send him a quick picture of my drink with a GIF of a cat with coffee jitters. About a minute later, he responds with a few laughing emojis, and I can't help but imagine Caleb opening the text from me and chuckling softly to himself. As I picture Caleb laughing, however, my stomach does this weird swooping thing—almost as if I'm riding a rollercoaster.

Huh. That's new.

Maybe I should add that to the ever-growing list of "Weird Things I've Felt Since Accidentally Recording Ghost Orbs."

Glancing at the door, then at my watch, I decide I might as well multitask while I wait for Sienna by updating the symptom list on my phone. I still really need to determine whether or not I'm being haunted.

So far, my research has been inconclusive. Most of what I've found when googling things like "am I being haunted" don't exactly line up with my experience. As I expected, typical haunting signs include objects moving on their own (none of that yet), strange sights (the orbs in the video but so far that's been it), feelings of being watched (eh, not really), disruption in electricity (intriguing, but not quite accurate), unexplained sounds (other than the weird sound in the basement of the church, no), and cold spots (not unless getting inexplicable chills at skin touching counts).

I've also tried googling most of these physical symptoms themselves—skin tingling, chest warm, feeling dizzy—but these results mostly just trigger my hypochondria, and now I'm worried I might be having a heart attack every time I'm with Caleb. Which, obviously that can't be it, right? So, I'm back at square one and thinking perhaps more extended time spent in close proximity with Caleb has to yield some results.

I'm honestly just excited for Caleb to be my friend. Again, maybe it's because we're trauma-bonded, or maybe it's because some weird spirit energy is compelling me to be his friend for some weird ghost reason, but at the end of the day, does it matter? We have a lot in common— we're both Triple H fans, we both like weird ghost stuff, and we both hate sports. Surely there's more, but that's at least a good start.

I hear Sienna arrive before I see her. I know that high-pitched bubbly voice anywhere. Sure enough, I look up from my phone to see a panicked Sienna waving to me from the counter and mouthing apologies. As usual, she's carrying a massive cross-body bag that looks like it weighs at least twenty pounds, and her wavy auburn hair sticks to her face in places where it's clear she's sweating.

"Goodness, I'm so sorry, Theodore," she exhales as she arrives at our table, dropping her bag on the floor where it makes a fairly loud *thunk*. Wow, it really is as heavy as it looks.

"It's totally fine, Sienna. It always is," I say, hoping my smile is convincing enough. "I'm just chilling. I don't have anywhere else to be today."

She flashes me a bright smile. "So! Tell me what's going on with you first because once I get started, I probably won't be able to stop. How has your last month been?"

Crap. I probably should have thought of something to tell her. Not a lie necessarily, but just something to fill the space. "Oh, you know me, nothing crazy. The usual."

"Really? Nothing interesting at all?"

"Well," I hesitate. "I mean, you might not think it's that interesting, but the crew and I went to one of those after-dark ghost tours at Saint Catherine's this weekend. You know that ancient catholic church on Holly Street?"

Sienna's smile vanishes, and her eyes widen. "A…ghost tour?"

I shrug. "Yeah, they have a pretty spooky history, and Triple H did an episode about them last week, so we figured we'd check it out, you know?"

She stares at me in horror. "You intentionally went to a place in search of ghosts?"

I'm quickly regretting bringing it up at all. "I mean, not literally, but—"

"Theo, that's really dangerous. You shouldn't put yourselves in those kinds of situations, you know? That's where dark spirits can manifest and attach themselves to you."

I blink at her. "What?"

"Ephesians chapter six, verses eleven and twelve. 'Put on the full armor of God so that you can take your stand against the devil's schemes. For our struggle is not against flesh and blood, but against the rulers, against the authorities, against the powers of this dark world, and against the spiritual forces of evil in the heavenly realms.'" She pauses before her big blue eyes bore into mine. "Spiritual warfare is no joke, Theo. Dark spirits are real. You need to be careful about putting yourself in places like that."

I stare at her in shock. I'm used to her quoting the Bible directly—she's done that around me dozens of times, so that isn't what surprises me. But I've never seen her look so genuinely *afraid* before. She really believes in this stuff—ghosts, demons, and spiritual warfare. And if the Bible mentions it, it must be real, right?

Shit. I mean—crap. Is that what's happening? A dark spirit has attached itself to me? Am I actually being haunted after all?

"Do you understand what I'm saying?"

"Oh, um, yeah," I stammer, nodding quickly. "No, you're absolutely right. I just—I don't know. Thought it might be cool to see…something."

Sienna shakes her head. "I understand your curiosity, but I just worry about your spiritual welfare, you know? Going into a dark place like that unprepared is just asking for trouble, don't you think?"

Maybe she's right. She knows way more about all this Christian stuff than I do. So much more, in fact, that it's the reason we broke up in the first place.

Finally, I nod, worried she might freak out if I don't say anything. "Yeah, you're right."

Sienna is quiet for a few seconds, curling a strand of her hair anxiously between her fingers. "So…did you end up seeing anything?"

"No," I say quickly. It's technically not a lie. I didn't see anything while I was down there. My phone captured something that neither I nor Caleb saw. I have to bite my tongue not to say more. I don't need her worrying about my spirituality any more than she already does.

"Oh, thank God," Sienna sighs in relief. "I'm so glad."

"Yeah," I add with a nervous chuckle. "Me too."

Sienna smiles brightly again, visibly happy to change the subject. "So, is there anything else new? How has your small group been going?"

Ah, small group. The way Sienna talks about her small group makes it seem that she's in a close-knit community of like-minded people who willingly gather every week to share life and build each other up. But my small group is nothing like that—it's just an arbitrary grouping of about ten guys in my grade at church that I've known since I was a kid. We meet for about an hour every Wednesday evening, follow a church curriculum, and share prayer requests with our adult leaders. That's it.

Admittedly, I don't really get much out of church outside of worship. Occasionally, a sermon, lesson, or small group discussion will stand out as impactful or eye-opening, but more often than not, it's just something I do because I always have. I don't dislike it enough to stop going, but it's not something to write home about. Or, in this case, tell Sienna about.

"It's fine," I offer. "Nothing new. You know me, my life is kind of boring compared to yours. We're here to talk about your trip!"

Sienna rolls her eyes at my self-deprecation, but her delight that she gets to take over the conversation is obvious. Or at least it's obvious to me. I guess that's one of the side effects of having dated her for five months after being close friends since elementary school: the ability to see through any masks she tries to put up. But if I'm honest, it's genuinely disarming how rare those moments are. Sienna is completely and earnestly herself. She truly is passionate about Jesus. She is sincere about her desire to better the world and help people.

It's inspiring at best. It's intimidating at worst. But that's Sienna.

"Okay, fine, I'll jump right into it then!"

And she does. She talks about how unbearably long the flight was, but she was led by the Holy Spirit to talk to some guy across the aisle from her. Unsurprisingly, it turns out the guy was just interested in getting her number, but she prayed with him, nonetheless. When they arrived in Johannesburg, they were able to stay in a nice hotel just one night before the next flight on a frightfully smaller plane going deeper into the country. Then, they piled up in a van and drove another four hours before they reached the village where the missionaries lived. The trip was mostly focused on the kids in this village and putting on a vacation Bible school for them so that they were taken care of during the day.

There are lots of tangents, lots of inside jokes, and lots of me listening quietly as Sienna gushes about her trip. She's honest about the parts that sucked, but the sincerity that pours out of her when she talks about the kids and the families she met in this village is genuine. It feels surreal; like she's talking about a dream she had one night, not a real experience that took her halfway across the world for two weeks. It's almost difficult to keep listening because I feel like I should have been there. Like maybe I was supposed to be there, but I missed the call.

Did I miss Your call, God?

The old familiar twist of guilt eats at my insides as I listen, wondering if this is how I'm supposed to feel about my faith. Why am I not this passionate about it? Why didn't I jump at the opportunity to travel to another country to show people the love of Christ? If it comes easily to Sienna, why can't it be like that for me?

I need to do more. I need to try harder. I need to be better.

Maybe I should ask her about it.

"So…" she trails off, her eyes still glazed over and slightly teary from an earlier story about a particular little girl she bonded with. "It was the best two weeks of my life by far. I will truly never be the same again, and I am definitely going back someday. Hopefully, in the next few years."

I swallow, wishing I had more of my Witches' Brew to drink, but the cup has been empty for at least an hour. "Wow. Yeah, that would be cool."

"You should come next time," she says softly, her eyes staring intensely into mine. "I truly believe if given the opportunity, you should take it."

I drop my gaze back at my empty cup, my fingers swirling the leftover condensation. "Yeah. Maybe."

Sienna reaches her hand across the table and holds my hand in hers. Her skin, while silky soft and gentle, is ice cold against mine, and despite the urge to recoil away, I stay still.

I try not to think about the fact that her hand doesn't feel electric when we touch.

I try even harder not to think about whose hand *does* feel electric when we touch.

I glance up at her warily, and she's staring back at me with a purpose.

"Can I pray with you, Theo?"

I want to say no at first. I really do. We're in the middle of the busiest coffee shop in town on a Tuesday afternoon. There's bound to be someone I know in this building—someone from school, someone from Cathy's, someone from church. It's embarrassing and awkward and unbearably cringe. The last thing I want is to sit here helplessly while my ex-girlfriend holds my hand over a sticky coffee shop table, praying for my soul.

But it's Sienna. She's not trying to embarrass me. She's not trying to make a move on me or rekindle our doomed romance.

She's genuinely trying to follow God's will. She cares about my salvation and loves me enough to try to intervene when she thinks I'm not living up to my full potential. Everything Sienna does is out of love—selfless love, even.

And as much as I hate to think about it, Sienna clearly knows what's best when it comes to spiritual welfare. Who am I to argue? She's truly an expert on this subject.

It's infuriating, but I can't say no.

So, I nod and close my eyes.

"Heavenly Father… We humbly come before You today, blessed beyond our wildest dreams with all You do for us."

Sienna's praying voice is a lot breathier than her normal speaking voice. I'm not sure what that means or why I notice it, but it's weird. I think I used to find it endearing. Now it's…not.

"Thank You for this fellowship Theodore and I share, and thank You for blessing us with a connection through your Holy Spirit—"

Fellowship? A connection through the Holy Spirit? Is that what we're calling this? Sure, fine. *God, You know how I feel,* I pray silently, feeling compelled to add my own inner voice to the mix so God knows I'm not just going through the motions this time.

"—to pursue Your Will and share Your love with the world. We thank You for the privilege that we have, and we ask that You show us how to use it for Your Glory—"

I cringe at that. *Ehh…not sure I want to be thanking You for our "privilege," but I'm sure You know what she means. Thank You for letting us be born in America in the twenty-first century so we have electricity and Wi-Fi and don't have to worry about the government killing us—most of the time, anyway. Help me find ways to maybe help people out who don't have it quite as good as I do.*

"Father, I thank You so much for blessing me with the opportunity to serve You in South Africa, and I pray that You reveal Yourself to Theodore in the same way You've revealed Yourself to me. Please open his eyes to see Your plan for his life, open his ears to hear Your voice, and open his heart to new opportunities to do Your will."

Yeah, I definitely second that. Just make sure that You're really obvious when You're speaking to me though, please. I can be pretty dense sometimes. I mean,

You know that, of course. But if I need to go on a mission trip or be a witness to somebody at school or something like that, please make it super freakin' obvious so I don't miss it. Please.

"We love You, Abba Father. We thank You for Your everlasting love, and most of all, we thank You for sending Your son to die for us."

Ditto.

"In Jesus' holy and precious name we pray, Amen."

"Amen."

I open my eyes to see Sienna beaming back at me. She squeezes my hand before letting go, and I try to relax back in my chair.

"Thank you, Theo."

I nod, staring at my cup again.

"Are you sure there's nothing else going on in your world?" Sienna asks after a few seconds of silence between us. "Anything specific you'd like me to be praying about for you?" I can feel her watching me as I fidget with my phone case. "Are you talking to any girls at school?"

I snort, perhaps a little aggressively. "Nope. Taking a break from dating for a bit."

Her smile vanishes, and her gaze drops to her bag. "Oh," she mumbles, nervously twisting a finger in her hair, clearly trying to think of something more to say but coming up empty.

To be completely honest, it feels nice to see her be the one to squirm a little for once. Perhaps not even the most spiritually mature people are immune to feeling guilt after all.

…which immediately makes me feel guilty for even thinking something like that. Crap.

I bite my lower lip. "Sorry. What I mean is, I'm just not interested in anyone right now, you know? Like at all. I'm not saying it's anyone's fault. I just haven't found anyone worth pursuing."

"Yeah," she replies. "No, right, of course!" The tightness in her expression melts away, and she's bright and sunny Sienna again. "Don't worry, she's out there somewhere! God already has a plan for both of you, and you'll meet her in His timing."

"I know," I say, smiling this time, making sure my tone isn't sarcastic or weird. I glance at my phone to see if I have any texts from Caleb but also to see the time. "Well, I think they're going to close soon, so we should probably get going."

"Okay!" Sienna is on her feet and struggling with her bag, but as soon as I'm up, she wraps me up in a hug. "I've missed you, and I'm so glad we were able to do this today!"

"Me too."

"See you tomorrow at church?"

"Yep. See you then."

TWELVE
CALEB

Friday, September 15

Wren's basement has always felt like a home away from home to me. There's just something so comforting about the worn, wood-paneled walls and the thick carpet that's been stomped thin enough in some places to see the backing poking through. Wren took over half of the space for their special effects set up a few years back, with clear plastic drawers stacked high, overflowing with countless colors and textures they use to make their looks. Over the summer, they revamped the corner where the bean bag chair used to sit and made it into a backdrop area for them to take pictures of their finished looks for their portfolio. I keep telling Wren they'd probably crush the Insta game if they'd just start posting those pictures, but they always shoot the idea down.

"You'd get thousands of followers like that—" I snap my fingers as I follow Wren down the creaky stairs from their living room. "And people would be able to appreciate your work!"

"We've been over this," Wren says with a sigh, collapsing onto the ancient plaid-patterned couch. "I don't do it for the clout. Anyone can get people to like a photo online. My art is personal. I'm literally transforming myself with it, and that's a really intimate process."

"I get it, I get it," I say, raising my hands in defeat as I sink into the cushion beside them. "Actually, I don't get it, but I don't have to. I just want everyone to tell you how awesome you are."

Wren snorts a laugh. "I am awesome, Caleb. I don't need a thousand followers to tell me what I already know."

"Fair enough."

Wren digs into the sofa for the remote, turning the TV—the only thing in this basement besides their make-up station that's from this decade—on and scrolling over to the YouTube app. It's just a few minutes till five, and Hudson never misses an upload deadline for a Triple H video.

"Do you think they're going to do a follow-up on Saint Catherine's?" Wren asks, settling into their seat and hanging one leg over the armrest.

"I doubt it. Hudson hardly ever does follow-ups. The last one I can remember is the one where that guy broke into that psych hospital outside Chicago and caught all that insane stuff on camera with the lights and the creepy EVPs."

"Oh right, wasn't that stuff all faked?"

"Yeah, that's why Hudson made another video to debunk all the shit that was on the recording. He called the guy out for being a fraud, and he got the bogus vid taken down in, like, three hours."

Wren clicks over on the app to refresh. "Well, here it is. Let's see what we're getting into today."

I pull out my phone, checking to make sure I didn't miss a text for Theo. We've been talking sporadically through the week, and I really wanted him to come watch with us tonight, but his shift at work started at five.

"Salutations, Haunties, it's your good friend, Hudson, back with another tale of high strangeness for you." Hudson intros the show like normal, his signature black t-shirt and perfectly parted hair a comforting presence in the room. "Before we get started, I wanted to talk about this clip that many of you have sent me over the last week. This apparently comes from a TikTok user, TheoreticallyTheo05, and was taken from the basement of the Saint Catherine of Bologna Church in Specter, Georgia. Watch closely now."

Wren turns to me wide-eyed. "Isn't that—"

"Shh!" I shush them, grabbing the remote and smashing the volume button. The screen goes dark for a second as Hudson's usual background is replaced by Theo's video of the classroom. I can hear his breathing as he pans across the room and the first orb comes into view. Then, the second floats into frame just before the video ends.

"There you have it, Haunties. Now, we haven't been able to authenticate this particular video, but it seems like there's something going on down in Specter. I don't know about you guys, but it's definitely caught my attention. Be sure and leave a comment below if you think this is legit or just another faker. Now then, let's dive into today's topic—"

I mute the video, pulling out my phone.

Has Theo already seen this? No way, it literally just posted two minutes ago, and he's at work. He's going to absolutely freak!

"What are you doing?" Wren asks, retrieving the remote and pausing the episode.

"Telling Theo he just got name-dropped by Hudson-freaking-Helter!" My hands vibrate with excitement as I type out the message, and I keep having to delete the extra characters I hit.

> **CALEB:** dude! Hudson just showed your TikTok on his new episode! i'm screaming!!!

"You actually have his phone number?" Wren asks, looking over my shoulder. "Or are you messaging him on Insta?"

"No, he gave me his number on Monday. Didn't I tell you that?"

Wren shakes their head. "I would definitely have remembered if you did."

"Shit, my bad." My cheeks burn for some reason I don't want to think about. "I was supposed to ask you about tomorrow too. He wants us to come over for a movie night."

"Like, at his house?" Wren questions, raising a dark eyebrow.

"Yeah. Apparently, he's got a sweet movie set up. But only if you want to. I know you don't know him—" My phone buzzes, derailing my train of thought.

THEO: !!!!!!!!!!
are you serious??? please tell me you're not joking.

CALEB: i'm not joking! the episode just went live a few minutes ago!

"Are you sure you want me there?" Wren asks, nudging me.

My phone buzzes again, but I look back at Wren. "Why wouldn't I?"

They shrug, rolling their eyes. "Do you think he wanted it to be just the two of you?"

Just the two of us? I'd be lying to say I hadn't thought about it. But he asked me to invite Wren and Freddy. I definitely remember that. Was he just being nice? Did he secretly want it to be the two of us alone in a dark room for hours? My heart hammers against my chest.

"No, he definitely invited you and Freddy."

THEO: I'll check it as soon as I swing a break! this is insane! I've got to tell Harrison!

"Well, I'm always game, but we'll have to convince Freddy. You know he's probably already got a date lined up with Andrew for tomorrow."

"Is that still a thing?"

Wren chuckles. "Apparently so. Maybe this one will stick around for a while?"

"We'll see. But, either way, yes, I want you there. He said we could watch a scary movie, so you should bring a couple of options!"

That excites them. Wren sits up, drumming their fingers together, till they've transformed into a Disney villain. "Interesting. How bad should I scar the poor boy?"

THEO: shoot, we're getting busy. I'll text you when I'm off work! Can't wait to see you tomorrow!

you know, so we can talk about the video and stuff...

I smile at his double message. My cheeks are on fire.

CALEB: yeah! can't wait!

Wren starts the video again, but the music slips into the background as I stare down the text, letting the words burn into my brain.

Can't wait to see you tomorrow!

Saturday, September 16

"Caleb, you're about to vibrate into a parallel universe over there. Can you at least chill long enough for us to get inside?"

The inside of Wren's car feels like a sauna, and no matter how many times I wipe my palms across my jeans, they remain moist. Theo's house is bigger than I imagined. It looms over us as we sit in the driveway, warm light spilling from the windows into the dusky evening air. We're technically still early, and

I don't want to appear too eager. What if that freaks him out? But I also don't want to be late and make him think I don't care, so how long do I think it'll take to get from here to the front door—

"Caleb, you're starting to freak me out, bro."

I exhale, looking over to Wren. "Sorry. I'm so nervous and have no idea why."

Wren raises an eyebrow at me. "You sure about that?"

"Okay, let me rephrase. I know why I'm nervous, but I don't know how to make it stop. I know that Theo isn't into guys, and I don't exactly have the best reputation for figuring out if someone is or is not flirting with me—hence the whole Logan fiasco—but I can't shake the feeling that there's something going on between Theo and me."

"Well, maybe it's a good thing I'm here tonight," Wren says, placing a hand on my shoulder. "Consider me your flirt-detector. If that boy so much as winks in your direction, I'll know it. You can look forward to my full report at the end of the night."

I nod. That actually does make me feel better. If only a little.

"I wish Freddy didn't flake on us," Wren adds. "I'll admit, he's the best when it comes to spotting longing glances. How else does he get laid so often?"

"I think you're confusing longing with desperation."

Wren smacks my shoulder, but they're smiling.

"Ow! It was just a joke!"

"Alright mister, you've made us a minute late. Now grab your gummy worms, and let's go see if this boy has a thing for you!"

I grab my bag of candy from the floorboard and bravely charge into the warm evening air. But as soon as I'm out of the car, my false bravado fails, and Wren moves ahead of me up the brick stairs to ring the doorbell.

"I got it!" a voice yells from inside.

Theo opens the door not ten seconds later, his chest heaving like he ran the fifty-meter dash just to get here.

"Hey! Uh, welcome! Come in." He shuffles to the side as Wren and I step into the foyer. "Glad y'all could make it."

"Thanks for having us," I say, eying the impressive chandelier hanging above our heads. Cue the intrusive thoughts about it falling and crushing me. Depending on how tonight goes, that may be the best-case scenario. "Um, Freddy already had plans, so it'll just be us coming."

"But we're way more fun than he is," Wren adds. "So it's not that great a loss."

Theo doesn't seem fazed. "No worries. We'll be downstairs in the theater room. The stairs are just through here. I've got popcorn and drinks already down there. So, we can just head down—"

"Well, hello there!"

A dark-haired woman appears at the end of the hall, all smiles as she makes her way into the foyer to join us. She looks a lot like Theo, with the same sharp features and strong nose. "I don't think I've met you two before. I'm Kora, Theo's mom. It's nice to see some new faces around here." She gravitates toward Theo, nudging him with her shoulder. "Theo, when you said you were having a movie night, I figured it would be the three musketeers coming."

The edge of Theo's mouth twitches. "Sorry, guess I forgot to mention it. And we talked about this, Mom. My friends don't like it when you call them that."

"Well, maybe your new friends will." Kora winks at us, and I can feel the embarrassment radiating off of Theo like a heatwave. The pink in his cheeks is kind of adorable.

"I'm Caleb," I say, offering my hand out to Kora. "It's nice to meet you."

Wren brushes their bangs aside and gives a polite wave. "Wren. Your house is cool."

"Thank you, Wren. That's so sweet of you to say! Theo, you should make more friends like her. She's got good taste."

Theo sucks in a breath. I open my mouth to correct Kora, but Wren beats me to the punch.

"My pronouns are actually they/them, Kora. Just so you know."

Kora blinks, her friendly smile wavering for all of half a second before she recovers with, "Right, okay, I'll do my best to remember that. Well, I won't hold you three up any longer. Theo, your dad and I will be up here if y'all need anything. It was great to meet you both!"

"Nice to meet you," Wren and I echo as Kora heads back up the hallway and into what I assume is the kitchen. I try not to count the number of crosses in the artwork she passes along the way. There's a lot of them.

"I'm really sorry about that, Wren," Theo says, leading us to the stairs that descend to the basement. "I should have told her beforehand."

"It's fine," Wren says with a laugh. "It literally happens every day. I stopped taking it personally a while ago. I just correct on the spot."

Theo nods, but his lips are pulled tight like he's deep in thought.

Stop looking at his lips, Caleb. Jeez.

At the bottom of the stairs, we head down a short hallway, and Theo opens another door into the theater room. Red curtains hang on either side of a projector screen on the far wall, and three rows of leather reclining seats face the screen, each row elevated slightly over the other. In the corner, a real-life popcorn cart sits behind a wet bar, the glass top filled with yellow popcorn. The smell of buttery deliciousness wafts in the air.

"Welp, this is it," Theo says, heading over to the bar. He squats down to open a mini fridge under the counter. "We've got soda and water. Help yourself to some popcorn."

"I brought sour gummy worms," I say, holding up the bag.

"Nice!" Theo grins at me, then seems to remember that Wren is here too, and adds, "Can I get you something to drink, Wren?"

"Grab whatever's got the most caffeine," they say, flopping onto the first chair in the middle row of seats. They waste no time fiddling with the buttons on the side, a devious grin taking over as they recline at a comically glacial pace.

"You got it," Theo replies, then he looks at me, and my palms start to sweat again. "What about you?"

"Coke's fine," I say, hurrying over to sit beside Wren because I don't trust myself to be one-on-one with him in this setting. I'll do something stupid for sure. On second thought, I move over so the middle seat is open. That way, Theo will have to sit between us, and Wren will get a clear view of any flirty behavior.

Theo brings us our drinks as well as two cartons of popcorn, then goes back to the bar to grab his own. "What movie did y'all want to watch?"

Wren pops up out of their seat, pulling a VHS out of their bag. "I was waffling back and forth most of the afternoon, but I finally decided on a classic. I hope you've got a VCR back there somewhere."

Theo laughs, pointing to the giant tower of equipment across from the bar. "Lucky for us, my mom collects classic Disney VHSs, so Dad had one retrofitted down here years ago." Wren tosses him the tape, and he catches it. "'*Killer Nuns from Hell?*'"

"You won't be disappointed," Wren assures him. "This movie is a spiritual experience. Plus, you'd never expect that nuns could kill people with a rosary in so many inventive ways. It really gets the creative juices flowing."

"Is that okay with you?" I ask, trying to get a gauge on Theo's reaction.

He eyes the cover of the VHS for a moment, then shrugs and plugs it in. "Killer nuns sound kinda fun. Let's do it."

THIRTEEN
THEO

My heart is already racing, and I haven't even seen a nun on screen yet.

As I happily play the role of host to my guests, I try not to panic at the empty seat between Caleb and Wren that they seem to have intentionally left open for me.

I can't say that I didn't already consider the seating arrangement for this movie night. It's not something I think about every time, but whenever we have new people, I try to be as considerate of their needs as possible, and some guests have very specific movie seating preferences.

Dad's pride and joy has three rows of black leather motorized-reclining movie theater seats. The first row has only two chairs, but the next two rows have three seats each. No one really needs to know this, but Dad did obnoxious amounts of research on the best viewing angles and distances between the viewers and the screen to the point that literally all eight seats are practically scientifically designed to be perfect. So, when people express that they prefer the back row because that's "the best distance to experience the movie," I have to remind myself not to ramble on about Dad's meticulous setup because that's insane. Who does that?

However, as I got older, I learned that there's a lot more to seating preferences than just viewing quality.

The problems start with the three-seats-per-row setup. On the surface, there's no need to overthink it: they're just chairs to sit on while you watch a movie, right? Why would it matter who sits next to you when you're going to be staring at a screen for however many hours the movie lasts?

Usually, that's true. For years, it was just me, Harrison, and Elise, so we all just plopped into the middle row and didn't think anything of it. It wasn't until Oliver joined our crew that we even considered the rows of three seats a little awkward because no one wants to be the fourth person who has to sit in a row by themselves when the other three sit together. But the solution was simple: two people per row. Done, easy.

However, Oliver invited a girl to a movie night one time in ninth grade and made a comment that changed everything.

"This setup could really kill the romantic vibe if you're not careful, dude. You know that saying, 'two is company, three is a crowd?' This is why."

Apparently, for couples, it's weird to have a third person in the same row.

It got worse once Harrison's feelings for Elise started to evolve into something more. He acted weird about it at first, wanting to sit next to Elise every single time and eventually insisting that he and Elise sit in the back row, too. But once the truth was out about their relationship, the arrangement made so much more sense for everyone because no one had to watch Harrison and Elise getting handsy, and Oliver and I got to use our middle seat to pile on our snacks or spread our legs across.

And even though I'm the oldest of my friend group, I'm a bit of a late bloomer and was the last of my friends to have a significant other, so it wasn't until I started having Sienna over for movie nights that I began to understand it myself. It *was* weird having Oliver sitting on the other side of me when I was holding hands with Sienna.

So yeah, seating arrangement anxiety happens a lot. Groups of more than three can be tricky, and teenage hormones sometimes need to be taken into consideration.

But tonight, I shouldn't have any seating arrangement anxiety at all. It's a perfect scenario—there are three of us, no one gets left out, and there's no coupling to worry about. Or at least, not that I know of. Would Caleb date Wren? I know he's gay, but like…would he be attracted to someone that's not a guy? Wouldn't that make him bisexual or pansexual? I don't know how all that works, and I'm not about to ask tonight, especially after Mom's slip-up.

Earlier this afternoon, I almost panicked and invited Harrison because it occurred to me that if Caleb brought Wren and Freddy, there would be four of us, which meant that we would need to split up into two rows. Would that mean that Caleb and I would sit together on our own row? Would he be uncomfortable with that? Would *I* be uncomfortable with that? Shit, shit, shit, do I need to get a fifth person to fix this?

But when I opened the door to find just Caleb and Wren, I felt relieved. All seating arrangement anxiety was dispelled. A perfect evening awaits us.

That is, until Wren claimed a seat in the middle row, and Caleb pulled a fast one, forcing me to sit between them.

It's fine. There's nothing wrong with that. It doesn't change anything; it doesn't mean anything. Why am I panicking?

"You good?"

I blink out of my stupor to see that Caleb and Wren are staring at me as I'm having a silent crisis about seating. I shake my head, embarrassed. "Yeah, sorry! Let's do this!" I grab the remote and hop into the middle seat as casually as possible.

Without further ado, I dim the lights and push play, reclining my seat back and settling in.

Caleb places his open bag of sour gummy worms in the cup holder between us. "Want some?" he whispers.

"Sure, thanks," I whisper back, reaching in for a handful.

The first forty minutes of the movie are pure camp, and it's fantastic. All three of us laugh out loud at scenes that are particularly silly and corny, which happens way more often than I expected. Caleb's laugh is also wildly infectious and makes me laugh even harder. Every time he laughs, I turn my head to watch how the screen lights up Caleb's face and makes his hair look more red than brown. His nose crinkles in this funny way that makes me want to keep him laughing, so I can't help myself from adding my own commentary in an attempt to have him doubling over.

A few times, we both reach for the gummy worms at the same time, and our hands bump into each other. The electricity is still there. Every single time.

In retrospect, maybe watching a horror movie wasn't the best way to research whether or not the weird feeling I get around Caleb is a result of being haunted. Whoops.

Oh well. I'll worry about the research later. Right now, I'm having a blast, and I honestly don't care what's causing it. I just like it.

When the gummy worm bag is empty, Caleb removes it from the cup holder so we're not continually disappointed reaching for it. But even when it's gone, he leaves his arm casually draped on the armrest with his fingers mindlessly fidgeting at the cup holder edge. The armrest is built for two arms, so I let my arm settle a few inches parallel to his, and it's almost as if there's a static electric buildup in the tiny space between us.

At some point, I almost jump as the electrified space is replaced by his arm brushing mine as he shifts in his chair. A chill shoots all the way down my spine at the touch. *Whoa.*

Caleb stiffens for a moment—does he feel it, too? —then settles in, allowing his arm to stay put against me. The contact of his skin is buzzing against mine, and my heart starts pounding a little harder.

I make a mental note to Google this later.

In the meantime, I refuse to move.

We're getting to the climax of the movie, and it's all jump scares from here. I anticipate most of them, but there are a few that still get me.

There's one scene, however, that gets all of us. Even Wren, who I was convinced was immune to all things horror, curses under their breath as the terrifying Sister Loretta emerges from the darkness to strangle Father Radcliffe to death with her blood-covered spiked rosary.

Caleb and I jump—I feel the shockwave of his movement through our touching arms—and he lets out a quiet yelp, and suddenly, his hand is clutching my hand in a death grip. I squeeze his hand back, adrenaline pumping through me to the point where I'm not entirely sure who grabbed whose hand first, but I'm not letting go.

A second or two later, Caleb whispers a barely audible "sorry" and tries to pull away.

I squeeze tighter. I don't want to let him go.

Eventually, he stops trying to free himself from my grip.

A few seconds pass where neither of us moves—I'm not even sure if I'm breathing—but when I'm sure he's no longer worried about it, I carefully loosen my vice grip on his hand, repositioning to a more natural hold. I finally release the breath I didn't realize I was holding and try to relax.

Caleb's hand also eases comfortably into mine.

The movie continues, but I no longer care about the fate of Father Radcliffe, Sister Loretta, or anyone in this movie.

My hands-on research approach—I laugh silently at my own pun—is producing far more results than Google ever did. Every point of contact with Caleb is electrified, and my insides are on fire. The heat seems to be emanating from my chest, but not exactly where my heart is. Interesting. But it spreads out across my torso, a heat just beneath my skin, and it's…*intoxicating*.

For a moment, the sensation seems familiar, but I can't place the memory. Have I felt this before? Surely not. Surely, I would remember something like this.

"Holy shit, I've completely forgotten the ending of this movie. I have to say, I did *not* see that coming."

My concentration is broken by Wren's voice, and I feel Caleb's hand quickly slip out of my grasp before I can stop it. Caleb's entire arm retreats away, and he folds both arms across his chest.

"Yeah," Caleb says softly, something indecipherable in his voice. "Neither did I."

"I mean, why would Sister Loretta kill the groundskeeper? They already established that he didn't see anything, so it's not like she was trying to cover her tracks. The motive doesn't make any sense. This is a serious plot hole."

I try to meet Caleb's eyes, but his gaze is fixed on the screen.

What just happened? Did I do something wrong?

Is he…embarrassed? Why would he be—

Oh.

The memory bombards me like a freight train. It's Valentine's Day. Sienna and I are in the backseat of my mom's SUV. Sienna reaches out and takes my hand in hers, her cheeks and her nose flushing a cute shade of pink. The touch sends shockwaves through my arm up into my chest. My throat feels dry, and I take a shaky breath, the sensation strange and overwhelming. *Intoxicating.* "Hand check!" Mom shouts from the front seat, eyeing me suspiciously through the rearview mirror. Sienna yanks her hand away from mine, shooting her arms up obediently to show her hands to my mother. I slowly raise mine, too, the feeling of shame and rejection immediately overpowering whatever feeling came before it.

Oh my God.

"I gotta pee," I blurt as I abruptly scramble out of the recliner, not even bothering to adjust it. I head for the bathroom.

"Want me to pause it, Theo?" Wren asks.

"No, it's fine. I won't be long."

I stumble out of the theater room into the hallway, then throw myself into the tiny half-bathroom and spend several minutes staring at my reflection. I didn't actually have to pee, but now I feel like I might have a panic attack, so escaping to the bathroom was a good call.

The *question*, the *realization*, the *dread* of what I may or may not have just discovered is threatening to pull me under very quickly.

Do I have a…

Am I…

Is this feeling…

I can't even allow myself to finish an entire thought. Not even my own inner voice will allow me to verbalize any of these ideas. That *can't* be what this is. It's not.

This is all coming from the ghost. That's it. This is that spirit from Saint Catherine's following me and messing with me.

Sienna was right. I shouldn't have gone to a place where I believed there may be a dark presence. That's all this is.

I'm confusing spiritual energy with something else. It just happens to feel eerily similar to what it felt like to have a crush on Sienna, to be attracted to Sienna, or to be close to Sienna. The ghost just wants to mess with me and make me think it's the same feeling with Caleb, but it's not. It's *not*.

Everything is fine. Everything is fine.

I splash some cold water on my face and spend a few more seconds to even out my breathing. Caleb and Wren are going to wonder if I'm okay if I stay away too long. I've got this. I'm fine.

Everything is fine.

I reach for the door but stop as three knocks sound against it.

FOURTEEN
CALEB

"No, it's fine. I won't be long."

Theo practically runs out of the room, and Wren turns to me with a look of confusion. "Is it the movie? That's totally my bad. I don't remember it being this bloody."

I unfold my arms, looking down at my palm. "No, I don't think it was the movie. I think I fucked up."

I can't believe I did it again. Why do I keep doing that? I mean, sure, he didn't shy away when our arms brushed against each other, but that doesn't mean that he was asking for me to hold his hand. Now I've gone and freaked him out.

"What do you mean?" Wren asks, leaning over their armrest. The movie continues in the background, the heroine explaining to a police officer about all the dead nuns. "What happened?"

Sure, he held onto it when I tried to pull away, but that doesn't mean anything, right? Surely bros do that sometimes when they watch a scary movie? Just because he held my hand doesn't mean he's into me.

Does it?

"Caleb, are you still with me?"

"Sorry," I apologize, shaking away my growing doubt. "Um, we may have been holding hands a second ago. Like, right before he got up and ran away."

Wren's eyes get wide. "Seriously? How did I miss that? Curse this incredibly entertaining movie!"

"What do I do?" I ask, my voice thick with desperation. Theo will be back any second, and I'm starting to freak out. "Do we talk about it? Should I just forget it happened unless he brings it up? I mean, you saw all the crosses they have in the hallway upstairs, so are his parents going to, like, flip if they find out? Oh my god, what if he's telling them right now? They're going to burn us at the stake, Wren."

Wren is laughing now, which isn't exactly a comfort. "Okay, let's take it down just a notch there, buddy. You two were holding hands, not signing the devil's book. I don't think they're going to start a witch hunt in their basement, so forget about the burning. The worst they'd do is sit us down for a lecture about our eternal souls, which can't last forever, so the odds of us making it out of here alive are still pretty good."

"I'm serious, Wren. I'm freaking out over here."

They wipe their eyes. "Sorry, I know. Look, you have to think about it from his perspective. If Theo really is starting to explore the possibility of having feelings for you, then even the small stuff, like holding hands, is going to be earth-shattering for him. You should probably talk to him about it and make sure that's something that you want to deal with."

Shit. I didn't think about that.

I've been so wrapped in trying to figure out if Theo has been flirting with me that I never stopped to consider what it meant if he was. What he must be thinking about himself right now, or what kind of battle must be going on in his head.

An ache flares in my chest. Suddenly, all I can think about is comforting him and making sure he's okay.

"Maybe I should go check on him?" I say, brushing off a layer of sour gummy worm dust from my shirt as I stand.

Wren nods in agreement. "I'll send a search party if you're gone longer than five minutes. Yell really loud if you get abducted by his parents. Oh! Do you think your mom would defend us in court if we end up having to kill someone in self-defense?"

"Let's hope we don't have to find out."

Out in the hallway, I spot a closed door with light shining from underneath. That must be where he went. I hesitate for a moment, listening, just to make sure I'm not about to interrupt an actual bathroom situation. I knock after I hear the sink cut on.

I hear Theo fumble with the knob on the other side. The door swings open, his figure backlit.

"Sorry," I stammer, taking a step back so he doesn't feel like I'm cornering him. His face is definitely flushed, and the tips of his bangs are wet. "I just—I wanted to make sure you were okay. I love watching Wren's movies, but they definitely get me sometimes, and I didn't mean to—I mean, not that I didn't want to—I just didn't want you to think that there was something implied—shit! I'm sorry. I don't know what I'm trying to say."

Theo chuckles, the serious expression on his face brightening like a ray of sunshine breaking through thick clouds. "It's okay, dude. Um, we were just caught up in the moment, right? I didn't think a movie about nuns could freak me out so much, but then I got thinking about being down in the basement at Saint Catherine's, and—I dunno, it just sort of all piled up at once. I'm good, though. Thanks for checking on me."

There's more he wants to say. I can see it on his face, but I don't push him. Instead, I nod and motion over my shoulder. "We can probably catch the finale if we hurry."

He grins again, giving me a nod. I step aside so he can lead us back into the theater room and to a very nonchalant Wren.

"Oh good, you're just in time, boys."

Theo takes his seat in the middle again, and I return to my side, crossing my arms over my chest again so I won't be tempted to reach across the armrest. I try and pay attention to the movie, but I find myself watching Theo out of the corner of my eye, waiting for his body language to tell me what's going on in his head. He trains his eyes forward, his hands gripping his knees and the rest of his body completely still. When another kill happens, spraying blood across the screen, he doesn't react. He merely sits there with this glassy-eyed stare, his posture rigid. By the time the credits roll, I'm almost convinced he's turned into a statue.

"Man, you really can't trust a nun, can you?" Wren jokes, getting up to adjust the lighting back to a normal level.

Theo stirs finally, getting up from his seat. "For real. I'll think twice about going to any midnight masses in the future, that's for sure." He laughs, but it sounds strained.

"Well, what now?" Wren asks, looking more at me than Theo.

Theo moves to the corner, ejecting Wren's VHS and returning it to its case. "Oh, um, it's still pretty early, so we could watch another one if y'all want?"

"We've actually got an early morning," I interject, standing up as well. Wren throws me a curious glance, and I nod to help them catch my drift. "We've got to, um, go on a hike with my mom. She's been talking about it all week, so I want to make sure I'm well-rested."

"Right," Wren adds, backing me up. "But this was fun! We'll have to do it again sometime."

Theo looks at me, his smile fading slowly. "Oh, okay. Yeah, I understand. I've got to be up early too, so it's no biggie. Let me walk you guys back upstairs."

Wren and I follow Theo up to the foyer again. We don't run into his parents on our way to the front door, and he steps out onto the porch to watch as we climb into Wren's car.

"Thanks for backing me up," I say to Wren once the doors are closed. "I panicked."

"No problem, but you'd better be joking because if you think I'm going hiking, you're delusional."

I snort a laugh as I look over my shoulder back at Theo's house. I swear, he's still watching even as we turn the corner and head for home.

"You're home early," Lola says from the couch as I walk in the front door. She's got the TV cranked up, playing an episode of *Friends,* and her laptop open on the coffee table. A stack of files sits on the couch beside her, and she looks like she's about halfway through whatever menial task Mom has saddled her with.

"It was a weird night," I say, falling over the recliner's armrest and propping my head on the opposite one.

"Does this weird night have a name?" Lola asks, hitting the pause button on the remote.

"He does, but I don't think I should be saying it just yet."

"Boo, you're no fun. Come on, Cal, I'm drowning in paperwork over here. One of us has to have a social life, and as you can tell, unless I start folding all of these documents into origami dolls, it's not going to be me. I want to hear about this boy!"

"Okay, fine. But this doesn't leave this room, got it?"

She zips her lips and locks them like we're back in elementary school.

"Me and Wren went over to his house tonight to watch a movie, and I sort of held his hand, which may or may not have caused him to run out of the room and sparked a possible identity crisis."

Lola blinks at me, then quickly unzips her lips. "All that happened because you held hands? I'm kind of impressed. If you'd kissed him, would his head have exploded?"

"It's not funny," I say, shaking off the image of Theo leaning in for a kiss before it can do any emotional damage. "His family is kinda super religious, so if he's interested in me, I don't want to be the reason that he gets in trouble with them, you know? Plus, how do I know he's not going to, like, snap one day and tell me I'm the one dragging him down to hell and try and whisk me off to some conversion camp?"

Lola sets the folder in her lap aside. "Okay, there's a lot to unpack there. But I think the most important thing to ask is: do you feel safe around him?"

All I can think about is the fluttery feeling that took over my body when Theo's hand was in mine. "Yeah. I don't think he's actually going to do any of that. It's just where my mind went first."

"Good, okay, now that's out of the way, how do you feel about being the one to help him work through those feelings? I'm assuming the two of you have a connection, right?"

"I think so. God, I thought my heart was going to burst out of my chest when I grabbed his hand."

Lola giggles. "Aww, that's so sweet."

Heat sears my cheeks. "Shut up."

"I'm serious! It sounds like the two of you are crushing, and if that's the case, you have to be willing to either help him through whatever processing he's doing or go ahead and cut ties now before anyone gets hurt, you know?"

I frown at her. "That seems like a pretty serious ultimatum. Can't I just flirt with him some more and not have to worry about the identity crisis thing?"

"Sorry, little brother, I don't think it's going to be that simple. It's better you prepare yourself now, so that way, you know what to do when the proverbial shit hits the fan. And, to try and lean to the side of optimism, if things end up working out for the better, you can look back and be glad that you had a game plan."

"Optimism? I think Mom's starting to rub off on you. How much longer do you have to work with her? I miss my sarcastic, pessimistic sister."

Lola lets out a groan, shoving the stack of paperwork beside her further away. "Too long. And I think you're right. I caught myself ordering a spinach salad at lunch today. Who the hell am I?"

"Yikes. Maybe you're the one with the identity crisis."

We both laugh, and Lola gets up from her spot on the couch to come and kneel next to me, running her fingers through my hair. "In closing, I'll say this. If you think this boy is worth the effort, then go for it. But if, at any time, you feel things start to spin out of control, come talk to me, okay? You're too young to have to solve all the world's problems. Leave some to your big sis."

"Okay. I can do that."

"Good. Now go get changed into your jammies, and I'll scoop us up a couple of bowls of ice cream, and we can watch *Schitt's Creek*."

"Oh my god, say less."

FIFTEEN
THEO

"I wanted to make sure you were okay."

My brain is stuck in a loop throughout the rest of the movie, replaying that sentence from Caleb over and over again, and it's impossible to focus on anything else.

Once Caleb and Wren's car is out of sight, I turn to make my way up the stairs, almost running smack into Grace. She smells like Cathy's and looks disheveled still wearing her uniform, makeup smeared and wearing off. But she's got a look in her eye that I know all too well.

"We need to talk."

"Grace, I'm really not in the mood—"

"Don't care," she snaps, then points upstairs. "My room?"

I roll my eyes, too drained to argue. "Fine."

I follow her up the stairs to her room, right next door to mine. Her room feels far less homey than it used to before she lived on campus most of the week, but it's not as cluttered as mine, so it makes sense to talk in here. I stand awkwardly by the bed, my hands going into my pockets.

She shuts the door behind me, then makes her way to her bed and plops down on it. "First things first, who were those two? Because I've never seen them here before, and I overheard Mom and Dad whispering in the kitchen about one of them 'not being a girl or a boy,' and Dad already looked uncomfortable, so… Nice job, kid, you're expanding your friend circle, and I'm proud of you."

She holds out her fist, and I stare at it for a second before bumping it with my own fist, offering her a weak smile.

"Thanks. That was Wren and Caleb. They're new friends from school. Well… Caleb and I are friends, but I told him he could invite his friends over if he wanted to. Not to say that I don't like Wren or anything. I just don't know them that well."

She's watching me again, waiting for more.

I honestly don't know what more to give her, so I just shrug. "That's it, I guess?"

"Nope, that's not it. Something happened." She's quiet for another few seconds, and my gaze drifts to the floor. I hate how perceptive she is. I hate that Grace knows something is going on. She always does. Is it just because she's my sister, or is it because she's actually a psychic?

"Are you confused about your feelings for Wren?"

I bark out a laugh, but the stress dissipates slightly at the relief that she got it wrong. "No, no, it's not like that at all. Look, we just watched a really scary movie tonight, that's all. I don't think I told you, but last week I went with the gang to Saint Catherine's, that old creepy church across town, and we did one of those haunted tours because Triple H did an episode about it recently. I snuck downstairs to the basement—it was stupid. I could have gotten in trouble, I know, but I wanted to maybe record something for TikTok, I don't know. But I felt something weird down there, and it really freaked me out. I've been feeling off ever since. And the movie we just watched was about killer nuns, so it just kind of triggered that weird feeling again, you know?"

Grace furrows her brow, still studying me, as if she thinks that if she looks hard enough, she'll find the cracks in my story, but I feel confident that what

I've said is absolutely true. It's leaving a couple of things out, but I hope it's enough to get her off my case.

"There's something you're not telling me," she says finally. "And look, I get it if you don't want to tell me. I can't force the truth out of you. But you need to know that I'm here for you if you need someone to talk to, okay?"

I nod and offer her the most genuine smile I can muster. "I know."

"Also," she reaches out and touches my hand. "I need you to know that there's nothing wrong with you."

I stare back at her and feign confusion. "W-What?"

"There's nothing wrong with you. No matter who you like. Okay?"

How could she—oh, *Wren*. She still thinks I like Wren. I mean, yeah, that would also be complicated for the same reasons that liking Caleb would be complicated. But I can't help the relief that washes over me that she didn't see through me completely. Caleb is still my secret, and I aim to keep it that way.

"Okay," I finally say.

She smiles and pulls away. "All right, you're free to go."

"Really?" I ask skeptically.

"Really."

I'm genuinely surprised she's not pushing me harder for the truth, but maybe I convinced her. Or maybe she knows I need space. Whatever the case, I'll take it. I turn and head for the door.

"Thanks, Grace."

"Anytime, bud."

I promptly escape to my room, select a moody playlist, and collapse on my bed.

Predictably, however, all I can think of is Caleb. And that terrifies me.

But should it terrify me? Is this all in my head? I try to replay the events of the evening, try to figure out where things went wrong, where things got…weird. We shared the gummy worms because he offered them to me. We brushed arms and it was an accident at first, but then Caleb left his arm there, and then a jump scare had us holding hands. I think he grabbed mine first, but I'm the one that held on. Then, when Wren spoke up, it spooked Caleb and he let go.

But as soon as I recall the feeling of his skin on mine, my body *responds*. Even right now. The heat in my chest, the chills up and down my arm, my heart pounding erratically—

Shit, shit, shit, this isn't helpful.

Part of me—the always-compliant, rule-following, goody-goody Christian side of me—knows that something deeper is going on, and I really should either pray about this, talk to someone, or maybe just break things off with Caleb altogether. If this…*thing,* whatever it is, is comparable to how I felt about Sienna, I should do the right thing and end it. Not just for my sake but for Caleb's, too. I can't give him the wrong idea. I can't spend too much time with Caleb if he thinks this is something it's not, so I might as well just let it go and move on like nothing ever happened.

However, that's only a part of me. The other part—the opportunistic side that trespassed into the basement of Saint Catherine's without caring about the consequences because the reward of internet fame outweighed the risk of getting caught—feels quite differently about the whole thing. So, the question is: do the rewards outweigh the risks in this situation? I think it depends on what the consequences of being caught would be, but the rewards? The rewards include having Caleb in my life. The reward is seeing how often I can make Caleb's nose scrunch in that funny way when he laughs. The reward is letting our hands touch sometimes, experiencing that intoxicating energy between us, and seeing what else happens.

And I mean, honestly, there's nothing *wrong* with holding hands. Sure, I've only ever really held hands with Sienna before now, but that was different. We went into it with romantic intentions. We were dating when we held hands. Caleb and I are friends, and that's it. Friends can hold hands. Right?

Maybe… Maybe we should only hold hands in secret, then. Just in case someone gets the wrong idea and thinks we're doing something wrong.

Because we're not doing anything wrong. And if we're not doing anything wrong, then what's the risk?

And if there's no risk, what am I so afraid of?

What if...

What if there doesn't have to be consequences because what if what is happening is actually nothing to be afraid of?

For the first time all night, I can feel the relief wash over me as I cling to this realization. It's enough. I'll take it.

If I'm going to be friends with Caleb, then it's probably time to make it official and introduce him to the crew.

Admittedly, I probably should have told my friends about Caleb sooner given how often we're texting now. Plus, having Caleb over last night will probably trigger some type of best friend alarm bells for Harrison. But the sooner I tell them, the less weird they'll be about it.

They won't be weird because Caleb is gay—not even the slightest. Harrison is the only one who might be the slightest bit hesitant about it, but that's for the same reason as my initial hesitance: the church has taught us that the lifestyle of being gay is wrong, but that doesn't mean we can't have gay friends. Gay people are people, too, and deserve just as much love and friendship as anyone else. As for Elise and Oliver, it won't even be on their radar as something to worry about. Elise already reads tons of gay comics and fanfiction, and I'm pretty sure her sister is dating someone non-binary, and Oliver doesn't care about anything. So that's definitely not what I worry about.

My friends will be weird because I don't just *make* friends. Before Saint Catherine's, I had a total of four people in my life that I consider my friends: Harrison, Oliver, Elise, and Sienna. I hate big crowds, and the idea of meeting new people freaks me out. In fact, when Oliver entered the picture, I was not initially on board with him invading our friend group because his golden retriever energy overwhelmed me so much. But Oliver was persistent, clinging to us like a goofy little parasite, and eventually, I got over myself and accepted it. Now I don't know where I'd be without him.

So, the idea of me inviting a new person into our crew with very little precedent? Especially since I haven't really mentioned how often I talk to Caleb already? Yeah, my friends are going to be weird about it.

I send the message to the group chat first, knowing if Caleb just shows up without their knowledge, it will be a nightmare.

> THEO: hey guys - so don't be weird, but I'm inviting Caleb Raynard to hang with us at the pool tomorrow, is that cool?
>
> OLIVER: oh shit isn't that the guy that went into the haunted basement with you?
>
> HARRISON: Uhhhhhhh what?
>
> ELISE: of course Theo! :)
>
> THEO: I said don't be weird Harry
>
> HARRISON: ??
>
> OLIVER: I mean it is weird that you're suddenly becoming friends with someone that isn't us dude
> > is he blackmailing you
> > oooh did you witness caleb murdering someone in the basement and now you've seen too much and he's threatening to kill you too if you don't do whatever he says
> > but all he wants is to hang out with a bunch of losers at your pool?
> > sounds like a pretty sweet deal honestly

THEO: guys seriously if you make it a big deal it's just gonna be even more weird. it turns out Caleb is actually a lot like us, like he watches triple H and likes ghost stuff and horror movies, idk. he seems like he'd be fun to hang out with

ELISE: yeah he sounds awesome! :) I'm always down for new friends!

OLIVER: i'm sticking with my theory of extortion

ELISE: that's not what extortion is Oliver

OLIVER: well whatever it is it's weird because Theo hates people

HARRISON: I'm with Oliver on this one.

OLIVER: see, harry gets it

HARRISON: You're gonna have to do better than that, Theo.

ELISE: y'all are being stupid. I support you, Theo.

THEO: ffs guys

Caleb and I hit it off at saint catherine's and we've been texting ever since, okay? it's not that big of a deal, isn't that how people make friends?

HARRISON: Theo, this whole thing is weird, so I'm going to be weird about it until you tell me the truth.

THEO: the truth is I think Caleb's cool and I think you guys will think he's cool too

idk man maybe I'm growing as a person? growing out of my weird social awkwardness? is that okay with you?

OLIVER: o_o

HARRISON: Whatever you say, dude.

I close the chat with a frustrated huff. This is so stupid.

All I want is to be friends with Caleb and for my friends to be friends with Caleb. Why does it have to be complicated?

This is why I don't make new friends.

SIXTEEN
CALEB

Sunday, September 17

My dreams are plagued by killer nuns—for obvious reasons—but also with glimpses of Theo around every corner. Every time I escape a deranged Sister from Hell, he's there, with that same look of panic I saw in his eyes last night. And, honestly, Theo constantly running away from me freaks me out far more than the murderous hell-spawned clergy.

When I finally wake up—an hour before my alarm is even set—I can't seem to shake the squeezing sensation in my chest, so I decide to head downstairs to see if a bowl of cereal can solve anything.

Dad sits at the breakfast table, his tablet propped up against a stack of files—no doubt left by Lola—and he looks up from his oatmeal to greet me.

"Good morning, Cal. Or should I say the alien inhabiting my son's body. There's absolutely no way he'd be up this early on a Sunday."

"It's me, unfortunately," I say through a yawn. Opening the fridge, the cold does little to wake me up. I grab the almond milk, setting it on the counter. "Couldn't get back to sleep."

"I hate it when that happens. Sorry, kiddo."

The pantry door opens with a creak, and I select my cereal from the top shelf. "It happens. Are you home today?"

Dad shakes his head, tapping his tablet to check the time. "I've got to head out in a few minutes. The director just ordered another set of reshoots, so we'll be on this project a while longer. Which isn't all bad since I get to come home at night and see you guys."

My cereal hits the bowl like rain on a tin roof. "You were already passed out when I got home last night. I could hear you snoring down the hall."

Dad laughs, rubbing the gray spot in his goatee. "Guilty, but you see how early I had to get up. Were you hanging out with Wren?"

I nod because it's technically not a lie as I debate telling him the whole story. But for one reason or another, I decide that it's best to keep Theo close to the chest for the time being, just in case things end up getting messy. No need to drag Mom and Dad into the drama if I can avoid it.

The milk washes over my sugary cereal, and I pat my pocket, realizing that I've left my phone upstairs. I set the bowl down on the corner of the table, wedging some space free from the mountains of paperwork.

"Hey, Dad, did you ever go to church growing up?"

Dad looks up from his tablet again, his thick brows furrowed enough that the lines on his forehead sink in. "Church? Yeah, a few times. Holidays, mostly, and it was only because your great-grandmother would guilt my parents into taking us. Why do you ask?"

"Uh, Freddy is interested in a guy who's pretty religious," I say, once again convincing myself there's just enough truth in my words to not be considered outright lying. "But I'm not sure it's a good idea. I mean, the guy isn't out or anything, obviously, and although Freddy's picked up some vibes, neither of them have explicitly brought up the possibility of them getting together."

"Hmm..." Dad ponders, tilting his head. "That's a difficult situation. But I think the best thing would be for Freddy to be clear and honest about his intentions. If he really likes this guy, it's better to clear the air of any confusion first. That way, if the other boy isn't ready to take that step, or if lines have gotten crossed and he doesn't feel the same way about Freddy, things don't have to turn awkward."

He makes it sound so simple. Is that what I should do? It would first require me to admit how I actually feel about Theo in the first place. I think it's safe to assume I've hit the point of crushing. But I also really enjoy him as a friend, too, which means if I mess this up, I could ruin a new friendship.

God, why does everything have to be so complicated?

"Tell Freddy I hope things go well with his new friend," Dad says, grabbing his tablet and collecting his oatmeal bowl. "I might be late tonight, so good morning, good afternoon, and if I don't see you, good night."

I grin as he kisses me on the head, then drops his dishes in the sink and heads for the door to the garage.

My cereal is getting soggy, so I scarf down my breakfast, constantly reaching for the phone that isn't in my pocket. I dump the remnants of my milk into the sink and head back upstairs to find my phone in the space between my nightstand and bed frame. It's still super early, but I've got a text from Theo.

> **THEO: hey Caleb - look, I'm sorry about last night if I made things weird. the movie just kind of freaked me out and that's embarrassing lol. but hey, I know it's last minute but do you want to come over to swim this afternoon? a few of my friends will be there and we'll probably order pizza or something for dinner, maybe play video games after it gets dark. you know, just chillin :)**

Well, at least I know I didn't scare him off. He still wants to spend time with me. That means something, right? But is it in an "I like hanging out with you, bro" way or an "I want to hold your hand and maybe make out with you in the basement" kind of way?

Great. Now all I can think about is Theo's stupid face and how his lips pull tight when he's trying not to laugh, or the way his eyes crinkle when he smiles every time I walk into the freaking room, or what it would feel like to wrap my arms around his waist and pull him close…

> **CALEB:** hey, no worries. yeah the movie was intense, I totally get it. this afternoon sounds fun. I'll have my sister drop me off.
> *gif of guy on unicorn float*

I hop back in bed, pulling the covers over my head as I open TikTok. Maybe after a little scrolling, I can at least get another hour of sleep.

"Jesus, you weren't kidding about this place, were you?"

Lola shifts her car into park, pulling her sunglasses down to stare up at Theo's house. It was surprisingly easy getting her to agree to bring me over on such short notice. Mom had a lunch date with a friend from college, and of course, Dad is on set today. But Lola was more than glad to take any excuse to abandon her paperwork.

"I know, right? If the pool is half as nice as the home theater set up, it'll be bougie as fuck."

Lola snorts a laugh. "Well, just text me when you guys start winding down, and I'll swing by."

"You're the best, Lo. And you're sure I'm not ruining any of your plans?"

"In case you haven't noticed, Cal, I have no life. I'll be at home, slogging through piles of depositions and, if I'm lucky, starting on the homework that's due tomorrow morning."

"God, your life sucks."

Lola rolls her eyes with a smile. "Tell me about it."

I give her a quick hug before hopping out of the car at the end of the driveway and wave as she pulls away. I walk around Theo's red Honda and another car I don't recognize to the side fence, looking for the gate he told me to go through. A booming laugh echoes as I pull open the gate.

"Cannonball!"

Harrison launches himself off of the diving board, pulling his knees in and hitting the water with enough force he soaks an entire corner of the deck.

"Jeez, Harry! You almost capsized me!" shouts Elise from her float. Her long, dark hair is piled on top of her head, and huge sunglasses hide most of her face.

Harrison resurfaces beside the float, a devilish grin on his face. "I guess I didn't try hard enough, then." He grabs the side and flips the float over, sending Elise into the water with a shriek.

"I'm going to kill you!" she yells, thrashing to get her footing, but they're both laughing, and it's honestly kind of cute.

"You made it!"

Theo stands on the pool deck, hair slicked to the side and water dripping down his bare torso. He's smiling—which he always does when he sees me—and I have to make a conscious effort not to stare.

"I made it."

Theo rushes down the hill to meet me, his arms outstretched like he's coming in fast for a hug. But all I can see is his exposed chest getting closer and closer and—he stops just shy of collision, dropping his arms to his side.

"Sorry, I just remembered I'm soaked. I don't want to get you all wet."

Yeah. That would be a tragedy.

I remind myself to breathe as we walk up the sloped hill to the pool deck. Although there was no hug, Theo does pat my shoulder as we go, and it's a little awkward, but maybe he's just looking for excuses to touch me?

Elise and Harrison are practically wrestling each other in the shallow end of the pool, and I notice Oliver reclining in one of the deck chairs, scrolling on his phone.

Theo's backyard is just as opulent as I imagined it would be. A wooden deck surrounds the inground pool, a row of chairs stacked with plush pillows and two striped umbrellas providing shade. Beyond the pool deck, the back porch is screened in, with a high-top table and chairs, a sitting area, and a TV mounted to the wall.

"You can drop your stuff over there," Theo says, pointing to the back porch. "And if you need a towel, there's a stash under the table."

"Thanks," I say, already feeling a bit out of place. I step off the deck and onto the cushy green grass. Even the lawn seems perfect, the deep color and thickness sure to be an envy of all the neighbors. Back home, Dad attempted to fix the lawn on his own one summer but ended up getting so frustrated he dug it all up the next year and smothered the backyard in stones. Now we've got a yard of rocks and dandelions, which honestly isn't that bad. No more lawnmowers.

I drop my bag off on the sofa, grabbing the towel I brought and tossing it over my shoulder. I already put sunscreen on before I left the house, so I pull off my shirt and shove it into my bag before heading back over to the deck. Theo's in the pool now, hanging onto the side of Elise's float as they carry a hushed conversation that I try not to assume is about me.

"Hey Caleb," Oliver calls from his chair, waving. "Welcome to Brigg's Oasis. It's going to ruin any community pool for you, so enjoy your last few moments of plebeian joy before you're corrupted by the luxury."

"Shut up, Oliver!" Theo yells from the pool, detaching himself from Elise's float. "You'll have to ignore him, Caleb. The rest of us do."

Oliver cracks a smile. "Don't say I didn't warn you."

"Your concerns have been noted," I say, giving him a thumbs up.

Harrison climbs out of the pool from the steps, and I realize this is the first time I've ever seen him without his glasses. "What's up, man? Been wandering around any good haunted basements lately?"

"Oh, you know it. I keep thinking if I hang around long enough, the ghosts will just accept me as one of their own. Then I can stop having to worry about college applications."

"Dang, alright," Harrison says with a chuckle. "Theo didn't tell us you had jokes."

I look over Harrison's shoulder at Theo, who's just a head hovering in the water. "Yeah? What did Theo tell you about me?"

This should be interesting.

"Just the fun stuff," Elise chimes in. "That you're partners in crime and your choice in movies is as sick and twisted as the rest of us."

I step down the first few steps into the pool, then sit on the edge, letting my legs dangle in the cool water. "It's true. Me and Wren like to traumatize as many people as we can with their mom's collection of terrible nineties horror."

Theo swims over to the shallow end, hovering close to where I am. He flicks his hand, splashing water onto my leg, and I respond with a kick that sends a stream right to his face. He laughs, and I can't help but smile.

"Terrible horror? Now you're talking my language," Oliver says, getting up from his chair. He sits down on the opposite side of the stairs, dipping his feet in as well. "Have you seen *Death by a Thousand Nails*?"

"Uh, duh. Wren made me watch that at their thirteenth birthday party. Freddy chickened out halfway through and missed the ice cream cake. Poor thing."

"Why can't y'all ever talk about stuff I like," Elise complains, paddling herself closer to the conversation.

"Because you only watch anime and troll AO3," Oliver replies.

Elise glares at Oliver. "There's horror anime, you know. It would bring all of our interests together."

"Like *I Love You, Seymour Shura*," I say before I think better of it. "Um, but you have to be okay with yaoi. It's about this guy whose boyfriend ends up turning into a monster at night and killing and eating criminals. It's very bloody, but also kinda camp. They released the first season of the sub a few weeks ago."

Elise perks up at the idea. "Ooo! I'm adding that to the list!"

"I'm in as long as there's blood and guts," Oliver adds.

"Tons," I assure him. I look over at Theo, but he's back in the deep end again, staring off into space. Damn. I was hoping that I could gauge his reaction. Maybe get an idea for where his head's at.

The door on the back porch opens and Kora waves at us. "Pizza's here! I've got it set up on the table when y'all get hungry."

Oliver bolts first. "I'm starving!"

Harrison helps Elise off her float, and the two of them share a smile that makes my stomach flip. Theo is still floating in the deep end, oblivious to the rest of us, so I grab one of the inner tubes and toss it at him. It lands perfectly around his head like a giant game of ring toss, and he sticks his neck through to look at me.

"Pizza's here," I say, motioning towards the rest of the group.

"Oh. Sweet. You go ahead. I'll be there in a second, okay?"

I nod, and he sinks back into the tube so I can't see him anymore.

Something is definitely up with him, but he obviously doesn't want to talk about it right now. Maybe some lunch will change his mood.

SEVENTEEN
THEO

Man, I'm in trouble.

I had fully convinced myself that I was fine. I had convinced my friends—and myself—that inviting Caleb over was perfectly normal and there was nothing else going on and that I really did believe that he was a good fit for our gang. The stuff I felt at Saint Catherine's and last night during the movie was directly correlated to the spooky vibes. This pool day would prove that. I could finally put this fear to rest, knowing that Caleb and I just accidentally trauma bonded over a haunted church, and we're just supposed to be great friends. That's all.

And then I saw Caleb again in the bright afternoon sun, with his curly copper hair and freckles dusting lightly across his face and down his arms. I saw him smile at me as I greeted him, almost tackling him in a hug before I realized I was dripping wet from the pool and he was still wearing a shirt.

But now he's not wearing a shirt. And I can't stop staring.

I swallow it down as best as I can, staying submerged in the pool and acting as casually as possible. I think I'm doing okay until Elise uses her trademark subtlety to get my attention.

"*Psst,* Theo!"

I roll my eyes and swim over to her float. "Elise, this counts as being weird."

"Were you about to hug him?" she asks, lowering her massive sunglasses down the bridge of her nose to give me a look. "How long have you guys been hanging out, exactly?"

"For the love of—" I grip her float tightly and lean in closer. "Drop it. Please. We can talk about it later."

"Oh my God," she whispers a little too knowingly, causing a spike of terror to shoot down my spine. "Oh yeah, we *definitely* will."

"Please be normal," I plead with her, stealing a glance toward Caleb to make sure he can't hear us. Oliver's attention is on Caleb now, a mischievous half-smile on his face, which means he's about to say something stupid. *Shit.* I turn my attention back to Elise. "Please."

She raises her eyebrows at me one last time before pushing her sunglasses back up on her face. "This isn't over, Theo Briggs."

"Welcome to Briggs' Oasis," Oliver says to Caleb. "It's going to ruin any community pool for you, so enjoy your last few moments of plebeian joy before you're corrupted by the luxury."

"Shut up, Oliver!" I shout, quickly distancing myself from Elise, thankful that at least Oliver isn't being a problem yet. "You'll have to ignore him, Caleb. The rest of us do."

Before I know it, everyone has congregated around the pool and they're talking and it's perfect. For a few beautiful moments, all my favorite people in the world are hitting it off, talking about horror movies, even bringing up horror anime, which of course piques Elise's attention, and I can't help but feel ecstatic.

Until Caleb brings up a horror anime that is...well, *gay.*

And suddenly, I'm trying not to spiral again. *Not now, not now, not now.* Stop thinking about it. It's fine. He's allowed to be interested in gay media. Elise talks about gay anime and fanfiction all the time.

I slowly drift further into the deep end of the pool, trying to swim away from the panic, away from the weirdness. There's no reason to panic. Nothing weird is happening. Everything's going so well. I'm fine, this is fine, and everything is normal and—

Suddenly, an inner tube lands around my head, shocking me out of my thoughts. I glance up and see Caleb watching me curiously, everyone else gone. "Pizza's here," he says, motioning to the porch.

"Oh. Sweet," I say, my voice flat. "You go ahead. I'll be there in a second, okay?"

Caleb nods, his expression still concerned, but he turns and walks away.

I take a deep breath and submerge myself under the water again, exhaling my breath so that I sink straight to the bottom.

Being a teenager sucks. Why do my emotions give me such whiplash?

I eventually force myself out of the pool and head to the porch for pizza, and by the time I sit down and start eating, I slowly start to feel normal again. I watch on as an impassioned Oliver recounts a funny story, and something Oliver says or does makes Caleb laugh, and somehow, my sour mood begins to fade away.

"So, we're *finally* watching it after literal years of convincing him to suck it up and watch the stupid movie, and Theo isn't even paying attention because he's too busy texting!"

Ah, of course, it's an embarrassing story about me. It's okay—I'm barely paying attention because I already know the story and lived through it. Oliver's dramatic retelling is doing a better job at telling it than I ever will anyway.

Also, it's too hard to concentrate when Caleb keeps laughing like that. He's leaning against the wall on the porch, plate of pizza in hand, his towel draped over his bare shoulders.

He has a lot of freckles. So many little freckles… They remind me of stars in the night sky.

"What text conversation could possibly be more important than *The Exorcist*?" Caleb asks with wide eyes.

I could probably take a marker and trace little constellations in those freckles. I can almost see them now if I look hard enough. Orion's belt. Cassiopeia. The Big Dipper.

"Psh, it was probably Sienna," Harrison mutters while taking another bite of his pizza slice.

Hearing Sienna's name violently yanks me out of the night sky, crashing back down to earth.

"Who is Sienna?" Caleb asks, and I try not to visibly wince as I brace myself for whatever unhinged answers my friends will provide to Caleb's innocent question.

"Theo's ex," Oliver replies quickly, his mouth very full of pizza, but of course, he wanted to be the one to say it. He swallows before adding, "The biggest Jesus Freak you'll ever meet in your life."

"Oh," Caleb says softly, his expression indecipherable. I try not to overthink it. Why would I overthink it?

"Yeah, she's—she's sweet, but a little intimidating to be around," Harrison adds, shooting a glance at me, then frowning. I guess whatever expression I'm making doesn't pass Harrison's vibe check. Shit.

"That's an understatement," Oliver continues. "Dude, Sienna is like, freakin' Mother Theresa or something. She goes on mission trips, she talks about the Bible all the time, she prays in public. It's wild. But hey, if that's what Theo's into…" he trails off, shrugging.

"Sienna was too much," Elise says bluntly directly to Caleb. "Theo's so much better off without her. I know I've said it before, but those five months were rough on all of us."

"Wow, five months?" Caleb says, finally looking at me. "That's a long time."

I open my mouth to answer, but Oliver interrupts. "Way too long. We threw a party when they broke up."

"It wasn't *that* bad," Harrison chimes in again, giving Oliver a look that clearly conveys he needs to shut up, but I'll be surprised if Oliver gets the message. "*She* wasn't that bad, she was just possessive of Theo's time, and we missed him, that's all. But that's ancient history, I'm sure Theo doesn't want to talk about—"

"Bullshit, that wasn't all," Oliver argued. "She made Theo think he was a bad Christian because he wasn't as brain-washed as her, and quite frankly that pissed me off."

"Same," Elise adds, taking a sip of her soda and eyeing Caleb as she says it.

Suddenly, I wish we were back in the pool so I could float back to the deep end and hold my head underwater so I could muffle all of this. I feel the tips of my ears burning with embarrassment. I can only hope it looks like sunburn.

"Can we not talk about Sienna?" Harrison says, his tone more serious now. "Again, ancient history and a real bummer to talk about. I think we should revisit the nineties horror movies you mentioned earlier, Caleb, the lesser-known stuff. You said Wren has a collection of old VHS tapes? They should bring them here sometime! Theo's parents have this crazy theater room setup downstairs. Has he mentioned that before?"

Caleb raises an eyebrow. "Yeah, I know. We came over last night to watch one."

Shit.

"Who did?" Harrison asks.

"Me and Wren," Caleb answers, though it sounds more like a question as he glances at me.

All eyes are on me. I shove a huge bite of pizza in my mouth and shrug.

"Oh, cool," Elise swoops in, her tone still casual. "It's super fancy down there. What did y'all watch?"

The conversation continues, but I can feel myself drifting again. This was a bad idea. Why didn't I tell them everything? This is my fault. I made this weird. Things were going so well, but I'm messing everything up. Stupid, stupid, stupid.

At some point, I notice Oliver throw his paper plate away and head back towards the pool.

"You're getting back in?" Elise asks.

"The sun is still up," Oliver replies as if it's the dumbest question he's ever heard. "So, yeah, duh."

Harrison and Elise exchange glances, shrug, and follow Oliver outside, shutting the screen door behind them.

Caleb is suddenly next to me, closer than I expected, and my stomach flips. "Hey, are you okay?" he asks softly, his brown eyes studying me.

"Yeah, I think so," I answer, fighting the panic away. "Geez, I'm sorry, man, I keep spacing out on you. But yeah, I think the food and the caffeine will help."

Caleb smiles hesitantly. "Are you still seeing killer nuns everywhere?"

I can't help the grin that takes over my face. "Yes, dude, they're everywhere! You too?"

"Yeah, I could barely sleep last night. Kept having nightmares of nuns chasing me and…" he trails off, looking down, but then he's back smiling at me. "Never mind."

"Well, let's definitely stick with the group. First rule of all campy horror movies: never split the party." My eyes land on his exposed shoulder, his skin there the lightest shade of pink. Before I even realize what I'm doing, I reach out to touch the back of my hand to his shoulder, and it's warm. "Hey, do you need some more sunscreen? I don't want you to fry out there."

Caleb's expression wavers, but only for a second before feigning offense. "Oh, is my paleness worrying you?"

"Look man, I don't want you to get sun poisoning because you came over to my pool! I can't have that on my conscience."

"Melanoma is no joking matter," Caleb replies. "Yeah, I could probably go for another layer, I guess. Thanks for looking out for me."

I bump our bare shoulders together and flash him a smile. "Hey, that's what friends are for."

And with that, I head back to the pool, determined to enjoy the rest of the day no matter what happens. No more weirdness. No more drifting away. No more worrying.

As I approach the pool, Oliver is already in an innertube, sporting his obnoxious holographic Pit Viper sunglasses. "Theeee-oooooo," he calls out in a sing-song voice.

I lay my towel across a chair to dry. "Yes, Oliver?"

He beckons me to come closer.

I very nervously comply, bracing myself for whatever unhinged remark is about to come out of Oliver's mouth. "What?"

"I like Caleb," he says very matter-of-factly. I can't see his eyes through the reflective surface of his massive lenses, but he sounds sincere. "Probably more than I like you, actually. He's way cooler."

Elise snorts, also floating on a tube with Harrison dangling off the side of her float, resting his chin on the tube and holding her hand in his. It's actually really cute, and I can't stop myself from picturing myself doing the same thing if Caleb was on a tube. Shit.

"Good to know," I say sarcastically, pulling over a chair to the side of the pool, my gaze drifting to Caleb in the shade, reapplying sunscreen. I wonder what color his hair will be when it's soaking wet. Probably darker. Maybe more brown than red.

"Although I have a new theory now," Oliver adds.

"A new theory for what?" I ask.

"I initially thought that you witnessed Caleb murdering someone in that basement, but now I'm convinced that it's actually the opposite."

"Wait, what?" Caleb asks, walking towards the pool and rubbing sunscreen into his cheeks. "What about me murdering someone?"

"Don't worry, Caleb, I'm convinced you're the victim now," Oliver reassures him. "I think that you witnessed Theo murdering someone in cold blood in Saint Catherine's basement, and he was going to kill you, too, because you'd seen too much. In a desperate attempt to save your own life, you agreed to do anything Theo wanted, and he forced you to spend your Sunday afternoon with a bunch of losers you don't know. Although now you know that we're not all losers, and there's at least one other cool person here, but still, you had no way of knowing that until you met me."

"Ahh, I see," Caleb says with a grin, glancing down at me. "Well, I guess the cat's out of the bag, Theo. Will you still let me live?"

I rub my chin thoughtfully. "Well, unfortunately, now I just have to kill all of you because you all know too much."

"Unless we all gang up on you," Caleb says with a mischievous smirk. "I mean, now it's four against one. You can't kill all of us."

"It's him or us, Caleb!" Oliver shouts. "Throw him in!"

"What, no!" I say as I scramble to my feet. "You wouldn't!"

"Oh, I think I would," Caleb says, his smile devilish and full of intent, which for some reason makes my insides feel funny, catching me off guard.

Caleb takes full advantage of my hesitation and lunges towards me, scooping me up in his arms in what I can only describe as a bridal carry, sweeping me off my feet with one arm and supporting my back with his other arm. It happens so fast that I'm barely able to register what's happening until I'm off the ground, legs dangling in the air, my bare olive skin pressed against his fair skin as he literally holds me in his arms. I can only stare up at him in shock.

"Throw him in! Throw him in!" Oliver is chanting somewhere in the background.

Caleb looks down at me and smiles. "Sorry, Theo." And he leans over the side of the pool to gently toss me into the water below.

The water is cold, shocking me initially, but I have the distinct feeling that the resulting adrenaline rush that follows is not related to the temperature of the water. I reemerge from the water, hearing laughter from several different directions, but my focus is solely on Caleb, who stands over the edge of the pool with a pleased grin.

"Traitor!" I yell after I gasp for air, then with herculean effort, I use my feet to propel myself upward out of the water and grab onto his arm.

"No, no, Theo, wait, *AHH—*"

I show no mercy as I cling to his arm with both hands, pushing myself off the wall with my feet as I pull him in to make sure he doesn't hit the edge as he tumbles into the water with me.

I resurface at the same time he does, and he's coughing and spitting, but he's laughing, and his nose is doing that little crinkle thing, which makes me laugh even harder.

I notice the sunlight bouncing off his wet curls. His hair *is* darker when it's wet, more of an auburn than copper. *Called it.*

"Asshole!" Caleb shouts, still chuckling. "My sunscreen hasn't soaked in yet!"

"Oh, crap, I'm so sorry, I totally forgot," I say between gasps of air, trying to stop giggling but failing miserably. My heart is racing, and my cheeks hurt from laughing, but I couldn't care any less if I tried.

After Caleb and I make it back to the shallow end of the pool, and he claims the last available inner tube, my heart finally stops pounding in my chest, and I can catch my breath. I grab a pool noodle and relax into it, floating effortlessly between my friends in a blissful daze.

As a bonus, every time Caleb and I make eye contact, he grins at me, and my chest feels warm. I tuck the image of this specific smile away in my brain for later study.

"So, I don't think we've talked about the Hudson shout-out of your video yet, have we?" Harrison asks out of nowhere.

"Oh shit, no, we haven't," Oliver answers, then turns to look at me. "Which is weird. Isn't that like your whole thing, Theo?"

He's right. I have barely even thought about it since Saturday afternoon before Caleb and Wren came over. Weird. "Yeah, I'm super psyched about it. It just hasn't come up yet," I say dismissively.

Harrison squints at me. "Well, what are we going to do about it? Have you tried reaching out to Hudson or anyone from the show to let them know you saw the shout-out?"

I run my fingers through my wet curls. "No, not yet."

"Dude, seriously, you're slacking," Oliver says, splashing himself with water to cool down. "What are you waiting for?"

"I mean, it was barely even two days ago," I say defensively. "I've had a busy weekend."

"Oh yeah, I forgot you had plans on Saturday that you forgot to invite us to," Oliver says with a smirk. "Rude, by the way. I would have loved to come watch a shitty horror movie with Wren and Caleb."

"Next time I'll invite everyone," I promise. I glance at Caleb and smile apologetically, and he returns it. I casually paddle a little closer to his inner tube, trying not to make it obvious that I'm doing so.

"You better," Oliver mumbles as he leans his head back against the tube again. "Man, you know what your parents need to do next? They need to install a giant screen out here and project movies on it. Can you imagine how cool that would be?"

"Mm-hmm," I answer half-heartedly. I stare up at the yard, imagining the set-up. Much like today, all my friends would be there, including Caleb. We'd both be in separate inner tubes beside each other, but we'd have to attach the tubes so they wouldn't float away from each other. Or hold hands, maybe. Hmm.

"Theo, are you still with us?" Harrison asks, waving at me.

"Yeah, I never left," I answer quickly. "I was just thinking about the logistics of the movie screen out here."

"Shouldn't we focus on the Saint Catherine's video? We need a game plan, dude. What should you say?"

"I'll figure something out tonight and text you," I say. "You're right. I'm sorry. I've just been distracted."

As I say "distracted," I unconsciously glance at Caleb again, and our eyes meet. I quickly look away, realizing that I literally couldn't be more obvious if I tried, and I just hope that no one else saw it.

But alas, I glance around the pool to see both Harrison and Elise watching me, Harrison's brow furrowed in confusion and Elise's eyes twinkling with revelation. Shit.

There will be an unfortunate number of conversations later tonight. I already feel it.

An hour or so later, the sun has set over the horizon, and the mosquitoes are beginning to swarm around us. Oliver heads out first, having procrastinated a book report to as close to the last minute as possible (apparently twelve hours before it's due is the sweet spot, he claims). Elise's curfew is 9:00 PM, so Harrison leaves promptly at 8:35 PM in case they run into any traffic on the way. Elise rolls her eyes because it never takes more than fifteen minutes to get from my house to Elise's house, but Harrison is terrified of upsetting Elise's father.

This leaves me alone with Caleb at 8:36 PM, and suddenly, I'm buzzing with nervous energy.

"Did you drive here?" I ask, glancing at the emptied driveway.

"No, my sister dropped me off. I'm about to text her to come pick me up."

"I could drive you home if you want," I offer without really even thinking about it. I just don't want him to leave quite yet. Or at least if he's going to go, I want to go with him, even if it's just for a few more minutes.

Caleb pauses, his fingers hesitating on the screen of his phone for a second or two, then looks back up at me. "Are you sure?"

I nod with a grin. "Yeah, I don't mind! I'll just change clothes real quick. Do you need to be home by a certain time?"

"Yeah, usually 10:00 p.m. is my curfew for a school night."

I consider it for a moment, then take the leap. "Do you want to hang out a little later and then leave? I can still get you home before ten. If not, it's totally fine. I can just take you home now. I won't be offended either way. Today's been a blast."

Caleb is quiet for a few painstaking seconds, making me regret even asking, and I'm about to open my mouth to say, "forget it, it's fine," when he finally gives me an answer. "Okay, yeah. I'd like that. If you don't mind driving me home, I mean. Will your parents mind?"

I try not to make it obvious how elated I feel at his answer. "Nah, they're fine! I drive my friends around all the time. As long as I let them know where I'm going and when I'll be back, they don't care."

Caleb smiles again. "Okay, I'll text my sister and let her know."

"Cool," I say as casually as possible and lead the way back to the porch.

EIGHTEEN
CALEB

Theo's friends are far weirder than I expected. But, like, only in the best ways. Mom always tells me how I've never met a stranger, that I can always find something in common with anyone I meet, but it's effortless to connect with Theo's friends. The afternoon shoots by in a blur of sunshine, pizza, and chlorine.

But even the best days have to come to an end, and one by one, his friends leave the pool until it's just me and Theo. This could be it. My chance to bring up this thing between us that neither wants to speak out loud. The advice from Lola and Dad circles around my head, and I try to figure out a game plan on how to approach the topic. I grab my phone, pretending to text Lola when really I'm asking for her input, but then he offers to drive me home, and all my plans sort of evaporate with the building heat behind my face.

Back inside, I change in the downstairs bathroom, stuffing my swimsuit and towel into a plastic bag in my backpack. When I finish, Theo is waiting for me by the stairs, his hair still damp but in dry clothes. I can't help but notice how the sun has left its mark on him, warming the tips of his cheeks till he's practically glowing.

"Want to smash?" he asks, but then his eyes go wide for a second, and he lets out a nervous laugh. "I mean, play smash. On the Switch. Sorry, when

Harrison and me play, we just call it smashing."

I laugh, too, mostly at his reaction and how much he's blushing. "Sure. You'll definitely wipe the floor with me, but I'll be a gracious loser, I promise."

"Okay, sweet. I'll go easy on you, then."

I follow him up the stairs and down the hallway till he opens the door on his left, leading into his bedroom. He pulls out his phone, tapping a few times, and an LED strip lights up around the molding along the ceiling. At first, they're harsh white, but then he clicks another button, and they soften to gold.

Theo does a quick three-sixty, then lets out a sigh. "Crap, I forgot I took my Switch downstairs earlier to show Oliver something on my Animal Crossing island. I'll be right back. Don't go anywhere, okay?"

"No worries. Take your time."

He dashes out into the hallway, and I'm left to take in all that is Theo's bedroom. The wall directly across from his bed is painted a dark hunter's green, the deep color broken up by rows of framed band posters, only some of which I recognize. In the center, under the mounted TV, is one of those consoles with the record player built into the top. The cover is open, and my curiosity gets the better of me, so I take a peek at what vinyl is loaded. Interesting, The Black Keys would not have been my guess, but the more I think about it, the more I can picture Theo reclined in his bed while the table turns and *Lonely Boy* plays in the background.

It makes perfect sense.

A stack of notebooks sits at the bottom of his nightstand, the one on top hanging open over the stack with a pen hooked onto the side. Are all of these full? Journals, maybe?

Theo reenters the room at a sprint, his socks skidding on the floor before he comes to a stop at the foot of the bed. "Got it," he says, holding up the rectangular device. "Sorry to keep you waiting."

"It's fine," I say, hovering by the bed because I'm not really sure where I should sit. Plus, his bed is actually made—like sheets tucked in and everything—and I don't want to mess it up.

He plugs the Switch into the dock, the TV coming to life. "Here," he says, handing me one of the controllers. "You can sit if you want."

"Here?" I clarify, pointing to the bed.

Theo chuckles, his dark eyes catching the lights from above and reflecting them like a starry sky. "Yeah, or wherever. Make yourself comfy."

I lower myself gingerly onto the bed, scooting closer to the end because I feel weird about my clothes touching his pillows.

Theo looks over at the chair by the desk in the corner, but then he comes over and sits on the other end of the bed, throwing the pillows behind him so he can lean against them on the wall. "Okay, let's commence the smashing. Who do you main?"

My face feels hot again, but this time, it has nothing to do with Theo. "You can't make fun of me."

"Oh no, please don't tell me you're a Kirby stan because if that's the case, I don't think we can be friends anymore."

I shake my head. "No, no, I'm not a child. But I suck the least when I play as Princess Peach. You can insert a stereotypical gay joke here."

"Dude, Peach is actually super balanced. Why would I judge you for picking her? Oliver kicks my ass as Peach half the time."

"Well, cool. I guess I make good choices then. Who do you play as?"

Theo leans forward, grabbing one of his pillows to hold in his lap. "It depends on the situation. Like, if I'm going against Harrison one-on-one, I usually play as Fox because he usually picks the slower characters, and I can run circles around him. Then, if Oliver and Elise join in, I'll pick a heavy hitter so I can maximize the number of launches I can get in a round and try and win that way. Then, if I'm just messing around with the actual game, I'll switch it up and play Ness or even Sonic if I want to give myself a challenge, but then again—oh, I'm sorry. I'm, like, really rambling right now."

"It's okay!" I encourage him, pulling my leg up onto the bed and tucking it under me. "It doesn't bother me in the slightest."

Theo clears his throat and switches his focus to the screen. "Anyways, let's play a couple warm-up rounds and see what trouble we can get into."

It quickly becomes obvious that Theo is the far superior Smasher. The first game is a massacre, with my score being somewhere in the negative double digits. After that, he suggests we play on the same team against some computer players, and that goes far better. Before long, we've killed half an hour, which means our day together is quickly coming to an end.

"Do you ever think about posting non-spooky content on TikTok?" I ask between rounds.

Theo sets his controller down, scooting himself to the edge of the bed so we're aligned. "What do you mean?"

"You know, like, stupid stuff? Dance trends or maybe one of those cool transition videos where you throw the shoe in the air and change outfits?"

"Dance trends?" Theo echoes, looking at me like I've just suggested he try jumping out of a plane. "Nah, no one wants to see that. I can't dance worth a crap."

"Seriously? They're never that complicated. I think I still remember the last one. Hang on." I hop off the bed, pull out my phone, and open my music app. I scroll till I find the song, hitting play and tossing it onto the bed. "Come on! You've got to at least try it. I'll show you how easy it can be. This one needs two people anyway."

Theo doesn't look convinced, but he does roll off the bed and stand in front of me, his arms folded across his chest. "Who do you usually do these with?"

"My sister, Lola. Or sometimes Freddy, but bless his heart, he was not gifted with rhythm, so I really only let him do one if I want to make myself look good."

The song hits the chorus, and I scramble to pause it.

"Okay, watch me and mirror what I do. Got it?"

Theo nods, shaking out his arms. "I'll do my best."

I shift my weight to one side, swinging my hips back and forth in a slowed-down version of the move so he can get a feel for the motions. His eyes watch me, lingering with each sway and causing a scorching heat to build beneath my skin. After a few demonstrations, he tries to match my movements, and it's all I can do not to laugh.

"How's that?" he asks, his voice thick with doubt.

"A little stiff, but it's fine. Here's the next part."

Stepping back on one foot, I raise my arms over my head, pulling them in one at a time, then switching sides and doing it again.

Theo's better at this one because it doesn't involve him moving his hips.

"There you go!"

"Was that good?" he asks, eyes bright with excitement.

He's never had bigger puppy dog energy.

"Yeah! Okay, for the next part, my right hand takes your right, and then my left takes your left, and we spin around over our heads till we're back-to-back."

Theo doesn't hesitate, closing the distance between us in a single step and taking my hands in his. They're warm and bigger than mine are, I notice for the first time, which I find amusing given our height difference. His skin touching mine is like dropping a match in a puddle of gasoline—instant ignition.

"How does this work?" he asks, his voice softer now that we're so close.

"It's easy; we turn this way and lift our hands over our heads, and we'll be back-to-back but still holding on. Ready to try?"

He nods, licking his lips.

And maybe that's what distracts me, or maybe Theo gets a bit overzealous with his turn, but our feet get tangled together, and before I realize what's happening, we're tumbling to the floor. Theo holds tight to me, and somehow, I end up on top of him, our hands still intertwined against his chest and our chins nearly touching.

My breath freezes in my lungs, my eyes trained on Theo's lips. How badly I want to let myself fall into them, to bridge the tiny gap between our bodies, and finally glean a clear answer as to whether or not we feel the same way.

Theo doesn't move, his body rigid under me. When my gaze meets his, it's impossible to miss the panic behind his eyes.

I let go of his hands, bracing myself against the floor and getting myself back into an upright position. "Sorry," I mutter, my lung function improving the further I get from Theo. "I'm not really sure what happened there."

Theo sits up, reeling in the panic and plastering a half-hearted smile onto his face. "It's okay. But, um, I think I'll probably just stick to the spooky content. Unless you think the outtakes of me trying to dance would kill because then I might consider it."

We both laugh, and it's like the entire room exhales around us. Reaching up, I grab my phone from the bed checking the time.

"I think we'd better get on the road," Theo says, hopping up and grabbing his keys from the bedside table. He offers his hand to help me off the floor.

I stare at it for a moment, quickly making note of the lines that run along his palm before I take it.

"Okay, okay. But only because I don't think we'd survive another dance."

That makes him laugh.

The roads between Theo's neighborhood and mine are empty this time of night. I spend the entire ride thinking of a way I can ask him about this thing between us, but the closer we get to my house, the harder it is to resist reaching across the armrest and taking his hand in mine.

You'd think I would be getting used to the sensation of touching Theo, seeing as we've been using any excuse to do so over the last week, but it only gets more intense each time, leaving me wanting more.

Before I know it, Theo pulls into my driveway, and I'm out of time. He shifts the car into park, switching off his headlights so the only illumination comes from his dashboard and the dim street lamp behind us. He turns towards me in his seat, a slight smile on his lips, obviously in no rush for me to leave.

I unfasten my seatbelt but don't reach for the door. "Today was incredible. Thanks for the invite."

"Sure thing," Theo replies, reaching over to turn the volume down on the stereo. Then he leaves his arm on the armrest between us, leaning towards me in his seat. "The crew really enjoyed hanging out with you, so don't be surprised if Elise finds you on Insta and starts sending you DMs."

I hold up my phone. "Too late. She found me, like, an hour ago."

Theo laughs, the corners of his eyes scrunching in that way that makes my stomach twist into a knot and my palms get clammy. And he's just so close to me right now. Does he realize how close he is? The dim light from the dash highlights the sharp angle of his jaw, and I can smell the minty scent of his gum with every word.

"Hey, Caleb, I was going to ask you about something," Theo starts, his gaze trailing down for a moment before it finds me again.

Oh my god, is this happening? Is this what I think it is? I'm not ready. Or maybe I am? I don't know. I need more time to think about it. Or maybe I don't?

My head is spinning, so I focus on breathing through my nose, my body locked in place like I've been turned to stone. "Okay, sure."

Theo licks his lips, and *god,* I can't take being close to him for another moment. The heat behind my face is going to start melting my flesh off any second. I need him to touch me again, to direct some of this heat so I don't burn up like a flashfire.

"This may sound weird, but ever since we went down into the basement at Saint Catherine's, I've been feeling—"

Before I even realize what I'm doing, my hand hooks around the nape of Theo's neck, and I close the distance between us, pressing my lips to his.

And suddenly, it's like every sense I have is in overdrive. The lingering smell of sunscreen from Theo's skin fills my nose as I inhale. The mildly sweet taste of mint from his lips as it hits the tip of my tongue. The explosion of sparks that bursts into the darkness even though I have my eyes closed. The sound of the surprised exhale that Theo makes when I pull away from him—

"Why did you do that?"

I open my eyes. There isn't a smile on Theo's face like I'd imagined there would be. His nostrils flare as he takes short, shallow breaths. His dark eyes are wide and shining like tears could roll at any time. I drop my hand.

Oh. Oh no, I had this all wrong.

"I-I'm sorry," I stammer, any lingering electric charge in my body purging itself in an instant. "I thought that's what you were—I mean, I thought we were—Shit. Shit, shit, shit."

Theo leans back from me, and it feels like we were tethered together, and he's ripped the connection off with a quick pull. "I didn't… I wasn't going to…"

"I'm sorry," I say again, clawing at the handle beside me. The door pops open, and I scramble out, pausing to add, "I'm so sorry, Theo," before closing it behind me.

I can hear his muffled voice from inside the car, but I can't make out what he's saying over the pounding pulse in my ears. My body propels me forward, up the stairs to the front door, and somehow, I manage to get the door unlocked and step inside before I slump against the wall and pull my knees into my chest.

Through the frosted window panel beside the door, Theo's headlights come back on, and a few seconds later, they're gone.

He's gone.

And it's all my fault.

NINETEEN
THEO

I don't remember the drive home. It's honestly a miracle I end up in my own driveway.

I turn off the ignition and sit paralyzed in my car for several minutes, trying frantically to come to grips with what just happened. Not just that, but what's *been* happening for the past week.

It was never the orbs. It wasn't a dark spirit or some ghost bullshit that I so desperately tried to believe in. Of course it wasn't.

Now that I know what this is… What am I supposed to do?

I can't be gay. It's not an option. It's never been an option. I've never considered the possibility of it being an option.

I can't be gay. I'm straight. I've only ever liked girls. I've only ever been with a girl. If I was gay, wouldn't I know by now? I'm seventeen, and I've never been attracted to a boy until now. That has to mean something, right?

I can't be gay. I'm—I'm a Christian. It's supposed to be a sin, isn't it? Immediately, my stomach twists with that familiar icy guilt, shame washing over me in waves. How big of a sin is kissing a boy, anyway? Does it matter if I wasn't the one who initiated the kiss? I've never had to give it much thought because I never imagined myself in this situation. Not in a million years.

To be fair, I remember that the last time homosexuality was brought up at church, I felt weird about it, but only because it felt like it was a surprisingly outdated stance for the church to take. I remember Grace bringing it up in an argument with Dad once, too. Something about how the Bible verses that Christians choose to demonize homosexuality are shaky at best, but I hadn't been paying much attention at the time.

Grace. Oh my God, I need to talk to Grace. She'll know what to do.

But will she? How can I tell her?

It's Sunday night. Grace has already gone back to school for the week.

I bang my head on my steering wheel and tightly grip the handle. Shit. It's probably for the best. I can't handle telling her right now. I can't handle telling anyone.

I make my way upstairs without incident from my parents—thank God. As soon as I hear my door click behind me, I collapse onto my bed, where not even an hour ago, Caleb and I were so happy, having so much fun, just hanging out. Playing games. Simply enjoying each other's company.

Then there was the TikTok dance. Holding his hands in mine, our feet stumbling over each other until suddenly I was on the ground and Caleb was on top of me, our faces mere inches apart…

If I'm honest with myself, I knew what I wanted at that moment. I knew what we both wanted. But I stayed in denial. Denial was safe. Denial was predictable.

If nothing is happening, then everything is fine, right?

But I can't deny the fact that every inch of me was on fire at that moment. What else could that mean? And when he—when Caleb *kissed* me, I felt electrified, as if Caleb's lips were a live wire and his current racked through me like nothing ever had before.

Kissing Sienna wasn't like that. The first time I kissed Sienna was memorable, sure, but it wasn't comparable to electrocution. It was more like having a pleasant fever. I felt hot and sweaty and clammy, so nervous I didn't know what to do with myself, but once the kiss happened, it was such a relief. Every kiss after that felt chaste, polite, domestic. As if I was training for the rest of our lives together. Because, in a way, I kind of was. My parents always assumed I'd end up marrying Sienna, so I started believing it, too. It wasn't until a few months into the relationship that I realized that Sienna and I were on completely different wavelengths most of the time, and even then, she was the one who ended it because we were "unequally yoked" or whatever spiritual mumbo-jumbo excuse she came up with. It was amicable, just embarrassing. But what we had for a while there was real, and I was definitely attracted to her.

So, what's different about Caleb? Aside from the obvious.

I honestly have no idea.

I roll over, grab my phone, and groan as I see the numerous messages in the group chat as well as private texts from both Harrison and Elise. I have a feeling Elise already suspects that something is going on between Caleb and me, and I know Harrison is going to get impatient if I don't come up with something for the Triple H video. I don't feel like dealing with either of them tonight, so I quickly text them both a vague "I'm too tired, let's talk tomorrow" text response and close my phone again.

For now, the only people who know what happened tonight are Caleb and me. And I, for one, would like to keep it that way. Denial has worked well enough so far; maybe it can protect me until Grace comes home this weekend.

That's fine. This is fine. Everything is fine.

As long as I can stay as far away from Caleb as physically possible.

Tuesday, September 19

Focusing on school is impossible.

It's not hard to avoid Caleb. We only share one class, and he seems just as keen on avoiding me, so the few times we accidentally make eye contact are quickly smothered. It hurts more than I expected, though, knowing that whatever friendship we had started is probably history now. But I try not to dwell on it. I can't afford to dwell on it.

It also doesn't help that Harrison knows me too well and knows that something is up, but there's absolutely no way in hell I'm going to talk about this at school. Or ever, if possible. I don't think I'll ever tell him what happened. I don't think I can tell any of them. It's too embarrassing. Too dangerous.

Plus, I don't want them to think Caleb did something wrong. It's not Caleb's fault. It's mine.

But it doesn't matter because they'll never know what happened.

I successfully avoid lunch on Monday and Tuesday by claiming I have a term paper that I had forgotten about.

Elise is the first to call me out, joining me for study hall on Tuesday afternoon.

"I know you're avoiding us."

"What are you talking about?"

Elise stares me down, her gaze unflinching. "Something happened that you're not telling us. Why?"

I shrug and glance back down at my notebook. "Elise, I'm just trying to finish this—"

"I saw you staring at Caleb, but I haven't seen you talk to him at all."

I feel the tips of my ears start to burn, and I can only pray she doesn't notice.

"Theo, what happened?"

"Look, can we talk about this later—"

"You keep saying that, but then you're always too tired, or too busy, or just outright avoiding us." She snatches my pencil out of my hand, forcing me to look at her. Her eyes are full of concern, more than I think I've seen from her in months. "What's going on, Theo? I just want to help, but I can't if you don't talk to me."

I lean my elbows on the desk and put my head in my hands, running my fingers through my hair in frustration. "I don't—I don't want to talk about it, okay? Maybe—" I'm already wincing before the words even leave my mouth. "—maybe it's none of your business?"

Elise recoils, stunned into silence for a few seconds. "Fine," she says as she abruptly stands up, tosses my pencil back to me, and storms out of the room, leaving me alone again.

Shit. That was really stupid. Not only did she not deserve that, but now I'm in trouble with Harrison, too. It's only a matter of time before this comes back to bite me.

And that time comes immediately after school.

"Theo, Harry's here!" Mom calls up cheerfully. "Go ahead and head up. I'm not sure what he's doing up there. Do you guys need anything to drink?"

"No thanks, Ms. Kora," I hear Harrison reply shortly as he makes his way upstairs.

Here we go.

Harrison opens the door abruptly and shuts it behind him. "Theo, what the hell is your problem?"

I stare at him, clinging tightly to my denial but also well aware that I've messed up. I sigh. "I'm sorry."

"You shouldn't be sorry to me. You should be sorry to Elise. She was trying to help you get out of your weird-ass funk you've been in lately because you clearly won't talk to me about it."

I shrug, feeling the guilt start washing over me like familiar waves of ice-cold water across my chest.

"She has some pretty wild speculations about what's going on with you, so if you don't start talking, I'm going to start embarrassing you with her theories."

Shit. Harrison doesn't have any idea how close Elise might be. "Okay, look, Harrison, I'm really sorry. I can't—I can't tell you."

Harrison stares at me. "What do you mean?"

"I—" I should have thought this through. I should have had a plan for this. "I had a fight. With Caleb. It's just… It's just been bumming me out, you know?"

"A…fight? With Caleb?"

"Yeah, but like, I promised to keep it a secret between me and him."

"Did he come on to you?"

My entire body goes rigid. "Wh-what?"

"Did Caleb try something on you? Like I know he's…"

"*No*, Harrison, God, that's—why would you say that?" Suddenly, every ounce of fear that I had turns to anger.

"Hey look, man," Harrison raises his hands defensively. "You're not giving me anything here. I'm trying to make sense of you acting crazy."

"By assuming that just because Caleb's gay, he'd—" I feel myself shaking. I did this. I messed up, and I shouldn't have brought Caleb into this at all. There's no way I can tell Harrison what happened now. He won't understand that what Caleb did wasn't unwarranted. "Harry, this is why I can't tell you. You're just assuming things about him because he's gay, and that's… That's not cool."

Harrison sighs, but I can tell he's considering my words. While he does, I wallow in the guilt, determining that I hate everything about the way this feels. Stepping on pins and needles for everything. Is this how Caleb lives every day? Never knowing who is going to be your friend or who is going to accuse you of doing something awful just because of who you're attracted to?

Does Caleb think that I think that of him? Does he think he scared me away because he finally made the move that we clearly both wanted, but I was too afraid and confused to make myself?

Shit.

"You're right, that was shitty of me," Harrison concedes. "I'm sorry. I really like Caleb, too. I'm not used to having gay friends, but that's not an excuse."

I nod, glad that Harrison and I are on the same page. Well, kind of.

"I can respect that you're keeping a secret for him. You're a good friend, Theo. I just worry about you sometimes, and you haven't been yourself."

"I know," I say softly. "I'm sorry I've been off lately. I've got a lot on my mind, and…yeah."

Harrison and I sit in silence for a while, my mind still churning with thoughts of Caleb. I need him to know I'm not mad at him. Or disgusted or anything bad like that. I was just…scared. Confused because of my shit, not his. He deserves that, at least.

"You still need to apologize to Elise, though," Harrison says, shoving an elbow into my side as he comes to sit on the bed beside me. "She's pretty pissed off at you."

I offer a half-smile. "Yeah, I figured she would be."

"So, now that all of *that's* out of the way," Harrison says after a few beats. "Can we *please* talk about the Triple H stuff now? You know, the episode that came out four entire days ago where Hudson literally gave you a shout-out, and you still haven't responded to it!?"

"Shit," I mutter, raking a hand through my hair in frustration. "Yeah, we really, really should." I pull my phone out of my pocket and sigh. "Just…give me a minute first, okay? There's something I need to do."

First, I type out a simple text to Elise apologizing for being an asshole.

The next text is a little trickier.

TWENTY
CALEB

My phone buzzes in my pocket, but anyone I would want to talk to at this point is already in the room. Wren digs through drawer after drawer, gathering supplies while Freddy spins in the make-up chair. He's still in his clothes from soccer practice, and his socks are covered in dirt and grass stains.

"Are you sure you don't want to join in on the fun?" Freddy asks, hanging his head over the back of the chair. "And by fun, I mean two hours of being poked and prodded, then washing all of Wren's hard work down the drain."

"I'm sure," I reply, sinking deeper into my spot on the sofa. "I'm really just in the mood to chill."

Wren comes up from their drawer spelunking long enough to add, "You've been really low-key since the weekend. What's up, buttercup?"

I haven't told either of them about my fuck up yet. I don't know why. Maybe I keep thinking that I'll wake up and the whole thing was just a terrible dream, and Theo doesn't hate me or think I freaking assaulted him.

But most likely, it's the horrible shame that's twisting my guts.

"I'm fine," I say, staring into the opposite corner of the room because one look at my face will probably give me away faster than telling the truth. "Everything is fine."

"It must be boy troubles," Freddy jokes. But then neither Wren nor I reply, and he sits up straight in the chair. "Wait, is it actually boy troubles? What the hell, Cal? You're having boy troubles, and you don't come directly to me?"

"I'm not having boy troubles."

"So, things are okay with you and Theo?" Wren asks.

"Theo?" Freddy echoes. "Wait, like, straight-church-boy Theo?"

"Everything is fine," I repeat myself. "Can y'all just drop it?"

Freddy spins to Wren, bracing himself on the armrests as he pulls his legs under him. "Is something going on between them? How'd I get left out of the loop?"

Wren squeezes a tube of foundation onto the back of their hand. "Well, you've had your head up Andrew Rhiner's ass for the last week, so you may have missed a few things."

"First of all, leave Andrew's ass out of this. It's perfect and blameless. Secondly, what the fuck? You guys can't just leave me out of these things! That's so rude."

"You haven't missed anything because there's nothing going on," I say, shoving my head between the cushions of the sofa. Wren and Freddy's voices are muffled now, and I don't care if they continue talking about me so long as I don't have to listen.

This is such a mess. As if I haven't felt bad enough the few times Theo and I have locked eyes at school, now I'm getting shit from Freddy. Why does everything have to be so fucking complicated? Why can't I just like a boy who likes me back, and that's all there is to it? No skating around religious prejudices or lying to my friends to spare myself the heartache. No misunderstandings or misread flirtations that cause me to make a complete *ass* of myself.

God, I was such an idiot for kissing Theo.

Someone touches my knee and I flinch, pulling my head out of the cushions. My vision is blurred with tears, so I quickly wipe them away. Freddy pulls his hand back, his usual smirk absent. Wren stands on the other side of the sofa, their arms folded across their chest.

Freddy scoots closer, pulling me into a hug. "Oh honey, there is not a boy on this planet worth crying over. And I was only playing. I'm not upset with you."

I wrap my arms around him, resting my chin on his shoulder. "I did something stupid."

Wren sits on the armrest. "You can tell us if you want."

I separate myself from Freddy, wiping my cheeks again. "Theo invited me over to his house on Sunday to swim with his friends. And I swear I thought he was flirting with me, like, all day. I was so sure. We even had a moment in his bedroom, just the two of us, and I felt something was going to happen, but then it didn't. He drove me home, but he lingered and wanted to talk to me about something, so when he leaned in close, I kissed him.

"But when I pulled back—when I saw the look in his eyes—I knew I'd fucked up. He freaked out, and I just left him there. Ran inside and hid under my covers the rest of the night. I mean, how fucking stupid can I be? Am I so desperate for someone to like me that I keep imagining things? Theo never wanted me to kiss him, and now he can't even look at me."

"I don't think you were imagining things," Wren says, getting up and coming around to the other side of me on the sofa. "There was definitely something going on between you two during the movie."

"Have you tried to talk to him since then?" Freddy asks.

I shake my head, the growing lump in my throat keeping me from answering.

Wren leans in. "Do you want to talk to him?"

My first instinct is to shout yes, to explain how much I want to fix things with Theo. But deep down, I know it's only because I'm hoping he actually does have feelings for me. And I have to stop seeing things that aren't there. I have to stop letting myself get caught up in these silly fantasies because, at the end of the day, I'm just hurting myself. And people like Theo. Good, kindhearted people who don't deserve to be kissed by desperate messes like me.

"I don't know," I eventually answer, exhaling a shuddered breath. "He'd probably run away from me at this point. I wouldn't blame him."

"Hey." Freddy cups his hands around mine. "We're here to back you up. If you want to talk to him, if only to clear the air, then just say so. Even if I've got to hunt him down and tackle him in the hallway at school, we'll make it happen."

"Maybe you could try texting him first," Wren says, patting my shoulder. "Before we resort to tackling."

Freeing one of my hands, I dig for my phone. "Okay, I can do that. Thank you, guys. I don't say it enough, but I really do love you both."

"Aw," Freedy coos. "We love you too, Cal. You're like the annoying little brother I never wanted. And Wren, you're the aloof, overachieving older sibling who makes our parents wonder why they ever had other kids. And I'm the problematic middle child with a heart of gold. What a beautiful little family we make."

"Oh." I stare down at the message that came through a few minutes ago. "He texted me."

Freddy and Wren both lean closer to read the message.

THEO: hey Caleb. I think we need to talk about Sunday, but before that, I want to say I'm sorry for freaking out on you. you didn't do anything wrong. I'm also sorry for avoiding you this week. do you want to talk about it? I'd really like to still be friends if you do :)

"What are you going to say?" Wren asks.

I pan between my two best friends, soaking in every bit of the love I feel from them.

"I think I'm ready to talk."

Wednesday, September 20

Theo and I agree to meet after school at Spookies. Wren offers to drive me, which I wholeheartedly accept, and Freddy says he'll head over the minute soccer practice lets out for emotional support in case things take a turn for the worse.

We pull into a parking spot outside the coffee shop, but I'm in no hurry to get out of the car. Wren doesn't rush me as they shut off the engine. We sit in silence, staring up at the inflatable ghost on top of the building as it bobs in the breeze.

"Are you sure you want to do this?" Wren asks, brushing dark bangs from their eyes as they turn to face me. "You can just walk away, you know."

I've been weighing that very idea in my head all afternoon. Especially when I caught Theo looking at me during English Lit. It would be the easy option, to rip Theo from my everyday thoughts and shove him in the corner of my subconscious till his name doesn't make my heart hammer or my palms sweat. But while it may be the easy way, I don't think it's the right choice. For either of us. I need the closure, and if there really is nothing between us, then maybe I can get to a place where being his friend will feel like enough.

"I want to. I've been playing the last week over in my head, trying to figure out if I've been reading signs that aren't there, but the more I think about it, the more I can't stop remembering every little gesture, every smile, or touch that screams something more. I don't know. Maybe he's too scared to admit it to himself because of the whole religion thing. But if that's the case, I think I need to be there for him. If only as someone who can listen and let him know it's okay to have these feelings."

Wren watches me, a shiny sheen in their pale eyes that's foreign to me. "You're a good person, Caleb. I want you to know that."

"Uh, thank you?" I say with a laugh, not sure how to respond.

They fold their arms, their features stoic. "I mean it. Call it fate or divine intervention, whatever vibes best with you, but I think Theo came into your life for a reason."

For once, there's no sarcasm to be found under their words.

"Are you okay? You don't usually get this philosophical until it's after midnight, and you've already shotgunned two Red Bulls."

Wren laughs, shaking their head. "Sorry, it just came over me there for a second. I guess what I'm saying is I think it'll all work out for the better. And even if today is hard and things don't go as planned, Freddy and I will be right there to pick you up."

"Thank you, Wren." I exhale, placing a hand on the door handle. "Okay, I can do this. I *can* do this."

"I'll wait a few minutes, then head in," Wren says, checking their phone. "I'll grab a table far enough not to spook him—" they pause, chuckling. "Get it? Spook him?"

"I do get it," I say, popping open the door. The afternoon air is thick with heat, even though it's late September. It rises up from the pavement in swirling tendrils of distortion. Going up the sidewalk, I pull open the cobweb-covered door and duck inside. The regular afternoon rush is in full swing, and the line to order is already long. I probably wouldn't be able to get any food or coffee around the squeezing sensation in my chest right now, so I just head into the cafe and search for Theo.

I find him in the corner booth, sliding his iced coffee cup across the table from one hand to the other. He doesn't see me till I'm slinking into the opposite side of the booth, and he jolts so badly he almost knocks his drink over.

"Hey!" he says, grabbing the cup before it can topple. "You snuck up on me, there."

"Sorry," I say, and it feels like I'm apologizing for a lot more than surprising him. "Um, hi, I guess."

Theo grins, pulling his hands into his lap. "Hi. Thanks for meeting me. I wasn't—I didn't know if you were mad at me or upset about the other night."

"Mad at you?" I echo, raising my brow. "What are you talking about? I thought you'd be the one that was upset. I was so stupid that night, Theo. I'm so sorry I sprung that on you."

Theo looks over his shoulder, leaning forward across the table as he speaks in a low voice. "It's okay. I'm not angry about it or anything. I want to make sure you know that."

Honesty. That's what Lola and Dad told me. I need to be honest with Theo and see if he'll do the same for me. It's the only way we're going to be able to figure this thing out without our friendship exploding.

I nod, lowering my voice as well. "I'm glad. But I have to be honest, Theo. I've been picking up some really mixed signals from you. And the reason that happened the other night was because I got the impression that you may have been interested in me. In, like, a more-than-friends kind of way."

"Oh," Theo mumbles, his gaze falling to the table.

"And I could be totally wrong," I continue, trying to steer the conversation away from the proverbial cliff. "And if I am, you can tell me, and I'll never bring it up again, but I just had to be honest with you for my own sake. You see, I have this bad habit of thinking that someone is flirting with me. Like, a few weeks ago, there was this guy at school, you may know him actually, his name is Logan—I don't know why I told you that—but anyway, I thought he was flirting with me by doing this thing with his foot, but Freddy told me he was just stretching his calves because of soccer practice and the coach—"

"What if I was flirting with you?" Theo interrupts me, his eyes still focused downward. "What if I was doing it and I didn't know it? What does that mean?"

"Wait. You mean I wasn't imagining it?"

Theo scratches the back of his head, frowning. "I… I don't think you were."

"Oh." It's my turn to mumble incoherently.

I wasn't expecting that. I mean, sure, I'd hoped I wasn't just imagining the chemistry between us, but the alternative comes with a whole other slew of implications. If he does feel the same way, why did he react like that when I kissed him?

He props his elbows on the edge of the table and covers his face with his hands. "I don't know what's wrong with me. Before meeting you, I never even thought it was possible for me to… feel like this. It was never an option. So, I've been wracking my brain trying to explain what changed." He pulls his hands away, really looking at me for the first time with wide eyes. "It's driving me crazy, man—to the point where I literally convinced myself that I was being haunted by some kind of ghost that followed me home from Saint Catherine's or something! But the more time goes on, I—I think it's just me. And if *I'm* being completely honest—" Theo glances nervously from side to side before lowering his voice to a harsh whisper. "I'm *fucking* scared. How can I go my entire life thinking of myself as one way, and it completely changes overnight? What happens if I wake up a year from now and I'm this entirely different person? How messed up is it if I don't even know who I am?"

I don't know what to do. I don't know what to tell him or how to comfort him, even though every fiber of me wants to. I have to try, though. If nothing else, just to let him know I'm here.

"Do you really feel all that different?" I ask after a moment. "Like your entire self has changed?"

Theo's eyes narrow. "What do you mean?"

I quickly organize my thoughts. "I mean, other than whatever it is that you're feeling about me, have there been any other changes? You still like the same things, right? Triple H and making TikToks, hanging out with your friends, playing video games with Harrison, that's all the same, right?"

Theo nods slowly.

"So, maybe it's not that you're a different person or somehow changed radically overnight. Maybe it's more like you've found something that's been there the whole time but socked away. People can't possibly know every detail about themselves, especially at our age. I mean, hell, I just found out I like Brussels sprouts, and I've been alive for almost seventeen years."

Theo cracks a smile, and it encourages me to keep going.

"I'm not trying to convince you of one thing or another. I just think maybe you've got it a bit twisted up? Maybe this is a part of who you've always been, and you're just now getting around to figuring out what that looks like."

Theo is quiet as he picks at his cuticles.

"I know you're scared," I add, reaching across the table to take his hand into mine before he picks himself bloody. "But if you need someone to talk to, I'm here. I can't pretend to understand all the things you're going through, but I am a good listener. And if we can't figure the problem together, there's always the internet."

That gets a chuckle out of him, and his grip on my hand tightens.

"I don't know where to go from here," he mumbles.

"And you don't have to. Just go at your own pace, and know that you've got friends who care about you and want you to be happy."

"Right. Thank you, Caleb."

"Anytime. And maybe tell me the next time you think you're being haunted? I at least want to get it on film to send to Hudson."

He laughs—a real laugh this time—and things feel like they're on their way back to normal between us. At least as normal as they can be.

TWENTY-ONE
THEO

The feeling of Caleb's hand in mine isn't like fire or electrocution this time. The initial touch was a spark, sure, but now it feels…natural. Like his hand is supposed to fit there.

I need to slow down. One life-altering discovery at a time, Theo.

I glance down at my watch. It's still early, only just after 5:00 PM, and suddenly I'm restless to get out of here, go for a walk, go for a swim, go for a drive, anywhere with Caleb as long as I can hold his hand. I've never been more grateful for Wednesday night small group to have been canceled, even though it took our leader Brandon getting the flu to do it. "So, uh, do you have plans for the rest of the afternoon?"

"Well," Caleb's eyes drift past me towards another end of the cafe. "Wren's my ride. They were kind of hanging back in case things here went…south."

"Oh," I say, trying not to sound hurt. "Were you really worried?"

Caleb shrugs, still not meeting my gaze. "I mean, you never really know."

Not for the first time, a surge of protectiveness overwhelms me, and I want nothing more than to protect Caleb from every jerk who has ever wanted to harm him. I gently rub tiny circles over Caleb's knuckles with my thumb. "I really like you, Caleb. Even if—even if we could only be friends, I'd still never try to hurt you."

Caleb glances up at me and smiles almost shyly. "Thanks. I like you, too."

His smile makes my chest warm again. "So…do you think Wren would let me steal you for the rest of the day? We can do whatever you want. My treat!"

"Okay. I'd like that. I'll text Wren."

He lets go of my hand to write a text, and I try not to get too excited at the possibilities of what we could do next. I finish off my iced coffee and lean back into the booth. I know that the reality of the situation—whatever this is between Caleb and me—will set in at some point, but for now, I just want to roll with it and see where it takes me.

Besides, it's Caleb. I like him. He likes me. There's no need to overthink it. At least not today.

"Alright," Caleb says as he puts his phone back into his pocket. "I'm all yours for the evening."

More than anything, I wish I could think of something funny, charming, or even flirty to say, but instead, I feel the tips of my ears turning red, and I snort. *Smooth.* "Are you hungry?"

"Starving."

I've never considered myself a romantic by any stretch. I've only ever been in one relationship, and it was with a girl who believed we should never even be alone in the same room or we might sin. And this day out with Caleb isn't a date—at least we haven't called it that yet—so I shouldn't feel pressured to do anything romantic, especially since we haven't even established what we are yet. But despite this, I am inexplicably overwhelmed with the desire to romance Caleb's socks off tonight. Nothing inappropriate, nothing too intense—just a taste of romance. Flirting. Talking. Holding hands. Maybe try the kissing thing again? God, I hope so.

However, I'm terrified I'm moving too quickly, and either Caleb's going to be freaked out, or my brain is going to catch up to what my heart is doing, and suddenly God is going to start talking to me, and I'm nowhere near ready for all of that yet.

So, for now, Caleb and I drive to Sonic for some burgers, fries, and milkshakes and just sit in the car.

"Okay, so I want to know everything there is to know about Caleb Raynard," I say between bites of fries.

"Okay, shoot. What do you want to know?"

"Favorite color?"

Caleb snorts. "Really?"

"Yeah, really! It's important!"

"Okay. It's seafoam green. Yours?"

"Hunter green. I like that we both like greens, though," I smile. "Your turn to ask me something."

"Oh, are we playing twenty questions now?"

"Sure! Unless you don't want to. If I'm being too nosy, you can always say 'skip' or something."

Caleb chuckles. "Okay. Favorite band or artist?"

"Ooh, that's a hard question," I bring a hand up to my chin and stroke it thoughtfully. "Man, I don't know if I can pick just one."

"Too bad, you have to."

"Ugh, fine. It's probably Sufjan Stevens, but I'm also going through a Djo phase. What about you?"

"I like a lot of lo-fi hip-hop stuff, but lately, I've really been into Charli XCX. 'Boys' is such a bop."

"Nice, I can respect that."

"So, before you think of the next question," Caleb asks hesitantly, and a spike of panic courses through my veins. Oh no, did I mess up? Am I rushing this? "Don't get mad, but—is it crazy that I don't know who Djo is? I don't think I've ever heard of them."

The relief at the question is immediate, but my jaw drops for a completely different reason. "You've never heard of Djo? What?? Oh, man, you are in for a treat, my friend," I scramble for my phone to play my favorite Djo song. "Fun fact: Djo is actually just Joe Keery, the guy who plays Steve in *Stranger Things*."

"Seriously?" Caleb's eyes are wide.

"Seriously! I was shocked, too."

We sit and listen to Djo for about a minute, and I try not to stare at Caleb's hands while we do. His hands are smaller than mine, his fingernails still painted with shimmery nail polish, but his hands are still decidedly masculine. The contrast is intriguing. I bet the polish would make his nails feel smooth if I touched them.

Then I remember—I *can* touch them. If he's still okay with holding hands, that is.

I place my hand on the console as casually as I can, trying not to be awkward about it but also not really caring to make my intentions subtle. We're at least at this stage, right?

Sure enough, he follows my lead and tucks his hand in mine. My stomach flutters at the touch, and I can't help the smile that takes over my face. I turn his fingers over so I can stroke a glittery nail. The texture is even smoother than I imagined it would be. "I like your nails," I hear myself say out loud. Smooth, Theo, real smooth. "I mean, I've never painted mine before. Never really even considered it."

Caleb is blushing, which boosts my confidence a bit. "Thanks. I really like painting mine. I don't think I could go back to not painting them now. It's such a small thing, but it's relaxing to do, and I don't know, I like how it looks. Adds personality. You should try it sometime."

"Maybe," I mumble, trying to imagine painting my nails a deep hunter green. I would make a huge mess, and it would probably look dumb on my long, bony fingers. Then I imagine what Harrison or Oliver would say when I came to school the next day with painted nails. Or what Nathaniel would say.

Or my dad.

Shit. Maybe not.

"You okay?" Caleb asks.

I nod, offering a smile. "Yeah. Where to next? Eileen can take us anywhere you want to go within the city limits of Specter, as I'm pretty sure we both have 10 PM curfews."

"Eileen?" Caleb raises an eyebrow. "You named your car Eileen?"

I laugh. "Yep. After the infamous Dexys Midnight Runners song, of course."

He stares at me with the same confused expression.

"'Come On Eileen'?"

He shakes his head.

"Oh, no, dude, are you serious?" I pull our interlocked hands to my chest dramatically. "You're killing me!" I pick up my phone with my free hand and immediately start playing the goofy 80s song that shaped my bizarre music taste.

Caleb grins, sly and skeptical at first, but then I start belting out the lyrics in a remarkably bad British pop accent, and it's not long before he's laughing. His laughter makes my chest swell, and it's by far the best music I've heard all day.

I finally stop singing, turning the music down to ask again. "Anyway, sorry, so where do you want to go now? The park? Target? Your place? My place? Your wish is my command."

Caleb pauses, considering the options. "Maybe my place? My dad should be home from set by now. He's pretty cool."

I smile as I enter Caleb's address into Maps. "You got it."

Once I'm out of the parking lot and back on the main road, my right hand falls back into Caleb's, our fingers interlocked, and it's incredible how potent his touch still feels to my senses. Does it feel this strong for him, too? Will the feeling fade eventually? Surely, it has to at some point. But for now, his thumb gently stroking mine still feels absolutely miraculous, and I never want him to stop.

"I guess I'll need to tell Harrison and the others at some point, huh?"

Caleb shuffles nervously. "About us?"

"Yeah."

"I mean, I guess that depends on what we are exactly. What *this* is."

I chew on my bottom lip. "Yeah."

"Are you ready to talk about that yet?"

"Probably not yet, but soon," I promise. "I just kind of…want to spend today without having to worry about it yet. Is that okay?"

Caleb is quiet for a few painful moments. "I think so."

"I don't want to give you mixed signals, though," I squeeze his hand reassuringly. "I want this. I just don't know what to call it yet."

Caleb doesn't answer. I let the silence settle over us as I drive, hoping he can understand and hoping I know what I'm doing.

TWENTY-TWO
CALEB

Theo sure is laying it on thick. But I like it. I like him. With his weird old lady-named car, his endless playlists, and the way he hangs on every word when I speak like he's drinking them all in alongside his milkshake.

And when he holds my hand, I can't help but wonder what he's thinking and if this simple gesture to him, too, feels like holding onto a firework as it explodes between our palms, sending sparks whizzing up my arm and across my body.

His hand tightens around mine. "I want this. I just don't know what to call it yet."

He wants this.

I'd be lying if I said I wasn't relieved to hear it. A reassurance that this is actually happening and it's not my imagination. And even though we haven't talked about what this means for his faith, I can't help but revel in the newness of the moment.

My house isn't far, so we're there in just a few songs. Theo is quiet, and I think he's nervous about meeting my family—I know I was walking into his house that first night—but he smiles at me after he shifts into park, pulling the keys from the ignition.

He takes my hand in his again on the walk from the car to the door, but when I find it locked, I have to pull mine away to dig in my backpack for the keys.

"Hello?" I call into the house once the door is open. I drop my bag on the stool by the door, waiting for Theo to come in before I shut it. "Dad, you here?"

"He's still on set," Lola's voice calls from the living room.

"Damn," I mutter, turning back to Theo. "Sorry, I really thought he'd be home by now. He's been working some long days lately. That's my sister in the other room."

"Did she say he was on set?"

"Yeah, they're shooting some drama near the old downtown area."

"Seriously? That's so dope! So, he's like working with famous actors and stuff?"

I snort a laugh. "Depends on the project. According to him, this project's pretty low-key."

"Is that Wren?" Lola asks from the living room. "Just warn me now if they've got you painted to look like some hideous alien before you round the corner and give me a heart attack."

"Oh, uh, it's not Wren!" I call back, shrugging my shoulders at Theo who's laughing.

"Hi, Freddy!" Lola yells, making another assumption. "I saw your post today. That new boyfriend is a cutie!"

"Not Freddy, either!" I respond. Theo's shoulders bounce with laughter as he covers his mouth.

There's a punctuated pause before Lola replies, "Well, are you talking to the wall then? Who is it?"

I wave for Theo to follow me, and we walk through the dining room, rounding the corner to the living room. Lola is sitting on the middle cushion of the couch, her laptop open on the coffee table and a textbook in her lap. Her coppery hair is pulled back off her face, and she's actually wearing her glasses, which means she must have been reading all day.

"You're new," she says as we enter the room, eyeing Theo over her thick frames.

"Lola, this is Theo. Theo, this is my sister, Lola."

Theo waves one hand, sticking the other in his pocket. "Hey, nice to meet you."

"Nice to meet you too," Lola says, smiling, but she's looking at me, not him. "What have you two been up to this evening?"

"Just chilling," I answer, suddenly feeling like I'm on the stand and Lola is getting ready to cross-examine me. "Grabbed some dinner. We're gonna go hang out upstairs."

Lola's smile doesn't fade. "Mhm. Well, I'll just be down here, doing homework and reminiscing on the years I used to have a life…."

Theo lets out a nervous chuckle, and I hook my arm through his, pulling him back toward the hallway. "Have fun!" I call over my shoulder to Lola as I lead Theo to the stairs. A bolt of panic shoots through me as we climb because I don't remember what state I left my bedroom in this morning, but it passes once I open the door and remember that it's mostly clean. Except for the bed, but I can count on one hand the number of times I've made it voluntarily.

"This is me," I say, walking him into the room.

"Nice," he says, admiring the stack of manga I have on my desk. He picks up the top volume, examining the cover. "Elise mentioned this one before. Is this one of those creepy series that you guys were talking about in the pool?"

The skin along my cheekbones ignites as I take the book from him. "No, nothing like that. It's just a story about a guy who runs a bakery. But you know, it's BL, so there's plenty of drama to keep things interesting."

Theo raises a brow. "BL? Isn't that some sort of Brazilian plastic surgery?"

"That's a BBL," I correct him with a laugh. "This is a 'boy love' series. It's just what they call it when the love interests are gay."

Theo nods. "Ah, I was way off."

"Yeah, they're kind of a guilty pleasure of mine. They're just fluffy and adorable, and I can't resist them."

Theo watches me for a moment, one side of his mouth twisted into a half smile. And even though we've been one-on-one all afternoon, here in my bedroom, with no one else around, the air between us feels charged, like any second a crackle of lightning could jump between us.

"You're judging me, aren't you?" I ask, setting the book back on top of the stack.

"Nah, no way." He takes a step closer, and it's like my lungs forget how to expand for a second. "I was just distracted by how cute you are."

"Wow, that was bold," I tease, even though my face is on fire.

He reaches for my hand again, and I let him, pulling him over to the foot of my bed. I sit on the edge, reversing the difference in our height as I look up at him.

"I've been feeling kinda bold lately," Theo says, his thumb tracing the back of my hand in small, steady circles. "At least, when I'm around you. I guess you bring that out in me. Hell, you even got me to dance—or at least try to."

All I can think about is how it felt when we were tangled on the floor.

"Yeah, that was kind of a disaster."

Theo's crooked smile slowly fades, and he licks his lips.

"Uh, Caleb?"

"Yeah?"

"Do you—" he pauses, clearing his throat. "I mean, is it okay if we—can I kiss you right now?"

He wants to kiss me. He's asking me, which in retrospect is probably what I should have done the first time. And although I want nothing more than to scream, "hell yes!" my voice is paralyzed by his dark eyes, and the next best thing I can do is give him a nod.

I sit up as straight as I can, suddenly caught up in a dozen different thoughts at once. Does my breath smell bad? Shit, I knew I should have told them no onions on my burger. What if he freaks out again? No, he's the one initiating. This is all going so fast—Theo's hand cradles the side of my head, his fingers falling around the nape of my neck, and all those noisy thoughts melt away with his touch.

His head dips slightly, and finally, our lips meet.

Where our first kiss had been a barrage on my senses, our second kiss is heated embers, stoked in my chest, flaring to life as if Theo's lips are a rush of oxygen. The heat spreads quickly from my chest, singeing the tips of my cheeks and running along my spine.

But Theo's kiss seems hesitant like he's still unsure. When he pulls away, he grins down at me, but he's left me wanting more. I tug the front of his shirt with my free hand, guiding him to sit beside me with the other. He lowers himself onto my bed, our hands still clasped, and he lets out a nervous chuckle.

"Are you okay?" I ask, wanting to gauge his reaction before I decide how I want to proceed from here.

Theo nods. "Yeah, definitely okay."

I squeeze his hand. "Good. Now, come here."

He leans again, his gaze falling to my lips. I move to meet him, resting my free hand on his knee. Once again, his kiss is slow and sweet, almost timid. Reaching for him, I twist my fingers into his shirt, pulling him closer to me and deeper into our kiss. A noise rumbles through Theo's throat, passing vibrations between us that sends a shockwave down my spine.

When he pulls away this time, we're both panting, and Theo releases his grip on my hand to run a finger along the collar of his shirt, tugging at it.

"Um, is it warm in here?"

"I think it's just this part of the room," I say with a laugh, gesturing between us. "Think we should cool it down a bit?"

A glimmer of mischief sparkles in Theo's eyes.

"Hell no."

Thursday, September 21

Freddy's jaw nearly hits the lunch table when I tell him about my day with Theo.

"For half an hour? Seriously? How can anyone make out for that long and *not* take their clothes off?"

Wren elbows him in the ribs. "Not everyone is as quick to pull off their pants as you, Freddy."

"Clothing stayed perfectly in place," I assure them. "I'm not trying to freak him out anymore, but he's the one who asked to kiss me to begin with. It's a good thing, right? It probably means that he's getting more comfortable with his feelings?"

"It definitely doesn't hurt your chances," Freddy says, rubbing his side. "I'm guessing he hasn't brought up making anything official yet?"

I shake my head. "I want him to worry about figuring out his own stuff first. Then we can talk about what the two of us are doing."

Freddy leans in over his lunch. "But how do you feel? Right now, I mean."

"Giddy," I admit, with a laugh. "Is that stupid? Wren, tell me I'm being stupid."

"Can't do it," Wren replies. "You're just way too cute when you're crushing. I can't dampen all the queer joy going on over there."

"So, I know that we know," Freddy says, pointing at himself and Wren. "But obviously, we're not going to say anything until the two of you make it official—which I am absolutely manifesting for you right now—but is Theo going to tell any of his friends?"

I give a shrug. "He mentioned it yesterday, but I told him it was best for him to move at his own pace and that he shouldn't feel pressured."

"He can always come hang with us," Wren says. "I always need a new victim—I mean, models to practice on."

"Yeah," Freddy agrees. "And me and Wren can sit awkwardly on the other side of the room while you two dry hump on Wren's couch."

"Oh my god, Freddy!" I grab a tater tot from my tray and fling it at him. "You're being completely wild right now."

"Oh please, I've said wilder things before breakfast. Hey, does this mean we can double-date with Andrew? Think about how many old people we can bother when there are two couples flaunting their homosexualities?"

"Maybe soon," I tell him, reaching for my phone. "We can drag you to all the new horror movies at the theater. I know how much you love them."

Freddy sticks his tongue out at me. "As long as I can bury my head in Andrew's chest, I'll be fine."

TWENTY-THREE
THEO

[10:48 PM]

THEO: hey Grace, are you coming home this weekend?

GRACE: yeah I am, why?

THEO: I need to talk to you about something kinda important.

GRACE: wanna talk now? I can be free in 5 mins

THEO: no it's cool - not an emergency. it's an in-person kind of conversation

GRACE: oh shit, yeah no problem. I'll actually be home tomorrow night around 8ish. no Friday class so I picked up a shift at Cathy's. will you be home?

THEO: yeah

GRACE: cool, I'll be wildly speculating what this could be about until then :)

THEO: I would expect nothing less :)

Thursday, September 21

I tell Harrison to come over immediately after school because I need to tell him something important. I have no idea what he thinks when I ask him to come alone.

But Harrison doesn't ask questions. He shows up alone.

"Okay, so are you finally going to tell me what's been going on with you?"

I stare at my bedroom floor. I wish Caleb were here. I wish I could be braver about this. I told him myself that he brings it out of me—maybe Caleb's the missing piece here. Maybe I should ask him to come over for support.

No. Harrison is my best friend. I can do this.

"I lied to you about Caleb telling me a secret," I finally blurt out.

Harrison furrows his brow. "What are you talking about?"

"Remember earlier this week, I told you that the reason I've been acting so weird is because I've been keeping a secret for Caleb?"

"Yeah?"

"I lied. It was my own secret."

"Yeah, no shit, Theo."

I take a deep breath and close my eyes, and when I open them again, I'm ready. "I like Caleb. A lot."

"Yeah, we all do," Harrison says slowly, still looking at me with confusion.

"No, dude. I *really* like Caleb. Like...we kind of made out on his bed yesterday?"

Harrison's eyes widen, and his mouth drops open. "Oh," he finally says, the gears turning in his head as he processes my words.

"I don't exactly know what that makes me, other than not one hundred percent straight, I guess," I continue. "I've decided it's a lot easier if I don't put a label on it yet. But you're my best friend, and I wanted you to know first. Well, I guess Caleb kind of found out first. He kind of figured it out before I did. Which makes sense because he's gay, so he's got a better eye for this kind of thing. But I don't think I'm technically gay because I still like girls and find lots of them attractive. I find a lot of people attractive, really, but I didn't realize that what I felt towards some guys was…attraction? Until spending time with Caleb made it really freakin' obvious because literally all I ever want to do is hold his hand and touch his hair and kiss his face and—sorry, that's TMI. But yeah, that's never happened to me before, you know? And I just—I don't know, but I—I wanted you to know because you're my best friend, and it's important."

Harrison is still staring at me, blinking rapidly like a malfunctioning robot.

"I hope this doesn't make things weird between us or anything," I hear myself keep talking to fill the silence, fear creeping in that maybe Harrison isn't going to react as positively as I'd hoped. "God, I really hope it doesn't, because I kind of need your help through this because if I think about it too much it freaks me out, like—I feel like this is going to need some kind of explanation, right? Like I have to tell Elise and Oliver, but also other people at school, right? And then there's my family—*fuck,* what am I going to tell my parents? I have to tell them eventually. I don't want to keep Caleb a secret like I'm ashamed of him because I'm not, but I'm scared. I'm scared that it's not going to go over well, and I really just need—"

"Theo," Harrison finally says my name and grabs my shoulder, and the relief that washes over me is instant. My voice was wavering the longer I rambled, and I've never been more thankful for a reason to shut up.

Harrison pushes his glasses up and narrows his eyes at me. "Theodore Briggs, you know me better than that. Of course this doesn't make anything weird between us. You're my best friend, and you liking a boy doesn't change a single thing about that."

I take a shaky breath, my eyes suddenly filling with very unwanted tears. I nod in his direction, knowing that if I open my mouth, the floodgates will burst.

"Shit, man, come here," he holds his arms open, and I practically collapse into him. He wraps his much bigger arms around me, enveloping me in a hug. "I'm so sorry you were ever afraid to tell me. You're my family. I love you exactly the way you are, no matter who you like or what you end up labeling yourself. Never be afraid to be yourself with me, dude. Never."

I nod into his shoulder, the tears flowing freely now.

"Alright, that's enough of that or you're going to make me cry," he mutters, his voice getting shaky, too. We pull away, and I quickly wipe my eyes on my shirt sleeve.

"Thanks, Harry," I say softly. "It means a lot. I knew you…I knew you wouldn't be—but I was freaked out. This is all really new and weird for me."

"I can't promise that I'll always understand, but I will always be here to support you," Harrison says, his expression extremely serious. "If anyone starts giving you shit about having a boyfriend, they'll have to deal with me. And Elise and Oliver, for that matter. Man, Elise is going to lose her mind, you know that, right?"

"What?"

"She tossed out that theory on Sunday, something about you and Caleb having something more going on, and I told her she was crazy. I'm never going to hear the end of it now."

I laugh. "Oh my God, I'm so sorry, dude. She's never going to let that go, either."

"Never," he says, smiling at me. "But it's okay. She's always going to give me shit for something."

"That's true. It might as well be about her gay-dar picking up on something no one else was getting."

"It must be the gay anime and fanfiction she reads," Harrison says thoughtfully. "Right? Caleb reads them, too, doesn't he?"

I snort and bump my shoulder into his. "That must be it."

We sit quietly for a few minutes, and I allow myself to sit comfortably in the silence. Harrison's not going anywhere. I think I always knew that, but it's something else entirely to be certain.

"So, when are you going to tell the others?" Harrison asks.

"Probably shouldn't do it over text, huh?" I say with a crooked smile.

"Yeah, probably not."

I nod. "Maybe Sunday? After church? It's Elise's week at her dad's, isn't it?"

"She's going to church with her dad, but then she's hanging out with me in the afternoon. So, we're free."

"I'll see if Oliver can come, too, then."

Harrison scoffs. "When is Oliver ever too busy for us?"

I chuckle. "True."

There's another few moments of silence before Harrison puts a hand on my shoulder again. "Thanks again for telling me, Theo. Also, for the record, Caleb genuinely seems like a good guy. I'm glad it's him. He's honestly a much better match for you than…" he trails off.

"Than Sienna?" I offer with a pained expression.

He winces. "Yeah. Sorry."

"Don't be. I couldn't agree more."

He sighs. "Not looking forward to hearing that conversation."

"What do you mean?"

"Are you going to tell Sienna about Caleb?"

I twist my face. I hadn't even considered that. "No way. Why would I? It's none of her business."

"Oh," Harrison raises his eyebrows. "That's a fair point, I guess."

Shit, *should* I tell Sienna? Is there any reason to? What if she finds out anyway? It's not very likely because she doesn't go to our school, and we barely spend any time together outside of church. But…rumors do spread. And if I want to bring Caleb around, she might just find out anyway.

Ugh. I'll cross that bridge when I get to it. For now, I have Harrison. I have Caleb. Soon I'll have Grace, Elise, and Oliver. For today, that's enough.

"Hey," Harrison says after a few moments of silence. He nudges my shoulder and nods towards my TV. "Wanna smash?"

I exhale a weak laugh. "Yeah, dude. I really do."

THEO: I told Harrison about us. I don't know why I was nervous, he was super supportive of course. threatened to beat up anyone who gives us a hard time <3

CALEB: that's great, Theo! <3

THEO: I'm telling my sister later tonight. she's bi and has a lot of lgbtq+ friends at school so I think she's going to be excited to find out I'm not straight lmao

CALEB: :D <3 <3 <3
I'll be right here if you need anything!

THEO: thanks. honestly, that's all i need.

I hear Grace's car pull into the driveway over my music, so I have time to brace myself. Harrison left about an hour ago, giving me some space to talk to Grace and promising not to tell Elise no matter how hard she pushes. Honestly, it could go either way, but I know Elise will act surprised even if Harrison slips.

There are approximately four minutes between the time Grace parks her car, walks inside, throws her weekend bag unceremoniously into her bedroom, and bangs on my bedroom door.

I'm laughing as I open the door, motioning for her to enter and quickly shutting the door behind her. I turn around to find her already sprawled out on my bed. She's surprisingly in a sunshine-yellow crop top (Mom and Dad must not have seen her yet), ripped jean shorts, and her trusty Doc Marten boots. Her long, multi-colored hair is thrown back in a messy bun on top of her head. She looks exhausted, but her eyes are focused intensely on me.

"Okay, do you want me to give you my theories first, or are you ready to spill it now?"

I laugh nervously as I sit in my computer chair, spinning it around to face her. "You probably won't be as far off as you think."

"You're in love."

I blink, turning the word over in my head a few times before answering. "I...think it's too soon to call it love, probably?"

"Is it Wren?"

"No."

"Damn," she swears quietly. "Harrison?"

I almost fall out of my chair. "Oh, *God*, no. Grace, come on."

"I know, I know," she grumbles. "Thought it would be exciting to get the gay theories out there first."

I chew on my lower lip. "Well..."

She snaps her head up, her attention laser-focused on me. "*Well?* What do you mean '*well*'?"

I shrug.

"So it *is* something gay."

"Kind of?"

"Okay, is Harrison gay?"

"No, you're getting colder."

"Ugh, okay, fine, I'm too impatient. Spill. Details. Gimme."

"I like a boy," I blurt out rather quickly.

Grace's face lights up immediately, her eyes widening and a goofy grin taking over her entire face. "I *fucking* knew it! Yes!! I'm so proud of you! How long have you known?"

I let out a nervous laugh again. "Umm… Well, I just officially met him two Saturdays ago. We've been kind of flirting for two weeks, but I didn't realize that's what I was doing until Sunday, so when he tried to kiss me, I freaked out, but then we talked on Wednesday, and now I'm kind of slowly coming to terms with the fact that I'm not as straight as I thought I was."

Her smile is genuine and excited, and it's honestly contagious. "I'm so happy for you, Theo, truly I am. So…bisexual?"

"I guess? I haven't put a label on it yet because this is really new and really terrifying, actually."

Grace takes my hand in hers. "I know, bud. It's okay. You can take all the time you need."

I exhale a shaky breath. This is way easier than telling Harrison, and I can't tell if it's because it's the second time I've had this conversation today or because I had no doubt that Grace would have the most positive reaction possible. Probably a little of both.

"Who all have you told?" she asks.

"You and Harrison so far," I answer. "I'm going to tell Elise and Oliver this weekend, but…" I hesitate to finish the thought.

Turns out I don't have to. "You're not sure about Mom and Dad yet."

I nod, my gaze dropping to the floor.

Grace sighs. "Yeah. I don't blame you. They don't exactly adapt to things very easily. So far, when it comes to me, they've freaked out about my choice in major, my nose piercings, my hair color, and most recently, my refusal to drag myself to church every Sunday. They might completely lose it when they learn that at least two of their three children aren't straight."

"Yeah," I grumble, raking a hand through my hair. "So, you never told them you're…"

"Bi? No, I didn't think it was worth the risk. But—" she trails off, gazing at me sadly. "I didn't realize I liked girls until I was already out of the house most of the week, so it's pretty easy to keep it from them for now. But you've still got at least a year before you're out of here."

"Yeah, and I don't want to keep Caleb a secret. I don't want him to think I'm ashamed of him. He deserves so much better than that." The thought of Caleb makes me smile despite the anxiety, and my stomach flutters. "He's really amazing, Grace. I can't wait for you to meet him."

Grace looks like she might explode as her hands cover her cheeks, almost like a real-life anime character. "Aww, oh my God, Theo! You've got it that bad already?"

I feel my face getting hot. "No. I don't know…I guess? I've never really felt like this about anybody before. Not even with Sienna."

Grace makes a face at the mention of Sienna. Man, did anyone other than my parents like Sienna? "Well, maybe this is the real deal. Or—shit, sorry, it's probably way too early to tell. You're seventeen, don't listen to me. But I'm just ridiculously happy for you."

"So do I need to like—" I fidget in my chair. "—come out on social media or something at some point? I don't know what I'm doing. I don't remember you coming out exactly."

"That's entirely up to you, bud. I only came out on the socials that I knew Mom, Dad, or old Specter friends wouldn't see, and there was nothing really 'official' about it. I think I updated my dating preferences on Facebook, and during pride month, I put a little ring of the bisexual flag on my profile picture, which flew right over the heads of anyone who would have had a problem with it. To be honest, Theo, I have it really easy. I get to just fly under the radar because I'm not in a relationship with anyone right now, and I don't live at home most of the time. For you, coming out will probably need to be a lot different. You have to decide if it's worth it to you to introduce Caleb as your boyfriend or keep it a secret to avoid the inevitable." She gives me that really serious look like she's about to drop some ancient, cryptic older sibling knowledge, so I lean in. "You have to decide if this is something worth fighting for. I can't make that call for you. Neither can Caleb, and neither can Mom or Dad. And if you feel like it might be safer to wait another year, that's up to you. Just make sure you're honest with Caleb and anyone else you date along the way."

I nod to show my understanding. I know she's right. It sounds so obvious—so simple when it's said out loud. But making that decision to tell people? Especially my parents, who may or may not even allow me to see him at all? It's terrifying. It would be nice to just keep Caleb to myself, to continue spending time with Caleb in secret, and never worry about telling my parents the truth. But I can't do that to Caleb. I don't want him to feel like a dirty secret. I want him to feel special. He deserves that.

I let Grace's advice sink in for a bit, dreading the answer to my next burning question. I'm honestly not even sure if I want to bring it up. Everything's so perfect—why ruin it now? I've been avoiding the topic so far. Do I really need to ask?

"Talk to me, bud. What's going on?"

Shit, she never misses anything.

"I...well, so, when you realized you liked girls," I ask nervously. "Did you still feel like you could still be a Christian?"

Grace's expression hardens. I know I'm striking a nerve, and I'm beginning to worry that maybe I should drop it. But before I can backtrack, she sighs. "Theo, I'm going to be as honest with you as I can be while also trying to respect your desire to keep being a good Christian. I don't want to take anything away from you. I know you're still technically a teenager, but you're practically a legal adult now, so you can make your own decisions. But you should also know that I do *not* identify as a Christian anymore, so my advice on this topic is going to be biased. Are we clear?"

I nod slowly.

"Okay. So, here's the thing. I believe that you can absolutely be a good Christian and also be gay. Or bi, lesbian, pansexual, asexual, whatever. I believe that most Christians use specific verses of the Bible out of context to justify their homophobia, but that inherently there's nothing in the Bible saying that men can't love other men, or anything like that."

Grace speaks very slowly and deliberately, clearly trying to make sure she's coming across as objective, but I'm hanging on to her every word. This is new information.

"There are lots of different translations and interpretations of those verses, most of them regarding the concept of 'sodomy,' but there's a lot of debate on what the original translation and context of those phrases even were. Also, sodomy and homosexuality are not the same thing. They weren't then, and they aren't now. That's an entire tangent that I could go into in more detail if you'd like, and I can get you some stuff to read on the subject, but I don't think it's necessarily what you need to hear from me today. Am I right?"

I stare at her, trying to understand. "I—I don't know. I mean, if you're saying that the Bible doesn't condemn homosexuality at all and it's just a big misunderstanding, then why is it even an issue at all?"

Grace takes a deep breath. "That's the complicated part that involves a lot of politics and centuries of heteronormative patriarchy. There's…a lot, Theo. I had never even heard of most of this stuff until leaving Specter, and I'm still digging into it even in my higher-level anthropology and sociology classes. What matters for you right now is knowing that your sexuality is not incompatible with your faith. If you believe in the basics of Christianity, you should know that wanting to hold hands with a boy does not take away from your salvation. If you believe that God created the world and that everyone is born into sin and is therefore deserving of hell, but then God sent Jesus to die for those sins so that anyone who accepts Jesus as their Savior will be saved from hell and will go to heaven… That's what makes you a Christian. That's it."

"So, what about the other stuff? Like, don't have sex before marriage, don't steal, don't curse, all of that?"

"Honestly? According to John 3:16, that stuff doesn't really matter, does it? 'For God so loved the world, that he gave his only begotten Son, that whosoever believeth in him should not perish, but have everlasting life.'"

"I—I guess," I mutter, trying not to make it obvious that my head is spinning. "I never thought of it like that."

"I know. That's intentional on the part of the church."

"Why?"

"As a means of—" Grace suddenly stops herself, smirking and shaking her head. "I've already said too much. Sorry. I need to stop." She reaches forward and takes hold of both of my hands. "All I want you to worry about is the first part of what I said. Being straight is not a prerequisite for being a Christian. Period."

"I mean, I can see what you mean, but like…will people at church feel that way?"

Grace sighs and closes her eyes. She hesitates for a few seconds, letting the weight of my question linger. "No, probably not."

I feel the familiar burn of tears prickling the backs of my eyes. "Then… that's bullshit, why even—" I swallow hard. "So, it doesn't matter if I know that I can be bi and still be a Christian because people at church are still going to tell me that it's wrong?"

"To be fair, I don't think all churches are like that," Grace offers. "In fact, there are a lot of churches in Atlanta that are very progressive and welcoming to the queer community. But, yeah, probably not SCC. At least not right now."

I chew on the inside of my cheek, willing myself not to cry. "That's…that's—"

"I know," Grace whispers, squeezing my hands. "I'm sorry."

I stare at the floor and focus on bouncing my leg. I know she's my sister, and she's seen me cry a million times before, but I can't stand the thought of losing it now. Everything was going so well. Shit, shit, shit.

"Listen, I know that this is a lot, and I'm so sorry you have to deal with all of this all at the same time. It didn't happen in this order for me, and your stakes are arguably higher than mine were, but I do understand a lot of what you're going through, and I'm here for you, Theo." I'm still burning a hole in my floor with my eyes, so it startles me when I feel Grace's fingers through my hair. "You just need to talk to me, okay? I'm here, and I love you, no matter what. You are stronger than you know, but don't be afraid to ask for help."

Completely against my will, a broken sob wracks through me, and tears start streaming down my cheeks. Grace pulls me into her arms and holds me as I cry, no longer trying to hold it back. All the fear, all the uncertainty, all the unfamiliarity, and all the unfairness of everything hits me at once, and I just can't keep ignoring it anymore. I cry until I can't cry anymore, all while Grace strokes my back and tells me that everything is going to be okay.

Finally, I pull away, sniffling. "Well, that was embarrassing," I mumble with a crooked smile.

Grace smiles at me, her eyes wet from crying, too. "Nah, you've been way more embarrassing than that, I can assure you."

"That's probably true."

"Well, I'm going to go get settled in," Grace says with a sigh as she stands up. "I have to be at work early tomorrow, unfortunately."

"Oh, I'm so sorry," I say with a wince. The breakfast shift at Cathy's is essentially torture. It's nonstop insanity, and the customers are always awful. "Godspeed."

"Thanks. But hey, text me if you need me. You know I'm always checking my phone on the clock."

"I know. Thank you, Grace. For everything."

"You're very welcome, bud. Anytime."

CALEB: how'd it go with your sister?

THEO: good. I didn't expect it to go badly, but it's nice knowing I have her support. I think it'll make it easier if I decide to tell my parents.

CALEB: definitely. I'm so happy it went well. how are you feeling?

THEO: a little overwhelmed. I think it's all starting to catch up to me, and I kinda had a bit of a breakdown while I was talking to Grace. ^.^; but it's fine.

CALEB: :(I know it sucks right now, but i just want you to know that i'm proud of you. and i'm right here if you need anything!!!

THEO: can we hang out after school tomorrow?

CALEB: sure!! We always hang out at Wren's on fridays. you can join us! if that's cool, of course.

THEO: definitely. Can I give you a ride over?

CALEB: *thumbs up* I'll meet you and eileen in the parking lot.
Theo: sweet. <3

TWENTY-FOUR
CALEB

Friday, September 22

Friday comes, and I can hardly focus on any of my classes. The dull droning of my teachers all blend together into a monotonous background noise of homogenized sameness. At lunch, I let Wren know that Theo is coming, much to their excitement. Freddy cancels his date with Andrew because he wants to be there, too, even though I tell him not to.

"Please! Andrew will understand, and to be honest, it gives me an excuse to bug out from the church event he wanted to take me to tonight. I refuse to go to any potluck dinner, no matter what religion they affiliate with. You won't see me eating green bean casserole."

"Things sound like they're getting pretty serious between you two," I say, happy to steer the conversation away from me and Theo for a change.

Freddy pokes at his lunch. "I guess so. He's a good kisser, at least, but he wants to take things so slow. I feel like I'm getting bored already."

"It's been, like, less than two weeks," Wren reminds him.

"Yeah, which is like a week longer than my last two relationships. I like the thrill of the chase, but once I catch them, what am I supposed to do with them?"

"Uh, get to know them?" I suggest.

"Form a lasting bond?" Wren adds.

Freddy makes a face. "I don't know if I'm cut out for all that. I just like making out with hot guys and sometimes having sex with them. And Andrew is adorable, in his own sweet way, and I don't want to dump him or anything, but the couple of times I try to take things to the next level physically, he shuts me down."

"Maybe he's just not into you?" Wren suggests with a chuckle.

Freddy smirks. "I mean, I don't like to be crass—"

"Since when?" I interrupt.

"Whatever," Freddy continues. "But Andrew is definitely into me. At least when we're making out in the backseat of his car. Trust me, I've seen the evidence. The hard evidence."

"Well, maybe he's not ready to take it that far?" I suggest. "Aren't you the first boyfriend he's had?"

Freddy nods.

"So, maybe he's not ready for anything like that. For him, everything must feel so new. Every first experience is stacking up on the last, and he's probably overwhelmed."

"Are we still talking about Andrew?" Freddy asks, "Or have we swapped back to Theo?"

"I think they both apply," Wren concludes. "You boys need to make sure you're listening to your boyfriends when things get hot and heavy. And I mean listen with your ears, not your dicks. If they say stop, you stop. If they say pause, you pause. If they say I don't want to do this, then you back the fuck off."

"Of course," Freddy says. "That's like the bare fucking minimum. I always do that. Consent is non-negotiable."

"And Theo isn't my boyfriend," I add. "So, I don't think any of that is going to apply to me anytime soon."

Freddy and Wren share a look between them.

"What?" I ask, even though I'm pretty sure I know their reasoning.

"Do you think he'll want to be?" Freddy asks. "Your boyfriend, I mean."

I want to say, "Hell yes, of course he does!" but I end up admitting, "I don't know. We haven't really talked about it yet. But he's still figuring a ton of stuff out, so it's not like the most important thing right now. All I know is that he likes me, and I like him, so we're just going to see what happens."

"We're just worried about you," Wren explains. "Not that Theo isn't a nice guy, but if the worst should happen, and he has to make a choice between, say, his faith or you, we don't want you to have to be in the middle of that kind of situation."

"That's not going to happen," I say, frustration stabbing through my words. "And even if it did, I know that Theo wouldn't do something that would hurt me. At least, not on purpose."

Freddy frowns. "Unintentional heartbreak still sucks. Trust me."

I wave my hands, signaling the level of "done" I've reached in this conversation. "Guys, it's fine. We're all getting a little ahead of ourselves. But everything is going to be fine."

"Okay," they both answer, and we finish the rest of lunch in a tense silence.

I practically bolt from my seat when the teacher dismisses us from last period. Sprinting outside, I scan the parking lot for Eileen's familiar red tone. Finding her, I do my best to act cool as I approach. Theo isn't in the car, of course, because I'm a weirdo who ran like he was literally on fire all the way out here. So, I lean against Eileen's passenger side and convince myself to calm the fuck down.

Theo shows up just a few minutes later, looking a bit surprised that I'm waiting for him. He wraps me up in a hug but keeps it brief. He looks over his shoulder after he lets me go, then says, "Sorry, did I keep you waiting long?"

I can't stop the smile that commandeers my face. "No, I just got here."

He unlocks the doors, and we both climb in. Theo starts the engine, and he's backing up before I can get my buckle on. I haven't even given him Wren's address yet, but he seems to be in a hurry to get somewhere. Once we're out of the school lot, he takes the next street, pulling into a strip mall and circling around to a spot on the backside of the building.

"Are we going shopping?" I joke as he shifts the car into park.

"Nah," he replies, unfastening his seatbelt. "I just couldn't wait any longer to do this."

Theo hooks his fingers through the space between my shirt's buttons, pulling me closer. He kisses me—a little too eagerly as his nose collides with mine—and we adjust quickly. The sudden rush of blood leaving my head leaves me dizzy.

"I missed you too," I say through my heavy breathing after he pulls away.

So that's what this is. He doesn't want to risk someone seeing us at school. I try to keep my feelings in check. I knew this would probably be the case, at least for a little bit while Theo figures his stuff out. But I didn't expect it to make me feel like this. Like I'm a secret waiting to detonate. Suddenly, Wren and Freddy's concern for me is making a little more sense.

Theo leans his shoulder into his seat, reaching over to turn the music down. "Sorry, I know we're supposed to be heading over to Wren's, but I just wanted you to myself for a few minutes first."

"It's fine," I say, popping off my seatbelt and mirroring Theo. "They won't miss us for a bit. Tell me about last night with your sister."

He nods, looking down at his hands. "Grace couldn't have been more chill. At least, about the 'me not being straight' thing. She kinda started to rant about the church, but she reigned it in before it got too bad."

"Oh, does she not go to church anymore?"

Theo shakes his head. "No. And it's been this whole big deal with our parents, but Grace really sticks to her guns. I don't know how she does it. The thought of having to trudge through that conversation with my parents every week—it's honestly exhausting."

"Do you—" I stop myself. "Never mind."

"What?"

"Forget it. It was something really personal, and I shouldn't be asking it."

"How personal?" Theo asks with a crooked smile. "It's okay. Really. You can ask me anything."

I shouldn't. It could erode all the groundwork we've been laying. But now he's looking at me, and I selfishly want to know the answer.

"Do you think liking me is wrong?"

Theo pulls back from me like I've struck him.

"I don't really know that much about your religion," I say, wanting to explain myself. "But isn't this—" I motion between myself and him, "—looked down on?"

Theo sinks his teeth into his lower lip like he's chewing on an answer.

"You don't have to answer," I tell him. "Like I said, it's really personal, and it's not even something we need to talk about right now."

"No, it's okay. I know it must seem weird. Honestly, I'm not the best student when it comes to the bible and all the rules, but even I knew that me feeling this way about you was going to make things complicated. I guess the short answer is yes. They don't really say it out loud a lot at church, but they'd definitely have a problem with the two of us being an item."

An item? Is that what we are?

"But if I'm being honest, I've kind of been feeling out of sync with the church for a few months now. Maybe that's when all this really started, maybe it's because of Grace, I don't know. I keep going because it's what my parents want me to do, but it's not like I'm really all there, you know? If it wasn't for Harrison, I'd be napping in the back row every Sunday."

"So... you don't feel guilty about us messing around or anything, right?"

Theo pauses again, dropping his gaze. "I can't say that. But it's not what you think, I swear. I feel guilty about a lot of things, not just that. It sort of comes with the whole Christianity thing. I'd feel this way no matter who I was making out with."

"Seriously? Are you just supposed to feel bad about everything you do?"

"Basically," Theo agrees with a half-hearted chuckle. "Anything that's not righteous, at least. Which is practically all the things I do on a daily basis."

"That sounds kind of impossible."

Theo shrugs. "It's all I've known."

Anger bubbles up under my skin. I hate this. I hate that Theo doesn't know a world without guilt and shame for just being human. I hate that he even has to think about what could happen when he leans in to kiss me.

It isn't right. It isn't fair.

"I'm still working through everything," Theo says, leaning closer to me again. "So, thanks for being patient with me. It's probably going to take a little while for me to come up with a final answer, but for now, I'm trying to put all that aside because what I feel for you is stronger than anything I've felt in a church."

And just like that, my anger morphs into something else, something warm and comforting. I wrap my arms around Theo's chest, pulling him into a hug.

"Take all the time you need," I say, resting my chin on his shoulder. "I'm not planning on going anywhere."

"Thank you."

"You're late!"

Freddy's voice echoes up the stairs as we descend into Wren's basement. I tighten my grip on Theo's hand as we round the corner. Freddy is already in Wren's makeup chair, his dark brown hair pushed back with a band, and his face covered with patches of something that kind of looks like oatmeal.

Wren steps back from Freddy to get a better look. They are wearing a pair of jean overalls—their normal outfit when it comes to painting, whether it's faces or canvas—and have their hair pulled back from their face. "Oh good, more victims. Don't worry. I've got something special planned for the two of you."

"Should I be nervous?" Theo whispers in my ear.

"Only if you're allergic to latex."

Freddy motions for me to come over, so I drag one of the old bean bag chairs and drag it over to Wren's makeup corner, plopping down beside his chair. Theo hovers by the couch, watching Wren work.

"We don't bite," they say to Theo, dabbing more of the oatmeal goo onto Freddy's forehead.

"Speak for yourself," Freddy adds, chomping his teeth together. "You are making me into a zombie, aren't you?"

"You'll see soon enough," Wren mutters under their breath.

"Have you seen any of Wren's work before?" Freddy asks Theo in a blatant attempt to rope him into the conversation.

Theo shakes his head. "I don't think I have. Caleb's mentioned it."

"You can look through my portfolio if you want," Wren says, pointing to the huge binder on their workstation. "You can even pick one out if you like. I don't mind repeating a look. I need all the practice I can get."

"Oh, okay. Cool." Theo looks quickly at me, then grabs the book, bringing it over and sinking onto the floor beside me.

"Don't feel like you have to," I tell him.

"How come I don't get to say no?" Freddy asks.

Wren snorts a laugh. "Because you're already my bitch."

Theo flips open the book, his eyes widening. "Oh my god, Wren. These are insane! How the hell do you do this?"

"A lot of patience and a shit ton of liquid rubber."

"They've been doing it since we were thirteen," I explain. "I wanted to be Legoshi from Beastar—he's this anthropomorphic wolf—for Halloween, so Wren offered to help with the face—"

"And it all went downhill from there," Wren adds. "It started as cute animals but quickly devolved into nightmarish creatures oozing puss and dripping blood."

Freddy groans. "Can't you make me into something cute for once?"

Wren shakes their head. "Sorry, that would take skills far greater than what I possess."

I pat Freddy's shin. "I think you're going to make an adorable… whatever it is."

"Gee, thanks."

"Less talking," Wren tells Freddy. "You'll mess up the peeling flesh effect."

Freddy rolls his eyes. "Great. Don't want to do that…"

Theo seems relaxed around us, which is comforting to know. He even reaches over and takes my hand while he browses, which makes my stomach flutter. Wren notices right away, giving me a wink and a smile. Theo finishes flipping through the portfolio while the rest of us chit-chat, mostly reminiscing about our favorite looks from the millions of times Wren has painted our faces.

"What do you think?" Wren asks Theo as he hands them back the binder. "Does anything pique your interest?"

"Um, actually, yeah. Would you be able to do this one?"

He passes over the photo of a younger Wren with a pale face, dark sunken eyes, black lips, and a top hat.

"The Babadook?" Wren takes the picture. "Yeah, totally. This one's simple enough. I'll have to see if I still have these claws lying around… it's been a few years since I did this one."

"Nice choice," I say, reaching for Theo's hand. "We love that movie."

"Even I watch it," Freddy chimes in. "But it's really only because he's an accidental gay icon. I mean, to this day, I'll still say I'm 'Baba-shook.'"

Theo laughs, leaning against my beanbag. His phone buzzes, and he looks up again. "Hey, it's time for the new Triple H episode. Do y'all mind if we watch it?"

"Nah, go ahead," Wren says, squirting a nasty-looking green color onto the back of their hand and dabbing it with a sponge. "I've got a ways to go with old moldy here."

Freddy's eyes get wide. "Moldy? I swear, I'll get you for this, Wren."

"Yeah, yeah. I'm shaking in my sneakers. Now, close your eyes, and it'll all be over soon."

The afternoon in Wren's basement flies by. After we watch the Triple H episode—a fascinating dive into an abandoned coal mine in Virginia—it's Theo's turn in the chair while Freddy's mold patches dry. I can tell he's uncomfortable as soon as the sponge hits his skin, but after a few minutes, he seems to relax. I stick by his side, distracting him with more stories of Wren's makeovers through the years and bouncing repartee with Freddy. After an hour or so, Theo's face is almost unrecognizable.

"I don't have the claws," Wren says, digging through the drawers. "But I still have the hat. So, if you want to do the complete look, I can just paint your nails black."

"Might as well," Theo says with a laugh. "I've come this far."

"You've been great," Wren says, grabbing the small glass bottle of nail polish from their station and shaking it. "Really, you fuss less than both Freddy and Caleb, and they've been my canvases for years."

"Hey," I interject. "I never complain."

"But you flinch every time I touch you."

"You have cold hands," I defend myself. "And most of the time my eyes are closed, so how am I supposed to know when it's coming?"

Theo laughs, the black paint covering his mouth stretching. "How do I look?"

"Terrifying," I assure him. "You're going to freak when you see it."

Wren takes Theo's hand, carefully coating each nail with the black polish. "Your cuticles are a mess," they tell him. "Hasn't anyone ever taught you how to buff?"

"I can honestly say I have no idea what you're talking about," Theo answers, pulling his other hand close and inspecting his nail beds.

"Look it up, friend. Add it to your self-care routine."

I'm pretty sure Theo is blushing under all that makeup.

After both hands have been painted, Wren disappears upstairs to get the top hat. Freddy is sitting on the couch, watching some guy on YouTube restore an antique desk lamp, so it's just me and Theo in the corner.

"You doing okay?" I ask in a low voice. "I kinda threw you to the wolves here."

"I'm good, I think," he says, staring at his nails. "I like your friends. They're funny but also kind of savage."

"Yeah, you get used to it after a while. You have to keep your wits about you, that's for sure."

He tears his attention away from his hands, looking at me now. And even with all the black and white makeup and creepy shadows, I can still see the shape of his features underneath.

"I bet I look so wild right now," he says.

"Just a little bit."

Theo leans in closer. "I guess this isn't the best time to kiss you then?"

I glance over my shoulder at the back of Freddy's head. He's entranced with his video, and Wren is still upstairs.

"I don't know how I feel about kissing a ghoul," I tease him, leaning forward. "What will people say?"

Theo picks up on my playfulness. "Let them talk. No one can get in the way of our forbidden love."

And even though I know we're just messing around, my heart skips a beat at his words, and I can't keep myself from wrapping my arms around his neck and pulling him into a kiss. He grunts with surprise, but then he's kissing me back, and his hands are on my waist, and I don't want him to ever let go.

"All that work I put in, and you two can't keep it in your pants for five minutes while I'm gone?"

I pull away from Theo to find Wren standing by the couch and Freddy watching over the back. They're both grinning like they've been let in on a secret.

"My bad," I say, dragging the back of my hand across my lips and pulling back a streak of charcoal-colored makeup. "In my defense, I do love the movie."

"Obviously," Wren says, walking over to their desk and pulling out a pack of wipes. They toss them to me. "Give me a minute to touch you up, Theo, and we'll get a picture taken and get you out of all that."

"Right," Theo says, looking at me with a sheepish grin. "Thanks."

I pull out one of the wipes, moving over to the mirror. "It kind of looks like I have a five o'clock shadow."

"More like you've been making out with a chimney sweep," Freddy calls from the couch.

Once I've removed the remnants of Theo's makeup and Wren has fixed the damage we did to their work, Wren sets up the backdrop, and Theo puts on the top hat, completing the illusion. Now it's time for the big reveal.

Theo takes a deep breath in, stepping in front of the mirror.

"Holy shit," he breathes, leaning in close and poking at his cheek. "This is insane, Wren. Like, I can't even recognize myself."

"Thanks. It's not my best work, but it's worlds away from the last time I did this look. Okay, now I'm just going to take a couple of shots for the portfolio," Wren says, pulling out their phone. "You stand over there, and I'll let you know when to turn."

They take a few shots from each angle. Theo asks for me to take a picture of him on my phone, too, so I can send it to him, so I snap a couple. How weird that these will be the first pictures I've taken of him. Maybe I should make it his contact picture.

After the photo shoot, Wren turns their attention back to Freddy and finishes up his moldy features while Theo takes one last look in the mirror before grabbing the pack of makeup remover wipes. A pile quickly forms on the table in front of him, each cloth smeared with gray smudges.

"How do I look?" he asks, turning to me.

"Like you missed a few spots," I say through a laugh. I grab a fresh wipe. "Close your eyes."

Theo does as I ask, and I set to work removing the last remnants of the Babadook from his face. I place my other hand under his chin, and he shudders.

"You okay?" I ask, pulling the wipe away.

"Y-Yeah, I'm fine. Sorry. Cold chill."

"Okay, you should be all good." I bundle up the wipes, tossing them into the trash can under the desk. "Do you want me to take the polish off your nails?"

Theo looks down at them, hesitating. "Um, no. I think I'll keep it on."

I take his hand in mine. "You sure?"

He nods, squeezing my hand. "Yeah. I want to try it out."

I check my phone. "It's getting late," I say, though there's still an hour before Theo has to be home. I want a little more time alone with him, so I add, "We should probably head out soon."

"Lame," Freddy says from the chair, his moldy complexion really taking shape. "You're not going to see my ultimate form."

"Send me a picture," I reply, already pulling Theo towards the stairs.

"Thanks for everything, Wren," Theo says, stumbling over his own feet as I pull him. "I had a lot of fun."

Wren doesn't even look up from their work. "Anytime, Theo."

Theo and I head up the stairs and out the front door to where Eileen awaits.

TWENTY-FIVE
THEO

I can't stop glancing at my black fingernails on the steering wheel as I drive to Caleb's house, rubbing the smooth surfaces of my nails against my fingertips at every opportunity. Of course, this is only a concern with my left hand. My right hand is currently in Caleb's hand on the console, our fingers interlaced, my thumb tracing little circles across his warm skin.

It still hasn't gotten old.

"I'm slightly concerned about going to work tomorrow with these," I mutter. "I don't think my supervisor will care, but I'm more worried that a grumpy old customer might say something."

"Do you have nail polish remover?" Caleb asks, that sweet, concerned tone in his voice.

"I'm sure Grace does, but I'm going to just see what happens. I mean, I'm a freaking busboy. Why should it matter if the kid who's clearing tables and cleaning up after customers has a little paint on their nails? I've had way worse materials splattered on my uniform after a busy day before."

"Yikes, I don't want to know," Caleb says with a grimace, and I laugh.

As soon as I put my car in park in Caleb's driveway, I resist the urge to immediately lunge for his face this time, opting to be a little more polite about it. I turn to him with a smile. "Is it okay if I—"

Before I can even get the question out, Caleb's lips are already on mine, and I melt into the kiss. It's soft and gentle at first, but his lips part against mine, and my chest ignites. His hand is wrapped around the back of my neck, and I reach up and run my fingers through his hair. God, his curls are so soft. The temptation to bury my face in them surfaces for a ridiculous second, and I almost laugh at the absurdity of it.

When our lips finally separate, I lean my forehead against his. "I had a lot of fun today," I say softly.

"Me too," he whispers back.

"I don't want you to go."

"Me neither."

I close my eyes against him, trying to memorize every detail of this moment. Now I understand why Harrison and Elise always linger alone at the end of our hangouts, taking any available opportunity to slip away just for a few minutes alone together. I get it. I never got it with Sienna, but I get it now.

"Text me when you get home, okay?" Caleb says, starting to pull away.

"*Waaaaait*," I whine, pulling him back for another kiss. He smiles against my lips, which makes me smile, too. As we pull apart, I nod. "Yeah, I'll text you when I'm home."

"Good luck at work tomorrow," Caleb says, opening the car door and climbing out.

"Thanks. Text me while I'm working? I'll be bored, and I'll miss you."

Caleb chuckles and leans down to look at me. "Sure thing."

"Cool. Bye, Caleb."

"Bye, Theo."

And with that, he closes the car door and walks to the front door. I watch him, frozen in place until he's safe inside his house, and even then, I stare at the door for a few more seconds, just in case.

Before driving away, I pull out my phone to queue up Charli XCX, the artist Caleb said was his current favorite. As I drive, bobbing my head to the music, I can't wipe the stupid grin off my face, replaying every moment we shared throughout the day.

The realization hits me fast and hard, almost knocking the wind out of me. It's been less than two weeks, but I think I might be falling in love.

Saturday, September 23

Work is as awful as to be expected for a Saturday. Thankfully, I do have a handful of coworkers who keep work bearable by goofing off in the back, making jokes in the kitchen, and tossing straw wrappers at each other in the breakroom. But if I'm being honest, escaping to the walk-in fridge or the bathroom to text Caleb is what gets me through the day.

I almost make it through the entire shift without even thinking about my nails. That is, however, until Antony, one of the waiters, gives me an intrigued look from the register as he puts in an order. "Huh, I didn't know you painted your nails."

I glance down at my hands, flexing my fingers, and then immediately shove my hands in my apron pocket. "Yep," is the best I can come up with for a response.

Antony doesn't respond right away, so I fidget with my apron, desperately surveying the dining room in hopes there's a table to clean off, but of course, there's not. I stand awkwardly beside Antony as he taps away at the screen, trying not to panic.

"I'd be careful with black, though," he finally says. "I don't want you to get in trouble with the higher-ups. You're one of the good ones, you know."

I turn to look up at him, not sure I heard him correctly, and Antony flashes me a kind smile before heading back into the dining room.

Part of me knows this should be encouraging that the one interaction I have about my nail polish at work is a positive one. But something dark and frightening curls in my gut as I consider the idea of getting reprimanded by "the higher-ups." Will they ask questions? Will they reconsider my employment there if they think I'm too feminine? Or maybe they think I'm being edgy since the paint is black? Or too…something else? Logically, I know that this trail of logic is stupid, but I can't stop it.

The nail polish has to go as soon as possible.

There is an immediate sense of shame that washes over me as I knock on Grace's door to ask for nail polish remover several hours later. I can tell she's disappointed by my request, too, but she doesn't say a word when she hands me the pink bottle and some cotton balls, watching me retreat quietly to the bathroom.

I can't do it. I can't risk my parents seeing it. Or Sienna. Or Nathaniel. Or Chase.

I'm not ready.

I try to remember that I've only been with Caleb for a few days and that all of this is uncharted territory for me. I've told Harrison and Grace that I like a boy now. I spent time with Caleb's friends, and Wren put makeup on my face and painted my nails. I was brave enough to keep the nail polish on at work, but that's as far as I can go for now.

The black paint comes off, but it's not easy. It's slow and agonizing, both literally and metaphorically. I can tell that this pungent stench of the chemicals is going to linger in my nose long after I leave the bathroom. With each finger I de-polish, I feel like more of a coward.

I'm too ashamed to tell Caleb yet. He'll see on Monday that I chickened out. I hope he's not too disappointed in me. I'm already disappointed in myself enough for both of us.

Maybe it's because I'm too lost in my thoughts, or maybe it's because I'm exhausted from work, or maybe it's because he's just too freaking quiet all the damn time, but as I exit the bathroom, I jump as I almost run smack into Nathaniel.

"What is that awful smell?" he asks, his face scrunched up in disgust.

"Nothing."

Nathaniel scoffs. "It's clearly something. Like some kind of chemical. What is that?"

I hesitate, but I sigh and realize there's no point in trying to hide it. "Nail polish remover."

Nathaniel tilts his head, studying me with a puzzled expression. "Did you…did you remove nail polish from something?"

How do I even respond to that? How do I tell my younger brother that I was just removing nail polish off my own fingers because, yeah, I'm a seventeen-year-old guy who gets his nails painted now, what of it? He's going to see right through that. That's not me. But then again, I guess it is kind of me now?

"Hello?"

"Yeah, um…I was helping one of my friends out yesterday with a costume—it's a long story, but they needed me to have my nails painted for it, that's all. So, I was just taking it off now before church tomorrow."

Nathaniel studies me for just a few seconds more, then shrugs. "Whatever," he says, then pushes gently past me to his bedroom door where he slips inside and shuts the door behind him.

I exhale a sigh of relief as I retreat back to my room. *It wasn't a lie,* I reassure myself. But it doesn't matter. I lie in bed wondering when I'll stop being a coward and just be who I want to be without fear. Like Grace. Like Caleb. Like Wren and Freddy.

Someday. Someday, I will.

Sunday, September 24

For the first time in my life, church makes my skin crawl.

Nothing happens, really. Nothing out of the ordinary. There's not a sermon on homosexuality, nor is there anything specific that happens that would remind me of my predicament. But it doesn't matter. I still feel it. Grace's words from a few nights ago bounce around in my head, and I feel...*wrong*. Like being here is wrong. No one knows about Caleb, but I fear every interaction and dread every conversation because what if they do? What if they figure it out? Will they kick me out? Will they try to "set me straight"? Will they tell my parents?

The storm brewing in my head is so distracting that I can't even focus on worship, the one aspect of church that has ever mattered to me. The music almost pulls me out of it, the soft, upbeat tunes nearly swaying me into a sense of peace, but as soon as I open my eyes, I just see Sienna with outstretched arms, Chase waving at me, or Brandon flashing me that friendly church leader smile and it all starts up again.

For the first time in my life, I seriously consider skipping church next week.

But that's a problem for future Theo to deal with. Today, I have to tell two more people that I like a boy and hope they don't freak out or abandon me or treat me differently. I know that none of those things will happen because it's Elise and Oliver, but the fear isn't so easily quelled by reason.

When the crew arrives at my house after lunch, we quickly head down to the theater room in hopes that whatever movie we put on will cover up the sound of our conversation. Elise decides on a classic we've all seen a hundred times before and could probably quote word for word: *What We Do In The Shadows*.

It's clear that Harrison has (at the very least) given Elise a heads-up that I'll be sharing something important, so poor Oliver is the only one who has no idea what's coming.

"So," I begin once the movie starts, making brief eye contact with everyone in the room. "There's something really important that I need to tell you guys, and I need you to keep it between us for now."

Oliver's face twists into confusion. "Wait, what is happening right now?"

Elise punches his arm a little harder than necessary.

"*Ow!* What the fuck?!"

"I'll make it quick, I promise," I say with a nervous smile. "So, um, Caleb and I have been kind of…seeing each other for a few days now. Like. Romantically."

Elise's reaction is immediate, which is a dead giveaway that Elise bullied the truth out of Harrison over the weekend. "YES!!" she squeals, which prompts Harrison and I to shush her. "Sorry, sorry," she says at a lower volume before continuing. "I knew it!! I *called* it, didn't I, Harry?" she punctuates "called it" with a playful punch to Harrison's shoulder. Harrison rolls his eyes.

Oliver is frozen in place, an unfamiliar look of shock on his face. His eyes are wide, and his lips are slightly parted as he stares at me.

"Literally a week ago, I saw it at the pool, and I told Harry immediately, didn't I, Harry? And he told me I was crazy! But you knew that I was on to you, Theo! You know that I knew something even then! We were supposed to have a conversation, remember? I told you this wasn't over. Wow, I can't believe it took you a whole fucking week to come clean!"

My eyes are glued on Oliver, panic shooting through my veins. I've never seen him look like this before. I fully expected him to make some dumb or inappropriate joke at the news because that's what Oliver does when people bring up anything serious. But he's silent. He's not laughing or smirking or anything. He's just staring—not even at me now, but just past me into space.

Harrison catches on and tries to help. "Oliver? You still with us, man?"

Oliver finally blinks a few times, snapping out of his statue form to look at Harrison, then at me. "Uhh, yeah. Sorry." He opens his mouth to speak, but nothing comes out, then he closes it again.

I feel like I might throw up.

"Dude, what is your problem?" Elise asks, waving her hand in front of Oliver's face.

Oliver shoots Elise an annoyed glare, then turns back to me with an expression that looks—apologetic? "Sorry, I'm—I'm not good at this kind of shit, okay? But like…I don't know, isn't that—like, aren't you not supposed to date guys? As a Christian or whatever?"

Harrison makes a pained noise. "Oliver—"

"No, I'm serious!" Oliver says, frustration clear in his voice. "Like, I don't know, I've heard horror stories of this kind of thing ending badly, so I guess I'm just trying to, I don't know, assess how big of a deal this is? Make sure we're all on the same page?"

It starts to click in my brain that this is apparently Oliver when he…cares? It's strange and uncomfortable, and Harrison, Elise and I keep exchanging confused expressions, seeking help, but no one knows how to proceed.

"Okay, look, sorry, I'm clearly not responding correctly. Let me try again." Oliver turns and looks at me with an intensity that makes me want to turn and run. "Theo. Thank you for entrusting us with this information. Does being with Caleb make you happy?"

I blink. "Yes?"

"Okay, good," Oliver continues. "You want us to keep this between us, though. So, do your parents know yet?"

"Oh my god," Elise grumbles as she rubs her face with her hands.

"No," I answer Oliver. "They don't know, and I—I don't want them to yet. I'm not ready for that conversation."

"Why not?"

"Oliver, that's enough," Harrison says with his Protective Best Friend voice.

"Let him answer the question," Oliver snaps. "Why not, Theo?"

"I—I mean, you know why," I say softly.

Oliver has that pseudo-apologetic look again. "Exactly. So that's why I didn't immediately get excited. Like, I'm happy that you're happy, but I'm worried for you. I mean, Theo, you're like the most goody-goody person I know. You don't break the rules. You don't rock the boat. You never break curfew, you always do your homework, and you go to church even when you don't want to. And now all of a sudden you have a boyfriend, and if your parents find out, they're gonna go apeshit, and I just—I don't know, that's kind of scary to me. So, like, if it's worth it—if Caleb is worth the risk to you—then I'm on board. I just want to make sure you know what you're doing and that the rest of us are all on the same page about this if shit hits the fan."

This was definitely the last thing I was expecting out of today. I stare at Oliver, searching desperately for something to say, but he's right. I'm terrified that shit is going to hit the fan. I'm terrified that my parents are going to lose their minds if they find out.

But then I remember that it's *Caleb*. Caleb, with his soft copper curls, warm brown eyes, and adorable nose. Caleb, with his love of sour candy, horror movies, and lo-fi music. Caleb, with his ever-present kindness, understanding, and patience as I stumble through all of this shit, never hesitating to support me.

Oliver may not get it, but Caleb *is* worth the risk. Being with Caleb makes me happy—happier than I've been with anyone else. My desire to be happy with Caleb overpowers my fear of the consequences.

"Wow, Oliver, you weren't kidding. You *are* really bad at this," Elise says after a few moments of silence. "Look, Theo, we're here for you. We all love you and would absolutely fight anyone who has a problem with you being with Caleb. Even your parents."

I laugh weakly at the thought. "Thanks, Elise."

"I'm also here for you, and I love you, man," Oliver says, sounding defeated. "That's why I'm scared for you. I don't know, I'm sorry. I just want you to be happy. People suck. You deserve to like who you like without having to worry about it, but it may not be that simple."

"You have a weird way of showing you care, dude," Harrison mumbles and slides back to Elise's side.

I ignore Harrison and put a reassuring hand on Oliver's shoulder. "I think I know where you're coming from, Oliver. Thank you."

Oliver tries to smile at me, but it doesn't meet his eyes. "Look, guys, I don't know how many times I've tried to warn you that I don't do serious conversations. Hopefully, now you'll finally believe me, and we can avoid this in the future."

"I'll say," Elise says. "I'm never sharing anything personal with Oliver for the rest of our lives. Jesus Christ."

Oliver turns dramatically and grabs both of Elise's hands, prompting a slightly frightening expression to flash across Harrison's face, but it quickly disappears. "Thank you, Elise. That means so much to me."

I laugh genuinely this time. "All right, do we actually want to sit and watch this movie or do something else?"

"Are you kidding?" Elise says incredulously. "How could we start a movie with Taika Waititi, the love of my life, and then not watch it?"

"Touche," I reply as I head to my usual recliner in the middle row. I gaze up at the screen just in time to see Taika's character, Viago, smiling into the camera. "You know, I'm starting to think maybe my admiration for him is a little more than just appreciation for his work."

"Get in line," Elise snaps. "Taika's my hall pass. Get your own."

"Your what?"

Harrison groans. "God."

"A hall pass is the one celebrity you're allowed to leave your partner for if an opportunity ever presents itself," Elise explains cheerfully.

"Ouch," I say as I look at Harrison.

"Nah, it's cool. It's a respectable choice," Harrison concedes. "Mine is Tessa Thompson."

I raise my eyebrows. "Okay, yeah, Tessa's also a fine choice."

"Oliver, who's yours?" Elise asks.

Oliver has been abnormally quiet so far, but it's understandable, given the conversation we just ended. He snorts. "Given that I don't have a partner, do I even need a pass?"

Harrison laughs. "I guess not?"

"Nice. Open season for me."

We all laugh together. The knot in my stomach finally loosens, and as the movie plays, I relax more and more in my seat. It's not long before I pull out my phone and text Caleb about how it went with Elise and Oliver, ask him who his hall pass would be—Logan Lerman, apparently—and babble on about the silly little vampire movie that makes me and my friends so happy even though we've watched it a million times.

TWENTY-SIX
CALEB

Friday, October 20

It's kind of scary how quickly someone can go from being a perfect stranger to the favorite part of your day. It's been a month to the day that Theo and I decided to give whatever this is between us a shot, and already, I can't imagine what my life would be like without seeing him nearly every day.

And everything *feels* different. Even small things, like riding to school in the morning, have taken on an entirely new excitement because I get to spend twelve minutes in the car, holding hands with the boy that I may or may not be head-over-heels about. We've set up a bit of a routine, Theo and I. He'll pick me up every morning for school, and we spend the ride trading the aux cord back and forth, playing music for each other. Then I have to go a whole four hours without seeing him again, which is fine but definitely isn't my first choice, till we get to lunch when I can sit beside him, knocking my knee into his the entire time. Then, in English Literature, I spend the entire class pretending to listen to Mrs. Hyung drone on about Shakespeare while I try not to stare at Theo from across the room. And after school, as long as Theo doesn't have a shift at Cathy's, we'll rotate between Wren's house and mine, hanging out and doing homework till Theo has to leave for family dinner, and I have to settle for texting him the rest of the night.

Our friend groups have even started to slowly meld together on the weekends—a master plan on my and Theo's part—with movie nights and trips to Pizza Palooza. Theo was even nice enough to let me drag him to one of Freddy's soccer matches, which earned him a lot of bonus points with Freddy.

And even though we're super careful not to be too lovey-dovey in public, Theo always finds a way to be touching me whenever possible. Whether it's hooking his pinky finger around mine as we sit in the dark theater, keeping his knee pressed against mine in the bleachers at the soccer match, or even playing footsie with me across the booth at Pizza Palooza—which did lead to a very funny moment when he got Oliver's foot instead—it seems like he can't help himself. Which I'm totally fine with.

But in those moments when it's just the two of us, and those prying eyes he fears are miles away from his mind, he'll wrap his fingers in my hair and run his hand across my chest as he kisses me over and over, and it honestly gets very difficult to think about anything but him and that moment, and what it would feel like to trace my fingertips along every inch of his body—

"Caleb! Theo's here!"

Mom's voice snaps me out of my early morning daydream. I close my laptop, abandoning whatever attempt I was making at a term paper and grabbing my backpack.

Downstairs, Mom is filling her thermos with coffee, and it looks like Lola has already left for her morning classes. Dad is probably still asleep, trying to recover from his late nights on set.

"Is this a regular thing now?" Mom asks, nodding her head in the direction of the front door and Theo's parked car.

"Seems to be," I answer, keeping it vague. Lola definitely knows what's going on between me and Theo, but I haven't decided to bring Mom and Dad in yet. It just feels like I'm going to jinx it somehow.

"Theo's very kind," she continues, shaking a pack of sweetener before tearing it open and dumping it into her coffee. "To drive you every day, I mean."

"Mhm." I stick my head in the fridge, mostly because I don't want to have this conversation right now, but also because I'm running late, and I won't have time to toast a waffle. I grab a yogurt cup and shut the door to find Mom staring at me. "Yes?"

"Nothing," she replies, breaking eye contact and screwing the lid onto her thermos. "I hope you have a good day, sweetheart."

"Thanks," I mumble, grabbing a spoon from the drawer. "Love you."

"Love you, too!" she calls after me as I head for the door.

Outside, the morning air is crisp with that early autumn chill that doesn't show its face till October in Georgia. Sure, it'll still be eighty degrees by lunchtime, but the mornings are here to remind us all that the heat does eventually come to an end. A breeze kicks up as I hop off the porch, raining leaves down on me as I cross to the driveway where Eileen is idling.

"Good morning!" Theo says as I slide into the passenger seat. Djo plays on the stereo, but he reaches over and turns it down while I buckle myself. He cranes his neck, surveying the area before he leans over for a quick peck on my cheek.

"You're bright and sunny today," I say, pulling the lid off my yogurt and stirring the contents.

"Can you blame me?" Theo asks, shifting into reverse and backing out of the driveway. "We've got an awesome weekend planned. I actually found time to study for my Geometry test last night, and I may have gotten an email from Hudson Helter this morning."

I nearly spit yogurt all over Eileen's dashboard.

"I'm sorry, what?!"

Theo is beaming, his crooked smile taking over. "He's coming to do an episode at Saint Catherine's in a few weeks. He asked if I would be interested in a short interview that he'd conduct before going in so we can talk about the video."

"And you said yes, right?"

"Of course!"

He's careful to keep his eyes on the road, but when we roll to a stop at a red light, he turns to me, unleashing all his Theo-sunshine-face energy on me, and I just want to wrap my arms around him.

I abandon my yogurt in Eileen's cup holder, suddenly too excited to eat. "Do you think I could go with you? I mean, I don't want to be in the interview or anything. I just honestly want to meet Hudson. Or maybe I shouldn't. You know, with what everyone says about meeting your heroes?"

Theo is laughing now.

"What's so funny?"

"You are. Do you think I'd go to an interview with Hudson freaking Helter and not bring you along? Of course you're coming! You're the first person I thought of when I got the email. Harry was a close second."

I was the first person he thought of. Why does that make me so happy?

He wraps his hand in mine, giving me one last look before the light turns green, and we speed off to school.

And even though his touch has become familiar at this point, my heart skips a beat. There can only be one explanation:

I think I'm in love.

"Over here!"

Elise shouts across the crowded dining room of Pizza Palooza. An old man sitting at the next table over shoots her a dirty look, and she responds by sticking out her tongue at him. Harrison whispers something into her ear, and she rolls her eyes.

I reach for Theo's hand but stop myself, pulling back.

Remember where you are, Caleb. Too many people to be doing all that.

Theo waves at his friends, then turns to me. "Are Freddy and Wren not here yet?"

I check my phone.

"Nope, looks like Freddy had to run home and change after soccer practice. They'll be a few minutes."

"Okay, cool. I'm going to go order if you want to go grab a seat. Still good with pepperoni?"

"Yes, please."

Theo moves like he's going to hug me but stops and just grabs my shoulder, giving it a quick squeeze.

We're really bad at being in public lately.

I weave my way through the packed dining room to the tables that Elise and Harrison have cobbled together. Oliver is here, too, scrolling on his phone. Elise waves as I approach, and I give a small wave back.

"Hey guys," I say, sliding into the seat beside Oliver. "Thanks for snagging a table. Hope it wasn't too hard."

"Nah," Harrison says with a smile. "We just had to fight off a couple of elderly patrons. No worries."

"They put up quite a fight for octogenarians," Oliver adds, looking up from his phone with a smirk. "But once you shatter a hip or two, they get the message."

Elise leans over the table, reaching for my hands. I let her take them. "Caleb, did you see that they're making season two of *I Love You Seymore Shura?*"

"What? No way! I thought they already covered all of the manga series?"

"That's just what they have translated. There are, like, five more volumes they're holding onto for some reason. I'm so excited, though! I even made Harry watch the first few episodes of my re-watch for season one. He didn't hate it!" "Why would I hate it?" Harrison asks, adjusting his thick-framed glasses. "It's got monsters, blood and guts, and a romance side-plot. It's all the ingredients of a good anime."

"Don't forget the cute dog," I add. "You gotta have a cute dog."

"The dog is a necessity," Oliver chimes in.

"What are we talking about?" Theo asks, sliding into the seat next to me. His knee collides with mine, and a wave of warmth washes over my face.

Elise raises an eyebrow. "Anime, duh."

Theo snorts a laugh. "Ah, how stupid of me."

"Did you get any more details from Hudson?" Harrison asks Theo.

"Dude, I promise. The minute I get the details, I'll let you know. But you've got to chill."

Harrison sinks back in his chair. "I just can't believe it's happening. You all know what a big deal this is, right? Hudson's got, like, three million subscribers. I said '*million*,' people. And he's coming to Specter!"

"Hudson Schmudson," Oliver says, leaning forward on his elbows. "I'm only here to talk Pumpkin Fair and all the delicious, deep-fried food I'm going to eat."

Theo snorts a laugh. "I refuse to ride the Gravitron with you this year. You ruined my favorite sneakers last time."

"Hey, I'm another year older and another year wiser. I'll wait at least ten minutes between snacks and rides."

"I'll believe that when I see it," Elise says, tucking a lock of wavy hair behind her ear. "Do y'all usually go to the fair, Caleb?"

"My family used to," I say with a nod. "But Wren, Freddy, and I have been going together since we were thirteen. My dad finally got old enough to admit the rides just make his back hurt, and Mom is usually buried at work this time of year. Apparently, a lot of people try to wrap up divorces before the Christmas season starts."

"Eww, did someone say Christmas?" A pair of hands seize my shoulders, and Wren's head pops into my periphery. "You better be talking about Jack Skellington, or else I won't hear it. October is a holy month, and I won't have you spoiling it with your peace on earth and goodwill towards men bullshit."

Freddy pulls out the chair at the end. "You'll have to excuse them. It's their high holy month."

Elise claps her hands. "I love it."

"Okay, we're all here," Harrison says once Wren has taken their seat. "Let's talk Pumpkin Fair."

The Pumpkin Fair—only called that because it used to take over a literal pumpkin patch back in the 70s—is a traveling fair that comes into town at the same time each year. It's only here for a weekend, so the whole town ends up there at some point or another. It's sort of a big deal, but that's only because there's not much else going on in Specter.

"Elise and I are planning on being there around noon," says Harrison, taking the role of lead organizer for the group. "Oliver, if you want to ride with us, then you'll need to be ready by eleven thirty—"

"I'll be ready whenever and wherever as long as I get deep-fried Oreos. God, I'm starving. Where is our pizza?"

"As I was saying," Harrison continues. "We'll be there around noon if we all want to meet up by the Ferris wheel."

"Sounds like a plan," Theo says, knocking his shoulder into mine. "I'll pick you up?"

I can't help but grin at him. "Yeah, thanks."

Freddy wraps an arm around Wren's. "Will you be my date? Andrew has choir practice or something church-y."

"I'm always here for you, Frederick."

"Yay!" Freddy bounces up and down in his seat. "You can buy me cotton candy and win me a prize at the dart-throwing game. I always try to win the unicorn but end up with some dinky little teddy bear."

Wren rolls their eyes.

"What do you like to do at the fair?" Theo asks me while Harrison and the others continue their planning in the background.

"I love the rides," I answer. "We always ride the Ferris wheel at sunset, so as long as we do that, I'm down for anything else."

Theo smirks at me. "Ferris wheel at sunset, huh? Who knew you were such a romantic?"

"I have my moments."

"Eighty-three!"

Oliver jumps up from his chair, "Bingo!"

The rest of us laugh as he goes to retrieve his pizza.

TWENTY-SEVEN
THEO

Saturday, October 21

I can barely sleep the night before the Pumpkin Fair.

Fall has always been my favorite time of the year. The colors, the holidays, the flavors, the weather—well, during the two or three weeks that Georgia allows us nice weather in October or November—everything feels new and exciting during fall. Halloween has always secretly been my favorite holiday, too. Or at least it used to be a secret. I used to feel a twinge of guilt that I enjoyed the spooky season more than Jesus's birthday—a stark contrast to my Christmas-loving family. It feels nice to be around people who unapologetically adore Halloween as much as or more than I do. I'm especially excited to share this season with Caleb for the first time. I feel a burst of warmth in my chest every time I think about it.

Since we're not meeting at the Pumpkin Fair until noon, I have to find ways to pass the time all morning. I saunter downstairs around 9:00 a.m., where both my parents and Nathaniel are eating breakfast at the kitchen table. We rarely all catch each other at the same time this early in the day, so I hesitate at the pantry before ultimately deciding to grab some cereal and eat at the table with them.

"Good morning, *aroha*," Mom says brightly.

"Good morning, Mom," I reply with a smile.

"Morning, Theo," Dad says, barely looking up from his iPad. "You're up early for a Saturday."

"It's Pumpkin Fair Day, Dad," I say as I pour my cereal and milk into a bowl in the kitchen. "I'm meeting up with friends at noon."

Mom's smile drops. "The Pumpkin Fair? Are you sure it's not going to be too crowded?"

I try not to roll my eyes. "I'll be fine, Mom. It's outside. I can just walk away if it gets to be too much."

"Are you sure?" Dad asks sternly.

"I'm positive," I insist. "Plus, my friends are going to be there. They'll look after me."

Neither parent says a word. Instead, they glance at one another for a moment, exchanging some kind of parental telepathy or something before returning to their breakfasts. That seems to have done the trick, so that's enough for me.

Once I'm seated at the table and eating my breakfast, Nathaniel finally glances up from his Switch to look at me. "Oh, yeah, can I get a ride to the Pumpkin Fair today?"

I freeze, trying to suppress the panic. "Uhh, sorry dude, I'm meeting up with the crew and some other friends from school. Plus, I'm already giving Caleb a ride."

"Dante and Ian are going. I was gonna meet up with them. I just need a ride there and a ride home."

Shit. If Nathaniel rides with us, I won't get to hold hands with Caleb while we drive. Or sneak a kiss or two at the red lights. It's the only chance we'll get to touch at all since we'll be quite literally surrounded by everyone in town. I can't stand the idea of missing a single opportunity with Caleb. We already have to be so careful all the time.

"Come on, Theo," Mom says, a frown on her face. "Give your brother a ride."

"Why can't you?" I ask before I can stop myself.

Mom narrows her eyes at me. "I've got a women's ministry meeting at church today. Your father will also be at the church for an elders' meeting."

I fidget with my cereal bowl. Shit. If I had just stayed in my room, this probably would have resolved itself. Stupid, stupid, stupid.

Nathaniel's eyes are on me when I look back up. He doesn't look angry or frustrated. He looks…curious. Like he's trying to solve a puzzle.

It sends a spike of anxiety up my spine.

"Theo, you really should give Nate a ride," Dad says with finality. "You're going to the same place; it's ten minutes away, and there's no reason not to. Do the right thing."

I clench my jaw, then release it. I'm out of excuses. "Yeah, okay."

Mom and Dad both smile at me, Dad turning back to his iPad and Mom continuing to eat her breakfast.

"Thanks, Theo," Nathaniel mutters, still watching me with that scrutinizing expression not unlike the way Grace looks when she's trying to pull something out of me. I turn my focus to my cereal.

"We need to leave here at 11:30," I mumble without looking back at him. "Will you be ready to go?"

"Yep."

"Good."

We eat the rest of breakfast mostly in silence except for Mom desperately trying to make conversation where she can. As soon as I'm finished, I make my way upstairs to get ready.

After a long shower and a borderline crisis picking out an outfit—I eventually settle for a solid burnt-orange t-shirt with an old flannel shirt consisting of shades of orange, red, and green, paired with some holey black jeans and sneakers—I'm finally ready to go. I grab my stuff and head out of my bedroom, where Nathaniel is waiting just outside my door. Together, we leave out the front door and climb into Eileen.

"Hey," Nathaniel starts as he climbs into the front seat. "Thanks for saying yes to driving me. I'm sorry if I'm annoying you."

I sigh. "You're not. It's not you."

"I'll move to the back when you get to Caleb's."

"Thanks."

We ride in silence for the first couple of minutes, but an inner battle rages on in my head.

What if I came clean to Nathaniel right now? Is it worth it?

As usual, I decide to weigh the pros and cons. The pros: Caleb and I still get to hold hands in the car. We probably won't sneak kisses at the red lights, but holding hands is better than nothing. Also, I don't have to worry about Nathaniel seeing anything or suspecting anything anymore, allowing Caleb and I to be able to relax around one more person.

The cons: Nathaniel might not take it well. He might tell my parents. He might be uncomfortable seeing me hold hands with a guy and ask us to stop—although that's very unlikely because he usually doesn't care about anything. Also, Caleb might be uncomfortable holding hands in front of Nathaniel, which would mean I told Nathaniel for no reason at all.

"Theo?"

"Hm?" I look over to see Nathaniel watching me again, his eyes flickering between my face and my hands on the steering wheel.

"Are you okay?" he asks.

"Yeah, why?"

"Because you've got a death grip on the steering wheel, and you're not even playing music."

I flex my fingers, relaxing my grip. Shit, he's right. "Oh yeah, I, uh, must have forgotten to put on a playlist. You can play something if you want."

"Are you worried that I might tell Mom and Dad about you and Caleb?"

I almost slam on the brakes. My leg actually twitches, and I almost get whiplash snapping my neck to look at him. "*What?*"

"Look, Theo," he says, hesitating. "I kind of…saw you and Caleb kissing in the car last week."

Fuck, fuck, fuck. "When? Where?"

Nathaniel shrugs. "In the driveway? I don't remember exactly when. It was after school one day."

My head is spinning. I should probably pull over. It's not safe to drive when I feel like I'm about to puke.

"Dude, it's okay."

"No, it's not."

"Yeah, it is. Dante is gay, too, actually. I get it, it's fine."

I exhale a shaky breath, trying to calm myself down.

"I'm not gonna tell Mom or Dad or Grace. I won't tell anyone if you're still keeping it a secret. Dante wanted to keep it a secret for a while, so I know what it's like. I just wanted to let you know in case that's why you didn't want me to ride with you to the fair today. You don't have to hide it from me because I already know, and I don't care. You can kiss or hug or hold hands or whatever. It doesn't bother me. And I won't tell anyone."

I take a minute to let all of that sink in, and then I glance at him again. He's looking straight ahead, relaxed and nonchalant. "You…you really don't care?"

Nathaniel shrugs. "I really don't. I see gay people at school, on TV, and in movies all the time. I know at church, they act like it's wrong, but I think that's dumb. You can't help who you like. Why should people be weird about it?"

The knot in my stomach begins to loosen, and the tension in my shoulders eases. "Yeah."

Nathaniel leans back in the seat. "So yeah, don't worry, you guys are safe with me. That's all."

By this point, we're already pulling up to Caleb's house, and I'm completely unprepared. I put the car in park, and Nathaniel immediately unbuckles to move to the backseat.

"Nate?"

"Yeah?"

"I—" my voice falters in my throat. "I really appreciate…you."

Nathaniel rolls his eyes. "Gross. Don't get sappy on me. Save it for Caleb." He gives me a grin before relocating to the backseat.

Caleb appears at the passenger door with a worried look as he glances from Nathaniel to me. "Hey," he says, a silent question in his voice.

I smile at him. "Hey."

As he buckles his seat belt, I lean over and kiss him on the cheek. His eyes fly wide open in panic.

"Nate knows," I say, nodding back to my brother in the backseat.

"Oh," Caleb replies, still sounding shaky.

"Hi, Caleb," Nathaniel says from the backseat.

"Hi, Nate."

Once I've reversed out of Caleb's driveway, I reach for his hand over the console. Caleb takes it, but I still see some flush in his cheeks. "Is this okay?" I ask, my voice just barely over a whisper.

Caleb smiles, giving my hand a little squeeze. "Yeah. Definitely okay."

As promised, Nathaniel disappears as soon as he sees his friends Dante and Ian, and it's just me and Caleb. And a couple of hundred Specter residents, of course. I try not to think about the crowd. At least everything is outside.

We make our way to the Ferris wheel, the agreed-upon meeting place for the crew. It's only 11:56, but I'm certain that Harrison, Elise, and Oliver will probably already be there. Harrison is a stickler for punctuality.

"Sorry, I kind of sprang all of that on you," I say as we walk. I've almost reached for his hand twice already, and we've only been out of the car for like five minutes. Today's going to be agonizing, but I'm determined to have a good time.

"It's okay," Caleb says, his voice bright and happy. "So, I take it he took the news well?"

"Well, actually, he already knew before today. Apparently, we need to be more careful in my driveway."

Caleb's eyes widen. "Yikes. Yeah, I guess we need to cool down."

There's a sinking feeling in my stomach at his words. I hate having to hide all the time. I know Caleb hates it, too, even though he'd never say it directly. I wish it wasn't a big deal. I wish I wasn't so afraid of my parents finding out. I wish we could just be ourselves. For a moment, I almost feel like we should just go back to the car and go somewhere else. "I'm sorry," I mumble, halfway hoping Caleb doesn't even hear me.

"What?"

"Nothing."

"Hey guys, over here!" Elise's voice carries over all the festival noise, and I see that everyone's already there, even Freddy and Wren.

As we approach, Oliver rubs his hands together, a wide grin on his face. "Finally. Now that everyone's here, I am starving. What are you guys thinking for lunch?"

"I want something fried, and I prefer that fried thing on a stick," Freddy answers.

"A man after my own heart," Oliver says, winking at Freddy. Freddy smirks at him.

"Should we just head towards where the food is and see what sounds the best?" Harrison asks. He's standing behind Elise with both arms wrapped around her waist, his chin practically resting on the top of her head. While he waits for an answer from the group, he plants a gentle kiss in her hair. I suddenly want nothing more than to try that with Caleb, but there's no way that would even work. Our height difference isn't as dramatic as Harry and Elise's, but as the shorter one, there's no graceful way I can just kiss the top of Caleb's head. I'd probably have to stand on my tiptoes or something ridiculous. And even if Caleb held me from behind like that, Caleb's head wouldn't tower over mine like Harrison's does for Elise. Caleb would probably be able to comfortably rest his chin on my shoulder from behind. The perfect position for him to whisper in my ear or kiss my cheek or—

"Theo?"

"Hm?" I blink a few times to shake myself out of my daze.

Caleb's grinning at me. "Are you coming?"

Everyone is already walking towards the concession stands, and clearly, Caleb had started walking only to stop and turn around before leaving me behind. "Yep, sorry, let's go!"

I intentionally brush my hand against his as we walk to catch up with everyone. He gives me a sideways glance. "What were you daydreaming about?" he asks, a playful tone in his voice.

"What do you think?"

Caleb smiles, and my stomach flutters.

The rest of the afternoon is full of extremely greasy food (Oliver was literally jumping up and down when he discovered the deep-fried Pop-Tarts), nauseating rides (that shockingly no one actually puked from this time), and occasionally overwhelming crowds (triggering only one mild anxiety attack, but Caleb helped keep me calm and I was fine again in less than five minutes).

I'm overjoyed with how much our friend group has melded together. Oliver and Freddy seem to be playing a strange game of flirting chicken, although I'm not sure what the desired outcome is, so it's fun to watch. Elise is captivated by Wren's horror makeup portfolio, and she continues pestering Wren to show her more pictures every chance she gets. Occasionally, the conversation will go back to horror movies, and Oliver and Wren's repertoire of obscure horror films they've seen is shockingly similar. At some point, someone brought up some indie comic book reference, and Harrison, Elise, and Freddy rambled on about it for at least twenty minutes.

As we're walking down a row of overpriced carnival games, something catches my eye. I gasp as I realize what it is. "Caleb, Caleb, look!" Without hesitation, I grab his hand and pull him to the booth, my eyes locked on the prize.

The booth itself is nothing special, and I don't actually see a game set up anywhere, but hanging from the tent ceiling and seated on shelves lining the back wall of the booth are dozens upon dozens of Halloween-themed plush toys of varying sizes. There are Frankenstein monsters, mummies, vampires, zombies, black cats, and witches—just about any cliche Halloween character imaginable.

But one sticks out above the rest. It's an adorable rust-colored puppy—almost the same shade as Caleb's hair but not nearly pretty enough—with a black witch hat and a seafoam green sparkling cloak. It's about the size of a basketball. It's *perfect*.

I point to the puppy as I nudge Caleb's shoulder. "I'm going to win that one for you," I say softly, with more determination than I've ever felt about anything.

Caleb snickers. "Really?"

"Hey, what did you stop for?" Oliver says as he appears on the other side of me. "You're not actually going to throw your money away on this shit, are you?"

I'm already digging into my pocket for my wallet. The attendant, a very bored-looking guy with messy blonde hair—probably only a year or two older than me—is scrolling on his phone when I clear my throat to get his attention. "Hi. Umm, what game is this, and how can we win one of those?" I point to the shelf where Witch Puppy sits.

The attendant looks annoyed as he casually stows his phone away in his pocket. He moves out of the booth and motions to a neighboring setup beside the booth, and my stomach drops. Apparently, in my tunnel vision, I completely missed it, and now I feel stupid for asking. "It's your basic Ladder Climb. Pretty simple. You just have to keep your balance on the rope ladder, climb to the top, and push the button up there."

I stare at the bright green and purple rope ladders in horror. Each end of the ladder converges to be supported at one point—one at the top and one at the bottom—suspended over an inflated bouncy house floor. The wobbly ladders provide a slight incline to get to the top, where there's a large red button. My confidence in winning Caleb's witch puppy is fading fast.

"Theo, this is clearly so rigged," Oliver says, not bothering to keep his voice down. "It's impossible to stay balanced. No one ever wins these things."

The attendant says nothing, his attention already waning.

"Come on, dude, seriously—"

"How much?" I ask the attendant.

"Five dollars per attempt," the attendant drones.

"Five dollars!?" Oliver shouts. "For one try?"

"What's five dollars?" Harrison asks as he approaches us now. I should have expected to have an audience, but the pressure of completing this challenge in front of the entire crew is mounting quickly.

"Harry, please don't let Theo waste his money on a stupid carnival game," Oliver says angrily.

Harrison laughs. "Yeah, right. Theo's literally the last person who would fall for a carnival game."

I bite my lip. "Well…"

Harrison's smile fades immediately. "Seriously?"

"This should be fun," Wren says with a smirk as they sidle up beside Oliver.

"Theo, you don't have to do this," Caleb says quietly, just to me. "I won't like you any less if you don't."

I find myself taking in Caleb's face for a few moments. We've been walking around in the sun all afternoon, so a few spots like the tip of his nose, his cheeks, and the top of his brow are tinted pink. His expression is gentle and kind, and I know he means what he says about not having to do this. I don't have to win his affection. I have it already. But this only makes me want to win him something even more.

After a few seconds, I turn back to the attendant with a crisp ten-dollar bill. "Let's do this."

Oliver groans loudly behind me. Freddy and Elise laugh. I don't hear any other reaction, but it doesn't matter. I need to get my head in the game.

The attendant takes my money and guides me to the rope ladder on the right. "Okay, the rules are no holding on to the rope or the outside of the ladder, no resting your elbows or knees on the rung or rope, and if you fall off, you lose."

"Is it timed?"

"Nope."

I nod and study the ladder. Theoretically, all I need to do is distribute my weight evenly across the ladder so that it stays level, right? It can't be that difficult. I've paid for two tries, so I use my first one to get a feel for the ladder, carefully placing my legs and hands equidistant from each other.

As soon as all of my weight is on the ladder, it immediately flips, and I fall to the inflated mat below. Shit.

"Told you!" Oliver shouts.

"Not helpful," I shout back. I glance at Caleb, who flashes me a sympathetic smile. Even though I know he's just trying to be supportive, I latch on to it as motivation to keep going.

I take my place back at the base of the ladder and survey it again. Maybe if I go fast, practically just run up the ladder and use it to propel me towards the button, I could make it.

Without trying to overthink it, I go for the running start approach. Once again, as soon as I'm on the ladder, it spins me off onto the mat.

"Come on, Theo," Harrison calls from behind me. "It's all about your center of mass. It's like a tightrope. You have to balance out your weight so that your center of gravity stays in the middle of the ladder."

"I'll need another five if you're attempting it again," the attendant says as I scramble to my feet. I nod and dig out my wallet.

"Theo, it's really fine," Caleb starts.

"No, I can do this," I reassure him—and myself. Harrison's right. I just need to maintain my center of mass.

After handing a five-dollar bill to the attendant, I'm determined that this is it. I'm going to get up there this time. I exhale slowly as I approach the bottom of the ladder, steadying my arms and legs. *I can do this. I can do this.*

I manage my way further up this time, taking my time as the ladder wobbles precariously beneath me. I hear several voices behind me offering advice and feedback, but I have to ignore them to focus on my movements. I've got it this time—

The ladder teeters aggressively and flips the other way this time, and I land flat on my back with a bounce. Before I'm even fully upright, I'm reaching for my wallet again.

"Theo, seriously," Caleb reaches out to hold my arm. "Don't throw all your money away for this."

I chew on my lip again. "One more. If I don't get it this time, I'll stop."

Caleb holds his gaze for a second but then lets go of my arm, smiling at me. "Okay. Last one. You've got this."

I grin widely at him as I hand the attendant yet another five-dollar bill. He takes it without making eye contact and leans back against the barrier again.

This is it. I stare at the ladder. *I can do this. I can do this.* I grip the rungs tightly, slowly moving one hand or one foot at a time, waiting for the wobbling to stop before making another movement. It's working—I'm so close. Just two more rungs, then I can lunge for the button.

Steadily, slowly, I'm just one rung away.

I slowly glance up at the button. It's close enough. I can jump for it.

I steady myself, then spring forward—

The ladder immediately flips, tossing me unceremoniously and gracelessly to the mat.

"Noooo!" the crew shouts in unison behind me.

I lay motionless on the bouncy floor, frustration, embarrassment, and disappointment swirling around behind my eyes, tears threatening to make everything so much worse.

Just as I'm about to close my eyes, Caleb appears above me, silhouetted against the bright blue sky. He's smiling warmly down at me, extending a hand to help me up. I try to return the smile as I take his hand, and he pulls me towards him. The desire to kiss him is overwhelming, but I sigh as I let go of his hand. Together, we climb off the inflatable floor and back to our friends.

"Sorry, Theo," Elise says as I rejoin the group. "It was fun to watch, though. Thanks for the entertainment!"

"That was a fun little detour," Harrison mumbles, giving me a weird expression. "But let's keep going."

"Uhh, hold up, guys," Freddy says, still behind us.

I turn around just in time to see Caleb handing the attendant a single bill and stepping towards the ladder.

"Cal, what are you doing?" Wren calls out.

My legs have already taken me back to the booth to watch. A few members of the crew make frustrated groans as they also return, but I say nothing as my eyes are transfixed on Caleb's attempt.

Caleb ignores everyone, steadies himself on the bottom rungs of the ladder, and begins his ascent. His movements are slow like mine, but the ladder wobbles significantly less beneath him. Each step forward is graceful and intentional. The ladder stays stable, and his grip remains secure.

Within seconds, Caleb has made his way to the top, where he carefully, steadily reaches up and presses the button, prompting a loud buzzer sound to emanate from the top of the booth. Only then does Caleb allow himself to let go of the ladder and fall, landing effortlessly on the inflated ground below.

"WHOA!!" The crew shouts gleefully around me, whooping and cheering for Caleb as he bounces off the mat. I haven't made a sound—I'm literally frozen in place, eyes glued to Caleb as he makes his way towards me. He's grinning ear-to-ear, only looking at me.

I almost feel dizzy watching him, heat rising in my cheeks. Am I…Am I turned on by this? Shit. Something to revisit later, I determine, trying to steady my own breathing.

"Holy shit, dude, that was amazing!" Oliver exclaims, clapping Caleb's back excitedly. "You've had to have done that before or something. Nobody gets it on the first try."

"Never knew you had it in you, Cal," Wren adds with a smirk.

"Seriously, how did you do that?" Harrison asks, almost suspiciously.

Caleb simply shrugs. "I took gymnastics through middle school. That game is all about balance, like Harrison said."

"Hey kid, come pick your prize," the attendant interrupts. Caleb spins around and heads to the prize booth. I watch him in a daze, still reeling.

"Look at you," Oliver murmurs to me, a mischievous grin on his face. "You've got yourself a gymnast boyfriend now, huh? That could be fun."

I try to ignore him even though his words make my cheeks darken even more, and instead, I make my way towards Caleb in the booth. He's carefully considering all the plush toys before him, which makes me laugh. "Hey, get the witch puppy. You earned it!"

"I want that one—" he says to the attendant, pointing to a completely different shelf from the one where the seafoam-green-cloaked puppy plush is sitting. I furrow my brow, trying to follow where he's pointing. "The green witch cat."

The attendant pulls a basketball-sized dark green cat off the shelf and hands it to Caleb. The cat is also wearing a black witch hat, and it's honestly one of the cutest things I've ever seen. "Congrats," the attendant says dryly, then returns to lean back against the wall and doesn't even wait for us to leave before he pulls out his phone.

"Aww, that one's cute too, but I'm surprised you didn't want—"

"It's not for me, dummy," Caleb interrupts, pushing the plush towards me with a smile. "It's for you."

My mouth hangs open, words stuck in my throat. "Oh. It's—really?"

Caleb laughs. "Of course it is. You couldn't win one for me, but I wanted to win one for you instead."

I feel like I might actually cry now—what the hell is happening to me? I've never been this flustered by a toy before. I take the cat in my hands and hold it close. "Thank you," I say, my voice cracking slightly. As if it wasn't already embarrassing enough that I feel like I'm going to cry, now my own voice is betraying me.

Caleb flashes the sweetest smile I think I've ever seen on his face, and suddenly, I'm feeling too much at the same time, and *God*, I just want to hold him.

Fuck it.

I wrap my arms around his waist and pull him into me, burying my face into his shoulder. He's stunned for only a moment, but it doesn't take long for him to hug me back, a low chuckle in his throat.

"All right, you two, come on," Elise says, a hint of anxiety in her voice. "Let's keep going. There's still more to see!"

I release Caleb from my grip, smiling up at him as we pull away. He's blushing when our eyes meet, and I feel like melting all over again.

There is not a single doubt in my mind that I'm in love with Caleb Raynard.

TWENTY-EIGHT
CALEB

The Pumpkin Fair is packed by the early afternoon. Our group ends up splintering after we eat lunch—if you call three rounds of fried Oreos and a bucket of fries lunch—each mini-group heading to a different corner of the fairgrounds. Oliver and Wren end up hanging out at the food wagons, waiting in the longest line for something called a "Giraffe's Neck," which I sincerely hope doesn't contain any actual giraffe. Harrison and Elise want to go check out the funhouse—which Freddy won't go near due to his irrational fear of inanimate clowns—so that leaves Theo, Freddy, and I to check out the rides.

Theo clutches the witch-hat-cat, finally tucking it into his burnt orange and brown flannel shirt so that the head sticks up over his chest. It's sort of adorable and also incredibly distracting because I just want to keep staring at it—at him—instead of avoiding bumping into the crowds of people.

"Which ride do you want to do first?" Freddy asks, our trio stepping off the main path for a second to try and figure out a game plan.

"How about the Viking ship?" Theo suggests adjusting the plush in his shirt, then giving me a smile. "I'm down for any ride right now, as long as it doesn't spin. I don't want lunch to make a comeback."

I graze my pinky finger against the side of his hand. "I love the Viking ship."

"Sounds like a plan," Freddy says, glancing down at our hands, then back up at me with a sly grin. "And if you two need this third wheel to roll away at any time, just let me know."

I pull my hand away from Theo's, shaking my head. "That won't be necessary, but thank you."

We make it over to the swinging ship ride, handing over our tickets to the bored-looking attendant and climbing aboard. The Vikings definitely haven't kept their vessel in the greatest condition, as there's paint peeling from every surface. Hopefully, all their efforts have gone into maintaining the mechanics so our first ride doesn't turn into our last.

I sit between Theo and Freddy, fastening myself into the seat. Across the ship, the other rows begin to fill as well, and I recognize a few people from school. By the end of the day, I'll probably have seen the whole town here at one time or another. It's just how it is at the Pumpkin Fair.

Once all the seats have been filled, the ship begins to move, swinging slowly at first but picking up speed with each pass until we're parallel with the ground. I can't help but let out a yelp as we plummet back down, and Theo's hand finds mine somewhere in the fall. Then we're moving upward, and I don't shout again, as I'm much too focused on his hand in mine to notice how high we go up for the final swing. He doesn't let go till the ride slows to a stop. As we unfasten ourselves, Theo checks to make sure his cat plush is still secure.

"Okay, what's next?" Freddy asks as we climb down from the ship.

"What about the freefall?" I suggest pointing to the towering steel structure just a few tents down. "Lola would never ride that one with me."

Freddy glances up at the tower, the color draining from his face. "If we have to."

Theo gives me a nod. "Me and Binx are ready if you are."

"Binx?" I repeat.

The tips of Theo's cheeks get pink, accentuating the light splotches of freckles brought out by the afternoon sun. "Yeah, you know. Like Thackery Binx. From *Hocus Pocus*." He pats the cat plushie on the head. "It fits, you know?"

My god, can this boy get any cuter? I want to drag him into the closest tent and kiss him till we're both gasping for air, but I have to be on my best behavior.

"It totally fits."

The lines stretch even longer this time of day, so we have to wait a while to get on the freefall ride. Theo and I spend most of the time playing an increasingly risky game of "find any excuse to touch each other" while Freddy scrolls on his phone. I didn't think it would be this difficult being so close to Theo and not being able to reach out for him. It seems like every day gets a little harder, and I want to bring it up, but it's not the right time. Still, I can't help but daydream about what it would be like to walk around the Pumpkin Fair with Theo's hand in mine for all the world to see. To wrap my arms around him whenever I wanted to and not have to have our friends remind us to break it up. To kiss him, drenched in the golden sunlight that transfigures his deep chestnut hair into hues of umber and honey.

"You okay?" Theo asks, shaking me from my stupor. We're almost to the front of the line, and both he and Freddy are looking at me.

"Yeah, sorry. All that fried food must have rotted my brain."

"Look, I want to dissociate from this ride, too," Freddy says with a wry smile. "But if I have to be present, so do you."

"I'm here," I promise with a chuckle. "Wouldn't want to be anywhere else."

"Are you sure you're okay?" Theo asks again, getting close enough that he can whisper it.

"I was just thinking. We can maybe talk about it later, okay?"

He nods, a spark of worry behind his eyes.

"It's nothing bad, I promise," I assure him, knocking my shoulder into his.

The next round of riders plunge down, their screams drowning our conversation. Then the gate ahead opens up, and we hurry along to get strapped into the ride. But by the time we get to the open seats, there are only two beside each other and a single one on the other side of the ride. Freddy looks like he's starting to hyperventilate, so I turn to Theo and ask, "Is it okay if I ride beside him? I think he needs the support."

Theo nods, giving me a thumbs up before he rounds the corner of the row and takes the single seat, pulling down the restraints. Freddy and I take our spots, doing the same and fastening the buckles.

Freddy lets out an exhale, clutching the bars on his restraint so tight that his knuckles blanch.

"Hey." I extend my hand out to him. "We got this. Everything's going to be fine."

Freddy takes my hand, nearly crushing it at first but then slacking the pressure a bit. "Don't let go," he says, a spark of sincerity in his voice.

The attendant completes their safety check, and the ride shoots us upward with a hiss of air and the teetering mechanical melody of a song. In seconds, we're at the top of the tower, the afternoon sun washing over the town of Specter below. To the north, you can just make out the hills that rise from the lower Appalachians, and if you turn in the opposite direction, you can see the cityscape of northern Atlanta. It's so wild how quickly I forget our town is tucked between such contrasts. The bustling city and the rolling hills of evergreen trees. It's beautiful—especially from up here.

"Shit, shit, shit," Freddy mumbles beside me, squeezing my hand till it aches.

"Breathe, Freddy," I remind him. "It'll all be over in a—"

The mechanical music ends, and the ride plummets, my dangling legs flying up and locking at the knee as gravity loses its effect on us. Then, halfway down, the ride stops, and we ricochet back up to the top for a split second before falling again, this time all the way to the bottom, slowing only a few feet from our collision with the dirt.

My heart is racing as the restraints lift up, and Freddy's hand is still wrapped around mine as we hop out of our seats.

"Oh my god," he breathes. "I think I'm with Lola on this one, Cal. Not for me."

The attendant—an older man with graying hair on the sides of his head—walks past us to get the ride ready for the next group, but I can tell he's staring at me and Freddy, or should I say, he's staring at our hands. I drop his, reminding myself that this is the reason I can't hold onto Theo the way I want to. It'll bring unwanted attention.

"That was crazy!" Theo says once he's rejoined us. "Did you hear me screaming?"

Freddy shakes his head, "Nah, I couldn't hear anything over my own blubbering."

"I heard both of you," I tease as we exit the gated area around the ride and step back into the crowds.

"Yeah, well, we can't all be as brave as Caleb," Freddy says.

"Wren is far braver than I am when it comes to rides," I correct him.

Freddy laughs. "That's just because they're dead inside."

"Did Binx make it through okay?" I ask Theo, turning back to him.

He untucks the plush from his shirt, giving me a thumbs up and a wink. "He was a trooper."

As we move towards the next ride, we're squeezed by the growing crowds. Theo does his best to stick by my side, but we keep getting separated by the endless stream of Specter residents. Again, I find myself wanting to reach out for Theo, to wrap an arm around his waist as we walk so he can't get washed away in the crowds, but I tamp that longing down.

"Hey, Freddy!"

Freddy stops in front of me, turning to scan the river of bodies around us. A tall boy with blonde hair and glasses waves over the heads of those around him, and it takes me a second to recognize him from school.

"Andrew!" Freddy calls, fighting his way through the crowd.

I take Theo by the elbow, pulling him out of the stream of traffic and over beside a cart selling kettle corn. We watch as Andrew and Freddy meet in the middle of the crowd, embracing each other and even sharing a quick kiss. I feel Theo tense beside me, and I realize I'm still holding onto him, so I drop my hold and mutter a quick, "Sorry."

Freddy and Andrew make their way over to us, hand-in-hand. "Caleb, Theo, you guys know Andrew."

"Hey," I greet Andrew.

"How's it going?" Theo adds.

"Sorry to crash," Andrew says, giving a sheepish smile. "I didn't think I was going to be able to make it, but our choir practice ended early."

"No worries," I tell him. "Glad you could come."

"Andrew hasn't eaten yet, so I was going to walk him over to the food trucks," Freddy explains, leaning his head on Andrew's shoulder. "Want to meet up later?"

"Sure, we'll check to see where y'all are in a bit."

It's probably for the best anyway. Things are starting to get really crowded, so maybe it's a good time for me and Theo to sneak away to someplace quieter.

"Okay, bye!" Freddy calls over his shoulder as the two of them disappear in the churning chaos of bodies.

"Hey, you want to go chill for a minute?" I ask Theo.

He brushes the hair from his eyes. "Are you sure? I'm okay to keep riding rides."

"I'm positive. Come on, we can cut through here around to the back of the tents."

Theo nods, following me along the grassy path between two white tarp tents to the backside of the fairground. From here, the old pumpkin patch sprawls out ahead, now just overgrown with local vegetation, but the remnants of an old wooden fence stick out of the ground every few feet.

Behind the wall of tents and trailers, the noise of the fair is muffled, mixed in with the sounds of birds and the road on the other side of the patch. Leading Theo, we walk along the tattered wooden fence, and after a moment, I stop, turning to face him.

"Has today been as difficult for you as it has been for me?"

Theo looks down at Binx, running his fingers along the brim of the witch hat. "It's not been easy, that's for sure. I can't help it. I just want to kiss you, like all the time."

"Same. And I love the Pumpkin Fair and all our friends, but I just… I wish there wasn't this weird tension distracting me. I want to enjoy myself and my time with you, but it's hard."

Theo nods. "I'm sorry. I don't really know what to say."

"I'm not sure what I want you to say either. I just wanted to be honest with you about what I'm feeling. And you don't have to be sorry about anything, Theo. I'm not trying to push you into anything you're not ready for."

Theo looks over his shoulder, scanning the area. He takes my hand in his. "I feel the same way. I wish we could be like Freddy and Andrew, that I could kiss you in the middle of a sea of people and not care about what others think… but I can't. I just need a little more time, I think. Is that okay?"

I pull him closer to me, leaning my forehead into his. "Of course it is, Theo. I'm not upset, I promise."

He closes his eyes, taking a deep breath. "I'm being a really shitty boyfriend."

My pulse jolts. "Did you really just say that?"

Theo pulls back, his face flushed. "Yeah, I did. Is that okay? That I call us that, I mean. Boyfriends?"

I nod emphatically. "Absolutely. One hundred percent."

His grip on my hand tightens. "I really like you, Caleb. And I'm trying my best not to screw this up."

"I like you too. And you're doing great, I promise. We'll get there."

Theo looks around one more time, then leans in close again. "Just to tie us over," he whispers, then his lips are on mine, and the tension that had been building all afternoon in my gut melts away.

And even when he pulls away and his hand drops from mine, I know in my heart he wants to kiss me again just as badly as I want the same.

TWENTY-NINE
THEO

The sun is starting to set, which means it's time to head to the Ferris wheel. I've been daydreaming about it all day. Theoretically, once we're at the top, I think we'll be far enough out of sight of the crowds for me to kiss Caleb. But I don't want to tell him—I want it to be a surprise.

Plus, the last thing I want to do is disappoint him if I end up chickening out.

We hurry to get in line for the Ferris wheel, anxiety gripping me that we won't make it in time. Caleb swears that it's okay if we're not on the wheel the moment the sun starts setting, but I refuse to keep disappointing him. I want *this*—just this one moment—to be perfect.

As we wait in line with the crew, I sneak in a few more casual touches with Caleb every chance I get. Bumping shoulders, feet, knees, whatever we can without drawing attention. As the sky darkens, I feel bolder. I link pinkies with Caleb or lean into his shoulder, feeling especially brave when I'm standing in Harrison's shadow. Surely, no one is paying attention to two random teenage boys barely touching in line for the Ferris wheel, right?

Besides, whatever anxiety I was feeling about people looking at us is occasionally overpowered by anxiety about the amount of attention Freddy and Andrew are getting. Not that it's anything direct—it's only a handful of people giving them side-eyed glances of confusion, disgust, or alarm. No one says a word or does anything, but it definitely has me tensing up every time they kiss or embrace, bracing myself for a consequence that never really comes.

If I'm honest with myself, ever since Andrew joined our crew today, I've been struggling not to feel jealous. I have no right to be jealous because the only reason Caleb and I can't be physical like that is because *I'm* afraid. I'm the one holding us back. It's agonizing. I don't know how much longer I can take it.

"Earth to Theo," Oliver says, waving a hand in front of my face. "Are you still with us, bud?"

"Yeah, I'm here," I respond, focusing my gaze on Oliver. I wonder for a moment what I was staring at before—hopefully not a person. "What are we talking about?"

"We're almost to the front of the line, so we've got to couple off," Oliver says. "Lucky for Wren, they're going to be coupled off with me."

"Lucky me," Wren replies with a grin. "Plus, you and I need to revisit our conversation earlier about the Stephen King IT movies, and I'm not allowed to talk about those within fifty feet of Freddy."

"That is correct," Freddy agrees, wrapping an arm around Andrew's waist. "Not another word until I'm out of hearing range."

We're finally approaching the front of the line, and Harrison, in his never-ending pursuit of looking out for me in every conceivable way, pushes me to the front of our group, and I tug on Caleb's sleeve to follow me—being sure to graze a finger across his skin while I grip his shirt. I look up at the sky. The sun is still above the horizon. *Yes!*

After securing Binx once again inside my flannel, Caleb and I climb aboard our gondola. There is no seatbelt—just a flimsy lap bar that the attendant casually lowers across our legs once we're seated. I keep a safe casual distance from Caleb in front of the attendant, but the second we start rising, I scoot over until our thighs and shoulders touch.

"We made it," I say, smiling as I look out over the park, and we rise up about halfway.

"We did," Caleb agrees. His hand is on the lap bar, but he inches it over a little. I follow his lead and put my hand on the lap bar, too, right beside his so that our pinkies touch. It's barely anything, but I feel the sparks like tiny fireworks erupting across my arms and into my chest.

"Have you had fun today, despite…everything?" I ask.

Caleb furrows his brow and looks at me. "Of course I have. I mean, sure, it's been…difficult, but I'm still having fun with you. With everyone else, too, but especially you."

My chest feels like it might burst. I wonder for a minute if I should tell him I love him, but quickly squash the idea completely. If I can't even hold his hand in public without being afraid of the wrong person seeing, it's not fair to start saying, "I love you."

God, Caleb deserves so much better than me.

"You okay?" Caleb asks, allowing his pinky to graze over mine.

"Yeah, I just—I don't know. Maybe—maybe I should come out to my parents this week."

Caleb doesn't say anything right away. I turn to see his expression, and it's thoughtful and only a little anxious. "Really?"

I look back down at our hands on the lap bar. "Maybe. My worst fear is that they'll take my phone or my car away and not let me see you. But assuming they don't do that, it would make things so much better because we could touch each other in public because I wouldn't be afraid anymore, but—" I exhale a shaky breath. "—if they freak out, I risk not being able to see you as much as we do now."

"So don't tell them yet," Caleb says gently. "If it's not worth the risk, don't do it."

I shake my head, then take Caleb's hand into mine, no longer able to care about the attendant or the crowds below us. "But you *are* worth the risk. It's not fair that you're stuck with someone that's afraid all the time. You deserve to be able to hold hands and hug and kiss your boyfriend whenever you want."

Caleb turns his body to face towards me. "Theo, you need to listen to me. I'm not 'stuck' with you. Okay? I want to be with you, too. I thought you knew that."

The gondolas start moving up again, and we're headed to the top. I glance up at the sun's position on the horizon. "I know. I'm sorry. We literally just had this conversation. I'm just being paranoid." I squeeze his hand. "No more serious stuff. Let's just watch the sunset."

Caleb studies me warily for another second but repositions to face the horizon, leaning against my shoulder again.

I look down and around us one last time. Surely, we're high enough. No one is watching. No one cares.

The gondola stops at the top, rocking slightly. I take a moment to look at Caleb, really taking him in. His face is glowing in this light, the bright orange sky making everything look radiant, but especially Caleb. The golden rays bounce off his hair, his freckles, his smile, his eyes—God, his *eyes*.

I reach across the distance between us, my body moving on its own without input from my brain. I gently cup his cheek with my hand to turn his head towards me, and I kiss him. I kiss him with everything that I am, with all the courage I wish I had, with all the love I can't speak of yet. And Caleb kisses me back, hesitantly at first, but it's not long before he melts into it, too.

Fuck Specter. Fuck potential witnesses. Fuck the possible consequences.

Right now, Caleb is mine, and I'm his, and nothing else in the world matters.

While his lips are on mine, something snaps in my brain, and suddenly, all I want is *more*. I need to be closer. I want to be lost in him. Everything else fades away as my hands slowly explore on their own, one moving up into Caleb's hair, the other down to his hip, basically wherever I can reach. I can smell his shampoo. I can taste the remnants of sour gummy worms. Every nerve in my body is screaming, but my brain feels like it's floating.

It takes the gondola moving again to pull me out of the dreamlike trance of kissing Caleb, and as we pull away, I also have to untangle my fingers from his hair and release my grip from his shirt. My entire being feels engulfed in flames, and I'm nearly out of breath from it. I risk a glance into Caleb's eyes, which are still way too big and gorgeous, and I almost dive in for another round before my brain finally kicks back on.

"Wow," Caleb says, his face flushed, but he has a nervous but genuine smile.

I hear myself laughing, which is probably the safest reaction my slowly rebooting brain can come up with. "Wow, indeed."

"Did—did you mean to do that?" Caleb asks while laughing.

"Kind of?" I say honestly. I finally look back out across the sky, and the sun is gone, dipped below the horizon, leaving brilliant pink and orange streaks across the sky. "Shit, I think I missed the sunset."

"Yeah, I think I did, too."

"I'm sorry."

Caleb raises his eyebrows and stares at me before bursting into giggles, which has me giggling uncontrollably, too. Is this what getting drunk feels like?

The gondola stops one last time, and I'm sure the Ferris wheel ride is almost over when I see her. I notice the familiar gleam of copper hair out of the corner of my eye, so I instinctively turn to see where it's coming from and freeze.

Sienna is staring up at me from the ground, her eyes wide with shock and… something else. My blood runs cold.

"Hey, what's wrong?" Caleb asks, but his voice feels far away. "What are you looking at?"

I open my mouth to answer him, but nothing comes out. I just stare at Sienna as she stares at me and—

Oh my God, she saw us.

Sienna finally breaks our eye contact and starts to walk away from the Ferris wheel, and the panic immediately sets in.

She saw us. She saw me kiss Caleb.

Not just that—she saw me *making out* with Caleb. It wasn't just a tiny kiss or a peck or holding hands or anything like that. Sienna saw me lose myself.

"Theo?"

For *weeks,* I've been living in fear of the wrong person seeing me with Caleb. For *weeks,* I've been too afraid to even hold hands with my own boyfriend in public. For *weeks,* we have deprived ourselves of even the smallest displays of affection around people.

All those weeks of caution, all those moments of self-control and restraint, all of it has been for *nothing* because I just ruined everything.

"Theo, you're scaring me."

"We have to go," I finally say.

"We do?"

I nod vigorously, panic spreading fast and quick. "We...we have to get out of here."

"Okay, sure, I think we're about to get off," Caleb says quietly. "Can you tell me what's going on?"

I keep my eyes on Sienna's orange hair as long as I can, but I'm losing sight of her. Shit, shit, shit, shit, I need to find her, I need to explain—

"Theo, talk to me."

"Ex-girlfriend. Saw us up there. Gotta find her."

"Oh. Oh, shit."

"Yeah."

The gondola rolls to a stop, and the attendant raises our lap bar. I hear Caleb mutter a "thank you" to him, but my eyes are trained on the direction Sienna went, and I start walking, but I don't see her anymore. Oh God, I have to find her. I walk faster.

"Theo, wait!" Caleb calls from behind me.

I don't wait. I start running.

"Theo, where are you going?" Harrison calls from the gondola he and Elise are still on above me. I don't answer—I don't even acknowledge them. I'll explain later. They'll understand.

I've completely lost sight of Sienna, and I can feel an oncoming panic attack as I find myself deep in a crowd of strangers. *No, no, no, no—*

My phone. I'm so stupid. We have phones. I can just call her. Text her. Something. Anything. I just have to get out of here.

I turn around, expecting Caleb to be behind me, but he's not. Of course he's not—I left him. There are only more people. So many people. Way too many people. Some of them look at me, but most of them don't. I stop walking and turn around to head back to the Ferris wheel, but a man rams into my back. He grunts and grumbles something about not stopping in the middle of the path, but I can barely hear him over the blood rushing in my ears and the noise coming from every direction. Kids are screaming and laughing. Adults are carrying on normal conversations. The ride machinery, the carnival games, the concession stands, and the merchandise booths are suddenly so loud, and every sound is overwhelming. It's too much, and I'm dizzy, and I need to sit down, but I can't sit down in the middle of the path, I'll get trampled, so I need to get out of the crowd, away from the people, away from—

"Theo!"

I hear Caleb's voice through the chaos, and I whip my head around to find him. Sure enough, his russet curls appear in my peripheral, and his warm brown eyes finally find mine. He extends a hand out to me, and I nearly crush it in my grip. Caleb pulls me behind him and out of the crowd, and we duck between two merchandise tents and out towards the parking lot.

As soon as we're out of the crowd, I collapse on the ground and hug my knees to my chest. "I'm sorry, I'm sorry, I'm so sorry—"

"Hey, shhh," Caleb crouches down next to me but maintains a few inches of space between us so that I don't feel cramped. God, he's too good to me. How does he know to do that? "It's okay. Just breathe."

It's only then that I realize I'm nearly hyperventilating, so I close my eyes and consciously try to slow my breathing. Caleb stays put, his presence grounding me.

"Can I touch you?" Caleb asks, and I open my eyes to see his hand hovering over my back. I nod once, and Caleb starts gently rubbing small comforting circles on my back, and I close my eyes again, focusing on the sensation of his hands.

We stay here like this for what feels like hours, but it's probably no more than a few minutes. My breathing is finally almost back to normal, and I open my eyes to see Caleb glancing down at his phone in his other hand.

"I'm sorry you had to see that," I say softly, my voice barely over a whisper.

Caleb immediately puts his phone away and leans in closer. "Don't apologize, Theo. You had a panic attack."

"I know, I just—I was stupid, I just ran off without you, I just thought I could…" I trail off, remembering why I ran ahead in the first place, and then I immediately wrangle my phone out of my pocket. "I need to text her."

"Who?"

"Sienna. She's—she saw us, she might—I don't know."

Caleb keeps his hand on my back, watching me silently as I frantically pull up the text conversation with Sienna.

THEO: hey Sienna, we need to talk about tonight, but you just disappeared and I couldn't find you. can we talk?

I stare at the text conversation, waiting for any indication that she read it or that she was responding. I exhale a shaky breath and shut my eyes again, concentrating on Caleb's hand still pressed against my back.

"The rest of the gang should be heading this way soon," Caleb says, looking at his phone. "Are you okay if they join us?"

I wipe my eyes with my sleeves and nod my head. Miraculously, little Binx is still secured in my flannel shirt, although his head is no longer poking up under my chin. He's fallen to my stomach where my shirt is tucked in, giving me a weirdly shaped bulge in my shirt.

"Are you worried she's going to tell someone?" Caleb asks quietly.

I nod without looking at him. "She'll think she's doing the right thing," I croak.

Caleb's hand stills on my back for a moment, but then he goes back to rubbing. "Is there anything I can do?" he asks.

I finally look up at him. The sky has darkened now, and the only light is coming from the large overhead lights set up around the fairgrounds, but here, between the merchandise tables and the parking lot is a strange liminal space where not much light is focused. But even so, I can see the concern in Caleb's eyes as he waits for my response.

God, I'm so pathetic. He deserves better. Better than a boyfriend having a panic attack while chasing down an ex-girlfriend because she's about to spill their personal shit all over the church.

If I wasn't so afraid of everything, none of this would have happened. We could have made out at the top of the Ferris wheel like every other young couple in Specter without a care in the world. It wouldn't have mattered if Sienna saw us, so I wouldn't have tried to run after her. If I wasn't so afraid of everything, I wouldn't be having a fucking panic attack that Caleb feels like he has to help me through.

"Theo, please talk to me," Caleb says, taking my clenched fist into his hands. "Please. I want to help."

"You're already helping," I say, trying desperately not to cry again. "Thank you."

"Do you want to leave?" Caleb asks, gently rubbing my hand with his thumb.

I shrug. "Probably should."

At that moment, Harrison, Elise, and Oliver appear beside me. I don't want to look at them. I know they've seen me like this before, but it's just as embarrassing every time. I also suspect that Freddy, Wren, and Andrew aren't far behind as well, and I definitely don't want them to see me like this.

"Is he okay?" Harrison says, presumably asking Caleb.

"I think so," Caleb says, still rubbing my back and holding my hand.

"Was he able to catch up to Sienna?" Elise asks.

"We'll deal with that later," Harrison declares, an edge in his voice. "Let's get you home, Theo. Elise, can you follow behind us in Eileen?"

"Of course," Elise says immediately, approaching me with an outstretched hand.

"Let me text Nathaniel—he rode with me," I say, reaching into my pocket for my keys to hand off to Elise and pulling out my phone. Sienna still hasn't responded. I swallow hard. *Stay focused, Theo.* I shoot Nate a text and try to breathe again.

"Caleb, do you have a ride?" Oliver asks.

"I've got him," Wren's voice says from behind us.

"I'm sorry, I'm so sorry," I whisper to Caleb. It's really an apology to everyone because I ruined everyone's night, but I'll apologize to my friends in Harrison's car later.

"Stop apologizing," Caleb says, his hand on my back moving to my shoulder and giving it a light squeeze. "I just want you to be okay. We all do."

My phone buzzes, but before I panic too much, I notice it's just Nathaniel saying he'll meet us by the car.

"Come on, bro," Oliver says, standing above me and extending a hand out to lift me up. "Let's get out of here."

THIRTY
CALEB

It all happens so fast. I try to comfort Theo the best way I can, but now Oliver has his arm around him, taking him to the parking lot, and I just feel so helpless. There's nothing I can do to fix it, and knowing that only adds to the swelling pit in my stomach as I watch the boy I possibly love crumble from the weight of his guilt and fear.

I want to hurl, and for once at the Pumpkin Fair, it has nothing to do with the rides.

"What the hell happened?" Wren asks once Theo and the others are out of sight. Now that the sun has set, the crowds are only getting thicker around the booths as more of the town shows up for the nighttime festivities. "I only got bits and pieces from Oliver. He was talking a thousand miles an hour on the way over here."

"We were on the Ferris wheel," I explain, the last ten minutes playing through my head in sputtering flashes like an antique movie projector. "He kissed me. And then… well, we were kind of making out at one point, and he saw his ex, Sienna, in the crowd below, looking up at us. And it freaked him out. He tried to go after her, but then the crowds set off a panic attack. I didn't know what to do, Wren. I didn't know how to help or—or—" My words get swallowed up by sharp inhales, and my vision blurs with tears.

This is all my fault.

"Hey." Wren takes hold of both my hands, steering me down so we're at eye level. They speak slowly, "You did the right thing by getting help."

It doesn't matter if I did the right thing in the aftermath. It doesn't change the fact that I'm the root of the problem. If Theo wasn't kissing me, there wouldn't have been anything for Sienna to see. Now, who knows what's going to happen? What if she already told his parents? What if they kick him out of his house when he gets home? Or worse, they whisk him away, forbidding him to contact me or his friends?

I've ruined his life all because I wanted a boyfriend. How fucking selfish is that?

"Jesus, Caleb, who died?"

Freddy is standing next to Wren now, his expression somewhere between confusion and concern.

"Shut up, Freddy," Wren steps in. "Not the time."

He holds up his hands. "Okay, jeez. Sorry. Hey, where did everyone go? Oliver said he wanted to challenge Andrew to a corn dog eating contest, and I was going to watch, you know, for science."

"They had to leave," Wren says, releasing their grip on me and pulling Freddy to the side so they can whisper in his ear.

Without Wren's grip tethering me to reality, my mind drifts back to Theo and all the ways I've screwed up his life. How can I face him again, knowing what I did?

"Caleb Reynard, look at me right this second."

Freddy is standing in front of me, his signature smirk nowhere to be found. He claps both his hands down on my shoulders, squaring me up. "Listen to me. I know what you're thinking right now. Don't bother trying to say otherwise. You feel shitty, and I understand that. The situation sucks, and you're looking for something—someone—to take the blame. But what happened tonight is not your fault."

It's easy for him to say it. He hasn't ruined anyone's life today.

I try to look away, but Freddy shakes me till I lock eyes with him again. "I'm serious! Do not blame yourself."

Before I can think, I shove him in the chest, and he stumbles back into Wren, who catches him. "What else am I supposed to do? I'm the reason all of this is happening to him! None of this would matter if he were kissing a girl on that Ferris wheel."

Freddy detaches himself from Wren, closing the distance between us once more. "I'm not arguing that fact. But think about it, Caleb. This was going to happen to Theo whether it was with you or not. Someday, down the road, he would have found another guy that brought up these feelings, and it would be the same story."

Maybe he's right, but it doesn't help the gnawing ache in my stomach, or dry the tears that slip from the corners of my eyes, or stifle the sob that breaks through the lump in my throat.

"It's going to be okay," Freddy says, pulling me into a hug. I wrap my arms around him as another broken noise escapes my mouth. "No matter what happens, you're going to be okay."

Wren is beside us now, too, weaving their arms into the mix. "It might get ugly, but we're here for you, Caleb. And for Theo."

"Right," Freddy adds. "So, don't beat yourself up. Theo is going to need all the support you can give him if the shit hits the fan."

I cling to my friends, doing my best to let their words sink beneath my skin as I focus on breathing. The longer I mull it over, the more Freddy makes sense. It's naive of me to think of my presence in Theo's life as some supernatural force that altered who he is as a person. He's always been this way, even if I'm the first boy that's made him aware of it.

With my breath no longer coming in heaves and a relatively good handle on the crying situation, Wren and Freddy let go, but they don't go far.

"Are you ready for me to take you home?" Wren asks, brushing a curl off my forehead.

"We can stay as long as you want us to," Freddy adds.

"Yeah, but you should go back to Andrew," I say, wiping my face. "I don't want to ruin your date any more than we already did."

Freddy raises an eyebrow. "Are you sure? Andrew is very understanding, so he'd be fine."

I nod. "Positive. Tell him we're sorry for keeping you."

"Okay. But call me if you change your mind. I'll be over in a flash. Unless, of course, Andrew finally decides he's ready for me to worship at his altar, then maybe there'll be a delay." Freddy flashes a devilish grin, and I can't help but laugh, which does help loosen the knot in my stomach.

"Come on," Wren says, hooking an arm around my waist. "I'll blast some really loud music on the way home to help us erase that mental image."

"Good luck!" Freddy calls after us, heading in the opposite direction.

"Hey, do you have a minute?"

Lola spins her desk chair around, abandoning whatever project she's currently working on. She's dressed in her PJs even though it's only a little after eight.

"For you, always."

I step into her bedroom, shutting the door behind me because it's one of those rare nights when both Mom and Dad are home, and the documentary they're watching isn't particularly loud, so I don't want them to overhear.

Lola's room is far tidier than mine. We may look alike, but we're different in pretty much every way. Her walls, which were once covered in ribbons and awards from her time in high school, are filled with framed pictures of her friends and the trips they take over the summer. The soft blue of her bedspread matches the color of the ocean in the photos that hang above it, and they fill me with the sudden urge to run along the beach, letting the water wash over my feet.

"Everything okay? You're back kind of early from the Pumpkin Festival." Lola watches me from her chair, her arms folded across her chest.

The knot in my stomach tightens again. "Yeah, um, there was a complication."

Lola gives me an encouraging nod. "Keep talking."

"Theo and I were on the Ferris wheel, and when we got to the top, he kissed me, and someone saw us. Not just someone, his ex-girlfriend Sienna, who apparently everyone looks at like she's some kind of living saint."

Lola sucks in a breath.

"When we got back down on the ground, he tried to find her in the crowd, but she was gone. And everything happening all at once sent him into a panic attack, which freaked me out because I didn't know what to do."

Lola stands, coming over to wrap me in a hug. "Oh, Cal. That must have been terrifying for you."

"I'm fine," I say, even though my throat is tight and my stomach is in knots. "Theo's friends took him home, but now I don't know what's going to happen with Sienna and his family, and I'm scared they're going to keep him away from me."

Lola guides me over to the bed, both of us settling onto the edge. "Have you heard from him?"

I shake my head. "It's only been an hour or so. And he's got more important stuff going on than texting me."

Lola frowns. "And you're sure that she saw you two? I mean, the Ferris wheel is pretty tall, so there's no way she could have seen a little peck."

Heat builds in my cheeks. "Um, it was a bit more than a peck."

Lola knocks her shoulder into mine. "All right, little bro."

"Shut up. This is serious."

"You're right," Lola replies, straightening up. "Well, it seems like you two will just have to wait and see which way the wind's going to blow. I know Theo's not out or anything with his family, so do you think his ex is going to tell his parents?"

"I don't know. I've never even met her before, so I can only go off the way the others talk about her, and if that's the case, it doesn't look good."

I can't imagine a scenario where she doesn't tell them. If she truly believes what Theo and I are doing is wrong, then I wouldn't be surprised if she went straight to his house from the festival to out him.

And no matter what Freddy and Wren say, I can't help but feel like this is my fault.

Lola taps me on the forehead. "What's going on in there?"

"Huh?" I blink at her.

"You're stewing, little brother. I can see it on your face. Are you just worried about Theo, or is there something else going on?"

A wave of heat to my face and fresh tears well in my eyes.

"Did I ruin his life?"

Lola pulls me in again, wrapping her arms around me. "Oh honey, no. Of course not. This has nothing to do with you and everything to do with people's ass-backward way of thinking. You did nothing wrong."

I exhale a shuddered breath as the tears spill over onto Lola's shoulder. "Then why do I feel so shitty? Why can't I get that look of panic on Theo's face out of my mind? Why does this hurt so much, Lola?"

She pulls back, taking a second to wipe the streaks of tears from my face. "Do you love him?"

"What?"

"Do you love Theo?"

My teeth sink into my lower lip. Sure, I've thought about it, but I can't say whether or not it's true. I've never been in love before, so it's new territory for me.

"How would I know?"

Lola chuckles, brushing the hair off my forehead. "I think you've got your answer. It hurts because you love him. It hurts because you're seeing him confused and in pain, and you don't know how to fix it. Love is that connection that lets you feel what Theo feels, both the good and the bad, and share those experiences with him."

"Well, right now, it kind of sucks."

Lola laughs again. "I know, Cal. But at the end of the day, you've got to ask and be honest with yourself. Is this something you want? No relationship is perfect, but is this one worth going through what you're feeling right now?"

Is she saying what I think she's saying? How can she suggest I break things off with Theo? Just thinking about it makes the knot in my stomach clench so tight I can't breathe. Of course he's worth it. I would do almost anything to see him smile again, to erase this image of him in my head, terrified and in pain.

I love him. Every confused, funny, frustrating, tender-hearted piece of him.

"It is," I say with confidence.

Lola grins. "I was hoping you'd say that. You two are just too cute together."

I give her a shove, laughing. "Gross."

"Little Caleb is in love," Lola sings at me, poking at my ribs till I'm crying from laughter instead of heartache. "Welcome to the club, little brother. I hope you find less heartbreak than the rest of us."

I lean into her, resting my head against her shoulder.

"Thanks, me too."

Sunday, October 22

THEO: sorry, I meant to text you earlier, but it was a rough night.

CALEB: :(i'm so sorry, Theo. can I do anything for you? Are you at church right now?

THEO: no, i told my parents I still don't feel good from the panic attack. I must look pretty rough because they didn't even try to argue. So Grace is hanging out with me this morning.

    but i'd much rather be snuggled up on the couch with you. <3

CALEB: smooth. ;)

THEO: I try.

CALEB: :P have you heard anything from Sienna?
    nevermind, we don't have to talk about it.

THEO: not yet. Maybe i should have gone to church today so I could talk to her.

CALEB: playing hooky is much more fun.

THEO: it would be way more fun with you.

CALEB: careful what you wish for :)

THEO: what?
    ???
    Caleb?

I knock on Theo's front door, waving over my shoulder to Lola at the end of the driveway. She agreed the very second I asked her to drive me over this morning. We've already discussed that she'll be back before noon, just to make sure that Theo's parents won't make it home before she picks me up.

After a minute or so, it swings open, a girl with multicolored hair and a nose ring standing there with a raised eyebrow.

"Oh, hi. You're Grace."

The girl smirks, nodding. "And you've got some balls, kid. Does Theo know you're here?"

"No. I knew he'd tell me not to risk it if I told him."

"Smart move." She steps to the side, sweeping her arm to usher me inside. "Well, come on in, Caleb. He's upstairs, hiding under the covers. Do me a favor and try to cheer him up, okay? I've got to head to work this afternoon, and I don't want him left alone like this."

"I'll do my best," I say as she leads me to the bottom of the stairs. "Thank you. For looking after him, I mean. He told me it was a rough night."

Grace grunts, then rests her chin on the handrail, looking up at me. "Yeah, we stayed up pretty late talking things through. He's got it pretty bad for you, dude. Just a fair warning."

"Oh, um." I clear my throat, a subtle heat building in my cheeks. "I feel the same way about him, to be honest."

She studies me for a moment. Her features are eerily familiar to me, even though I've never actually seen her in person, and for a split second, it feels like Theo's eyes are staring at me. But then she blinks, and I exhale, and she says, "Okay, you pass the vibe check. Carry on, dude."

"Thanks," I say because nothing else really seems appropriate. At the top of the stairs, the hallway is dark, but I spot the door to Theo's room cracked open, a sliver of green light spilling out onto the floor. Muffled vocals drift from within, along with a percussive piano melody. The song sounds familiar—he's probably played it in the car for me before—but melancholy. I reach for the doorknob but hesitate, instead rapping my knuckle against the door.

"Grace, I already told you I'm not hungry."

I push the door open, letting the green light wash over me. "That's a first."

Theo bolts upright in his bed, his dark hair sticking out in a dozen different directions. "What—how did—why didn't you tell me you were coming over?"

I make my way over to the foot of his bed. "Because you would have told me not to risk it, but I would have done it anyway, so I just decided to cut out the middleman." Sinking a knee into the mattress, I lean forward to kiss him on top of his head. "But if you'd rather I leave, I'm sure I can tell Lola to turn around and come get me—"

Theo's arms wrap around me, pulling me into a bone-crushing embrace. He buries his face, saying something that gets muffled against my chest.

"What—hey! That tickles!"

He looks up, resting his chin against me. "I said there's no way I'm letting you go now."

I run my fingers through his tangled hair. "That's what I thought."

THIRTY-ONE
THEO

"I said there's no way I'm letting you go now."

"That's what I thought," Caleb says, running gentle fingers through my hair, sending electricity across my entire being. I feel like crying again, which I'm surprised is even possible, given how much I've cried over the past twelve hours. It's getting ridiculous.

But at least this type of crying is the good kind. The kind of crying that happens when you finally feel relieved. Loved. Safe.

Fuck, I'm so in love with him.

"So, how are you feeling?" Caleb asks. "You look a lot better than you did last night."

I scoff, loosening my grip so that Caleb can sit next to me if he wants. "I mean, you literally saw me at my worst yesterday. I can only hope I look better today."

Caleb sits on the bed with me—above the covers, always the gentleman—watching me with eyes full of concern and kindness. I can only imagine what he sees: my hair is definitely a disaster, my eyes probably have dark circles under them, and I have no idea what pajamas I ended up throwing on before collapsing in bed last night.

I suddenly realize that I haven't brushed my teeth since last night, and that absolutely won't do.

"Oh shit, let me, umm...I'll be right back," I mumble, awkwardly maneuvering the sheets off me and sliding out of the bed. Luckily, I had enough lucidity last night to at least put on some old gym shorts and a T-shirt without any holes. "Stay there. I'll be back."

"Okay," Caleb replies, a question in his voice.

When I return with fresh breath, a washed face, and calmer hair, Caleb has moved so that he's leaning against the headboard of my bed, still on top of the covers, but my nest of tangled sheets and blankets open for me beside him. The sight of him there—sitting like that in my bed, waiting for me to join him—immediately sends heat to my face and my stomach.

"You good?" Caleb asks with a crooked smile.

I take a deep breath, remembering why he's here in the first place and trying to get my thoughts together. The fact that I'm so flustered pulls that old familiar guilt straight to the surface, and I wince. *Wow, first you skip church, next you're going to start furiously making out with your boyfriend in bed and fantasizing about doing more? So much for being a good Christian.*

"Yeah, sorry, I just had to...freshen up a little," I finally answer Caleb and carefully crawl into the covers on the bed next to him.

Once I'm settled in, Caleb reaches for my hand and holds it in his. The sparks are still there. Even though it's been well over a month since the first time we held hands; even though Caleb has seen me at my absolute worst, despite the constant guilt I'm trying to ignore, and despite the possibility that this entire relationship might blow up in our faces any second—the sparks and flames I feel whenever Caleb and I touch are still there.

I lift his hand to my lips and press a soft kiss to it. "Thank you."

"For what?"

"For being there for me last night. For helping me through it, for pulling me out of the crowd, for giving me space when I needed it but holding me when I was ready." I stare into his eyes, making sure I convey how serious I am. "I can't imagine it was easy, but…you have no idea how much it means to me that you were there and that you're still here."

Caleb turns to face me, gazing back with intensity. "Of course I'm still here, Theo. I care about you. A lot. I'll always be here for you."

I can't stand the distance anymore. I lean in and press my lips to his, and everything else melts away. Like yesterday, it starts as a gentle kiss, an outward expression of my overwhelming love and adoration for him, but that same switch flips in my brain, and the kiss becomes something more. And I want more. And I need more. And so I reach for more, pull him closer, and—

Caleb pulls away. Not aggressively, but it stings just the same.

My eyes fly open. "I'm sorry, was that too much?"

Caleb presses his forehead to mine. "No, it's not—I'm just trying—" He sighs. "Last night was a lot for you. I don't…want to take advantage of that."

I exhale a laugh and close my eyes again. There are so many things I want to say, both seriously and jokingly, but they all fall flat. In the end, I know he's right. My emotions are still running wild, hormones all out of whack.

I really don't deserve him.

When I finally catch my breath, I lean back against the headboard again. "I'm a mess," I mutter. "You must really like me to stick around."

Caleb smiles and leans back with me. "You're worth it."

I lean my head on his shoulder for a few minutes, letting myself just be in this moment.

I almost tell him I love him three times before Caleb speaks up. "You also have some really great friends, Theo. Like, they were there so fast, mobilizing and moving as if it was something they'd rehearsed. Like, I knew Harrison was a ride-or-die kind of friend, but damn."

I chuckle. "Yeah. They've had practice." Caleb starts to look upset, but I shake my head. "I mean, we're all a little messed up. I think that's why we're good for each other. Oliver has had a couple of panic attacks in the last year, and Elise had one a few months ago. This is probably my third in like…two years? I don't know. We all just kind of know what to look for, and we've learned how to respond."

Caleb looks relieved. "That's good. It's good to know that even if we don't end up—or we can't—be together, you still have them."

My chest tightens, and I find myself scooting impossibly closer to Caleb, clinging to him. "Don't say that. We're going to be okay. We—we have to be." I should be embarrassed by my sudden neediness, but I don't care.

Caleb nods, strokes my hair again, and kisses my temple. He doesn't say anything, which causes the anxiety in my stomach to swell, but I try to ignore it. I can't think about the fact that Caleb knows just as well as I do that everything is about to come crashing down around us, and there's nothing either of us can do about it.

Fuck it. If this is the last time I can spend time in Caleb's arms, we might as well enjoy it the best we can.

"Hey," I say with a smirk, waiting for him to look at me before continuing. "Wanna smash?"

Caleb's body stills beneath me for just a second before he remembers, then he laughs and gives me a small shove. "Always."

Lola comes to pick Caleb up at noon, just in case my parents decide to come home right away to check on me. It's a smart move because I hear the garage door open and my parents' car pull in at 12:17 p.m.

As I head downstairs to eat lunch with my family, my phone buzzes. Expecting a text from Caleb or someone from the crew, I casually pull out my phone from my pocket but then freeze halfway down the stairs. I have to grip the handrail and ease myself down to sit on the middle stair to make sure I don't fall.

THEO [7:18 PM]: hey Sienna, we need to talk about tonight, but you just disappeared and I couldn't find you. can we talk?

[9:02 PM]: Sienna seriously we need to talk. please call me or text me?

[8:42 AM]: I'm not gonna be at church this morning - had another panic attack yesterday so I'm not feeling good so when you get a minute, I really want to talk to you.

[9:06 AM]: please don't talk to anyone about what you saw on the ferris wheel until we talk first.

SIENNA [12:29 PM]: I'm sorry for the delayed response, Theo - I needed to pray on it. I love you so much, and I'm worried about you. Please don't hate me.

"*Please don't hate me.*"

Oh my God.

She told them.

"What are you doing?" Nathaniel asks from behind me.

I look up to see that he's trying to get down the stairs, looking completely like his normal self, only frustrated that I'm in the way. If Nathaniel knew something, I would be able to see it on his face. He'd warn me of what was coming. It's an unspoken Briggs sibling agreement: We look out for each other.

Maybe my parents didn't talk about it in the car on the way home. Maybe Sienna didn't tell them after all. Maybe she told someone else. Chase, maybe? Brandon?

"You okay, man?" Nathaniel asks again, quieter this time. "Is this another panic attack?"

I shake my head, pulling myself up as casually as possible. "No, sorry, just...got a weird text." Which isn't a lie. It is a weird text. Cryptic. Ominous. Terrifying.

Nathaniel eyes me suspiciously, then continues past me into the kitchen. I brace myself, putting on a brave face as I follow behind him to join my parents and Grace already seated at the table.

Grace. Grace is still here. I'm suddenly overcome with relief. No matter what, Grace is here, and she'll have my back for this.

Everything's going to be okay.

"Hi, sweetie," Mom says as I enter the kitchen. "How are you feeling?"

"I'm fine," I reply. "Better."

She steps closer and runs her fingers through my hair. I can only hope there's no remnant of Caleb on me. Shit. She has such a sharp eye. I forgot to check my shirt for any loose copper hair.

"Did you get some sleep?" she asks, touching my forehead, even though I never claimed to have a fever.

I nod, smiling at her as genuinely as possible. "It was just a panic attack, Mom. I just underestimated how big the crowds would get at the fair. I'm good now."

"We talked to Sienna today," Dad says out of nowhere. His voice almost startles me because I forgot he was even in the room. I turn to look at him. He looks…off. A fresh wave of nausea washes over me.

"Oh yeah?" I say, my voice cracking slightly.

Dad's eyes meet mine. There's something in his expression that scares me, but I can't let him know that. "Yeah, she said she saw you at the Pumpkin Fair last night."

Grace and I make eye contact. She knows the whole story, so I imagine alarm bells are ringing in her head, too.

I look back at Dad. "Yeah, I saw her from a distance, but she didn't stick around to talk."

"Hm," is all Dad says in response before returning to his burger. I glance at my fast-food bag at my seat and realize I've never been less hungry in my life.

I look back at Grace, who subtly shrugs and sips her soda.

A false alarm, maybe?

"Are you going to sit and eat, hon'?" Mom asks, watching me with a raised eyebrow.

I quickly nod and sit down. "Oh, yeah," I laugh, but it comes out nervously. "Sorry. Still tired."

As I sit, Grace stands up, gathering the remnants of her lunch and throwing it away. "Thanks again for lunch. Unfortunately, I've got to get to work," she says, looking directly at me.

My stomach drops, and my blood turns to ice. *No, no, no, no—*

"Have a good day, sweetheart," Mom says, her voice far too flat.

"I'll try," Grace replies, still watching me but with an apology in her eyes. "Don't do anything crazy while I'm gone."

Don't leave me alone with them, please, please, please—

"Drive safe, Grace," Dad calls out as Grace heads to the front door.

"Love you, bye!"

"Love you, bye," everyone at the table says in unison.

The front door closes, and I feel like I might throw up.

The table is silent for at least a minute as I slowly pull my carton of fries and foil-wrapped burger out of the fast-food bag. It's not really warm anymore, and the fries feel more like Styrofoam, but I eat them anyway. If I can make it through this lunch, everything will be fine.

At some point, Nathaniel breaks the silence by standing up. "Thanks for lunch," he mumbles. "I'll be in my room."

"Okay, hon'," Mom says with a smile. Is it just me, or is her smile forced? *Breathe, Theo, breathe.* Nothing is happening.

I return to picking at my Styrofoam fries, very intentionally controlling my breathing and any facial expressions that might betray how I'm actually feeling. Surely, the Sienna thing was a false alarm. If something was up, my parents wouldn't wait this long to—

"Theo, your mother and I need to talk to you," Dad says abruptly, his voice terse. Strained. Frustrated.

Shit.

"About what?" I ask, refusing to look up at him. I stare intensely at a fry on my plate and focus on my breathing again.

Mom moves to sit beside me, leaning in. I know I shouldn't, but I look up at both of them and regret it immediately. Dad's expression is stern and serious. Mom's face is…*shit.* Mom's face is sad. Worried. Anxious.

"Sienna told us what she saw you doing, Theo," Dad states very calmly. "I didn't get the impression she was lying, and I can't think of a reason why she'd lie about something like this, but we want to hear your side of the story and go from there. Okay?"

I swallow, still trying to breathe. "Okay."

"She said you were with one of those new friends you've brought over a few times. Caleb, wasn't it, Kora?"

Mom nods.

"She saw you two riding the Ferris wheel together, and from where she was standing, it looked to her like—" he hesitates, his voice halting abruptly as if he can't even say it. As if the very idea of what we were doing is so repulsive that he can't even speak of it.

The agonizing silence feels like it goes on forever, but Mom eventually chimes in. "Kissing. Sienna said that she saw you and Caleb…kissing."

I look up at Dad and notice his jaw clenching. Mom puts a comforting hand on his forearm, and it makes me feel sick.

"Well?" Dad asks. "Is that true?"

I stare at him, my heart hammering violently in my chest. I want to bolt. I want to scream. I want to cry. But I'm paralyzed. I can't move. I can't speak. I just stare.

"Theodore, I asked you a question," Dad says, the volume of his voice rising just slightly.

"Michael—"

"Yes," I finally croak.

Dad's eyes widen, and Mom's mouth hangs open. They're both silent for a moment, so I say it again.

"Yes, that is what Sienna saw."

Dad finally snaps out of his shock to give me a very disdained look. "Okay, so it sounds like we need to have a talk then, don't we?"

"About what?" I ask, a little more aggressively than I probably should, but this is all uncharted territory, and I have no idea how to traverse it.

My dad barks a nervous laugh, but then the room goes silent. No one moves or makes a single sound. I don't dare even breathe.

"Theo, I'm being serious," Dad says. "We raised you better than that."

I feel my blood begin to boil. "Better than what, Dad?"

"Better than to go around Specter kissing *boys*, that's what."

I clench my fists, tears pricking at the backs of my eyes. "That's not—that's not even remotely what I'm doing, Dad!"

"Then explain to me exactly what you're doing, then. I'm listening."

I open my mouth but close it again. *Breathe, breathe, breathe.* Mom tries to put a comforting hand on my shoulder, but I flinch away. She winces at that, but I press on.

"Caleb is my boyfriend," I declare. "He's the only boy I've ever kissed and the only boy I plan on kissing."

Dad is glaring at me now. "Theo, what are you talking about? You can't have—are you joking right now?"

"Why would I joke about this?"

"Then why—why are you saying that Caleb is your—" he stops again, unable to say it, and I feel myself being consumed with fury.

"*Boyfriend,* Dad," I say through clenched teeth. "Boyfriend."

Dad's face twitches as he chokes out another humorless laugh. I stand to my feet, but Mom reaches for my arm. "Theo, please—"

"Caleb is my boyfriend. It's not a joke," I say furiously.

"How long has this been going on?" Dad demands.

I shrug. "A few weeks," I answer flatly, trying to control my breathing again.

Dad finds a place on the table to stare at, refusing to look at me.

Mom speaks up instead. "Honey, you have to understand that this is...a bit shocking for us," she says gently. "You know how we feel as a family about this. And where the church stands on—" she clears her throat. "—this kind of thing."

I shake my head furiously. "Honestly, 'this kind of thing' shouldn't really matter all that much in the grand scheme of things, and I think the church needs to get over it."

"Excuse me?" Dad says, his eyes locking on me again.

"I've been talking to Grace, and there are apparently a lot of things that were mistranslated and stuff in the Bible about—"

"Theo, you can't just take everything Grace says at face value," Dad interrupts. "She's going to a very liberal school that is intentionally trying to deconstruct her faith. That's just what happens when you go to a secular college."

Now, it's my turn to laugh angrily. "Oh, so anything Grace says is dumb because she learned it at a secular school? Dad, she's actually studying things. Researching, using legitimate sources to learn things about the world." God, I wish Grace were here right now. She'd know what to say. Not that it would matter.

"Are you saying the Bible isn't a legitimate source?" Dad asks, a challenging tone in his voice.

I take the bait. "Maybe not as legitimate as you think it is."

Mom gasps. Dad's face is turning red. I'm still standing in front of my chair, and I've never felt a stronger urge to bolt out the door as I do right now, but I'm frozen in place.

"Go to your room," Dad says quietly. "We'll continue this discussion later."

I don't second guess or question it. Without a word, I make my way to the stairs.

"Leave your phone."

I freeze. "What?"

"Leave your phone on the table," Dad says flatly. "You'll get it back later tonight."

I pull my phone out of my pocket and stare at it in my hands. Oh, God. Can they unlock it? Are they going to read all my texts? Are they going to see my Twitter? TikToks? Look through all my pictures?

There's nothing I can do now, so I put it on the table, turn, and leave the kitchen, heading upstairs. As soon as I close the door behind me, I collapse on the bed and cry myself to sleep for the second time today.

Knock, knock. "Theo?"

I'm pulled from a restless sleep by the soft, sad voice of my mother on the other side of my bedroom door. I don't answer. Instead, I close my eyes and refocus on my four-hundredth replay of "Two Weeks" by Grizzly Bear.

"Can I come in, *aroha*?"

Shit, I can't believe she's using *aroha* against me. "Yeah," I croak. "Sure."

The door creaks open, and I reach over to the stereo to reluctantly turn down my favorite song. Mom cautiously sits at the end of my bed and is quiet for what feels like an eternity but is likely only a few minutes.

"Where's Dad?" I finally ask flatly, surprised he hasn't also come upstairs for the inevitable lecture I'm due to receive.

Mom doesn't look at me. She's surveying my music wall where I have framed posters of all my favorite artists. It's one of the things I'm most proud of in my room, and Mom should be familiar with it since she and Grace helped me hang everything up there last summer. But here she is, studying every single poster as if it's the first time she's ever really seen them. Part of me wonders if she's looking for some secret message about my sexuality in my music choices.

Finally, she looks back at me and smiles weakly. "He went to the park. He said he needed a run to sort his thoughts."

I nod. Of course. I guess I should be grateful for more time. And grateful that he's at least thinking it over and letting his emotions settle before he takes everything away from me.

"Theo," Mom says, staring at me. "I really want to talk, just you and me for now. Is that okay?"

I shrug. It's not like I have a choice.

"I just feel like…this really came out of nowhere, and I just want to understand how this happened." She pauses, then continues. "Because here I thought I was your mother, and I should have seen the signs or at least had an inkling of a hint that my own son was gay before—"

"Bi."

She frowns, blinking a few times. "What?"

I'm genuinely surprised at myself for interrupting her for semantics, but now that I have, I continue. "I'm not gay, Mom. I'm bisexual."

She considers this for a moment, a flicker of hope crossing her face. "So, you still like girls?"

I chew on my bottom lip, determined to handle this patiently, even though she's definitely already drawing the wrong conclusion. "I am attracted to girls sometimes, yes. I was attracted to Sienna when I was with her. But right now, I like Caleb."

Mom is silent for another few seconds as she processes this information. I focus on appreciating that it's just me and her. Mom actually listens to me most of the time. She genuinely wants to understand where people are coming from. Dad doesn't always have the patience to listen. If something goes against his belief system, he tends to dismiss it immediately.

"I know you said you'd been with Caleb for a few weeks, but—" she hesitates for a moment but presses on. "How long have you been…bisexual? When did you—when did you decide that?"

A nervous laugh escapes out of me. "I didn't *decide* to be bisexual, Mom," I say with a shrug. "I just am. You know me. I would never choose to be something that broke any rules."

"Then, why?" she asks suddenly, almost desperately.

My mouth hangs open as I continue shaking my head. "Why? Wh-What do you mean 'why'? Why are you attracted to men, Mom? Why were you attracted to Dad and not some girl?" I run a hand through my hair, frustrated that I have to explain this to someone else when I barely understand it myself. "I don't know why. I didn't have a choice, I didn't want this, it just…is."

Mom's quiet again, absorbing it. When she doesn't say anything, I keep talking.

"I think I've been bisexual all along. There just wasn't a boy I really liked until Caleb. But now, looking back, a lot of things make sense, you know? Like, remember when I got really obsessed with Sufjan Stevens a few years ago, and I couldn't stop watching his live performances on YouTube? I thought it was just because of his music, but—" I stop myself and shake my head again. "N-Nevermind, that's probably TMI. The point is, I've been bi all along, but something about being around Caleb made me…realize it, I guess."

"So," Mom starts softly. "You didn't know you liked boys until you started hanging out with Caleb?"

I inhale sharply, anger rising in my chest. I know exactly where this is going. "Mom, he didn't peer pressure me into liking boys. It's not like that. I just—he just makes me really happy. Happier than anyone."

We sit in silence for several minutes. I have a feeling this isn't going well, and I'm terrified that Mom is going to come out of this conversation, blaming Caleb for turning me gay and never letting me see him again. I try desperately to think of something more to say to convince her, but I keep coming up empty. All I want to do is bury my face back into my pillow and scream.

"Theo, I'm trying to understand this from your perspective because I love you, and I need to understand how we got here. I can only pray that you know that," Mom says, the softness in her voice starting to falter. "But you also need to understand that this isn't—this isn't *right* in the eyes of God, nor is it right in the eyes of the church, and as your parents, your father and I can't just stand by and watch you go down a path that leads you away from God's Will for your life."

"Mom, I'm not doing anything—"

"We only want what's best for you. You're young, and you may feel this way now, but remember that Scripture tells us that the heart is deceitful above all things."

I feel sick. "Mom—"

"Your father knows more specific verses about homosexuality and how God feels about two men having…*relations*—"

"*Mom*, we're not having—"

"Even if you're not now, you'll want to later if you continue down this path, and that's—"

"I love him."

Mom's mouth hangs open, and she goes silent mid-sentence. I'm shocked that I said it, too, but now that I have, I can't turn back.

"Mom, I'm in love with Caleb. I love him more than I've ever loved anyone, and you and Dad and the church might think that's wrong, but I don't think God does. Why would He make me like this if being myself is wrong? Why would He allow me to fall in love with Caleb if it's a sin?" When Mom doesn't interrupt me, I keep going. "Caleb makes me feel like I can do anything. He—he believes in me, and he encourages me and supports me, and he makes me feel brave. He cares about me, and he understands me, and I care about and understand him. Being with him doesn't make me feel dirty or wrong. I've only been keeping our relationship a secret because I'm afraid of losing him. I'm only afraid of people seeing us together because I'm afraid you'll take him away from me, and I can't—" my voice breaks, a sob threatening to claw its way out of my throat. "I love him, and I don't want to lose him. Please don't take him from me."

Mom has tears in her eyes now, but she doesn't say a word. Tears are streaming down my face, but I can't think of anything else to say. Because I know deep down that none of this matters. Me loving Caleb isn't going to change her mind. Her mind's made up. Not being straight is not okay. It never will be.

"I…Theo—"

"Please," I sob. "Just…please think about it?"

Mom stands up and walks to the door. "We'll talk again when your father gets home." And with that, she leaves the room and closes the door behind her.

THIRTY-TWO
CALEB

Monday, October 23

I haven't heard from Theo since I left his house yesterday. All of my messages have gone unread, and when my phone finally did buzz, it was Harrison letting me know that my worst fears had come true.

Theo is on lockdown.

I'm honestly a little impressed that his parents thought of everything when it came to cutting off my connection to him. I mean, I've tried everything from email to TikTok messenger, even the word puzzle game that we like to play when we're procrastinating homework. I try to spell out a message to him, but it goes unanswered.

By the time I get to school, I practically sprint through the halls to his locker. He's not there, of course, but I'll just wait here till he shows.

But he's still not here when the first chime rings and that just ratchets up the anxiety in my stomach till it feels like there's an entire beehive buzzing around. I hustle over to my first class, checking my phone one more time before taking my seat. Freddy catches my eye from the other side of the room, giving me a quizzical look, but I wave him off. I don't know enough about what's happening to try and explain it right now. I need to talk to Theo. To make sure he's okay. To make sure he's safe and not being carted off to some conversion camp where they electrocute his brain till they're convinced he's straight.

Isn't that what they do at those places? I've honestly never looked it up.

Class begins, and I have to at least pretend like I'm not freaking out, but I quickly begin to unravel by the time lunch rolls around.

"What is going on?" Freddy asks. He and Wren are already at the lunch table when I join them.

I scan the dining room, searching for one of Theo's band T-shirts for a glimpse of his dark hair. He's got to be here. He's got to be safe. I can't think about the alternatives.

"Caleb."

A tater tot bounces off my chest, falling onto my tray. Freddy and Wren are both staring at me now.

I set my tray down, taking a seat across from them. "Theo isn't answering me, and Harrison messaged me last night saying that his parents had locked his phone. Which means they definitely know about us, and now I can't stop thinking about all the terrible things that could be happening to him because of me—"

I exhale, forcing myself to hold for a few seconds before I take another breath.

"Have either of you seen him today?"

"He wasn't in first period geometry," Wren answers. "He missed the test and everything."

"I don't have a class with him till the afternoon," Freddy says. "Have you talked to Harrison or the others about it?"

Before I can answer, I spot Harrison across the cafeteria, his sights trained on me. I give him a wave, and he hurries over, Elise just a few steps behind him.

"Hey guys," he says, sliding onto the bench beside me. "Caleb, I—"

"Where's Theo?" I interrupt, not able to contain myself. "Is he here? Did you talk to him? Have his parents shipped him off halfway across the country? Are they shocking his brain—"

"Breathe, Caleb." Wren's hand reaches across the table, wrapping around mine. "Let him finish."

"Sorry," I say through an exhale.

Harrison gives me a pitying look. "He's here. He came in halfway through second period. He's making up his Geometry test right now. But he asked that I tell you he's okay, and he'll see you in English Lit. I'm one of the only people his parents are letting him talk to right now."

Okay. He's here. He still wants to see me. That's a good sign. Surely, things aren't as bad as I've drummed them up to be in my head.

"Thank you," I say, giving Harrison a nod. "Is he… is he really okay?"

Harrison's gaze drops down to the table. Elise puts a hand on his shoulder, leaning over to answer, "I don't think so. His parents—well, mostly his dad—aren't exactly the most open people when it comes to change. We're hoping things turn out for the best, but you should prepare yourself for a bumpy ride. And maybe try not to worry too much. We're here for Theo. For you both. If I have to fight Theo's dad myself, you'd better believe I'll throw hands."

"He's also got Grace, who will defend him tooth and nail," Harrison adds, looking up from the table. "She's not going to tolerate any radical bullshit from their parents."

Right. He's got a support system in place. Everything doesn't rest squarely on my shoulders. That's a comfort.

"Where's Oliver?" Wren asks during the lull in Theo-related conversation.

Elise rolls her eyes. "Standing outside Mr. Brenner's classroom, waiting for Theo to finish his test. I keep telling him to give Theo space to breathe, but he refuses to leave his side."

"Aww," Freddy coos, unwrapping his sandwich. "That's really sweet, actually."

Elise shakes her head. "It's something, alright."

The rest of lunch carries on without much talking on my end. Elise and

Freddy somehow get caught up in an argument I only hear half of, but it has something to do with who is the gayest member of the X-Men.

When the chime sounds for the next period, I bolt from the table, tossing my untouched lunch into the trash on my way out the door.

I'm the first student in the classroom, huffing and puffing from sprinting all the way here from the cafeteria. Mrs. Hyung looks up from her desk, puzzled, then goes back to her Sudoku. I set my backpack down at my desk, then step out into the hallway and lean against the wall, waiting. It's five minutes till class is supposed to start, but I'll be damned if I'm going to miss out on a single second of time with Theo.

I spot Oliver first—he's easier to find in a crowd—coming around the corner. He scans the hallway like he's a drug-sniffing dog, ready to bust the closest offender. Then he sees me, and he stops, turning to the side. The milling crowd of students parts, and my chest squeezes as I finally catch a glimpse of Theo.

In the few agonizing seconds it takes to close the distance between us, a thousand thoughts run through my mind. But when I'm standing in front of him, taking in his crooked smile, they all fade away, and all I can do is wrap my arms around him, holding him tighter than I've ever held anyone before.

Theo lets out a sigh as he tucks his head against my chest, his body melding into mine.

And for a blissful second, I'm so happy to be here, holding on to the boy I love.

Then I remember where we are.

"Shit," I whisper, slacking my hold on him. "Sorry."

But Theo clings to me, refusing to let go. "No, it's okay. Just a little bit longer."

I happily comply, resting my chin on top of his head and closing my eyes. Who cares if people see us now? The fallout has already happened. The only benefit is maybe we don't have to be so guarded anymore.

"What are you looking at? Have you never seen people hug before?"

Theo lifts his head off my chest, turning to Oliver. "Calm down, man. It's okay."

Oliver nods, folding his arms. "Yeah, sorry. That one got away from me. Are you good?"

"I'm good," Theo replies, pulling away from me but taking my hand in his.

Oliver looks at me. "I'll leave him in your capable hands. Theo, I'll see you after class."

"What's all that about?" I ask as Oliver strides away from us.

"He's just being overprotective," Theo says, lifting his free hand to stifle a yawn. "It freaked him out when I stopped replying to his messages yesterday."

"I know the feeling."

Theo glances up at me, and for the first time, I get a good look at him. Dark circles under bloodshot eyes—the poor thing needs a nap in the worst way.

"I'm sorry," he says, looking down at his shoes.

"No, don't be. I didn't mean it like that."

He nods slowly. "It's bad, Caleb. Like, really bad. My dad won't even look at me. We got into a shouting match last night, and he just—he won't listen. Then Grace came home in the middle of it, and that only made things worse."

I don't know what to say, so I just hug him again, hoping it at least gives him a little comfort.

"They don't want me to see you," Theo continues. "But they can't keep me from school, so I'm under strict orders to come home right after, and I'm not allowed to go anywhere else, but Cathy's for my shifts and church."

"But we can still see each other here," I say, trying to focus on the positives. "So that's something. And maybe, with a little time, they'll come around."

Theo barks a broken laugh. "Yeah, maybe."

The hallways are almost empty now as the next chime sounds, signaling the start of the period.

"We should get in there," Theo says, sniffling as he rubs the end of his nose.

"I think my dad will have an aneurysm if he has to deal with my sexuality *and* being tardy twice in one day."

I squeeze his hand.

"We're going to get through this," I say as we walk towards Mrs. Hyung's room. "I know everything sucks right now, but it's going to get better."

Theo pauses at the door, turning back to me with a timid smile. "I hope so."

The school day comes to an end, and I make a mad dash for the parking lot. Freddy catches me in the hallways, but I just spout something closely resembling an explanation on my way to find Eileen.

Theo's car is near the back of the lot—as he was probably one of the last people here this morning—and he's waiting inside, music drifting from the cracked windows. I swing around to the other side, open the passenger door, and climb in. Theo jolts, sitting up straight in his seat with half-lidded eyes.

"Oh shit, did I wake you up?"

" 'Isfine," he slurs, rubbing his eyes. "I must have nodded off."

"How long have you been out here? I thought for sure I was going to beat you."

"Mr. Laugherty let us go ten minutes early."

"Did he have to make another court appearance?"

"That's the rumor. To be honest, I was only half listening."

We both laugh, and for a moment in time, nothing outside this car matters. There's only me and Theo, and I couldn't be happier.

But then reality seeps in along with a breeze, and I figure I've put it off long enough.

I reach over, taking his hand in mine. "I know we don't have a lot of time, but do you want to talk about last night?"

Theo sighs, reaching over to adjust the volume on the stereo. "There's not really much to say. Sienna told my parents, and they freaked out. I'm grounded for the rest of my life, and who knows what else they'll do? I'm stuck, and I don't know how to fix it."

"Do you—" I stop myself, shoving the question back down. It's a selfish thing to ask, especially when he's so miserable.

"What?" he asks, his dark eyes pleading.

"It's nothing," I say, shaking my head. "I'm sorry, I wasn't thinking."

Theo shifts in his seat, turning his body towards me. "Tell me."

I sink my teeth into my bottom lip. I can't deny that I've been wanting to ask this question, but now I can't stop thinking about how it might make Theo feel worse. And that's the last thing I want to happen. But he's asking me, and I'm incapable of telling him no.

"Do you regret it? Being with me, I mean. Do you regret starting this relationship?"

Theo doesn't answer right away, leaning back against the door. My heart hammers against my chest like a rabid animal trying to thrash its way out of a cage.

"You don't have to answer," I say quickly, trying to backpedal. "It was a stupid question—"

"No, it's not. I'm just—I'm having trouble getting the words right. Give me a second?"

I nod, too scared to say anything else, or I might dig myself a deeper hole.

Theo exhales after a moment, his eyes finding me again. "The short answer is no. The longer answer is a bit more complicated. But what I want to make sure I get right is I am so glad to have you in my life, Caleb. When I think about how we spent our entire lives in this town, going to the same schools, I can't help but wonder what would have happened if I'd met you earlier. Would it have been such a shock if you showed up when I was ten, and this connection of ours could have happened gradually instead of all at once?

"But I can't answer those questions. I can't go back in time or play this forever game of 'what if?' All I can do is tell you how I feel right now. There was this moment last night when my parents were arguing when I truly thought I would never see you again. Looking back, it sounds silly, but at the moment, I was petrified."

I tighten my grip on his hand.

"It wasn't my parents yelling, or getting kicked out of my house, or being shunned by the church—none of those possibilities scared me more than waking up every day and knowing that I wouldn't get to hold your hand."

"Theo…."

"I love you, Caleb. And I know it sounds stupid, saying it out loud, but I think that's how I know things will be okay, no matter how they turn out with my parents. This—" he holds our hands up between us, "—feels more real to me than anything else. So even if people tell me that it's wrong, or if my dad tries to argue theological semantics, they can't take away the honesty of how I feel about you."

"It's not stupid," I say, my voice cracking. "I feel the same way about you, too."

Theo lets out a shuddered laugh. "That's a relief. It would be really awkward if you said you just wanted to be friends."

I pull him forward over the armrest, planting a kiss on his forehead. "Not a chance."

He laughs again, this time wholeheartedly, but it gets cut short with a yawn. "Sorry, I'm running on half an hour of sleep and a prayer."

"What time do your parents expect you home?" I ask, checking my phone.

He rubs his eye. "I told them I was working on a project with Harrison, so I've got maybe another hour before they'll start getting suspicious."

"Then you need a nap. Come on." I let go of his hand, climbing into Eileen's back row and throwing one leg up on the seat. I pat the open space, beckoning for Theo to join me.

"God, I love you so freaking much." Theo adjusts the volume dial again, then joins me in the back, nestling himself up against me and leaning his head on my chest.

"Sweet dreams," I whisper, brushing a stray strand of hair from his face.

Not a minute later, he's snoring.

THIRTY-THREE
THEO

Waking up next to Caleb feels like nothing short of a dream.

Unfortunately, the dreamy feeling doesn't last long, having to rush home quickly before my parents start wondering what I'm up to.

Thank God for Harrison covering for me. Thank God for Caleb insisting I nap with him instead of trying to talk more or even make out—which, quite frankly, I would have preferred over the nap, but I was so freaking exhausted I don't think it would have been very romantic. Thank God for Eileen giving Caleb and me a place to be alone without fear.

I haven't really felt like thanking God for much else lately, but I'll thank Him for those things, at least.

When I get home, only Dad and Nathaniel are home, and I say nothing to either of them. I go directly to my room, and I don't come out until dinner.

Mom tries desperately to pretend that everything is fine as we eat together at the table, but I don't have the energy to placate her. Nor do I have the energy to fight. I just sit and eat my roast chicken in silence, avoiding eye contact with everyone. So does Dad.

Dad doesn't look at me. He hasn't looked at me since Sunday.

It hurts, but not any more than anything else does.

After dinner, I perform my required chores. Load the dishwasher. Take out the trash. Put away the leftovers. Then I go back to my room.

I can stomach a routine as long as I don't have to interact with Dad.

At some point, while I'm working on homework before bed, there's a knock at my door.

"Theo?" Nathaniel's gravelly voice comes from the other side of the door.

"Yeah, come in."

Nathaniel quietly enters, shutting the door behind him. He's not carrying his Switch, which is surprising. "Hey."

"Hey."

He watches me for a moment before he speaks. "Are you okay?"

I snort, looking back down at my Chromebook. "Really?"

"Yeah, it was a dumb question," Nathaniel says, sighing as he sits on the edge of my bed. "I'm…I'm really sorry."

I shrug. "I knew it was only a matter of time."

Nate is quiet for a while, and I almost ask him what he wants, but he speaks first. "I think it's bullshit."

His swearing startles me a bit. I'm so accustomed to filtering, feeling guilty about, and second-guessing everything that comes out of my mouth that I even get second-hand anxiety on my brother's behalf, worried someone might have heard him. That's how deep this bullshit goes, I suppose. I smirk. "Yeah. It really is, isn't it?"

"Is Grace really going to get proof from her school about homosexuality and the Bible?" Nathaniel asks. "Like to show Dad that it's actually okay to be gay?"

I have to look away. Nate looks so…hopeful. Like he believes it's actually possible that something Grace brings home from Emory University is going to change Dad's mind about anything Biblical. It stings. "I don't know, Nate," I answer honestly. "I don't doubt she'll build a case. She will. But I just doubt it'll change anything."

Nathaniel considers this for a moment. "It might. It might at least convince Mom, maybe?"

"If it doesn't convince Dad, it doesn't matter. Mom believes whatever he tells her to believe." I frown, then look back at Nate. "Which is also bullshit, by the way. Mom should be able to think for herself."

"Yeah," Nathaniel mutters. "I know."

The two of us sit in silence for a few minutes, and I try to focus on my homework again. There's nothing more to say, and thinking about it just makes me feel worse.

"I'll let you get back to what you're doing," Nate says eventually, standing up from my bed and making his way toward the door. "But I wanted you to know that I think Dad's wrong. There's nothing... *wrong* with you. For liking boys."

I sigh. The inclination to cry is there. The desire to feel warm and fuzzy about my younger brother accepting me for who I am is definitely in there somewhere. Unfortunately, it's too far beneath the heavy weight of apathy to make its way to the surface. "Thanks, Nate," I say as earnestly as I can. "It means a lot."

And with that, Nathaniel leaves the room.

About an hour later, as I'm about to climb into bed, my phone buzzes to indicate a text message. I shouldn't get a jolt of hope that it's Caleb because of course it isn't, but it happens anyway. Fortunately, though, it's Grace, so I open the message.

>   GRACE: how are you holding up, champ?
>   got a minute to talk?

>   THEO: I was just about to go to bed actually. I'm really tired.

>   GRACE: that's fair, no worries. I just wanted to let you know I've been

> thinking about you all day and I'm hard at work putting something academic together to show Dad this weekend. I know it might not go very far with him but I'm determined to try. I've got a few other friends, classmates and even one of my TAs helping out too. we're all victims of religious trauma in some form or other so your situation has inspired some serious academic mobilization.
>
> me and my squad of sociology/anthropology/religious studies nerds are gonna fuck shit up trying to bail you out of this <3

I read her texts over and over again, letting the weight of her words settle over me. I revel in the warmth that envelops me as I imagine Grace leading a rag-tag team of nerdy college students huddled around a table covered in books at a giant library, all on a mission to convince my homophobic dad that homosexuality isn't a sin after all. I picture a wild-eyed Grace with her multi-colored hair in a messy bun, standing in front of a comically chaotic conspiracy board with cut-out Bible verses, historical blurbs about Ancient Rome, and rainbow stickers all messily strung together with red string and thumbtacks.

The mental picture alone is enough to make me laugh out loud, thawing the apathy weighing heavily on my chest and bringing tears to my eyes.

> THEO: holy shit Grace. thank you. seriously you have no idea what this means to me that you're trying. even if it doesn't work, I appreciate it so much.
>
> please thank your friends for me

> GRACE: you're so welcome, bud - I'm happy to do it. my friends are too, we're already having fun
>
> also, they said they want pics of you and Caleb together but I assume Mom and Dad probably took those off your phone, correct?

THEO: yeah, I assume Dad deleted them.

but if you text Harrison, he can probably get them from Caleb

GRACE: hahahaha yes perfect

you guys are too cute, I'm going to use your cuteness to get more people to join the cause

hang in there, bud - I love you. you're worth fighting for, don't forget that.

THEO: thank you Grace. I love you too.

Wednesday, October 25

The rest of the week marches on. I wake up, I drive to school, I spend as much time with Caleb as possible, then I drive home and stay in my room.

On Wednesday evening, I am forced to go to church.

The good news is that no one in my small group seems to have any idea of my predicament. Sienna must have only told my parents, and my parents must be too humiliated to tell anyone else. I'm not even worthy of a prayer request. It hurts in a way that it definitely shouldn't, so I don't dwell on it much.

But the bad news is that Sienna is there.

I don't think I've ever hated a person until now.

Each time our eyes meet, I look away as quickly as possible. She looks like she's trying to smile at me gently, but I can't—I won't look at her.

Thankfully, it's fairly easy to avoid her. She doesn't try very hard to get my attention or talk to me until Nathaniel and I make our way to Eileen at the end of the night.

"Theodore?"

The sound of her voice immediately makes my skin crawl. For a moment, I want to tell Nathaniel to run so we can jump in the car, lock the doors, and make our escape, never looking back. But there isn't enough time. She's closer to Eileen than we are. Was she waiting for me?

Sienna stands rather awkwardly a few feet from the driver's side door, holding her massive purse, weighed down with her Bible, journal, highlighters, and pens. I wonder if I'm in that journal now, my name recorded onto a page as a grave prayer request. Or maybe a new project for her to work on. More of a renewed project, as I'm sure her dating me earlier this year wasn't entirely without some type of ulterior spiritual motive. Maybe if she hadn't broken up with me, I never would have kissed a boy. Maybe she feels guilty about it.

I shove my hands into my pockets, gripping my keys tightly as I approach her. "Sienna."

Her wavy burnt orange hair is tied back into a messy high ponytail, a few stray strands dangling in her face. Honestly, she looks rough— at least rougher than I'm used to seeing her. I hope she's missed as much sleep over this as I have, but not for the same reasons. She stares at me for a few moments, searching my face. I genuinely have no idea how much of my resentment is in my expression as I stare back.

Sienna's eyes dart over to Nathaniel for a moment, then back to me. "Can—can we talk for a minute before you go?"

"No, I need to get home," I reply flatly. "I have a strict curfew now, you know."

"Please?" She takes a step closer to the door. "I'm—I'm sure your parents would understand—"

"Oh, I'm sure they would if *you* talked to them, right?"

Sienna recoils slightly. "That's—that's not what I—Theo, I really need to talk to you."

"Leave me alone, Sienna," I say as I unlock the car doors from the fob in my pocket.

The sound of the car unlocking makes Sienna jump, but she doesn't move from her spot, blocking me from getting into the driver's seat. "Look, I just wanted to say I'm sorry. I did what I thought was right, but I never meant to hurt you. I—I saw you and that guy up there, and it was—it was *wrong*, so I had to—I had to do something, and I didn't know what else to do, so I panicked and told your parents, and I'm sorry."

I feel my jaw clench, rage boiling beneath the surface, but I swallow it down. "Apology not accepted. Move, I need to go."

"I didn't know what they would do, but I had to—I had to do *something*, you know? I knew you wouldn't want to talk to me about—"

"I *did* want to talk to you!" I snap at her, my voice raising, but I keep my distance. "Maybe my parents didn't mention it, but I had a fucking panic attack at the fair trying to chase you into a crowd of people! And I texted you like six times that night, begging you to talk to me before you went and did something stupid, but you ignored me. So don't even try that shit with me."

With each expletive, Sienna flinches. It makes me angrier. It makes me want to curse more. "I—I'm sorry, Theo. I really am. I didn't know about—I didn't know you had—" Her face flashes several emotions at once. Confusion. Guilt. *Pity.*

Unfortunately for her, none of those tricks work on me anymore. "Oh, so you 'didn't know' about the panic attack? Or is it that you 'didn't know' that large crowds trigger them? You know what else you probably 'didn't know?' That one of the *shittiest*, most *fucked up* things you can do to a non-straight person is to out them. Especially to their conservative parents, but really, just outing, in general, is a really shitty move. But you did that anyway."

She stares at me with tears welling up in her eyes. "I—I'm—"

"My dad won't even look at me anymore, Sienna," I continue, my voice breaking, but I don't even care anymore. "*You* did that. I was going to tell my parents about Caleb in my own time on my own terms, but you took that from me! I'll *never* get that back. My relationship with my parents will never be the same because of what you did. Do you understand?"

"Theo," Nathaniel says quietly, putting a hand on my shoulder. "We need to go."

I nod my understanding, but my eyes are glued to Sienna, unblinking, unrelenting. Tears are rolling down Sienna's cheeks, and I know it's wrong, but I'm *glad*. "So, no, Sienna. Apology not accepted. Please get out of my way."

Sienna finally drops her gaze and steps aside, and I move swiftly past her to get in my car. She stands frozen in place as I shut the door behind me, start the engine, and back out of the parking spot.

"Are you okay?" Nathaniel asks from beside me.

I take one last glance at Sienna, still a tear-stained statue with big, wet blue eyes, gripping tightly to her purse. "I will be eventually," I reply as I put the car in drive and pull away.

Friday, October 26

On Thursday, I have to work after school. It's the first time that work has actually been refreshing because it keeps me busy. I have full conversations with a few of my coworkers, putting on a happy face like everything is fine. Maybe they even believe that it is.

When I get home, I raid the fridge for a snack and a soda, then begin my ascent upstairs to finish my homework when I'm stopped by a quiet voice from the living room. "Theo?"

"Yeah, Mom?"

She doesn't answer, so I reluctantly walk into the living room to investigate. Mom's sitting on the couch, almost completely in the dark, her form only illuminated by a single lamp on the end table next to her. She has a family scrapbook open in her lap, head tilted down as she gazes intensely at a page.

"Mom?"

Mom looks up slowly, and I can tell now that her eyes are wet with tears. "Oh, I was making sure it was you. I thought I heard you get home, but I just…wanted to make sure."

I nod hesitantly. "Yep. It's me. Just got home from work. Gonna work on some homework and then go to bed." I linger for another moment, an internal battle in my brain trying to decide whether I should continue sulking and ignoring her since I'm still mad at both parents for grounding me or asking her if she's okay. Because clearly, she's not okay, but…

"Are…are you okay?" I hear myself ask.

Mom sniffles. "Not really."

I chew on my bottom lip as I wait for her to continue, but she doesn't. "Do…you want to talk about it?"

She sniffles again, gazing back down at the scrapbook. "I don't—I don't know."

Apprehensively, I make my way to the couch, dump my soda and snacks on the coffee table, and sit next to her on the couch. I peer down to see which scrapbook she's cradling, not surprised to find that it's one she made of our family vacation to Yellowstone National Park three years ago. It was our last big family vacation that we took before Grace went to college, and Mom frequently revisits this album when she's feeling particularly nostalgic or sad about us being "all grown up." My eyes land on the focal photo on the page: it's of all of us—Dad, Mom, Grace, Nathaniel, and me—standing in front of a picturesque valley with an impressive waterfall in the background.

"That was a fun day," I mutter, not really sure what else to say.

"It was," Mom says quietly. "Do you remember when we were driving between the different landmarks, sometimes for hours, and you and Nathaniel wouldn't stop bickering about and playing video games on your Nintendo…?" she trails off, trying to remember what the console is called.

I let out a weak laugh. "Nintendo Switch. Yeah, I remember." I smirk.

"Nate kept ignoring the low battery alerts and kept letting it die, and he would lose all his progress and try to blame me."

Mom laughs. "But then you would always help him get it back. He'd whine to you about it, and sure, you'd get frustrated sometimes, but you were always there to help him get back to where he was before."

I nod. "Yeah."

Mom sighs shakily, a wistful smile on her face as she stares at the photo. "You were always the best big brother to him. You still are."

I shrug. "I try to be. Nate's a pretty cool little brother anyway, so it's not hard."

She sits quietly for a few seconds, then her gaze turns to me, and she reaches out a hand to touch my hair. I let her, closing my eyes as she runs her fingers through my unruly curls. It feels nice, but resentment from the past several days is bubbling just beneath the surface, causing a whirlwind of contradicting feelings that I eventually ignore because I'm just too tired to fight.

"I look at these pictures sometimes," Mom says after a while. "They're pictures of all of us, of course, but…recently, I've been paying attention to the ones of you." She pauses, tracing the picture of fourteen-year-old me on the page with her finger. "I look at these from three years ago, and I look at newer pictures from a year ago, and then I look at you here and now, and while I can clearly see where you've matured, gotten bigger and taller, and how your face looks more grown-up, there are so many things about you that are still just as 'you' as they were three, four, five years ago."

I frown, watching her curiously. "Yeah, that…that's how aging works, right?" I ask, somewhat playfully but cautiously.

Mom chuckles, nudging me slightly. "Of course, you goofball, I know that's how aging works. I just…" she hesitates, gazing back down at the scrapbook, her eyes getting sad again. "I keep looking at these photos trying to figure out when something…*changed*. I don't know when it happened, and I don't know how I missed it. Because for so long you've been Theo—my Theo—and you have your own special light about you—and you still do, but something must have changed for you to…I don't know, I just…I should've seen it. I should have seen it and…" she trails off, staring down at the page as if she's looking for the rest of her words there. "I just can't figure out how you've changed this much so quickly without me being able to notice."

Immediately, Caleb's words from Spookies all those weeks ago come rushing back to me. "Mom, I didn't—I'm not a completely different person just because I like a boy. Everything else is the same. I'm still me. I still like playing video games and hanging out with my friends. I still listen to music 24-7, and I get super fixated on the bands I like. I still eat too much pizza, and I still get freaked out in big crowds. I still get self-conscious about being shorter than most of my friends. I'm still trying to blow up on TikTok and get a million followers, and I'm still obsessed with Triple H and spooky stuff." I glance down at the Yellowstone family photo and laugh nervously. "I still wish more than anything that I had not been wearing that cursed t-shirt for this picture because now I'm embarrassed by it."

Mom exhales a shaky laugh. "Wh-why are you embarrassed by it?"

"Because it's a stupid Shaggy and Dragon Ball Z crossover shirt referencing a meme that was probably already dead when I was wearing it," I say with a wince. "The idea that this t-shirt is immortalized in a scrapbook and exists online somewhere literally makes me want to crawl under a rock and die."

Mom starts laughing in earnest now, which makes me laugh, too. When the giggling subsides, I look at her with as much seriousness as I can muster. "So, I'm still Theo. I just found something else about myself that has been there all along. It was just locked away."

Mom considers this silently for a few moments. I can only hope that she's considering it, anyway. She finally looks back up at me. "I want to understand, *aroha*. I truly do. And I want you to understand why—why your father and I have responded the way we have to all of this."

I sigh and stare back down at the scrapbook, specifically at Dad's face. Deep down, I know he means well. They both do. They're worried about their son's salvation, which is something I'll never truly understand and probably won't unless I have kids of my own. They genuinely believe that my being anything other than heterosexual is endangering my chances of spending eternity in Heaven after I die. When I think about it like this, their reaction makes a lot more sense, but it doesn't make it hurt any less.

"So…hypothetically," I begin hesitantly. "If Grace were to convince you and Dad that the Bible maybe doesn't actually condemn homosexuality, would that make you feel better?"

"It's not that simple, Theo," Mom says quietly. "Whatever proof she's bringing to the table is from her secular school, and that's—well, you know how your dad feels."

I swallow down the anger that threatens to bubble over at that. Of course. "Well, could you at least believe me when I tell you that this isn't just something that's going to go away?"

Mom's brow furrows. "What do you mean?"

"You keeping me away from Caleb and grounding me isn't going to make me stop being attracted to boys. You know that, right?"

Mom swallows audibly, her gaze shifting out into the dark living room at nothing in particular. "I don't…I don't know."

"Well, I do," I press on, suddenly feeling bold. "This isn't just a phase or some rebellious stunt. You know me better than that. I don't act out like that."

"I know, that's why I'm so confused," Mom says, her voice cracking. "That's why this whole mess didn't make any sense to me from the start. This just… it isn't like you."

"But this *is* me, Mom," I insist. "The real me. It's not a stunt. Not a phase. Just…me."

We sit in silence for several minutes before I stand up from the couch and grab my things from the coffee table. This conversation is pointless. A complete waste of time. We're just talking in circles, and Mom's never going to—

"Does he make you happy?"

I pause for a moment, taken aback by her question, but then answer without hesitation. "Yes. He really does."

Mom stares past me again, her face thoughtful, but she doesn't respond. A few more seconds of silence later, I slowly make my way towards the stairs. Before I start my ascent, I turn back to speak one last time. "You'd really like him, Mom. If you just gave him a chance—gave *us* a chance—I know you'd love Caleb, too." And with that, I retreat to my room and shut the door behind me.

THIRTY-FOUR
CALEB

THREE WEEKS LATER

Friday, November 17

The worst of the fallout is behind us. I'd hate to ruin my reputation as a pessimist, but things between Theo and me are actually going really well. All-things-considered.

    I'm still avoiding his house—not that I'm officially banned or anything, but it's awkward for me, and I don't want to cause any additional stress for Theo. His mom is starting to come around to the idea of us being together, which is way more than I ever expected. He says things are getting better between them, but he's not telling me the whole story. And that's okay. It's going to be a long process, and I'm just glad he's able to talk to me again. Of course, now that the cat's out of the bag and his parents know we're dating, there's a whole host of new rules inflicted on Theo—like Nathaniel has to ride to school with us so we're not alone in the car—but we've found workarounds for almost all of them by now. Ways to steal away, even just for a moment, so I can have him all to myself. And in these moments, I cram all the desires I can't act on under watchful eyes—which mostly boils down to a lot of making out. But it's also when we whisper to one another, trading secrets and hopes and dreams for the future.

I love these stolen minutes most of all.

"Are we still on for the movies tonight?" Theo asks, laying his head back against my chest. Eileen's backseat has become our own little slice of paradise as we soak in the last remaining minutes before Nathaniel finishes up at his robotics club. I run my fingers through his dark, wavy hair. "Yeah, Freddy and I already coordinated seats. He and Andrew are going to meet us there at seven."

Theo nods, grinding the back of his head against me. "Sweet. I'm glad we're finally getting around to our double date. I feel like you two have been plotting this forever."

There's a reason it's taken us this long, but I don't have to say it out loud. He already knows. And it's not like I'm upset about it. He apologizes all the time when we have to work around his parents' rules, but I always tell him he doesn't have to. Whatever hoops I have to jump through, I'll do it. He's worth it.

"We should have invited Harrison and Elise too," I say. "Made it a triple-date."

"Nah, those two have been insufferable lately. They'd be swapping spit the whole time. They can't keep their hands off each other."

"How are we any better?" I ask with a chuckle.

"Hey, at least we have the decency to not make out in front of our friends."

"What about last weekend at Wren's?"

Theo goes quiet for a moment. "Okay, point made. But in my defense, I thought no one was looking."

"Mhm. Sure."

Theo elbows me in the ribs, and I wrap my arms around him, pinning him in place against me. "Now, don't go starting something you aren't prepared to finish."

He wrestles himself out of my grip, laughing as he plants a knee into the seat and turns to look down at me. "I'm going to make you regret those words."

"Well, you'd better get started then—"

Theo's lips silence me as he crashes into our kiss, pressing me back against the car door. His hands rest on my shoulders as he steadies himself, then drift down my shirt, and I jolt as his fingers slip between the top buttons of my shirt, leaving trails of fire across my skin as he unfastens them.

And then his lips are on my neck, and I can't think anymore. I can't breathe except in these small gasps as Theo's hands trace my collarbone. I hold onto his waist as he comes up for air, grinning at me before he leans down for another kiss, letting the weight of his body fall against me. And there's friction between us—the kind of friction that shoots electricity up my spine. The kind of friction that clouds my head in a fog, pushing away all other sensations till there's nothing left—

A soft *ding* emanates from Theo's pocket. He breaks away, his heavy-lidded eyes lingering on me as he digs his phone out.

"It's Nate's five-minute warning," he explains, falling back into the open seat.

I'm trying to catch my breath, so I just nod, hoping he doesn't notice how much of an effect he has. Now that Theo isn't on top of me, my brain is catching up to the rest of my body, and I pull my knees up toward my chest, wrapping my arms around them.

"Guess our time's almost up," I say, and even though I don't intend it, I can't keep the sadness from my voice.

"Just till tonight," Theo reminds me with a grin. "Hey, don't look so sad."

I dig a finger into either side of my mouth, lifting my frown. "Is that better?"

Theo cringes. "Horrifying, actually. Hold on, I should take a picture for Wren so they can recreate the terror."

I roll my eyes, an actual smile taking over. "Very funny."

Theo laughs, stowing his phone back in his pocket before falling silent. He stares through me, eyes unfocused.

"Everything okay?" I ask, straightening my leg to tap him with my shoe.

"Hm?" Theo blinks, coming back down from outer space. "Yeah, sorry. I was just thinking about the interview tomorrow. I'm still trying to wrap my head around it."

"You're going to be great," I assure him. "Hudson is going to love you so much. He'll invite you to co-host with him."

Theo snorts a laugh. "Yeah, totally. It'll be the Triple H and Theo show. It just rolls off the tongue."

"The whole crew is going to be there to cheer you on," I keep going, making it my mission to keep him from psyching himself out. "And if the worst should happen, at least we'll have a great video of you fainting to post on your TikTok."

"Oh, great. I wasn't even thinking about passing out. That's totally going to happen. I'm going to hyperventilate and fall out right in front of Hudson."

"Hey." I catch his hand, holding it in mine. "If that happens—which it absolutely will *not*—I'll be right there to catch you."

He gives me a small nod, taking a deep breath.

"But let's be honest," I continue, "I'm going to pass the fuck out right beside you, so Harrison will have to catch the both of us."

He laughs, which seems to dissolve the tension from his shoulders.

Damn, I don't know if I'll ever get tired of looking at him. Sitting across from me, the curls of his hair illuminated by the later afternoon sun as it streams through the window, I can't help but stare. He's beautiful in so many ways I'm not. Strong in so many ways I'm not. How could I do anything but love him?

A sharp knock raps against the window, and I spot Nathaniel's hoodie lurking behind Theo's head. He reaches behind to open the door, sliding out.

"Hey, Caleb," Nathaniel says, lowering his head to greet me.

"Hey, Nate."

"Are you coming around for Thanksgiving?" he asks, slinging his backpack onto the empty bench beside me.

The driver's door opens, and Theo hops in just in time for me to shoot him a look.

"Um, we haven't really talked about it."

"Talked about what?" Theo interjects.

"Thanksgiving," Nathaniel repeats. "He should come over for dinner. Hannah and Jessie would probably like him."

I pop open the door, stepping out of the suddenly warm car. "I don't think your parents—"

"It's not gonna happen, bro," Theo cuts me off with a little more finality than I care for.

Nathaniel steps around to his brother's window. "Why not? Mom and Dad know the two of you are dating. Why would they say no?"

I hold my tongue, letting Theo answer.

"Because the whole family doesn't know. And yeah, Hannah and Jessie would probably be chill, but that doesn't mean Uncle Tim will. Or Granny. Caleb doesn't want to be around people like that."

"Don't you think you should ask him first?" Nathaniel looks up at me over Eileen's roof. "I hate it when people speak for me. Would you like to come over for Thanksgiving dinner? Mom always says the more the merrier."

Theo gets out of the driver's seat, looking at me too. I can't read his expression—maybe somewhere between curiosity and annoyance. "Well? What do you think?"

"I don't think it's a good idea," I say slowly, trying to pick my words carefully. "Not that I don't appreciate the invite, Nate, really I do. I just don't want to force your brother to do anything he's not ready to do. If he's not out to your extended family, me being there is just going to raise too many questions."

Nathaniel nods. "Oh, right. I didn't think about that. God, it's so stupid that you guys even have to worry about that. Like, I've never had to tell Aunt Susan I'm attracted to girls over a bowl of mashed potatoes. It shouldn't even have to be a thing."

A snort escapes before I can catch it, and Theo laughs, too.

"You're absolutely right," I tell Nathaniel.

"Well, I'm still in favor of you being there," he says, looking over at Theo. "No offense, bro, but Caleb is much more fun to hang with. He lets me win at Mario Kart and doesn't listen to depressing vinyls."

Theo slaps a palm to his chest. "Ouch, man. What the hell?"

"I said no offense." Nathaniel shrugs, closing Eileen's back door and walking around to the passenger side. He pauses, glancing up at Theo again. "Maybe it would be easier if you just made a big announcement. Like, 'Hey, Caleb is my boyfriend, and it's not a big deal, get over it.' Then you wouldn't have to worry about telling everyone."

Theo frowns. "It doesn't work like that, unfortunately. Hey, we can keep talking about this in the car, okay?"

"Okay, yeah. See ya, Caleb."

"Bye, Nate."

Theo rounds Eileen's hood, wrapping me up in a hug. "Sorry about that," he mutters in my ear. "I don't think he really understands."

"I think he gets more than you give him credit for," I say, resting my chin on his shoulder. "And for the record, if you wanted me there for Thanksgiving dinner, I'd be there in a heartbeat. Homophobic-Uncles-be-damned."

Theo pulls away, giving me a look. "Really? You'd do that?"

"Of course, I would. Your family is not going to scare me away. I think we've already established that."

He smiles, giving me one more squeeze before letting me go. "Okay, I'll think about it. We can talk more tonight."

"Okay. I love you, Theo."

"Love you, too."

Saturday, November 18

The cracked and splintered parking lot of Saint Catherine's church has been roped off; tours canceled for the night as Hudson's camera crew set up out front under the crooked steeple. A yellow lanyard around my neck proves that I'm allowed to be here as people dressed in black shirts hurry to and fro, working against the clock of the setting sun.

"Where's Theo?" Harrison asks, slipping his own lanyard on. The rest of the crew are still checking in, but Theo and I have been here for an hour already. He was nervous about being late.

"I think he said he was going to the bathroom." I check my phone. "But that was fifteen minutes ago, so I might have to go on a rescue mission."

Harrison rubs his hands together, then lets out a puff of breath between them. Now that the sun's going down, the temperature is dropping fast. "Have you spotted Hudson yet?"

I shake my head. "Not yet, but he should be here any minute. They want to get started as soon as it gets dark."

"You won't think less of me if I squeal like a fangirl when he gets here, will you?"

I clap him on the shoulder. "I'd only think less if you didn't."

Harrison pulls out his camera. "I'm going to go get some shots around the lot before it gets too dark. Would you let Elise know where I am?"

"You got it."

It's only a few minutes before Elise and Oliver find me. Elise pulls the scarf around her neck tighter as she shuffles over to me. "Jesus, it's freezing out here. Where is everyone?"

"Harrison is taking some shots before it gets dark," I explain, pointing him out across the lot. "Wren is almost here, and Theo is taking a moment to himself, I think."

Oliver nudges me with his shoulder. "Are you excited to see Hudson in the flesh?"

I hesitate, not really sure how to answer that. If he'd asked me yesterday, before I was standing by myself, before last night's double date where Theo hardly said two words, before all this weird energy got in the way of me enjoying what was supposed to be an incredible moment, I would have said "hell yeah!"

"Yes," I settle on, because there's not enough time to get into all the other things I want to say.

"Are you good?" Oliver asks, raising an eyebrow at me.

"Yes," I say again, shaking my head to try and cut through the noise of my thoughts. "I think I'm just nervous for Theo. I'm going to go find him. Will you guys grab Wren when they get here?"

"I'm on it," Oliver says with a grin.

"Thanks."

I head over to the row of blue portable toilets, but they all say "vacant," so I scan the parking lot, searching for Theo's jacket, but I come up empty. Where could he have snuck off to? Circling the church, I still can't find him, and I'm starting to worry. But then I spot the side door of the cathedral cracked open.

Maybe he's inside?

The door creaks as I push on it, echoing up the angled ceilings. Rows of worn wooden pews sit in the dim light, and at the very back, I spot a familiar head of dark curls.

Sliding into the seat beside him, Theo barely even registers my arrival, his arms folded on the pew in front of him and his chin resting on them.

"You found me."

"I found you."

The silence settles over us like the layers of dust covering our surroundings. It's peaceful here, even in the twilight. I should feel uneasy—this place is literally about to be filled with people trying to capture evidence of a haunting—but with Theo beside me, there's not even a drop of fear in my veins.

"It's weird being back here," Theo says, his eyes trained forward, staring at the stained glass that hangs over the altar. "The place we met. Everything's so different now, and yet I still feel the same as I did back then."

"What do you mean?"

"I was looking for something that night. I didn't know what it was at the time—or maybe I thought I did. But what I actually found ended up bringing me back to this place."

"The orbs," I say.

Theo leans back against the wooden seat. "No, it was you."

My breath catches as he wraps his hand around mine.

"You crashed into my world that night, Caleb, and just by grabbing my hand, you set off this chain reaction that led me here. And I don't think I'll ever be able to express how much you mean to me."

"I was so scared after it happened," I say, tightening my hold on him. "I kept thinking you were going to punch me or something."

Theo smirks. "Wow, glad you thought so highly of me."

I bump my shoulder into his. "Can you blame me? I didn't know anything about you. And now… well, I won't say I know everything. That would be wild, but I know enough. And I love it all."

Theo laughs again, and I can see his face flush, even in the dim lighting. "I don't know how you do it, but I'm not complaining."

"Loving you was never the hard part," I assure him. "Sure, there's been challenges. There's going to be a whole lot more of them waiting for us down the line. But they never change how I feel about you, Theo. They never take away from this—" I hold up our intertwined hands, "or how happy you make me, just by smiling."

And he gives me what I want, that half-cocked smile that stokes the fire in my chest and draws me close. Before I can think, my lips are on his, and I feel that smile spread against my skin, morphing, changing into something more, something sacred in this dilapidated place of worship.

It's the closest thing I've ever felt to a spiritual experience.

And when Theo pulls away from me, the electricity he leaves on my lips surges through my veins. And when he kisses me again, this time with an open mouth and hot breath, and an urgency that doesn't scare me but shakes me to my very core—I want nothing else in this world.

Only him.

Only Theo.

THIRTY-FIVE
THEO

Saturday, November 18

GRACE: Theo, I'm so devastated that I have to work and can't be there tonight, but you're gonna kill it, bud!!
I can't wait to hear all about it as soon as I get home tonight!

THEO: thanks Grace <3 don't worry, I'll tell you everything

GRACE: You better!!

When Caleb and I reluctantly leave the peaceful quiet of the cathedral, we're immediately confronted with a chilly gust of evening autumn air. I only let go of Caleb's hand to quickly zip up my jacket before quickly grabbing it again. The cold feels amazing, especially after such a long, hot summer. I love it.

"Shit," Caleb curses. "How is it even colder?"

Before I can respond, a guy in all black with a headset and an iPad appears behind me, seemingly out of nowhere, startling us both. His eyes are wide—almost manic. "You're Theo Briggs, right? The TikTok kid?"

I nod nervously. "That's me."

"You need to come with me. We're set to start in about seven minutes."

"Oh, okay," I reply. Squeezing Caleb's hand, I go to follow iPad Guy, tugging Caleb along with me. I'm not ready to be apart from him yet.

Caleb tries to slip out of my grasp, but I tighten my grip. "Theo, I'm not supposed—"

"Just stay with me for a few more minutes," I beg softly, flashing what I can only imagine are desperate puppy eyes in his direction. "Please?"

Caleb's resolve crumbles in an instant. "Okay, I'll stay as long as they'll let me."

My heart is hammering violently in my chest as we approach the area where the lights and cameras are set up. I still can't believe this is actually happening—I keep expecting to wake up in my bedroom from this dream. But sure enough, there's a bus parked a few hundred feet away with the familiar *Hudson's Haunted Habitats* logo plastered across the sides. And just a few more yards from the bus sits my beloved Eileen—my shiny red sanctuary, ready to whisk me away as soon as all of this is over.

As my eyes scan the scene, they eventually land on familiar faces—Harrison, Elise, Oliver, Wren, and Freddy are all standing a few feet back from the film equipment. Elise spots me first and waves excitedly with a gloved hand. Harrison smiles and nods at me. Freddy also waves, and then Oliver and Wren shoot me a thumbs up.

They all came. Not for Hudson, but for me.

I mean—okay, probably for Hudson, too, but I'm still counting it.

A moment later, I see where we're probably headed—two director's chairs are set up in front of the cameras, perfectly positioned to frame Saint Catherine's behind them. The chair on the left has Hudson's name on it, and the other is blank.

Oh, God, this is happening.

"Hey, kid," a different guy with a different iPad calls out, gesturing to

Caleb. "Only purple lanyards past this point."

Caleb and I stop in our tracks, and my stomach churns with anxiety. Even though I knew this was coming, I had hoped I would be ready. But I'm not. I'm not ready. Fuck, I'm really not ready.

Caleb takes both of my hands in his and smiles at me. "Guess this is it, then," he says, giving my hands an excited squeeze. "You've got this, okay? I'll just be right over there with the others. It'll be over before you even know it."

He's right, of course, but it doesn't make me feel any better. "Yeah. Okay."

"I love you," he adds—not quietly, but not loudly, either. As if we were alone and no one else was around. For some reason, though, I don't panic about people hearing him. Maybe it's because I'm already panicked about everything else. Or maybe it's because I'm not afraid of people hearing anymore.

"I love you, too," I say back, matching his volume. There's a sizable surge of adrenaline as the words leave my lips, but not in a bad way. It's comparable to how it feels at the start of a rollercoaster, creeping up the lift hill. Frightening but exciting.

Maybe I can do this after all.

"This way, Mr. Briggs," iPad Guy says, impatiently waving me forward.

Caleb lets my hands go and waves one last time before making his way towards the rest of our crew. I take a deep breath and follow iPad Guy to the set.

"Okay, let's get you mic-ed up," iPad Guy says, waving another crew member over towards us. "You'll be in this chair here on the right."

I simply nod and step towards the chair. My chair. The chair that's adjacent to Hudson's chair. The chair where Hudson will be sitting in just a couple of minutes to interview me in front of all these cameras.

Breathe in. Breathe out.

While the new crew member works on attaching a small microphone to my jacket, iPad Guy continues with his instructions. "Okay, so Mr. Helter is on his way now. He's going to brief you on the questions he'll be asking so that you're not caught off guard, but they should probably resemble the questions from the email you received last week."

I nod again. I've read that email so many times at this point I could recite it backward and forwards. But that's not going to help if I just black out, is it?

"As you know, this shoot won't be live, but we're hoping to get this in no more than two takes, so just try to relax, all right?"

"That feel okay?" the microphone crew member asks.

"Mhm," is all I can say to both of them. I'm starting to feel dizzy, and suddenly, my throat is dry. Why didn't I think to bring something to drink?

"Can we get a water here, please?" iPad Guy barks at someone else, and before I even have time to thank him, a tiny bottle of water is pressed into my open hand. I lift it up to take a sip with trembling hands. Shit.

"Okay, everyone, three minutes!"

Breathe in. Breathe out.

Caleb. I spot him in an instant because he's already watching me. He smiles calmly as our eyes meet across the parking lot. "You got this," he mouths to me.

I take another calming breath and try to believe him.

"You must be Theo!"

The all-too-familiar voice of Hudson Helter immediately grabs my attention. I spin around, carefully placing the water bottle on the ground beside my chair before finally meeting Hudson's gaze. "Y-Yes, hi, that's me!"

Hudson is grinning ear-to-ear—a genuine, friendly smile that warms me to my core. His jet-black hair is styled straight up in his trademark fauxhawk, piercing blue eyes taking me in as I stare up at him reverently.

While preparing for tonight, I had read dozens of other fans' descriptions of meeting Hudson in person, so in theory, I knew he was outgoing, sincere, and good-natured. I already couldn't wait to meet him, but now I was even more excited knowing he was such a great person off-screen, too.

What I had not prepared for, however, was the fluttering in my stomach and instant heat rising to my cheeks the second we made eye contact.

Caleb was right. Hudson is hot. Very hot. Even hotter in person than on camera.

"It's a pleasure to meet you!" Hudson continues, reaching out to shake my hand.

I shake it eagerly. "I—uh, wow—the pleasure is all mine," I stammer, desperate not to sound as cringe as I feel. The Triple H fanboy in me is screaming. "I'm a huge fan. Obviously. I mean, I guess that wasn't necessarily obvious, but yeah, I've been a fan for...ages. Me and all my friends, we're huge fans," I say, pointing over to where Caleb and the others are standing. "They're all here, too."

"Excellent!" Hudson says before spinning around to wave at them. The crew eagerly returns his wave, and I'm pretty sure I faintly hear them squealing with delight when Hudson turns back to me. "I'm excited about this episode! I'll mention this once we start rolling, too, but I'm genuinely impressed by the footage you captured on TikTok back in September."

"Thanks," I croak before taking another gulp of water.

Hudson goes to sit in his chair and motions for me to do the same. "Here, have a seat and get comfortable. Did you get a chance to look over the questions we emailed you?"

"Yes, sir," I reply without thinking.

Hudson scrunches his nose. "Please, none of that," he says with a chuckle. "I know we're in the south, but you don't have to call me 'sir' or anything. It'll just make me feel old."

"Sorry," I mumble sheepishly. "Old habits."

"No sweat," he insists. "So, do you have any questions for me about what we're going to discuss?"

I shake my head. "No, I think I'm good."

"Great! I'll just stick to those questions, then, if that's okay with you."

"Yep, sounds good."

"One minute!"

Hudson claps his hands together. "Excellent—you're going to be great! And again, this isn't live, so if we need to do a retake, it's okay."

I turn to look at Caleb again—just one more time to calm my nerves—when another familiar face catches my eye instead.

There, standing in between Caleb and Harrison is a shorter woman with olive skin and dark, wavy hair bundled up in a massive red puffer jacket. She catches me staring, so she smiles and waves at me.

No way.

I have to blink a few times to make sure I'm not hallucinating.

Mom?

"Thirty seconds!"

I stare back at her, dumbfounded. *She came.*

My parents have known about this interview for weeks. They were aware of it even before The Pumpkin Fair Disaster and all the fallout that directly followed. I never directly invited them to watch the interview because they've never expressed any real interest in Triple H or my videos before, so why would they care?

I definitely did not invite Dad. We're still not on the best of terms. It's certainly better than it was at the beginning—he'll actually look at me now, and we've made small talk a time or two over the past couple of weeks—but neither of us seems ready to reconcile, and I'm mostly at peace with that.

Even though Mom and I are getting along far better than Dad and me, I don't remember asking Mom to come tonight. She knew I was excited about it, but she never gave any indication that she planned on showing up. Maybe Grace told her to come. Grace wasn't able to get out of her shift at Cathy's tonight, but maybe she convinced Mom to go on her behalf? But why? No one outside of the Triple H crew is allowed to film or record any of this, so… what difference would it make?

Did Mom just come because…she wanted to?

"Ten seconds!"

Maybe Mom is here because she wants to be. She's here to support me.

"Five, four—"

Because, despite everything that's happened, she really loves me.

"Salutations, Haunties," Hudson begins, and I quickly shift my attention back to him. "It's your good friend, Hudson, back with another tale of high strangeness for you! We're here in a little town in Georgia that you all might remember from a few weeks ago called Specter!"

I take a steady breath, trying to subtly straighten my posture and pretend that I wasn't about to start crying about my mother when I'm supposed to be participating in an interview with my celebrity idol.

"You may also recall that a certain TikTok garnered a lot of Haunties' attention because the user really captured something incredible down in the basement of Saint Catherine of Bologna Catholic Church. As soon as I watched the video, I just knew I had to fly down to Georgia to check it out for myself! But while the team discussed whether or not we wanted to do another episode on this habitat, we received a message from that TikTok user, and it turns out he's a fellow Hauntie! So here we are on the grounds of Saint Catherine's, getting ready to do some good old Triple H exploration! But before we get into that, I've got our viral videographer Theo here to talk to us for a bit about his experience here all those weeks ago."

I give the camera a slight wave and a shy smile before turning my attention back to Hudson.

"Thanks for agreeing to come on the show, Theo!"

"Of course! Thank you for having me."

"So, let's jump right into it! Tell us how you came to be in the basement of Saint Catherine's on that fateful night!"

"Well, my friends and I had just listened to the Saint Catherine's episode the night before, so we wanted to come check it out for ourselves. Specter doesn't get noticed much, so it was extra exciting for us. We had heard rumors about this place being haunted, but we'd never been, so we figured we would try to do one of the haunted tours. The guide wasn't taking us down to the basement as part of the tour, so I kind of ventured off on my own to see if I could capture anything."

"That's the true Hauntie spirit," Hudson interjects with a grin. "As long as you were being safe about it!"

I nod. "Oh, yes, of course. My friends knew where I was, and I was sure not to touch or disturb anything."

"Excellent! But I understand you weren't completely alone venturing into the basement that night?"

I smile as a flash of copper curls flickers through my memory. "Yep. Unbeknownst to me, someone else caught a glimpse of me, so they came down to investigate. Scared the crap out of me, too."

"So, who was this stranger?"

"His name is Caleb," I answer, unable to stop smiling. "We sort of knew each other from school, but not that well. While we were down there, we realized we were both into Triple H, so he continued with me further into the basement, and he was with me when I found the chalkboard. He's even in the video for a few seconds, but you can barely see him because he was waiting for me out in the hallway."

"That's great! I always love hearing about Haunties finding each other like that. Friendships forged in spooky places. I love it! Do you guys still hang out?"

"All the time, actually," I start, glancing over to where Caleb, Mom, and the rest of my friends are watching. "As a matter of fact, he's—" Caleb and I lock eyes, and my heart swells. "Caleb is my boyfriend. We've been together for almost two months now."

Caleb's eyes go wide, and his hands move to cover his mouth. Freddy and Wren grab Caleb's shoulders, shaking him excitedly. Elise gasps so loud that I'll be surprised if the microphones don't pick it up. Harrison and Oliver exchange a look, but they're smiling at me.

I make a conscious effort not to look at Mom. Just in case.

"Whoa! I did not see that coming at all!" Hudson exclaims, looking genuinely delighted. "Congratulations! Well, there you have it, folks! Let it never be said that you can't find love in a haunted basement!"

I laugh. It's not a fake laugh for the camera, either—it's real, uninhibited, wholehearted laughter bursting out of me, and it feels incredible. It's euphoric. Cathartic. Ridiculous.

It's all so silly, so absurd. But that's exactly what happened, isn't it?

I found love in a haunted basement.

And I'll never be the same again.

The rest of the interview is a bit of a blur. The realization that I outed myself publicly to my hero, his entire crew, and every single person in the world who watches Triple H hits me in waves, and by the time the cameras stop filming and iPad Guy is ushering me off the set, nothing feels real anymore. My ears are ringing, and I feel like I'm in one of those dreams where my legs can't keep up, and I'm somehow moving in slow motion while everything else around me continues as normal.

This is, of course, until my favorite pair of freckled arms are wrapping around my waist, lifting and spinning me several inches off the ground. Warmth fills my chest as I instinctually wind my own arms around his neck. I cling to him tightly, breathing in his familiar, sweet, and comforting scent.

Caleb.

"You were amazing!" Caleb says excitedly, his breath hot next to my ear, sending shivers down my spine that have nothing to do with the dropping temperatures. "As soon as Hudson started talking, literally every bit of anxiety drained from your face. For a second, I thought maybe you'd been body-snatched or something!"

I try to laugh at his joke or maybe make a self-deprecating quip about my anxiety, but I'm too full of relief that I was able to appear composed on camera to come up with anything clever. "Ha, thank you," I exhale as I squeeze Caleb back.

"Theo, you fucking nailed it!" Oliver shouts, wrapping his long arms around both Caleb and me and slapping me on the back. "I never doubted you for a second!"

"That's a lie," Elise interjects. "He was literally planning out which crew members he would need to beat up to get to you if you passed out."

"Wow, Elise, way to be cool," Oliver grumbles.

"Anytime!" Elise snaps back cheerfully. "But seriously, Theo, we're so proud of you!" She joins in on the group hug, and Harrison joins directly behind her.

"Was it everything you thought it would be?" Harrison asks eagerly, gripping my shoulder firmly.

"Everything and more," I reply reverently.

"And seriously, can we talk about how much hotter Hudson is in person than on camera?" Freddy chimes in, appearing with Wren behind Caleb. "Like, oh my god?"

"Oh, one hundred percent," I reply, and everyone voices agreement, even Harrison. As Harrison has said before, no one is that straight.

"I think it's safe to say we're all a little envious of you now," Wren adds, also placing a gloved hand on top of the friend huddle. "But none of us could have done it better than you, Theo. You did good."

As we slowly pull apart, I make eye contact with everyone in the circle. "Thank you, guys, for being here. It means the world to me."

"We're not the only ones, you know," Harrison says quietly, looking past me and gesturing toward something behind me. I turn around to see Mom standing a respectful distance away, now donning a black knit beanie with her hands shoved deep in her puffer jacket pockets.

"Mom," I say aloud, taking an apprehensive step towards her.

Mom outstretches her arms to me. "Come here, *taku tama*."

I close the distance between us and bury myself in a warm, poofy hug. I'm suddenly overwhelmed again, fighting back the urge to cry yet again.

"You were wonderful, Theo," Mom says softly, pressing a light kiss into my hair. "I'm so proud of you."

"Thanks, Mom," I rasp, willing my voice to stop cracking. "I didn't…I didn't know you were coming."

"Of course, silly," she replies. "I'm your mother, and this is something very important to you. I wouldn't miss this for the world."

"Well," I sniffle before continuing. "You didn't have to come, but you did, and that means a lot. So…thank you. Really."

As we pull away, she gives me a serious expression. "I've been doing a lot of thinking and a lot of praying over the past few weeks, Theo, and I've realized a few things."

My stomach drops. Oh no. Not here. Is she about to ruin everything by bringing up my sexuality again? In front of everyone?

"As a mother, there's nothing more important to me than the happiness and the well-being of my children. Nothing in the whole world matters more than that. You are my precious son, and I will always want the best for you. I'll always want to protect you. To love you and support you. To teach you right from wrong and hopefully show you how to live by example. But at the end of the day, all those things can only go so far. You're almost an adult now, and pretty soon, you'll go your own way, and I won't be able to protect you from the evils and cruelty of the world anymore. I can only pray that what I have given you will be enough."

I shuffle uncomfortably. This feels like a lecture, but it also feels like something…else. Something different.

She reaches her hand out towards my face, brushing a loose curl away from my eye, smiling wistfully at me. "Right now, you are still my child, and you're still under my protection and guidance. However, as much as I might want to use this time to control you or try to convince you to make choices that align with what I believe is right…none of that matters if it just ends up pushing you away."

I stare at her in shock, the backs of my eyes burning with tears.

"I love you, *aroha*. I want you to be happy. I want to support the things that make you happy. Like this interview—I may not understand the appeal of ghost stories and exploring abandoned churches, but if watching those shows and making those videos makes you happy, then I'll be right here to support you." Her eyes flicker past me, and I follow her gaze to see Caleb standing with the rest of the crew while watching me with a protective, worried expression. "Caleb makes you happy," Mom continues. "I may not understand it yet, but I am trying. I've been reading the material that Grace gave me, by the way, and it's giving me a lot to think about. But more importantly, you're my son. My Theo. And if being with Caleb makes you happy, I'm not going to stand in your way."

The rest of my composure crumbles in an instant. I collapse back into my mother's arms, choking out a broken sob into her shoulder. She holds me tight against her, whispering "it's okay, sweetie" and "let it out" while gently rubbing my back, and I can't hold back my tears anymore.

"I love you, Mom," I finally manage to say, my voice cracking all to hell, but I can't find it in myself to care anymore.

"I love you, too, Theo. So, so much."

We stay like this for a little while longer until Mom clears her throat, and I finally remember where I am.

"Come on over, Caleb," Mom says a moment later. "I'm sorry to keep him from you for so long."

I peel myself out of my mother's arms to face Caleb, who is studying me closely with a worried brow. "Sorry," I mumble, wiping my sleeve across my face.

"No apologies needed," Caleb says, seemingly at both me and Mom, but then he focuses on me. "So, um, the gang and I were just talking about dinner.

Are you hungry?"

"Starving, actually," I answer.

"That reminds me," Mom pipes up. "I was actually going to propose something to the two of you."

Caleb blinks at her, then looks at me. I just shrug.

"So, I don't want to intrude on your time with your friends tonight, but I was wondering if you two would like to join me for dinner another night sometime soon? My treat, of course," she adds, then smiles warmly at Caleb. "I feel like you and I got off on the wrong foot, Caleb, and for that, I'm sorry. But I would love nothing more than to try again and get to know you better...as Theo's boyfriend."

Caleb's face goes blank for a second or two before he breaks into a shy smile. "Yeah, I...I think I would like that. Theo?"

My heart feels like it might burst, which unfortunately sends one more tear rolling down my cheek before I can stop it. I nod. "Yeah. Me too."

Mom's face lights up, and her smile is by far the brightest thing in the whole lot.

Caleb and I slip away from the gang shortly after dinner. We have forty-eight minutes before our curfew, and we have no intention of letting a single second go to waste.

The parking lot of Saint Catherine's is completely deserted now. I imagine Triple H will be back tomorrow to finish filming the episode, but for now, the lot is empty. Well, almost empty.

Surely, no one will notice a little red hatchback tucked close to the building, just out of sight from the main road. Even if we are spotted, it's very hard for me to care.

What can I say? I'm a bit of a bad boy now.

The windows fog up quickly from our shared body heat despite cracking all the windows to let the crisp November air inside. But it's perfect.

After about twenty very hot, breathless minutes of making out in Caleb's lap in the backseat of my car, we both know it's time to stop.

We finally talked about sex a few days ago. For now, we've agreed to wait a little while. It's only been two months. We want to wait until we're both ready before we take that next step. Honestly, if making out is already this good, I don't think I can even handle sex yet. I think I might die from being too happy. Or maybe my heart would explode. Who knows?

Once we catch our breaths and allow things to simmer down, I find myself gazing at Caleb, cataloging my favorite features for the hundredth time. His adorable pointed up nose. His beautiful curls. His soft, plush lips. The angle of his jaw and the slope of his neck.

I'm about to tell him how gorgeous he is, but Caleb opens his mouth to speak first.

"So, are we going to talk about how you told Hudson Helter on camera that you have a boyfriend tonight?"

I exhale a nervous laugh. "I should probably feel more freaked out about it, but…" I trail off, searching for the right words. "I don't. It feels good, actually."

"Yeah?"

"Yeah," I echo. "It feels like I'm free. I hadn't planned on saying anything, but…I just pictured you, and the words just kind of flowed right out of me. It felt…easy."

Caleb smiles, but it doesn't quite reach his eyes. Shit, something is wrong.

"Hey, you okay?"

Caleb's gaze drops to his hands, then back up to me. "I've been meaning to ask this for a while, but…I can never tell if it's the right time. But it's going to eat me alive if I don't ask, so here goes."

I wait for him to continue, offering my hand between us. Caleb takes it in an instant, interlocking our fingers.

"Do you...still feel guilty about us? Like...being with me. Are you still able to call yourself a Christian?"

I chew my bottom lip, considering his question for a few seconds. "I...I don't think I feel guilty anymore. It still happens sometimes for other stuff, and if I'm honest, once we revisit the sex thing, the guilt might come back to haunt me, but...being with you doesn't make me feel guilty at all. At least, not anymore."

Caleb nods, then looks at me inquisitively. "So, you're still able to be a Christian with me?"

I sigh. "To be honest, Caleb, I don't really know. I mean...I'm technically still a Christian because I was baptized and all of that, but...I haven't really felt close to God in a while. I don't really talk to him much anymore, and I feel like he hasn't talked to me, either. But that's not because of you. I was already feeling distant from my faith long before you came along."

"Really?"

"Yeah," I insist, squeezing his hand. "So, sure, it's complicated, but...I don't know. I'm not really worried about it anymore. I know that sounds weird, but...I'm just kind of taking it one day at a time, and the further along I get, the more okay everything feels. Does that make sense?"

Caleb rubs his thumb over mine. "I think so. But...are you sure you're not missing anything because you're with me? Like...do you think God stopped talking to you because you're sinning with me, or whatever? Does he do that? Can you get blocked by God—"

"Hey," I interrupt softly. I lean closer to Caleb, reaching out my free hand to gently cup his chin, tilting his face towards me until our eyes meet. "Listen to me. I promise that none of my faith stuff is your fault. I don't know what I believe in when it comes to religion anymore, but I do know that I believe in you, and I believe in us. Okay? I'm so happy with you, Caleb. Happier than I've ever been. Even my mom can see it. You make me happy, and that's all that matters."

Caleb's shoulders seem to relax, tension leaving his body. "Okay."

"Do you believe me?"

He nods, his lovely brown eyes locked with mine. "I do."

I pull our conjoined hands up to my lips and kiss the back of his palm. "I love you so fucking much."

"I love you, too."

"Good, because I'm going to make it everyone's problem from now on," I say with a smirk, making my way back to the front seat of the car to start the engine.

Caleb follows my lead to the passenger seat. "What do you mean?"

"No more hiding. No more stealing touches in secret. No more acting like we're just 'good buddies,'" I declare excitedly. "We are official, we are out and proud, and we're going to start acting like it. I'm talking *disgusting* amounts of PDA, babe."

"Babe?" Caleb squeaks, and it's the cutest fucking thing I've ever heard in my life.

"Shit, is that okay?" I ask quickly, eyeing him seriously.

Caleb is blushing furiously. "Yeah, more than okay."

I beam at him. "Okay, cool. So, what do you say, *babe*? Are you down for being the most obnoxious, sickeningly sweet couple in Specter?"

"I've never wanted anything more," Caleb proclaims. "It's about damn time someone put the Straights to shame!"

We both erupt into giggles and just as I go to buckle my seatbelt, warm hands cup my jaw and pull me into a kiss. This kiss is softer, gentler, and less heated than the kisses from earlier, but if I'm honest, it's my favorite kind of kiss. Unexpected, but welcome. Electrifying, but in the best way. The sweetest surprise that I never knew I needed.

Just like Caleb.

ACKNOWLEDGEMENTS

Thank you so much for reading! This book has been such a treat as it's the first time I've been able to write alongside my best friend Amy since we were teenagers, trolling the message board role-play sites of the early '00s. A lot has changed since then. However, coming back together to create Theo and Caleb's story feels just like old times. So, my biggest thank you is to you, Amy. Thank you for allowing me the honor of co-piloting this new adventure, and I hope it's just the first of many more for you.

There are so many others to thank, but I'll try and keep things brief—a huge thank you to my husband, Cecil, my biggest supporter and cheerleader. I love you to the moon and back! Next, a big thank you to Molly at We Got You Covered Book Design for helping us make **THEORETICALLY STRAIGHT** look its best! I can't recommend her services enough! And, of course, a colossal thank you to Sara Pulsifer, for their fantastic artwork used in the cover design. You brought our boys to life, and I cannot thank you enough!

And lastly, thank you to all the readers who have supported me over the years. Whether through purchasing my books, leaving reviews, or reaching out to me, I want you to know that I appreciate each and every one of you and thank you for making this dream of mine a reality.

Till next time,
ALEXANDER

If someone had told me two years ago that I would be writing acknowledgments for a real, published book, I would have laughed in their face. I have so many people to thank, and I tend to be a bit long-winded, but I'll do my best!

First and foremost, I'd like to thank Alex—my best friend, my co-author, and my constant supporter for twenty freakin' years. Thank you for always believing in me, even so much that you were willing to share this creative project with me. Thank you for holding my hand through this whole book-writing process and allowing me the time and space to work through all my emotional baggage to breathe this story to life. You're such an inspiration to me, and I'm so honored to see my name next to yours in print. I love you so much!

To Jackson—my partner, my soulmate, my rock, and the love of my life—where do I even start? Thank you for being the best husband ever. Thank you for always encouraging me to pursue my passions, even (and especially) when I don't believe in myself. Thank you for going above and beyond to support me in every conceivable way—not just for the duration of this book, but always. No matter what life has thrown our way, you have never stopped advocating for me, and I can never thank you enough. I love you, you dork!

Thank you to my endlessly supportive circle of friends and family: Jess, Patrick, Cecil, Mal, Laurel, Anna, Anthony, my brother Matt, my sister-in-law Clarice, my in-laws Staci and Robert, and so many others—if I listed everyone out by name, this section would be as long as the book itself!

On the publishing side of things, I want to thank our amazing beta readers: Jess, Laurel, Esther, Nel, and Jodi. I'd also like to thank Sara Pulsifer for her incredible illustration of Theo and Caleb on the cover, and Molly Phipps for her amazing cover design, formatting, and overall beautification of our book! Thank you all for everything you've done to bring our beloved boys to life.

This may be where I lose some of you, but I am compelled to include a special thanks to David Jenkins and the amazing writers of the television series *Our Flag Means Death*. I watched the first season of OFMD in April 2022 and was fundamentally and irrevocably changed as a person. For the first time in over a decade, I was inspired to write again, and I haven't been able to stop since. It started with fanfiction, but *Theoretically Straight* wasn't far behind. My love for this series has also introduced me to so many incredible people in the OFMD fandom—some of whom are now my close friends. This book simply would not exist without the influence of *Our Flag Means Death*, the beautiful queer story it tells, and the wonderfully diverse community it brought together.

And along those lines, thank you to all the readers of my work thus far. You have cheered me on every step of the way, encouraging me to keep writing, and even made me believe that I might be kind of good at writing! Wild!

Finally, to my loving parents: thank you for raising me to believe in love, redemption, and empathy. We may not agree on everything nowadays, and you may not even read this book due to its content, but you always taught me to work hard, love unconditionally, and be true to myself, and that's what I've done. Thank you for everything.

All my love,
AMY

ABOUT THE AUTHORS

AMY BAILEY (she/they) and **ALEXANDER EBERHART** (he/him) have been best friends for almost twenty years. They both grew up in the Metro Atlanta Area, bouncing from suburb to suburb until they eventually landed in the same church as preteens, and they've been pretty inseparable ever since.

Alexander has always had a passion for writing, even from a young age. He still lives on the cusp of Atlanta with his husband and their pets. He has penned five Young Adult novels, all revolving around the Atlanta area, and enjoys bringing an underrepresented setting to life in imaginative and (sometimes) hilarious ways. When not crafting quality queer fiction, Alexander works for a local company in the service industry and enjoys running D&D campaigns for his friends. Explore the library of his work at **alexanderceberhart.com**.

Amy (known as Bailey to their online friends) has dabbled with creative writing sporadically over the past two decades, but it wasn't until recently that the creative floodgates truly opened up for them. They've written roughly 250,000 words of fanfiction over the past year and won't stop until they've reached a million! When they aren't hunched over their laptop, Amy can be found playing Dungeons & Dragons, going to the movies with friends, or backseat gaming on the couch with their wonderful husband, Jackson, and their beloved pets, Olive and Ruby.

www.ingramcontent.com/pod-product-compliance
Lightning Source LLC
LaVergne TN
LVHW041743060526
838201LV00046B/898